The Black Pearl is one of the most extraordinary and fascinating accounts of one man's 'secret' erotic life ever to emerge from the late-Victorian and Edwardian age of public morality (or, at any rate, public moralizing) and private sexual excess. The title indicates that the anonymous author was influenced by that classic journal of 19th Century erotica, *The Pearl*, and there is much of *The Pearl*'s flavour of outspoken rebellion against the official prudery of the time in these uninhibited memoirs.

But there are intriguing additional dimensions to the writings of 'Horby' (the pseudonym adopted by the author of *The Black Pearl* to disguise – very effectively so – his true identity). It is clear that the financial freedom that his independent income gave him, together with his aristocratic status, allowed him access to the inner circles of the artistic and occult worlds of his time. As a result, alternating with graphic accounts of sexual adventures are anecdotes – many of them wonderfully scurrilous – concerning some of the most famous creative talents of the age: Frank Harris, Lillie Langtry, Arthur Machen, Aleister Crowley, G. B. Shaw and H. G. Wells, to name but a few. But above all it is 'Horby's quest for his own sensual variety of enlightenment through the study and practice of sex-magic that provides the main theme and fascination of *The Black Pearl*, now at long last available for the first time to the wide audience it so richly deserves.

Also in paperback from New English Library

The Pearl: volume 1
The Pearl: volume 2
The Pearl: volume 3
The Pearl Omnibus
The Oyster: volume 1
The Oyster: volume 2
The Oyster: volume 3
The Oyster: volume 4
The Oyster: volume 5
The Oyster Omnibus
Rosie – Her Intimate Diaries: volume 1
Rosie – Her Intimate Diaries: volume 2
Rosie – Her Intimate Diaries: volume 3
Rosie – Her Intimate Diaries: volume 4
The Rosie Omnibus

The Black Pearl: Volume 1

The Memoirs of a Victorian Sex-Magician

Anonymous

NEW ENGLISH LIBRARY
Hodder and Stoughton

This edition first published in 1995
by Hodder and Stoughton
A division of Hodder Headline PLC

A New English Library paperback

10 9 8 7 6 5 4 3 2

British Library Cataloguing in Publication Data

Black Pearl: Memoirs of a Victorian Sex
Magician
823 [F]

ISBN 0-340-62568-6

Typeset by
Letterpart Limited, Reigate, Surrey

Printed and bound in Great Britain by
Cox & Wyman Ltd, Reading, Berks

Hodder and Stoughton
A division of Hodder Headline PLC
338 Euston Road
London NW1 3BH

PUBLISHER'S FOREWORD

The Black Pearl: The Memoirs of a Victorian Sex-Magician is a legendary classic of Victorian underground writing. Although the identity of the author presently remains unknown, it is clear from the text that he was a member of the aristocracy who knew all the leading figures of his age, both male and female. This eminently respectable figure obviously enjoyed the hidden and lascivious side of high life in his time: and he was also drawn to low-life. As such, we have a unique portrayal of the undertones of life in the 1890s and after.

His title obviously indicates that he was influenced by that classic journal of Victorian erotica, THE PEARL. The date of composition cannot be ascribed with exactitude though the text indicates that the author was recalling events some years after their happenstance. The edition discovered by Dr Geraldine Lamb, the editor, indicates on the publishers' notes opposite the title page that this work was privately printed in an edition of 156 copies by Van den Haagen of Amsterdam, 1925. It was set in 12pt Bembo, 1 pt leaded, printed on Japanese paper, crown quarto in size, bound in black buckram, with gold-stamped lettering which has led some bibliophiles to identify the latter work as that of Spalding & Hodge of London.

This book is of value to the sociologist, the psychologist,

the historian, those fascinated by literary anecdotes and political tales by a man who knew personally all those of whom he speaks; and above all to those who find in the study of human sexuality, a key to human nature.

EDITOR'S PREFACE

It is not often that one comes upon a classic of Victorian erotica whose very existence is a matter of speculation and rumour. Much Victorian erotica was written by debauched aristocrats in their leisure hours, then privately printed for presentation to friends. Some of these works were issued during the 1890s by the drug-addicted publisher, Leonard Smithers, who also published works of genuine literature by Oscar Wilde and works of art by Aubrey Beardsley. Others were not set, bound, printed and presented until many years later in order to protect both the name of the author and the reputations of those he mentioned.

Such is the case with *The Black Pearl: The Memoirs of a Victorian Sex-Magician*. If the publisher's notation can be trusted, it was not issued until 1925 and then only in a strictly limited edition. I came upon it in a curious way.

Following on from my B.A. at Cambridge, I went on to pursue M.A. studies at Harvard and it was there that I found myself debating issues of sexuality with distinguished men and women such as Norman Mailer and Dr Camille Paglia. Although both of them appeared to venerate the penis, they both seemed to see it as a tool of vengeance. Both, however, in their separate ways, seemed to be committed to the idea that human evolution could be advanced by sexuality. I was discerning a similar ideal in the poetry of England's Fiona Pitt-Kethley.

My essay *The Penis: Tool of Vengeance or Tool of Love? An Exploration of Socio-Phallicism* was eventually printed (1992) in *The New Rationalist*, published out of Harvard. I received a number of letters on account of it, some of them dismally predictable, but one, at least, was extraordinarily interesting. This was from an English baronet who has insisted that he remain anonymous. After a lengthy correspondence, he invited me to his castle, where he was a kind, courteous and considerate host.

It was during my stay that he showed me a copy of THE BLACK PEARL. I was absolutely astonished by this work. Most pieces of Victorian erotic writing show us simply the sleazy tenderloin of the repressed sexuality of that time. We get certain insights and there is entertaining rebellion against prevailing official mores but precious little more, even when the descriptions of the sexual encounters themselves are very well-written. Yet here was a rake who came to perceive sexuality as the holiest truth between man and woman – and as a way of advancing human consciousness.

In the text, he was at first simply a man of late middle-age recalling his youthful sexual exploits. He was reminiscing too about his encounters with celebrities such as Oscar Wilde, Lillie Langtry, Bernard Shaw, Ellen Terry, Frank Harris and Mrs Bram Stoker, among so many others. Yet he was also searching for something more and ventured into the many esoteric orders of his time such as the Hermetic Order of the Golden Dawn, the German Ordo Templi Orientis, the American Female Flagellants of New York, the Temple of the Smokers of the Sacred and numerous others. It was clear to me that in the course of his curious quest, he had become learned in many arcane techniques of expanding consciousness, which he refers to in the text as both 'Magick' and 'Mysticism'. There was much too about the use of plants and minerals to achieve a state he calls 'ecstasy'.

Who was he? My host refused to tell me, other than to state that he was the friend of a distant elderly cousin. In the text he makes it clear that he was an independently rich Viscount with access to both the rich and the poor – and the middle classes. The memories he records of his contemporaries have the ring of truth and yet it is so far impossible to identify him. My host showed me a stack of papers which had passed into the hands of the family. From these it is obvious that he chose to operate under the pseudonym of 'Horby'.

'I see that boys and "feasting with panthers" are not to your taste, Horby,' reads a scribbled card from Oscar Wilde, adding: 'but hock and seltzer should be. Do delight me at the Cadogan, 1.00, Tuesday.' The following telegram is obvious: 'LUNCHEON STOP TWO CAFE ROYAL STOP BE THERE HORBY STOP FRANK HARRIS'. Harris was then Editor of *The Saturday Review* and one of the most influential literary figures in London. Another telegram: 'SORRY CANT AND WONT STOP GBS' is obviously (and typically) from Bernard Shaw. 'Glad you appreciate poetry, Horby, but there's more to it than that,' is the inscription in the author's handwriting on Aleister Crowley's WHITE STAINS, which was privately printed (1898) and which has subsequently been criticised for its scandalous obscenity. A copy of the 1895 John Lane, The Bodley Head edition of *The Great God Pan* contains the following message by its author, Arthur Machen: 'Come to wine on Wednesday rather than to whine. And then you too, Horby, can sample the Jar of Avallaunius.' 'Absinthe any time, so get in touch, Horby, be pleased to hear from you, John Davidson,' are the drunkenly scrawled words on another bespattered postcard. 'Horby' must have stayed in touch with some of his old friends from the Nineties, for in this collection I discovered a 1921 edition, published in New York, of *Oscar Wilde: His Life and Confessions* by Frank Harris with the inscription: 'Horby, you old rogue! Don't forget your old friends! And don't you miss those glad, erect days!? – Frank Harris.'

Unfortunately for the researcher, there are no compromising documents from identifiable women. One assumes that either Horby or his family destroyed any letters of this nature. However, there are some perfectly proper signed photographs of beautiful and fully-dressed celebrities of the Nineties, such as Lillie Langtry, Ellen Terry, Florence Farr and Florence Balcombe. Lillie Langtry was, of course, the leading courtesan of her age and was for a time the mistress of the Prince of Wales. Ellen Terry was the leading actress of her era and was celebrated most in her role of Lady Macbeth. Florence Farr, a leading actress and dramatist, was also the lover of men such as Bernard Shaw, William Butler Yeats and Aleister Crowley. Oscar Wilde wanted to marry Florence Balcombe on account of her exceptional physical beauty but she spurned him in favour of Bram Stoker, author of *Dracula*. On the back of each one of these photographs, erasures have been made.

There is no doubt whatsoever in my mind that *The Black Pearl* should be published in the 1990s, giving us a quite unique insight into the 1890s. For my own part, I am still tracking down clues which will lend insight into this remarkable author. He has given us a document of great human interest which spans the academic disciplines of sociology, psychology, history, literature and sexology. It will surprise and possibly shock those who have a clichéd view of Victorian attitudes. It certainly lifts the manhole cover off a steaming underworld. The author explores every facet of his own sexuality and that of those he encounters. At times his interests are simply those of dissipation and debauchery. At other moments he relates the strange kinks of those he meets, which embroider the rich tapestry of human sexuality. For me, however, the most remarkable feature of this book is that its aristocratic Victorian author, outwardly a veritable pillar of the Establishment, comes to look upon sex as the holiest sacramental act in the known Universe.

Geraldine Lamb PhD.,
University of North Texas.

AUTHOR'S INTRODUCTION

As I take up my pen to write of my life, I remain convinced that fighting and fucking are when two people come closest. You can grow close to a man either by fighting against him or by fighting with him on the same side as one slogs along through various battles. However, I am of the opinion that it is not possible to grow close to a woman unless one fucks her.

My personal view is that when fucking a woman, one should jolly well roger her brains out and give it some arse. I'm well aware that this view is thought unfashionable in our degenerate modern times. Female emancipation has indeed proceeded apace and I have never opposed it but the results have not been precisely what I wanted nor, one suspects, exactly the results desired by the fairer sex. It is indeed a delight to regard our modern young girls in their slim, short skirts but they lack the mystery and romanticism of the long, rustling white petticoats of yesteryear. These days, they all wear rosy red-leaf lip-stick and they all smoke and they pout sexily but despite all that delicious expanse of white thigh and ankle, they lack the eroticism of the women of my youth. These days one takes a girl for morning cocktails at 'The Apple Tree', goes on to luncheon at 'Pietro Le Fueno', proceeds to an afternoon session at 'Dolly's', where one's ears are deafened with jazz, takes afternoon tea at The Connaught, goes on to cocktails at the

Ritz, sees the latest play at the Theatre Royal, The Haymarket, has drinks and then dinner at The Savoy, and all the thanks you receive is 'Cheerio.'

Ah! It wasn't like that in the days of my golden, gilded youth! Women really were women in those spacious times! They certainly weren't boys with short bobs for hair, flat chests and thin skin and bone where their buttocks should have been. It is said that times have become increasingly sexually free. It is so and I welcome the development yet some inscrutable element has been lost. How is the matter best put? I am reminded of Lady Charlotte X, who always used to defend the institution of marriage on the grounds that it lent so much spice to the pleasures of adultery. Forbidden fruit does indeed taste so much sweeter. In a similar vein, one could advance the proposition that the very restrictions of my youth gave each forbidden encounter an exquisite charm that is wholly lacking in these present days that are so permissive and yet so cold.

Nevertheless, it is impossible for me to complain about a life indefatigably blessed by good fortune. I am hardly a rich man but even in these inflationary times it is just about possible to jog along on £100,000 a year. The only duties incumbent upon me are maintaining the lands, a job done most capably by the family stewards; and turning up at the House of Lords occasionally whenever there is a vital vote. My quiet position has enabled me to meet some of the most interesting men and women in the land and also to travel abroad to meet more.

Throughout my life, I have been a lover of Woman, in all her intriguing shapes and guises. Although I have enjoyed the good fortune of meeting with some of the strongest, most powerful and most intelligent men of my era, and although I have assuredly learned wisdom from their lips, I have received yet greater education from the labia of ladies.

This may be thought a peculiar view but I shall demonstrate my case.

Too many men of my acquaintanceship, however illustrious, have informed me that they regard the sexual act as being merely the prodding of a stiff rod between soft thighs into a soft and welcoming female orifice. Although their joy in this glorious matter can hardly be denied and although I take a deep share in their joy, knowing of it to my own good, I nevertheless insist that there is something more to the matter.

The sexual act, properly understood, is more than merely the delights of animal gratification, splendid though these are. It is more than the doing of a deed alleged to be 'dirty' and therefore somehow sinful, in consequence of which its execution imparts a sinister thrill, an added *frisson* of forbidden pleasure. It can be the holiest, most religious act in the World when a man and a woman come together and create energy between one another as a sacrament. It can elevate one's consciousness and enable one, if one dares say so, to evolve beyond the level of the apes who originally sired us.

During my life, I have been able to acquaint myself with a number of occult groups, from some of whom I learned much and from others of whom I learned nothing at all. Most of them have taught me techniques, nevertheless, which I have found to be useful. It is my willed intention to put down here all I know before I die so that possibly some others may benefit from the recounting of my experiences.

In the beginning, I knew nothing other than my rampant rod and of its lust for a slick, juicy cunt. By the end, I had discovered the Holy Grail. I shall begin, then, amidst the mist of ignorance, continue through a hard middle and, one trusts, finish with a flourish at the end.

CHAPTER ONE

I've never forgotten the day when she returned from her mid-morning ride, for I had stared admiringly at her beautiful bottom. She seemed heated and excited, her face was flushed and she breathed so heavily that her protuberant breasts threatened to split the linen and lace of her fussy white blouse.

'Get your Latin book,' she said, 'I'll be with you shortly.'

Miss Rosemary Radcliffe entered the schoolroom in her usual fashion twenty minutes later. As was her custom, she wore a green floppy hat, angled slightly to the right, and long, green silk gloves adorned her arms. As was usual, her thrusting young breasts were tightly encased in a fussy, white satin blouse with frills around its frontage. Her hips and legs were swathed by a long, green pleated skirt, underlaid by petticoats which swished and crackled as she walked. There were high-heeled laced boots of leather upon her feet and the effect of her high heels was to make her glorious bottom stand out. I could not take my eyes away from her bottom. It seemed to have a life of its own as it wiggled and waggled and as each movement caused a fluttering of the pleats in her skirt.

'Let's get on with Latin Unseen Translation,' Miss Rosemary Radcliffe said briskly. 'Translate the first sentence on page 56.'

'Caesar,' I said, 'having drawn up his battle-line, and

fearing a shortage of corn, departed to the plains with his cohorts, before the advance of the Gauls from their camp.'

'Satisfactory,' she said. 'But if you come here a moment, I will show you how to translate it with greater elegance.'

I arose and walked towards her with a throbbing erection in my trousers. The bulge was unmistakable. 'You naughty boy!' she squealed, and then she touched me, to my inexpressible delight. The touch of her finger upon my rigid rod evoked an immediate ecstasy and I sank to my knees and for a moment buried my face in her lap, breathing in the aroma of her voluminous skirt. Her thighs moved and her petticoats rustled and crackled. Her small, soft hand gently unbuttoned my fly and sought inside for the treasure after which she lusted. Her fingers played delicately up and down my stiff and throbbing member.

'Ohh . . .' she sighed, 'never forget this . . .'

I could no longer help myself and nor could Miss Rosemary Radcliffe. We kissed with our tongues intertwining and as we did so, I unbuttoned her blouse. Beneath it, there was a scarlet corset, which explained her erect stance, but I removed that from her nubile body and admired her delicately smooth skin and her breasts with their shouting erect nipples. A pull of a zip saw her skirt come away and I lost no time in disabusing her of her two petticoats, one soft and silken and the other stiff and crackly. Beneath these there was a suspender belt and stockings, which I swiftly removed to behold her glorious quim. Its lips were utterly enchanting.

'Oh! . . . oh! . . . oh!' she sighed as I entered. 'Now fuck me all the way to Paradise!'

Her cunt was deliciously warm and wet as I pumped her with my prick, my hands holding her beautiful, silken-soft bottom with a finger up the rose-bud of her arse. Her cunt gripped me and gripped me again and I shivered with the sheer delicious pleasure of it.

'Just fuck me!' my governess shrieked and as I rode her, her loins went into a series of spasms, shaking her gentle cunny. 'Ohh . . .!' she gasped as I realised that my hands beneath her gorgeous bottom her soaking wet with the juices of her love.

'That was good,' she sighed languidly. 'I can see, though, that I must teach you more.'

CHAPTER TWO

Miss Rosemary Radcliffe must be among the most extraordinary women that I have encountered during my life. In later years, she went on to teach other scions of the aristocracy and the gentry. One could always tell the difference between, say, a chap who had merely been to Eton and one who had enjoyed the benefits of Miss Radcliffe's tuition in addition. Although I believe that many virtues can be imparted by a public school education, one nevertheless finds it an embarrassment to witness inexperienced public schoolboys endeavouring to disport themselves in ladies' company. They appear to be awkward, sweaty and ashamed. Their mode of attracting a female more befits a drunken clown. This has never been the case with anyone who has had the good fortune to benefit from Miss Radcliffe's sound teaching.

I doubt if I shall ever forget her long, straight, brown hair, gloriously free and hanging whenever she entered from the riding stables yet in the evenings always strictly piled in an immaculately tailored bun. I shall never forget the look of her crisp, clear blue eyes nor the sound of her ice-clear voice. Her sessions of supervision were equally unforgettable.

I did not know what to say when I entered the schoolroom the morning after my first initiation into the joys of womanhood. Everything had changed for me and yet the room had not. I was still sitting behind a walnut desk in a diminutive attic room and staring at a blank blackboard. The room smelled of dust, chalk and wax polish. To my right, there was a lattice window which supplied a view of meadows populated by grazing sheep. I was wearing the clothes which Miss Radcliffe had demanded of me: a grey flannel suit with knee-length shorts, a crisp white shirt and light blue tie and grey socks up to my knees with shiny, black buckled shoes. Miss Radcliffe had given me to understand that once I had surpassed her exacting standards, I would be allowed into long trousers.

'Just give him a sound education,' my pater had said, adding; 'Y'know.' This included ensuring that I would be up to taking a place at Trinity College, Cambridge. Since my academic standards were little more than mediocre, my governess and tutor had been allotted quite a task.

On this particular day, though, with the sun glaring through the window so as brightly to illuminate all the dancing chalk dust, I must confess that I awaited the coming of Miss Rosemary Radcliffe with some considerable trepidation. The subject to be taught was Ancient History and it was difficult to concentrate upon the warlike deeds and domestic doings of the ancient Egyptians, Babylonians, Assyrians, Greeks and Romans. I stared hopelessly at the books before me and wondered how I might face Miss Radcliffe after all that had transpired on the previous day. I sat in the silence and stared gloomily at the blackboard with its tray of multi-coloured and excruciatingly squeaking chalk. The silence was eventually broken by the rustle of a skirt with swishing petticoats ascending the staircase, then Rosemary Radcliffe entered the schoolroom.

On this day, she was wearing a long, black bell-skirt which clung tightly to her voluptuous bottom. Her high-heeled, shiny leather ankle-boots made her buttocks stand out and tremble as she strode. Her breasts were neatly restrained within the confines of yet another white blouse of satin trimmed with lace. Around her trim waist, there was a wide belt of gleaming black leather with a sparkling silver buckle.

I know now that I was not alone among males in possessing a peculiar fascination for skirts. *Skirt*: the very word provokes my nerves into a tingling of anticipated erotic delight. The garment conceals joys whilst at the same time offering so desired an accessibility. That morning I thrilled to the toss of Rosemary Radcliffe's skirt-hem and as she smoothed her slim white hand over her bottom just before she sat down, I was compelled to adjust my trousers in order to free my rampaging erection. I fear that my face was flushed but hers was white and pale as though nothing untoward, other than the natural matter of education, had transpired.

'Good morning, Horby,' she spoke evenly.

'Good morning, Miss Radcliffe.'

'Tell me about the latest state of your reading in Ancient History.'

I endeavoured to mask a nervous gulp. One wondered if she were being serious or simply playing with me. Only yesterday I had been squeezed within her luscious thighs to be initiated into an unknown joy I had yet to fathom deeply and the event had perplexed my mind. I had not gone to bed to read Ancient History.

'A little Ovid . . .' I faltered feebly.

'Ah, yes.' Those damnable blue eyes of hers speared straight through me. It was obvious that she knew that I was telling a lie, equally that I knew that she had ascertained that fact. 'And did you find Ovid interesting?'

'*The Metamorphoses* is a splendid book,' I replied.

'So it is,' she responded crisply, 'and so is his *The Art of*

Love which awaits us in due course.' I blushed furiously but she did not. 'What is your opinion of the pagan religion as described in Ovid?'

'Very interesting indeed, Miss Radcliffe,' I replied politely, though if the truth be known, I was uncomfortable then with questions of religion. My parents had not raised me in terms of any particular structure of beliefs, my Mama was dead and Papa was an avowed agnostic who went to Church every Sunday simply to maintain his social position as squire among the countryfolk.

'To begin with,' said Miss Radcliffe, 'there was worship of the female.' She shifted her skirt across her legs, those lovely legs I had known only yesterday, and I could see her doing that through the gap in the desk at which she had ensconced herself.

'Yes . . .' I said dreamily.

'This was thousands of years ago,' Miss Rosemary Radcliffe continued with maddening calm, 'The sky, the stars, the sea, the Moon and the Earth were worshipped and all of these were personified as aspects of The Goddess, a great and all-embracing female deity.'

I was not sure if it were my imagination or no, but I fancied that beneath her voluminous skirt, she was squeezing her thighs together tightly.

'Men were at that time so unintelligent,' Rosemary Radcliffe continued coolly, 'that they were incapable of associating the biological fact of sexual intercourse with the birth of a child nine months later.' I flushed furiously and nodded. 'Males had to evolve,' she continued relentlessly, 'if human beings were to evolve. Women encouraged them so to do. Eventually some men discerned that the Sun is what gives life to this planet and that the phallus is what gives life upon Earth.' I glanced down briefly at my throbbing erection and acquiesced in the manner of a keen and willing student. 'The Goddess has many forms,' she resumed with remorseless calm. 'She is called Nuit in Egypt, also Isis, and was known in Ancient Greece as Hera, wife of Zeus the King; as Athena, Goddess of Wisdom; or as Aphrodite, Goddess of Love and Beauty.' She stroked her hair and fluttered her eyelids demurely whilst I hoped I wouldn't come into my short trousers.

'Men, meanwhile,' she said, 'saw another truth, the truth of the Sun and the phallus which they called 'God' under many names. Zeus, Apollo, Dionysus, Ra, Horus, Adonis Attis, Osiris and Mithras are but a few examples. Unfortunately, in establishing this religion, they oppressed the very women who had nurtured them towards the accomplishment of his execution.'

'Quite so . . .' I murmured, unable to tear my eyes from the black skirt which swathed her belly, thighs, knees, calves, ankles and feet and which hid her glory of female flesh.

'Would you like to make amends?' she demanded fiercely.

'Yes . . .' I whispered hoarsely.

'Then come to me on all fours, as men did once, lift my skirt and place your head between my thighs.'

I hastened eagerly, hot and panting, to comply with her command. Crawling beneath the desk, I flipped up her long, black skirt and its white petticoats beneath to discern that she was not wearing knickers. There, in front of me was her beautiful pearly oyster, surmounted by a bush of feminine hair, encased by satin-soft thighs and exhaling an odour of attar of roses. I placed my head between her soft, warm thighs and they responded by embracing my cheeks.

'Kiss me . . .' she sighed, then with an imperious gesture, she tossed her skirt and petticoats over my head and placed the high heel of her boot upon my bent back. My face, already well above her knees, came to embrace her silken skin. My nose, mouth and chin were now tickled by her pubic hairs. My governess and tutor gave a wriggle and holding me close with her thighs, rubbed her hairy moist cunt all over my face, my eyes, my nose and my mouth in a very lingering manner. In the midst of her hair, I found her nether mouth and felt a little protuberance near its tip, which she pressed with increasing force against my own lips and which appeared to be quite quiveringly sensitive. The instant that I felt her heel pressed into my spine, I gave it a kiss. Instantly she pushed it into my lips and my mouth was forced wide open. Unable to kiss it, I tickled it with my tongue.

As I did so, the movements of Miss Rosemary Radcliffe became more and more vigorous, her hold on me grew tighter and tighter and she pressed me still more closely. Feeling the increasing pressure of her sharp heel upon my back, I continued to play with her soft flesh as I inhaled its perfume, to bite it gently with my teeth and to lick it with my tongue, especially that little protuberance, as soon as I discovered the transports of delight which this gave her. To my enraptured amazement, the aperture grew still greater and greater until I seemed actually to lose my face in it. It had wet me and seemed to cover me all over in it. I felt as if I was some distance inside her body and I grew furious with a strange excitement which increased with her own. Miss Rosemary Radcliffe's throbs and sobs became more and more convulsive, as she squirmed and writhed in a coming rapture.

At last, centring herself upon my mouth, there came a series of violent spasmodic throbs lasting for some seconds then becoming gradually slower and slower, whilst there spilled into my mouth a warm, sticky fluid tasting something like a mixture of dry sherry and bitter almonds. I could hear her exclamations although her skirt and petticoats were smothering my hearing of the sounds. Eventually, her efforts ceased, her grasp relaxed and she reposed as my head sank against her thigh.

Myself, I was experiencing my own rapture. How delightful that Woman should be so formed and possess an organ so receptive, so responsive, so capable of appreciating and returning the passions of my own, which, indeed, I longed to place inside hers once more. How exquisite would be the pleasure if our movements could take place simultaneously and whilst I was inside her. I was overjoyed at the intimate knowledge of a woman who had taught me so much and wondered whether everyone had equal good fortune, feeling convinced that they could not otherwise obtain anything like a perfect acquaintance with her.

I burned to express my feelings in words, to implore her to permit me to carry out my idea of inserting in her the engine of mine which she had manipulated. Unfortunately I could not speak for I did not know what to do with the liquid love-milk with which my mouth was permeated. I needed to rise and gasp some fresh air but I was trapped beneath her skirts and she was clasping my head tightly beneath her thighs. A horse's strength is in his loins, a lion's in his jaws, an elephant's in his trunk and weight, an ox's in his neck, and a woman's is evidently in her thighs. I again tried to free myself only to receive a tighter and more prolonged and suffocating squeeze followed by a smart blow on my back from her heel. A little chagrined and disappointed, I thought it wisest to give in and resolved to await events, passing my time in contemplation of my delicious situation under a young lady's petticoats. To enhance my sense of it, I recalled her lovely facial features and figure to my mind, picturing her to myself seated there. And then I remembered that I was in full possession of the secret of her most private charms. I gently rubbed my head against her, up and down the insides of her thighs. She relaxed her hold and her lascivious motions told me how this pleased her.

I revelled in the contact of her undergarments and in the warm atmosphere and pungent scent of the locality. I gloried in the discovery of what petticoats actually did conceal and I swallowed the liquid in my mouth with a voluptuous thrill. I revelled in the contact of her undergarments once again as I wondered whether there was anything wicked in all this – whether it was impure? Was it adultery, fornication or lasciviousness to be beneath a maid's legs, kissing them and gratifying her and myself by dalliance with my lips and tongue with her exquisite and enticing 'mouth' simply because that second mouth was between her legs and usually hidden? This concealment was as conventional as dress, founded on the decorum and decencies of life. Was it wicked to kiss the mouth of an Eastern woman because, when walking abroad, it was covered by a Yashmak? Brushing aside the conventionalities in the shape of skirts and petticoats gave a poignant relish to an embrace that seemed perfectly legitimate. So I hugged Rosemary closer and kissed her legs again.

In a few minutes, any further disposition on my part for reflection and analysis was cut short by a firm but gentle pressure of her dainty leg and little heel on my back. Again I glued my mouth to what seemed the compendium, the embodiment, the full divine revelation of Rosemary Radcliffe herself in her most intimate soul, and, on this occasion, with fewer scruples and with more avidity, with greater knowledge and keener skill, I nipped the tender, succulent lips. I inserted my tongue further and tickled the little protuberance more persistently, absorbing the yielding flesh more greedily. Miss Radcliffe's motions were in proportion more violent, her transport, her loss of self-control more complete. All our efforts were directed to bring about a repetition of that convulsive and spasmodic agitation of her being which appeared to delight her and affected me. It took much longer this time and required more effort. Her legs were thrown wider apart and she exerted herself more vigorously. At last it came! The spasm took place more slowly and endured longer. She lay back with a gasp of relief and satisfaction and I was released.

'You dear boy . . .' she sighed dreamily. I glanced at her with adoring eyes. 'We will have some tea now. I want it, I can tell you . . .' She rang for the maid as I stretched myself, looking at the clock to note that I had been under her petticoats and in close communion with her for over two hours; and made sure that I looked properly respectable when Meggs the maid entered. Of course, Miss Rosemary Radcliffe was looking equally proper and one could attribute the flush on her cheeks to her passion for instilling the truths and beauties of Ancient History to her keen and willing young pupil.

When the tea arrived, we both drank it gratefully and in silence.

'Energy, energy, energy,' she murmured at last. 'The male and the female.' She rose, smoothing down her skirt and looking so unutterably demure. 'That's IT.' Then she swept from the room with her skirts swishing in a rapture of female joy.

For a long time afterwards, I sat in the schoolroom and gazed at the bare blackboard. I'd been taught one of the best lessons I had ever learned. There'd be English Poetry this afternoon: that was something to which I truly looked forward.

In later years, I told the story to Frank Harris and I will relate it in the ensuing chapter. For the present I wish to state that I duly proceeded up to Trinity College, Cambridge and Miss Rosemary Radcliffe proceeded duly to marry one of the wealthiest and most handsome young Earls in the Kingdom.

CHAPTER THREE

'Wouldn't you agree, Horby,' Frank Harris roared at me over a Café Royal table littered with bottles of champagne and cognac and drunken guests, 'that the first really good fuck *really* is the bloody best!?'

Ah! How sweet it was to be young and rich in early 1895 with all the World before me!

'Frank,' said Oscar Wilde, who was sitting next to me. 'Our young friend here may share my ignorance of what a rugby scrum is, but I imagine it's like a conversation with you.' He glanced briefly at seven men who were placidly snoozing upon the table-top. These men were either very aristocratic or very rich or both. Only the artists and I were still conscious. Bernard Shaw, who had ignored the ten-course luncheon in favour of a nut cutlet with a green salad and who had eschewed wines of the rarest vintage on account of his peculiar preference for mineral water, remained his annoyingly sober and pleasant self. Aubrey Beardsley, pale, thin and skeletal, did not seem to be affected by the vast quantities he had quaffed at all. He was sketching idly, his long fingers flicking his Swan fountain pen in swift streaks over a napkin. 'Are they going to take out the guests along with the dishes?' Oscar enquired gently.

'I hope they don't take you out, Oscar,' Harris retorted. 'You see, what I was telling our young friend here – unlike some of the boys you know, Oscar, isn't he? eh? – is that I'm not talking about a mediocre first fuck.' He seemed blithely oblivious to the consternation he was causing amongst some of our fellow diners though our fellow artists at other tables merely laughed. 'That's merely a grope and a squirt. Let's face it, gentlemen, bad sex is simply two and a half minutes of squelching!' he boomed.

A prim-faced gentleman and his ugly, prissy lady both choked on their wine. Raucous roars of approval came from the opposite major table, where the Duke of Devonshire was hosting the artists James Abbot McNeill Whistler and Edgar Degas, briefly visiting from Paris. They were accompanied by three stunningly good looking young women who added to their laughter a throaty, sexy chorus.

At last I was really starting to enjoy myself. The past six months had been hard, for Rosemary Radcliffe had performed her duties immaculately and left to take up another post; and my pater had died, following my mater who had passed away some years earlier. There had been an inevitable period of grief and sorrow at my bereavement. Eventually, I had pulled myself together on New Year's Day 1895 to realise that I was the heir to a Viscountcy, that I had a small stately home, a town flat, 10,000 acres of prime land, the nation's fourth largest collection of antique silver and an income from the funds of £100,000 a year. I had a place at Trinity College, Cambridge, to be taken up this October; there was my relationship with the Hon. Claire Woodrough, of which more anon; and Rosemary Radcliffe continued occasionally to write to me. I always wrote back to her. Here and now, I had nothing of which to complain, for my family connections and my claim to be a budding artist and poet had won me a seat at the Café Royal at the table of the fabled Frank Harris.

What an extraordinary man he was! Stories abounded

concerning him. One heard that he'd been a cowboy in the American West, then a student of Philosophy at the University of Heidelberg, next an intrepid journalist reporting front-line dispatches from the Russo-Turkish War; after that, the Editor of the London *Evening News*, who tripled its circulation via sheer sensationalism whilst winning serious literary acclaim for his hauntingly sensitive book of short stories, published as *Montes the Matador*. He was a short, thick-necked, furious fighting man, yet whenever it suited him, he could play his voice like a cello. His fierce, challenging blue eyes glowered at you as his thick, handlebar moustache appeared to bristle with incipient anger at unmanly conduct. Although he was then married and living near me in Park Lane with the noted Society heiress he had married, he was accounted among the most notorious rakes of London. Presently, he was Editor of the *Fortnightly Review*, sneered at but bought by an older generation, and venerated by all emerging writers and artists.

'Don't have another, Frank,' Oscar Wilde said as Harris sloshed out generous glasses for the three of us and Aubrey Beardsley.

'Why not?' Harris asked.

'It might make you drunk.'

'Oscar, have you ever seen me drunk?'

'No, Frank,' said Oscar, 'and never sober either.'

'Ha! ha! D'you hear him?' Harris roared with laughter. 'Here.' He placed a hand on Oscar's arm, preventing him from lifting the brandy to his mouth. 'Don't do that, Oscar, it's bad for your health.'

Instantly, Oscar passed his glass to Bernard Shaw, who took it politely and gazed at it thoughtfully.

'Don't do that, Mr Shaw, it's bad for your health,' said Oscar.

'What exactly is your point, Mr Wilde?' Shaw responded.

'It's Frank's good advice,' Oscar chuckled. 'The only thing to do with good advice is to pass it on.'

'Good on you, Oscar!' Harris roared and raised his glass.

'Don't you ever worry about your liver, Mr Harris?' Shaw asked soberly.

'We're just good friends,' Harris returned. 'Anyway, if you drink less than your doctor, you'll be all right. What is life anyway? It depends on the liver. But enough of this. I wanted young Horby here to tell me all about the first really ace fuck he ever had. Go on, young man. Or don't you dare?'

'Oh, Frank . . .' Oscar Wilde sighed, 'mine was like cold mutton.'

'How interesting,' Aubrey Beardsley said loudly. It was the first time he had spoken in the past two hours.

'Mr Harris,' said Bernard Shaw, 'I feel that you are pressing this young man into a mere relation of what is simply, in the last analysis, a biological imperative.'

'Ha! ha! Excellent!' Frank Harris bellowed, and the prissy couple at the corner table fled in terror. 'Now, young Horby, listen to me. Fighting 'n' fucking are the only serious things, y'see? And these distinguished gentlemen around us don't realise the bloody fact. I assemble the greatest men in the kingdom – or should I say the queen-dom? – to discuss these vital matters and look at it! Seven of my guests are asleep. Go on, snore on!' he shouted at them. 'Look at Bernard Shaw, finest critic of music and drama of our benighted age! He might even make it as a dramatist some day; heaven knows he's got the ability. But when did he lose his virginity? Twenty-eight.' The voice of Harris dripped with scorn. Shaw stared moodily at the bubbles in his mineral water. 'And when I asked Oscar and Aubrey here when they thought sexual feelings began in the male, why, Aubrey told me eleven and Oscar told me thirteen. Frankly, if you'll pardon the pun, I've been having sexual feelings ever since I was born. And here's to that!' He tossed back his Napoleon cognac and poured himself another. 'Now, young man,' he demanded, 'can you tell us about a really good fuck?'

'I certainly can, Mr Harris,' I replied. He looked delighted and ordered more champagne and cognac as I explained briefly to him the background of Rosemary and myself. 'And so it came to that afternoon,' I said, 'when the lesson was English poetry.'

'Love it,' said Harris, tweaking his moustache, 'but don't be too long on getting to the juicy bits, as the actress said to the Bishop. Come on, boy, don't be bashful.'

'Frank, I think you're interrupting,' Oscar Wilde murmured gently, adding: 'And even I am interested here.'

'On this occasion,' I resumed, 'Miss Rosemary insisted that the Poetry lesson be conducted in her boudoir, where she eagerly devoured crumpets and muffins and plum-tart and cups of delicious, fragrant tea. She made me sit near her and follow her example. Her manner towards me was most winning and affectionate, with a strong spice of tantalising coquetry. She even indulged in some little endearments of a particularly alluring character, occasionally brushing her long, pink-taloned fingers against the renewed stiff swelling in my crutch. I sighed with the pleasure of it.

' "Oh, do you want me . . .?" she sighed.

' "Yes . . ." I breathed as her fingers flicked over my fly to unbutton it and to release my throbbing member.

' "Poor fellow," she murmured softly, "how swollen, how red, how inflamed he is! I must set him right." Her soft, cool and delicate hand was very soon upon me. There was a strange gleam in her eyes as she spoke these words which immediately excited my wonder. She flung herself back upon the sofa and pulled open her blouse to reveal pale, pouting white breasts with shouting erect nipples. I had never seen a sight quite so alluring, so desirable. Her severe black skirt had ridden all its way up to her luscious thighs. One slender leg was completely unveiled to display the proud flesh beneath the suspenders of her stocking tops; and the other was far away from its sister at the other side of the sofa. When a young lady sits edgewise upon a table, she is said to be in want of a husband; when she rests on her back in the presence of a growing young man with penis rampant and poking stiffly out of the fly of his trousers, careless about her clothing, her eyes aflame and her legs well separated, it may safely be affirmed that she wishes to welcome this young man to her arms. No doubt the idea that I was six years younger excited her. The idea of being possessed by and yielding to her pupil gave a peculiar, a poignant zest to it, which the ordinary humdrum everyday copulation of a youth and maiden would have been without.

'I slipped my hand on to the lovely leg nearest to me and let it move upwards. I felt that once again she had no drawers on, my hand was around the smooth roundness of her gorgeous bottom. I moved up her clothes and saw the delicate pink flesh which I kissed. Her own left hand upon my shoulders drew me from my position over her.

' "How dare you?" she said.

' "I love you, Rosemary," I replied, gazed into her eyes then kissed her ruby lips.

'She put her right hand round my back and holding my mouth to hers gave me a long, clinging kiss, inserting her tongue between my lips in quest of mine own, moving hers up and down as she did so.

' "You – you . . ." she gasped, "must say what you want,

you must ask me – to – let you . . ."

'I guessed what was necessary. How strange it is that the more refined the girl, the more she loves to be shocked.

' "Oh, Rosemary . . .!" I sighed.

' "Rosemary?" she echoed scornfully.

' "Miss Radcliffe . . ." I murmured back softly; and she melted in my arms.

'With my lips upon her warm, wet, open mouth and my eyes fixed upon her angelic, cold-blue stare, I removed her petticoats and ensconced myself between her limbs, naked from the tops of her stockings, rejoicing in the contact of her flesh with mine. Her legs enlaced themselves at my back and made me a happy prisoner. I caressed the full round globes of her bosom, removing my mouth from hers to cover them and her neck with burning kisses. Her right hand had meanwhile not been idle. It had been playing delectably with that instrument which was to outrage her so sweetly and she had excited it greatly and enlarged it even further.

' "Do you want to fuck your governess and tutor . . .?"

' "Yes . . ."

' "Then say it." That high, crisp, clear voice.

' "I want to fuck you, my governess and tutor, Miss Radcliffe."

' "Then it must be put in *there*," she returned sweetly, guiding my prick to her cunt with the delicate flute-playing of her fingers.

' "Oh, Rosemary!" I gasped as I entered her.

' "It's nicer, isn't it," she sighed, "having itself uncovered by me there than by my hand, isn't it, Horby?"

' "Oh!" I was beside myself.

' "Oh!! Oh! Oh! Naughty, naughty boy!" So was she. "Oh, darling! Oh, Horby! Oh, Baby! Push him further in – there," she spoke as she embraced me with all her strength.

' "Oh, Rosemary! Oh, Miss Radcliffe!" I exclaimed as, after a few blissful moments of sweet tossing by her, which I felt to my finger tips, and a moment's determination to keep the position I had gained, from which, indeed, her strong legs at my back made any retreat impossible, I shuddered, and sank upon her luxurious form, as, with passionate force, the spasmodic injection of the essence of my being into hers was accomplished. Her bottom rising and falling rapidly, herself in a lovely exquisite love sickness, she held me tightly, scarcely relaxing her grip.

' "You've done it to please yourself," she breathed. "Now do it to please your lady." Naked, I lay beside her, caressing her neck, arms and hips. My mouth gave her its true appreciation of her beauty, sucking at her thrusting breasts as though they contained the milk of paradise, then giving her delicious cunt long, loving and lascivious licks. Her moans grew louder as her pretty, dimpled bottom wriggled upon the satin surface of the sofa. "Come to me," she called like a woman wailing for her demon lover, "come to me!"

"I entered her slowly and deliberately, rather like a giant iron-clad steam-ship coming into port. Then I rammed my sex inside hers right up to the hilt, and she kept gasping. She carried on gasping as I rode her in and out, going all the length, all the breadth and all the way, commencing slowly, then working up to a quick-thrusting serenade which turned into a joyous succession of staccato stabbings and she moaned with the rapture of it. I moved my prick in strong, sweeping circles, rubbing every pore of that soft, wet cushion within her as her hips gyrated with pleasure. Our loins fused together in a gallop so hard and fast, it was a blur of ecstasy that made my hips throw her cunny that extra inch, which as I was later to learn, means yet another mile higher than the sky – and then my arms held her close and tenderly as she came.

"The spasms that shook her body jolted me like an electric current. Then I blasted away with my prick shooting for the stars, Rosemary all the while moaning her soft delights at the sunbursts of my throbbing.

"For a few minutes, she lay quite still, her blue eyes closed, as I gazed down upon her face. Its contours had softened into an almost child-like vulnerability, which made me feel protective. I kissed her soft, ruby lips once more.

' "I love you," we both said simultaneously.'

CHAPTER FOUR

'Thank you, Horby, you've acquitted yourself well. I thoroughly enjoyed that,' said Frank Harris. There was a merry twinkle in his eye. 'You've certainly woken up everybody else.' I looked around the table to see that seven slumberers were now fully awake and staring at me with considerable interest. 'Waiter!' Harris roared; and the waiter came instantly for Harris was renowned as the terror of waiters. 'Bring another half-dozen of the champers and another couple of the brandies. Sickert!' he shouted at a gaunt man in a threadbare suit who had just cruised in to seat himself at a corner table only to order merely a small beer. 'We can't have you on your own with just a beer. You're an artist, for fuck's sake!' Harris roared. 'Pull up a chair, my dear fellow, and join us for copious quantities of champagne and cognac.' As this fellow with a haunted, melancholy cast of features nodded, smiled thinly and complied with the request, I remember feeling so young, so keen, so eager to learn things. That was the Café Royal in those golden days. One could go there and dine on steak tartare followed by a well-hung pheasant and drink the rarest of vintages: yet an impoverished poet or artist could also go there for the price of beer. These days, one gathers, it has degenerated into being an uninteresting public house with a bad and over-priced restaurant attached to it. The exquisite private rooms where one could once entertain young ladies are no more also, one is given to understand.

'So what did you gain from this experience?' Frank Harris boomed at me.

'Long trousers,' I replied.

'Oh, God,' Aubrey Beardsley sighed wearily as he continued to sketch relentlessly, 'you're not seriously telling me, surely, that you have to give a woman an orgasm before you're allowed to wear long trousers, are you?'

'Now, now, Aubrey,' Harris smiled genially, 'no attacks on our young friend here. He's told us a damn good story about the male and the female. When does your art ever encapsulate images of the male and the female in the same sort of way?'

'It just has, Mr Harris,' Beardsley replied icily, holding up an inked table napkin which showed Salome holding up the severed, bloodied head of John the Baptist upon a plate.

'Art is the art of repeating oneself effectively,' Harris said. 'I think I've seen that image before,' he added coldly. 'In Oscar's *Salome*.'

'But done like this?' Beardsley queried. I regret that I never knew Aubrey Beardsley that well, though I was a great admirer of his art. As a person, I always found him to be rather cold and cutting. Of course I was familiar with his illustrations to Wilde's *Salome*. They had caused a scandal, made Beardsley famous, increased Oscar's infamy when the play was performed in Paris but banned in London and made of Mr Beardsley the most fashionable and sought after artist in London, for the time being. I stared at this thin, short-haired, tubercular-looking and frail young man with his frigid pride. Then I stared at the visual image upon his napkin. It jolted me out of my momentary complacency. In addition to the drawing with which I was familiar, he had drawn a crucifix above the severed head of John the Baptist and inserted a large penis in the gaping mouth of *Salome*.

'Your attitudes towards Christianity, Mr Beardsley,' Bernard Shaw said levelly, 'are perhaps somewhat ambivalent.'

'Not at all, Mr Shaw.' Beardsley quaffed three measures of cognac in one gulp and then coughed horribly. As he spluttered his way to his recovery, he put his beautiful drawing on the candle-flame before him and ignored the involuntary gasps of 'No!' which went up around the table as his artwork burned within his fingers. 'Nero used the Christians as human torches,' he observed drily, 'which is the only light the Christians have ever given to the World.' His artwork passed into ashes within his long, slender fingers. He arose. 'I am going now. Thank you for the luncheon, Mr Harris.' He picked up the walking cane he'd kept beside him, one of ebony topped with pewter that had been delicately engraved, then coughed hard once more. 'My apologies, gentlemen, for I have a cold. My fault. I have left the tassel off my cane.'

'Where're you off to?' Oscar Wilde demanded. 'And why in such an inglorious hurry? Why such reckless folly in one so young?'

'I'm going to France, Oscar,' said Beardsley. 'The real France. Not the places you frequent.'

'Dear Aubrey,' Wilde sighed, 'he knows France so well. He has been to Dieppe once.'

'Watch your weight, fatso,' Beardsley retorted and strode swiftly out of the room. It took Oscar a couple of minutes to recover from that shot.

'Women!' Frank Harris pronounced, returning to his favourite theme. 'Here's to 'em, those gorgeous little bitches, those sucky-cunty satin-bottoms!' He tossed back a glass of champagne. 'Don'cha know what the wife of the General Boulanger said when he called off his intended coup d'état in France? Well,' Harris lit a big, fat Havana cigar, 'I said: "Madame Boulanger, what are you most looking forward to now that your husband has retired?" She replied: "A penis." I couldn't exactly print that in the *Evening News*, now, could I? And it's just as well I didn't because what she'd intended to state was the French pronunciation of "Happiness". Not that she had it. No, no,' Harris wiped away a tear from the corner of his eye, rather as though Madame Boulanger had once been a true love of his, which for all I knew, she might have been. 'General Boulanger, at one time the new Napoleon and the coming dictator of France lost his nerve on the eve of his intended coup, ran away to Belgium and shot himself over the grave of his mistress. As George Clemenceau, y'know, that leading French Minister said to me only the other day: "He died as he lived. Like a subaltern". But I digress. The question I am putting to the company generally and particularly to this young man here,' he gave me a big, toothy grin appropriate to a man of the world, 'is whether the first real fuck is the essential one. I mean, what you described for our delectation, Horby, was that the time you lost your virginity?'

'Not at all, Mr Harris,' I replied coolly. 'I think I made it clear earlier that I'd already lost my virginity. What I described was not an experience which I found to be just good. I was trying to describe an experience which for me was truly great.'

'All right!' Harris responded. 'Now my point is simply that this great fuck etches such a powerful imprint upon the male mind that one is always searching for it ever after and yet one can never recapture that first fine sacred rapture . . .' He sighed dreamily and quaffed more champagne.

'I don't quite agree, Mr Harris,' I answered. 'Much as I

love and revere the memory of my tutor and governess who initiated me into these mysteries of joy, I nevertheless experienced another form of sexual ecstasy shortly after I had won my place at Cambridge and my governess had left the household.'

'Tell us about it, my boy!' Frank Harris bellowed.

'It was with a cousin of mine called Claire.' Now it was my turn to sigh dreamily as I thought of Claire Woodrough. 'She'd come to stay at our country seat. She was about my own age and what a gorgeous girl she was! She had a fine head of blonde curls, striking eyes flecked with blue and gold, small breasts like ripening apples, a neat waist, a pert bottom that thrust out and seemed to take a secret joy in every swish of her skirt and lean, lissom legs with well-turned ankles. How can I forget that enchanting evening, after a dinner party, when I found her in the Conservatory musing over the cacti and Venus fly traps.

'She looked so very beautiful. She was flushed with wine and music, her cheeks were aglow, her eyes sparkled, her bosom heaved, her form was dilated with pleasure and vivacity showed in her every movement, mischief in her every glance.

' "Are you enjoying the evening?" she enquired, putting down her candle and giving her skirts a whisk.

' "Very much so, Claire." I gazed admiringly at this girl in her dinner dress, decorated with frills, which displayed nearly all of her pert breasts. With her slim, bare arms and smiling countenance, she was the personification of grace, beauty and girlhood. "Would you care for a walk in the garden beneath this marvellously romantic moon?"

'She nodded her assent, we slipped out quietly onto the lawn and soon vanished from view among the trees and bushes. A queer light came into her eyes and she twitched her bottom in a way which I recognised and knew to portend mischief. Then she sat down by an oak tree and her skirts rode up to her knees. When she saw me staring at them, with a becoming consciousness, she tried to shake the garments down. I quivered with a delighted apprehension. Then I kissed her full on the lips and my tongue explored the inmost recesses of her delectable young mouth.

' "Please please me," she murmured. "I do not like force. I think its employment inelegant," she said, with a most winning air of pretty embarrassment, coyly looking down as if frightened of her own temerity and uncertain of the response.

' "Indeed," I answered instantly, with a look freely expressing the admiration I felt. My frank tone conveyed the sincerity of my conviction. The effect was magical.

' "You darling boy," she answered, embracing me with girlish abandon and kissing me. Then with her hand upon my shoulder, she looked into my eyes and declared: "Undress! Now . . . we shall both enjoy it and I will help you." Affairs had indeed taken a very pleasant turn. It had become a task of love to obey her and the sacrifices involved were sweet and thrilling. We were both in a flutter of pleasant excitement as I yielded to her wishes. There followed enticing moments as she unbuttoned the fly of my trousers then fumbled with their fastenings. Her taking them off caused us both an infinity of delightful confusion. I felt the night air against my bare legs and made a vain attempt to catch the mischievous pair of hands that were so ruthlessly invading my privacy with the undisguised intention of entirely depriving me of it.

'She slipped lower on the ground in front of me to pull away my socks. Again a thrill and a gasp as she petulantly pulled away my shirt and I felt her soft cool hands on my bare and rampagingly erect member. With a pretty pout and an amused air, she took my penis in her mouth and licked it lasciviously. I was beyond any kind of resistance as her tongue darted in quick flicks up and down my stiff shaft. I threw my arms around her and kissed her ears and neck. We lost ourselves for some seconds in the sweetness of our embrace.

'She pulled away, passed her hands over my legs and thighs and between them, then played with my rigid member in a most tantalising fashion, observing that she was glad to make the acquaintance of so handsome a gentleman.

' "How it grows even more when I play with it!" she exclaimed. With a quiet sigh, she fell to sucking it again, kneeling between my legs. Her heavily drooping lids, the swimming eyes I had seen just before she sucked my prick, her quickly heaving bosom and the voluptuous movements of her twitching bottom gave a promising and encouraging account of her own condition. By a dexterous movement, I slipped my hand under her petticoats while she was thus interested in studying me. She started, grew fiery red, made a pretence of resistance which was, even to my inexperienced eyes, plainly unreal – instinctive not intentional.

'It is at this juncture that a man loses, if he is faint-hearted, but I was far too much excited to be faint-hearted. I insisted and I touched her. A complete change came over her instantly and it seemed to me miraculously.

' "Oh, darling . . .!" she ejaculated. "You mustn't . . . Oh, you mustn't!" Then, after a pause. "How would it tell me?"

' "It would tell you there," I said, placing my finger on the spot.

' "There! Oh – oh – should you put it there?" she asked, awaiting the answer with evident anxiety.

' "Yes, there!" I replied. I had got hold of her completely; her legs were well separated, and she moved lasciviously backwards and forwards, rubbing herself against my hand.

As I repeated the words, I pressed my middle finger well into the lips of that feminine mouth to which Rosemary had first introduced me.

' "Oh-oh-oh! You bastard! What would it do?"

' "It would throb-throb-throb," I answered, poking her with my finger each time I said the word and gazing laughingly at her, "and make his way right – into – you!"

' "Would it? This long thing . . .?" She held it tightly. "Just fancy!" She laughed lecherously. "All this inside me!" Her words were accompanied by a delicious blush and exquisite confusion, and as she moved lasciviously, I felt my hand being moistened. "Oh how dreadful – but how nice it would be – but wouldn't it be awfully naughty? Have you," as a thought struck her, "ever done it to any girl before? I mean, are you sure it is right – the right way, I mean?" She covered her words with a look of arch simplicity, endeavouring to conceal her rosy face as she knelt over me.

'I could not but smile. I felt triumphant. A beautiful girl of my own years was delivering herself into my hands. There was a friend within the citadel who would hand the fortress over to me. So, for all answer, I moved my hand again. It was a most potent and convincing argument. After some inarticulate sounds and one or two impassioned movements, she cried out, so I followed up my advantage and pressed the matter home.

' "You must – you must – you must!" The words came from deep within her. "How shall I lie?" Now, I was still something of a novice but I had at least been taught the elementary stages.

' "Lie on your back, my darling," I said, then withdrew my hand and made room for her. The late spring grass was agreeably accommodating, warm and damp.

' "So?" this charming girl enquired as in pretty disorder she abandoned herself helpless and absolutely to the divine impulse of nature and cast herself down – her legs wide apart, her petticoats up to her knees, her immaculate white drawers positioned around one slim ankle. I gazed enraptured at her lovely, uncovered limbs in their white silk stockings, at her heaving bosom, at her beautiful features.

' "How dare you look at me like that!" she squealed. "Come! come!" Before I had time to throw myself into the Elysium beneath me she had twined her arms and legs about me and clasped me in a close and firm embrace. The voluptuousness of the position was most intoxicating.

'My naked thighs pressed against hers underneath her skirts, ruthlessly encroaching upon the sanctuary of feminine divinity. My breast oppressed her palpitating bosom, her throbbing form lay vanquished and confined beneath mine. No maidenly coyness, no ladylike reserve could avail her to the smallest extent now. Her face was a sweet and close prisoner which I could kiss at pleasure. I myself was a close captive between her legs, two warm round soft cushions, two wilful and unrelenting gaolers grasping me with arch feminine severity.

'There was a delicious scent of summer flowers emanating from her, and her violent and unembarrassed movements as she adjusted herself to her satisfaction, thrilled my sense of touch. She settled herself without the slightest hesitation or awkwardness and with a bewitchingly careless disregard of me, retaining her tight grasp of my body all the while. Her magnetic power gradually stole over me and possessed me. Her touch thrilled me through and through.

' "There," she sighed in a transport of delight, speaking with the clear distinction of one who knows her own mind exactly and is determined to fulfill it at all hazards. "Pull my petticoats out of the way – come up closer – now . . . so," wriggle, wriggle, "now put it right in there, directly right through me or – or! – or! – or! – I shall squeeze you to death!"

All my fatigue vanished as if by magic. I was carried away by the realisation of my fondest dreams before me and the intensity of the physical happiness of my situation. I knew instinctively that I was on the brink of tasting the fullest earthly bliss and of draining the cup. It could not be dashed from my lips now.

' "Oh . . ." this lovely girl gasped as I sank into her embrace. Our youth and inexperience stimulated our ardours all the more, working us up into a yet higher pitch of excitement with its continually recurrent thrills of exquisite sensation.

'At last to my astonishment and alarm she cried that I was hurting her and the tone of her inarticulate expression of pleasure changed. Her eyes were suffused with tears. I began to have misgivings as to whether I was right after all. She was courageous, however, and she insisted. There appeared to be some obstacle. She complained of being sore, that I was tearing her. She bit me as my mouth sought hers to silence her protests with kisses. She asked me to draw back for a moment and even tried to push me away. But my transport was such that, even had I wished, I could not have complied. Carried away by my feelings I only pressed onwards the more. I felt that the climax had come and holding down her wrists upon the grass, I forcibly overcame her resistance.

'In a paroxysm of passion I threw myself upon her with fresh vigour and forced myself well into her, despite her opposition. I felt mad, furious, like an animal which has tasted blood. The obstacle soon vanished; I burst through it; and not heeding her screams, I thrust forward inside her; holding her with my arms about her neck as in a vice, pressing her down against the ground so that she could not retreat. Throb – throb – throb. I sank onto her breast and she seemed to faint in a delirium of joy, her pain gone with the sound of her screams.

'At that instant, she was stamped upon my mind with such strange and astonishing vividness that I still recall it with awe and wonder.

'At the moment of consummation, when her response and my convulsion satisfied the hunger I had not until then known how to allay, there was a perfect picture of her impressed upon my sensorium. And as our flesh mingled, it was as though I fed upon her beauty and tasted the loveliness of her ankles, her thighs, her bosom, her features, her whole form – drank it in, absorbed it, lived upon it.

'This, then, is love, I reflected, as we reposed in ecstasy within each other's arms and I gazed upon her as she lay with her head resting on my shoulder and a leg still thrown across me as if to signify that she had not yet done with me.'

CHAPTER FIVE

'Ah! Young love! Nothing like it!' Frank Harris exclaimed heartily, then inhaled the bouquet of his brandy. 'The trouble is, Horby, dontcha know, that when you're young, you're given a Gatling machine gun and you don't know how to use it. The instant that you learn, it's taken away and you're given a Winchester repeating rifle. The moment you become expert with that, it's snatched away too, and all you're left with is a single shot Colt .44.'

'Oh, Frank, you're so coarse sometimes,' Oscar Wilde protested. 'I found young Horby's tale of adolescent love quite hauntingly sensitive whereas you merely relished its juices. You have no feelings, Frank,' Oscar sipped champagne, 'it is the reason for your success.' He lit a black cigarette with a gold tip and added: 'Just as it is the reason that will explain your failure in later life at some forthcoming time.'

I liked Oscar Wilde, though I did not share his notorious sexual tastes. At the time I was acquainted with him, he was the most celebrated dramatist in London, with *An Ideal Husband* and *The Importance of Being Earnest* running simultaneously. Champagne and success had spoiled him, however. He carried himself with an ungainly paunch and his facial features were unnaturally bloated. Notwithstanding these initially unprepossessing physical characteristics, it must be stated that he was renowned for his kindness and generosity. He had a voice like a cello. He was also known for his fondness of bar-boys and stable-lads.

'Failure?' Harris retorted scornfully. 'The word does not exist in my dictionary!' he declared with a sweep of his arm. 'Well, well, that's rich, coming from you, Oscar.'

'What are you talking about?' Oscar returned testily.

'Oh,' said Harris, 'you *know* what I'm talking about.' He swallowed a goblet of brandy at one gulp. 'Our friend Shaw here can explain it to you more succinctly than I can.'

'Basically, Oscar,' said Bernard Shaw, 'you are getting yourself into a right mess. If I understand the matter correctly, the Marquess of Queensberry, an infamous brute, is jealous of your close friendship with his son, Lord Alfred Douglas, known in other circles as "Bosie." The father and the son both hate one another. Queensberry has spread rumours, some on paper, throughout London, claiming openly that there is something sexually improper about your relationship with his son. Urged on by the son, you have embarked upon a legal case against the Marquess, accusing him of the most serious offence of criminal libel. In a word, don't.'

'Succinct,' Wilde murmured. I could now see why people respected Shaw, this rabble-rousing socialist agitator who was writing disreputable plays which upset people and did not entertain them. His 'rational dress', a Jaeger suit of brown woollen cloth, lacked all degree of elegance. One wanted to punch that firmly outstanding jaw and as for that long, red beard, one wanted to tug it, preferably pulling this vegetarian's pale face down into a steaming bowl of oxtail soup. Nevertheless I could not deny that he was talking uncommon sense. A wide-eyed Wilde was staring hard at Shaw.

'Don't . . .?' he faltered. 'Are you sure?'

'No,' snapped Shaw, 'I'm positive. And, incidentally, the name *is* Shaw.'

'Listen to him, Oscar,' Harris urged. 'No middle-class jury would entertain some of your writings for a moment. You don't stand a ghost's chance on a dark night. I couldn't give a bloody damn about your pleasures, Oscar, certainly they're not mine, but I'm telling you that Queensberry has already got a private detective on your tail, recording everything you've been up to. You'll lose the case. Then they'll prosecute you and throw you bang up inside chokey. Prison, Oscar, you understand?'

'I have some friends . . .' Wilde said slowly.

'Oh, you mean the aristocracy, do you, Oscar?' Harris returned. 'Well, let me tell you that at the first positive whiff of scandal, they'll desert you in droves. You'll be lucky to share a cup of tea and a fruit pie in a railway waiting room with a disabled dwarf.'

'He's right,' Shaw said simply.

'Oh, Frank,' Oscar smiled scathingly, 'you know the aristocracy so well, don't you? You have been in every great house in England – once.'

'Please yourself, Oscar,' Harris returned calmly, 'for I can't imagine you'll be pleasing anybody else.'

'Would you go to bed with me for a million pounds, Oscar?' Bernard Shaw asked suddenly. I started. It was such an unusual question to come from him. Oscar looked utterly astonished.

'Goodness, you do surprise me, G.B.S.,' he returned with a sardonic chuckle. 'I don't really fancy your tall, muscular, lean scrawny body at all, but for a million pounds . . . yes, I suppose I would.'

'Would you sleep with me for tuppence?' Shaw demanded.

'Really!' Wilde looked indignant. 'What do you think I am?'

'That we know,' said Bernard Shaw. 'I'm just trying to establish the price.'

'How amusing,' Oscar said acidly. He added sarcastically: 'I wish I'd said that.'

'You will, Oscar, you will!' Whistler cried out from the Duke of Devonshire's table.

'With you, James,' Oscar faced Whistler, 'vulgarity begins at home and should be allowed to stay there.'

'A poor thing,' Whistler retorted, 'but for once, I suppose, your own.' Then he added concernedly: 'Don't go to court, Oscar.'

At that moment, Lord Alfred 'Bosie' Douglas entered the Café Royal. He was a blond and strikingly handsome young man who walked with an arrogant swagger and who had an unendearing supercilious sneer upon his lips. He looked at Frank Harris and it was obvious that they didn't like each other.

'Ah!' Douglas curled his lip. 'I espy Ancient Pistol.'

'Well roared, Bottom!' Harris boomed back. Douglas turned away, hissing some furious words into Oscar's ear. Oscar made his farewells and they left together, arm in arm.

'Oscar's not well,' said Shaw. 'When he's on form he can blast my own wit out of the water any day of the week.'

'Many thanks, Harris!' a pudgy faced young man called out from the other end of the table as he rose. 'Most enlivening as always.'

'If that horrible little man weren't a major shareholder in the *Fortnightly Review*,' Harris muttered as soon as he had gone, 'I couldn't bear to have that bore at my table.'

'He has his special quality,' Shaw commented. 'It's called money.'

'Any pump will give water if you piss in it,' Harris growled. Now he became morose. 'Never understood these peculiar types who want to bugger boys. Never have, never will. Now, women with women, that's quite another matter, wouldn't you say?'

'Certainly would,' I responded. 'And I received a letter today on precisely that theme from my dear tutor and governess, Rosemary.' This letter was so hot that it was virtually burning holes within my pocket.

'Read it to us,' Harris sighed, 'read it.' The other luncheon guests, who had been temporarily snoozing, suddenly perked up attentively. 'It goes as follows:

Dear Horby,

I promised that I would keep my favourite pupil informed of my doings. It seems like ages since we have been together. I miss the feel of you between my thighs. O my darling, I have just laundered my cami-bockers and my cami-knickers especially in loving memory of you. And you say that you admire me? Perhaps it is because my drawers are so frilly, the lovely ones that I want to wear, that go past my knees. You know the ones I mean, with the broderie anglaise. *In the meanwhile, my heart throbs and I have been thinking of you.*

Do you remember the day of our picnic? Your masterly member was so prominent in your britches. The moment it started to throb, I had to take my knickers off. You were a little disconcerted, as I recall. I had made cucumber sandwiches and had cut off the crusts in order to please you. I wanted to take the salad dressing and lavish it all over your lovely bottom. You were reading to me of the great works of Literature: Charles Dickens, William Shakespeare – of course, for we must not forget him – Ovid, Aesop, Lord Byron, Dante, Samuel Pepys and Chaucer. My love, on that day, was I really interested?

I appreciate your application to your studies but enough

is enough. I long to feel you prod your rod into me once again. I would love to suck your phallus, all stiff and unmoving in its throbbing gristle. Please lick and kiss my pudenda once again. My cunt is yearning for your stiff prick. I await your next coming eagerly. I still recall the feel of your sperm between my legs and am itching for more.

O my darling, sweet one and beloved, why can you not come and visit me tonight? Are you really that preoccupied? For you, my love, I would have oysters, scallops and asparagus in a fine buttered sauce. I'd wear my bustle as I know how it excites you. Surmounting it would be my chemise, and my stiffest white petticoat would surround my legs. Over and above all that, there would be my scarlet, silk ball-gown that is enhanced with brocade. Of course, I would also be wearing my black suspenders and my white silk stockings which always seem to arouse you – and a red-flowered lacy black garter on my naked thigh. My stockings are of sheer silk.

I'd be willing to wear my muffler for you, the one that is made of mink. Do you remember the evening we went ice-skating and I wore my mink with chinchilla at its edges? You are an excellent skater. You certainly charmed me on that occasion. Your figures of 8 are so precise. On the ice-rink that night, we were the perfect couple. You had waxed your budding moustache into a potential handlebar and you looked so dapper. All the girls were looking at you and suddenly I felt jealous of your tender youth. You are a bit of a naughty one. Is this why you did not come and surprise me last night?

Yesterday I went riding. I go riding most days as my new horse Pegasus is a stallion. Oh Pegasus! You the winged horse of Bellerophon – you my lovely Pegasus that caused the fountain Hippocrene to flow on Mount

Helicon . . . sometimes I feel like you – like a volcano about to erupt within me. In common with Vesuvius, I may seethe for years. Meanwhile, amidst these thoughts, I rode naked upon my lovely stallion and down to the beach. I was hoping to pluck cockles and mussels but instead I met my dear friend Elizabeth, a gorgeous, slim-buttocked young lady. She was studying a book and she told me of Saul the son of Kish and first King of Israel and of how the Witch of Endor called upon the ghost of Samuel before the fateful battle of Gibaon.

'Would you like to go swimming?' I asked. She nodded. Elizabeth, I should explain, is my 18-year-old pupil whom I am tutoring for London University. As she pulled off her clothes, I was surprised to see that she was not wearing any undergarments. Her breasts were as pure as those of a virgin and the golden down of pubic hair matched the colour of her crowning glory. We swam and then lay on the beach in our nakedness. So innocent! yet I felt there was someone watching us. From the gleam of the sunlight, I could discern field glasses positioned above a hill-top. To be candid, I was not terribly worried. I knew it was Simon, a former pupil of mine who still has so much to learn.

The sun was warm upon my breast. Elizabeth lazed next to me. Suddenly I felt a hand upon my breast and a butterfly kiss above my eyebrow. Then Elizabeth kissed me – first of all on the cheek and then full on the mouth, cleverly inserting her tongue. My thighs started to twitch as well as other parts of my anatomy. Then she wiggled her finger within my vagina, I'm sure that Simon was still watching us through his field glasses. Her fingers probed also and she started to caress my breasts. All of a sudden, her tongue was within my vagina, endeavouring to prod and lick my vulva, my clitoris, the whole of my entire fucking cunt – and I wanted more. She gave me more. She was my pupil but these were lessons I had never received before. She persuaded me to lie on my stomach and elevate my bottom, then she kissed it sweetly and licked the backs of my knees. The sun was so warm.

Sun! – the Gods of Apollo and Helios, come down and take me now! I am such a rampant bitch! But I had Elizabeth beside me and I took her into my arms once again.

'Let's swim,' I murmured, 'let's swim to the Rock.' She regarded me quizzically. 'You'll know, if you don't do already. It is low tide now and if we swim quickly, we can enjoy this rock. It is like the Rock of Gibraltar, though without the baboons.'

The sea was highly salty and for a short time, we simply floated on our backs. On arriving at the rock, which resembles a woman's bosom, we gazed upon its smooth surface, interrupted only by occasional eruptions of green and yellow lichen. Once more we caressed and fondled one another in the dying red glow of the sunset. I stroked her clitoris and her gorgeous, slender cunt.

I put my mouth to her delectable quim and gave it three long, strong strokes with the rough edge of my tongue. She shuddered and she shivered as her hips undulated and her erect nipples shrieked out a yearning for the crimson sky. Then she quivered and she sobbed and I hugged her closely to me.

Horby, my darling, you really must come and visit me before you go up to Cambridge and also tell me all about London life and what you have learned there. One trusts that this letter will inspire your desire.

With Love,
Rosemary.

'Letters of Introduction for this young man anytime,' Frank Harris commented jovially. 'Take up that invitation, Horby, or else you're an even bigger fool than you look! Ha! ha! I mean no offence, my friend. All this lesbianism, eh, gentlemen? But I tell you, you can't beat a good, stiff prick. Oh, no. "A penis tense, not penitence," as Sir Francis Dashwood used to say in the more spacious days of the so-called Hell-Fire Club. Anyway, young man, it's time I went. Come again any time but allow me to attend to the insignificant trifle of our bill of fare. Oh, and one other thing I don't want you to forget!' Harris held up a thick, admonishing finger. 'If you can get a woman to hold a stiff penis in her hand as you weep softly all the while, you've got the bitch, damn me, you've got her!'

CHAPTER SIX

When I entered the Great Gate of Trinity College, Cambridge in the Autumn of 1895, I found myself to be in an entirely new situation. There was certainly no matter concerning which any discerning gentleman could complain. My rooms looked out onto the delectable Wren Library. Whenever I felt dispirited, I could cure the matter speedily enough by a stroll in Great Court or else by the Backs, where it was such an unalloyed delight to watch the sluggish flow of the River Cam. The dons were learned and charming and had the wisdom to leave me to my own devices. As heir to a not inconsiderable fortune, I could do as I pleased.

I lost no time in investigating the matter of the girls and women in the town. Here there was news which gladdened my heart, for the domestic servants earned little more than £120 a year and the shop assistants were lucky to have as much as £150.00. I always had a purse full of gold sovereigns, having discerned that five of these represented more than a week's wages, and was soon swiving merrily enough. There were some inns which rented rooms by the afternoon to 'young gentlemen' and their lady companions and there were also a couple of brothels. This was all entirely appropriate for one who was reading for the Tripos in Moral Sciences.

It was during this most pleasant period that I became

acquainted with an interesting fellow-undergraduate, one Edward Alexander Crowley. He was reading for the Natural Sciences Tripos and he appeared to be enjoying the delights of University life as much as I was. He was a tall, slim, handsome young man with a mane of abundant dark hair and fiercely penetrating dark eyes. He had swiftly become captain of the Cambridge University Chess team, where he had gained his half-Blue with distinction. He had already established a national reputation as a mountaineer with unguided climbs in the Alps and in the Lake District which have yet to be repeated. It was said that he'd virtually strolled up the 'unclimbable' and treacherous chalk cliffs of Beachy Head, taking with him his mother and her dog.

I first met him at a brothel in Bateman Street. He was going into it and I was coming out. He invited me to sherry in his rooms on the following evening. By this time, he had changed his name to 'Aleister', for reasons best known to himself, and had published a privately printed poem called *Aceldama*. I rather liked Verse XIII:

'All degradation, all sheer infamy,
Thou shalt endure. Thy head beneath the mire
And dung of worthless women shall desire
As in some hateful dream, at last to lie;
Woman must trample thee till thou respire
That deadliest fume:
The vilest worms must crawl, the loathliest vampires gloom.'

It did not surprise me at all that in later years he became a recognised poet although I gather at the time of this writing (1925) that his work has presently fallen out of fashion. At the time I called upon the young Aleister Crowley, he had an apartment at 27, Trinity Street, which was stacked with books and pervaded by an atmosphere of furious study and harsh effort. He wore a great floppy bow-tie around his neck and his fingers sparkled with rings of semi-precious stones. His white shirt was of the purest silk. Looking around the room, I could see an ice-axe and a salmon fishing rod. I ventured a few words to compliment him on his poetry and asked him if he had since been inspired by his Muse to write any more.

'Oh, it depends what you mean by poetry.' He laughed sardonically and held up a stack of papers. 'That's next for the printer. It's called *White Stains*. Here I demonstrate that alleged "sexual degeneracy" ' – he spoke the words with withering scorn – 'is merely the result of the Christian sin-complex. And here,' he waved the backs of envelopes in the air, then refilled my glass with exquisite amontillado, 'are some crude, rough limericks, music-hall style. Like to hear 'em?' I nodded acquiescence.

'Paul Proper vowed virtue a cinch is.
His tool was four feet and five inches.
He vowed it was legal
To bugger an eagle
But utterly wrong to fuck finches.'

'Here's another,' Crowley said cheerfully.

'There was a young man called Seemu
Who wanted to bugger an emu.
He said, when he lost;
"Though our love has been crossed
"I shall always sincerely esteem you." '

'A couple more,' Crowley murmured.

'There was a young gaucho named Bruno
Who said: "There's one thing that I do know:
"A woman is fine.
"A sheep is divine.
"But a llama is *numero uno*." '

'There was a young woman called Gloria
Who was had by Sir. Frederick Wistoria.
And then by ten men,
Sir Frederick again,
And the band at the Waldorf Astoria.'

'But forgive me, my dear Horby, I digress,' said Crowley. 'Here we are talking about sex when we should be doing it. On for the Bateman Street brothel, are you?'

Five minutes later as we were marching eagerly down King's Parade, Crowley continued to regale me with limericks:

'My dear Mrs Ormsby-Gore
I simply can't do any more.
I've done and I've done
And you still haven't come –
And my God! It's a quarter to four!'

'That'll happen to the best of us, Horby,' Crowley remarked cheerfully, 'but here's a final one for old age . . .

'There was a young lass from Pitlocherie
Who was raped by a man in a rockery.
She said: "Sir, you have come
All over my bum.
This isn't a fuck! It's a mockery!" '

'Birth, copulation, death,' Crowley murmured as we strolled past Peterhouse. 'And what's the good of it all? I was seriously thinking of becoming a diplomat. Been to St Petersburg, Scandinavia, Holland and Switzerland, y'know. Got all the connections. But I'll just end up lying for my country and I'll be forgotten. Poetry? Even here in Cambridge, cradle of poets, how many people have even heard of Aeschylus? I must find a material in which to work which is immune from the forces of change.'

'Such as?' I enquired.

'Magic, perhaps,' Crowley responded; then before I could pursue this matter he declared: 'Ah, here we are! The brothel beckons. Did you know that this used to be my prep school? Ghastly place.'

The house itself was a tall, unprepossessing building of grey sandstone brick. We rang three times and were admitted by a demure maid in lace cap and apron. She ushered us into a bar peopled by confident men of business, undergraduates who were either very nervous or very brash and a dozen ladies in the most flattering of finery. Madam Harriet, an enormous woman, was sitting at the bar and chatting pleasantly with her clients. She greeted us warmly since she had seen both of us before. We resolved upon a double whisky with seltzer while we made our choices. I liked the look of a freckled young bitch called Sophie, whom I hadn't had before. Crowley had his eye on the tall and slender Elsie, whom I could recommend with genial confidence.

'You know, Horby,' Crowley drained his glass, 'I find that even forty-eight hours of abstinence is enough to dull the fine edge of my mind. I think women ought to be brought round to the back door every day with the milk.'

'Such a joker, aren't you?' said Elsie. Crowley responded in taking her by the arm and vanishing upstairs. I bought

Sophie a drink, then we went upstairs too. One of the reasons that I patronised this establishment is that there wasn't anything sordid or sleazy about it. The bedrooms were most comfortable, with pleasant and erotic pictures upon the walls. On this occasion, though, I did not wish to regard pleasing pictures. I had whispered what I wanted to Sophie and she gladly obliged.

I laid down on my back.

'Pull your legs as wide apart as they will go,' she said. I did. I'd been told that she had the most beautifully shaped, dimpled bottom in England.

Then she briskly stood over me, so arranging her petticoats that I was right under her bottom, with nothing between it and my face, but here and there her drawers, and these she rubbed away, relishing the contact of her naked flesh with mine. She caught me in front with both hands, rolled the testicles, slipped her hands down and endeavoured to excite each nerve in turn. She evidently knew all about it. I rejoiced in my contact with her flesh and with her lower lips, which were in a state of great excitement, very wet, and constantly rubbing and pressing my mouth and all over my face. I was overwhelmed by that sense of the female sex which exacts immediate sexual acknowledgement from anything in the least degree worthy of being called masculine. This exaction was made yet more irresistible by the delicate use of her hands.

I was making contact with her secret anatomy and Sophie was beautiful. I felt as though I was becoming as well acquainted with women's private parts as with their faces. While my head was beneath her buttocks, Sophie sucked Mons Priapus, bit him and pulled him unceremoniously about. By this time I was rampant.

She turned over and I thrust my rampaging member into her wet, warm vagina and her eyes swam and were kindled by what I knew to be desire and her cheeks burned with the rosiest, loveliest blushes. I threw myself upon her in an animal rage and fury, driving all before me, only too eager to deluge her with the essence of myself.

'Oh – it's so dreadful!' she gasped. 'Putting this terrible *thing* of yours into – into *me* – where – where you have done.' I could feel her flush as she said this. 'And now it's going into such a fit, coming on strong with such throbs, like a steam engine. I can feel it to my finger-tips – to the tips of my ears. O, it's nice! And really, I believe, because it is so naughty. Is my delicious wet like balm to you?' Sophie's limbs were beautiful, round, and plump, her skin was white and clear and my happiness as I rogered her was great. Her entire body was suffused with a warm glow.

She twiddled my testicles, interlaced her legs with mine, stroked my bottom and pressed her fingers forcibly against my rear. When she did that, Lust used his wings and I felt myself become a beast. Her evolutions and undulations seemed to excite her even more than myself. Pressing her lips against mine, she inserted her tongue into my mouth.

'You love to put your nasty rank smelling stick into my body, don't you?' she teased. 'A fine, a modest idea! How dare you suggest such a thing to a lady!' she continued, exciting me to distraction. 'Fuck me,' she breathed.

'Oh,' I sighed, 'I want to fuck you, Sophie.'

She moved lasciviously.

'Do you want to, very much?' she enquired coquettishly. 'Must you now? – an hour hence, will that do?'

'Now, now,' I replied, catching fire from her. 'Now let me, oh, pray let me fuck you now!'

She placed her lips to mine, clasped my shoulders with her arms and gripped my body with her legs. One hand she put underneath me behind. Her cunt gripped my prick so fiercely, I thought she might be sucked off by her contractions. I was inside her up to the very hilt. As she moved up and down, I felt myself melting into her. Her soft breasts, her pert bottom gave me so much pleasure by their very silken contact. I forgot who she was individually. As I came in a showering spasm, I recollected only that she was a woman.

' "Love," says the poet, "is woman's whole existence," ' Crowley remarked as we were walking back afterwards. He'd obviously enjoyed a jolly rogering too.

'It is all she wants, whatever she may affect,' I replied. 'If you can tickle her cunt and her clitoris with your fingers, your prick or even your imagination, she will obey you exactly as a vessel with steerage obeys the helm.'

'Would Madam Harriet agree?' Crowley returned genially and then burst into verse:

'There was an old lady of Cheltenham
Said "Cunts? Why, of course, dear, I dealt in 'em.
I thought it my duty
To make 'em so fruity
My clients used simply to melt in 'em" '

CHAPTER SEVEN

Of course, the brothels of the town were forbidden to undergraduates and so were public houses. We were meant to go out of College dressed in gown and mortar boards or else face arrest by the Proctors, the University police force, but Crowley and I had worked out ways of outwitting them, as had many others.

By the beginning of his final term, Crowley had acquired an increasingly formidable reputation. I can lend no credence to the tale that some Trinity hearties threw him in the fountain for 'being dirty all over.' Crowley was an astonishingly athletic young man and if anyone had been foolish enough to lay a finger upon him, he would have broken his antagonist's jaw with one punch. No bully would have stood a ghost of a chance against a man who was performing Alpine climbs the like of which had never been seen before.

However, I did find the rumours of his involvement in 'Black Magic' to be disturbing. I had heard it alleged that when the Master of the College had forbidden him to put on a performance of bawdry in Ancient Greek, *Lysistrata* by Aristophanes, he had responded with a magical ritual. It was said that he had collected a devil's dozen, then, having made a wax image of the Master, he stabbed a blade into the ankle of the waxen image; and the next day, the Master fell down the steps going out of Chapel and broke his ankle.

'No, no, not at all, my dear Horby,' he replied with a light laugh when I called upon him to hear his version of the tale. 'That was all some nonsense that I invented and told to the foolish.'

'That may be so,' I replied, 'but I saw the Master in Great Quad today. He was on crutches and his ankle was in plaster.'

'Then he was foolish enough to believe it too.'

'What's that?' I queried. My finger flicked to indicate a volume entitled *The Book of Black Magic and of Pacts* edited by one A.E. Waite.

'Superstitious peasant nonsense,' Crowley returned scornfully. 'Does anybody really want to know how to bewitch his neighbour's cattle or ensure how his maid-of-all-work will fart continuously in the kitchen? If you want to know how to do that, you may have to waste your money on this wretched book. No, no, I'm after much bigger game than that.' His expression suddenly became dreamy and thoughtful. 'The author of this rubbish about Black Magic also insists that there is a Secret Sanctuary of Wisdom, governed by Masters, Adepts and Initiates, in which all the Truths concerning Man and his place in the Universe may be found.'

'Sounds a wonderful idea,' I said. 'Wouldn't it be nice if I could believe a word of this myth?'

'Myth, is it?' Crowley murmured back. 'Well, I'll be finding out. I've pledged my last penny to go on a quest to find it.' He was a visibly rich young man but I wondered if he were merely being frivolous. 'And if I do, Horby, interested?'

'Yes. If you do.' I sipped his fine tawny port reflectively. At that instant there was a delicate tapping on the door and a beautiful woman strode into the room, draped in a shimmering purple evening gown with absurdly high-heeled shoes. I was sure that I had seen her before but could not quite place her. She had a fine, slender figure and seemed to be well acquainted with Crowley, for they embraced with some passion. When Crowley introduced her to me as Liane de Pougy, I realised the nature of the situation.

I had seen Liane de Pougy dance once on a drunken night at a Smoking Concert of the Cambridge University Footlights Club. 'She' was in fact Henry Jerome Pollitt, a graduate of Cambridge University, who delighted in impersonating the celebrated beauty and music hall entertainer, Diane de Rougy. I had subsequently heard of Pollitt via his close friendship with Aubrey Beardsley.

'Just been in Oxford, my dears,' said Pollitt/Liane as he/she accepted a glass of port from Crowley. 'Met a frightfully interesting young man up there, a gentleman of the name of Beerbohm, Max Beerbohm. Remarkable young dandy. When I asked him about the difference between Oxford and Cambridge, he replied: "The Oxford man comes down thinking he owns the World. The Cambridge man comes down not giving a damn who owns it." ' Crowley and I both burst out laughing. Pollitt/Liane whisked his/her skirts with flattered pleasure.

'I like that,' said Crowley, 'that is very fine. But I give you my own definition. Cambridge makes you the equal of anyone in the World. Oxford leaves you in the invidious position of being his superior.'

'That depends on the position,' Crowley's strange friend replied and Crowley laughed sardonically. I was starting to feel rather *de trop*, for I was never of particularly peculiar persuasions, so I bade my farewells and left into a fine night with the prospect of pleasant adventure before me. My destination was the house of a woman I shall call Lady Clarissa. She was a most remarkable woman.

Her father had died when she was just twenty-three and had unconditionally left her the sum of one million pounds. Among her many properties, there was a neat, Queen Anne house mid-way up Jesus Lane and that is where she entertained her many admirers. She had a passion for male intelligence and wished always to sample it directly and at its root. On sunny afternoons, she could often be espied in her gleaming black carriage, staring out eagerly through her lorgnettes at the undergraduates on King's Parade and noting them for future reference.

Although it was my first time in calling upon her, I felt no cause for any apprehension. A solemn and demure maid opened the door. Then I heard strange cries, just as I was showing the maid my invitation card. Soon enough, I saw the cause of these cries. A slim, young man with a very weak chin, dressed in all the Season's finery, was being unceremoniously marched towards the front door by an exquisitely beautiful woman whom I knew to be Lady Clarissa. She was wearing a very tight, white blouse with frills and a black skirt slit as if for bicycling.

'Come back when you can behave yourself, Hugh!' she snapped in icy tones of cut glass, then kicked his arse out into the street, turned on her heel and strode away. Hugh span out into the street and landed in a muddy gutter. The maid closed the front door having admitted me. She had a fine, full figure and a lascivious face. I liked the way in which her body was swathed in a satin dress like a sheath. It was so tight that she could only take little, mincing steps, and with each step she took, her voluptuous bottom switched enticingly from side to side, and the purple, satin material shimmered softly in the light of the chandeliers above. As she led the way into the drawing-room, I had to remind myself that I was here to seduce Lady Clarissa, rather than her maid.

Lady Clarissa was of course an enticing and delectable prospect. She received me well with vintage champagne. I sat upright whilst she reclined languidly upon a sofa like some great and supple cat. For a short while, we discussed Philosophy, a subject in which we both displayed much evidence of study and reading. It was increasingly obvious to me, however, that my philosophical aphorisms were merely her *hors d'oeuvres*. As soon as the maid was out of the room, I helped her to a second glass of champagne and then I kissed her.

It was as though an electrical current had been abruptly connected. The bodies of both of us were jolted, yet I persisted in my kiss, as she did so gladly, and our tongues explored every inmost recess of one another's mouths. At length, she pulled away, sighed, then said: 'Across the hall in ten minutes. Directly across.' With that, she arose with a swish of her skirts and swept out of the room.

I quaffed my champagne but stared moodily at the oaken grandfather clock on the wall. This showed 9.20 p.m. I padded silently to the drawing-room door – which she had fortunately left half-open – and discerned through the spaces between the hinges that there was indeed a door across the hallway. It was closed and there was no sign of the maid. I decided to light a cheroot and help myself to more champagne. At 9.30 precisely, I strode swiftly across the hallway and smacked smartly on the door.

'Come in . . .' sighed a dreamy female voice. I marched in with my throbbing penis going before me only to be astonished.

Slim, willowy, slender Lady Clarissa was entwined naked upon a four-poster bed with her voluptuous, buxom maid. They were nestling in each other's arms, nuzzling one another's necks and nipping each other playfully on the lobes adorned with bejewelled ear-rings.

'Say, "Good afternoon," Bridget,' Lady Clarissa commanded as she slapped the younger girl's pearly, white bottom. 'Say: "Good afternoon, sir." '

'Good afternoon, sir,' Bridget simpered as Lady Clarissa's long and delicate fingers teased her pink nipples into a state of shouting erection. She responded by cupping Lady Clarissa's slim breasts with the palms of her hands and stroking them gently. Clarissa shuddered and when Bridget drew the back of her hand softly down Clarissa's satin-smooth body and towards her quim, the belly of Her Ladyship fluttered. Bridget started to suck Clarissa's small, hard nipples, her own rubbing against Clarissa's navel.

'Oh! Oh! OH!' Clarissa squealed. 'How exquisite! Give me more.'

In answer, Bridget drove her finger-nails deep into Clarissa's pert bottom. There was another cry, then Bridget withdrew her hand to reveal immaculate white flesh rudely bruised by red marks. Clarissa shuddered and came in Bridget's arms. I was too fascinated at that instant to do anything other than watch.

'Your bottom, darling,' Clarissa murmured, running her fingers down Bridget's miraculous curve, 'it's so delectable.'

'As is yours, darling.' Suddenly, Bridget was diving between Clarissa's legs. An impassioned kissing of smooth and slender thighs soon persuaded the lady to part them wide-openly, displaying the majesty of the oyster within which the discerning could perceive the pearl. Bridget avidly applied her mouth to Clarissa's oyster as her tongue sought after the pearl. Her hands dug into the bed so as to cradle Clarissa's tender bottom. I saw Bridget insert a finger in between the thrusting cheeks. A cry came from Clarissa, ensued immediately after by the extravagant heave of breath that told me Bridget's tongue had located her clitoris.

Now, as Bridget sucked greedily, Clarissa's loins were unable to keep still. They twitched and tried to twirl but Bridget was remorseless in her thirst for Clarissa's juices. Suddenly Clarissa shouted: 'Fuck men!', her bottom entered a series of quite uncontrollable spasms, her thighs gripped Bridget's head in a threat to envelop it altogether, her sleek white arms were flung wide open – then she sighed delightedly and relaxed and the only sound in the room was that of Bridget lapping up her cup.

' "Fuck men," did you say?' I enquired genially. 'What a good idea!' With that, I whipped off my clothes and climbed into bed between the pair of them. Both were moaning softly, languorously and lasciviously. A woman can make love to another woman far more adroitly than a man can. She can often sexually satisfy a woman more pleasurably than even the most vigorous of bullish studs. Nevertheless, a man has something which every woman wants and no woman has and it is called a stiff prick.

Clarissa drew me to her breast and fondled my erect member as it lay between her legs. It was wonderful to lie before these gates of paradise that I longed so ardently to enter. Bridget passed a strong but gentle arm over my body. Two women? I never until then felt what true nakedness was. My intense appreciation of it transfigured me with passion.

'I must feel how he does it,' Clarissa sighed, placing both hands upon my shaft, opening her thighs wide and moaning with joy as I thrust into her warm, wet and welcoming cunny. Bridget slipped a wicked finger within my bottom and wriggled it, urging me on in the delicious task I had undertaken. Her hand upon my highly excited nerves and sensitive organ, stimulated them almost to frenzy. I begged her to remove it.

'No, I shall not!' she snapped, still holding me tightly.

A pause, another long sigh, Clarissa's eyes softly closing, her mouth apart, her lips deliciously moist, as I entered further and beyond the gate, as she came more and more under the divine influence. My whole being seemed to be concentrating itself in the spasm that was about to overtake me – it came.

'Aaargh!' Clarissa shrieked; her bottom undulated within my eager grasp and my hands became soaked in the juices of our lust. My love, my soul, my existence were conveyed to my sweet lover amid her soft inarticulate murmurs more graceful to my ears than any other music could be.

'Mmmm,' Clarissa added. I cuddled up against her beautiful, smooth, soft flesh, dozing in satisfaction.

What was this? Bridget had just drawn her finger-nails down my back.

'A young gentleman,' she declared indignantly, 'does not come into a lady's bed in order to sleep!' I turned onto my back, finding myself with another full-blooded erection. She extended herself upon me, holding me close with one arm, while, on the other, she excited my virility in a ticklish way she knew to perfection. Her being over me like this was a strange and new experience. She pressed me down and I lay completely at her mercy. Her legs held me. She slipped her fingers up and down Mons Priapus until he was beside himself with pent-up lust.

'Not until I tell you, sir,' she whispered slyly. She proceeded to work herself up into an ecstasy of excitement, positively perspiring, glowing with her efforts, kissing me passionately. The contact of her breasts, of her hair, of her bottom, the extent to which she made me feel the fire of her eyes, excited me to distraction.

'Oh! Ah! Oh, Bridget! Oh, I must, I must!' I cried out.

'Not yet,' she answered. 'You must not yet. You must

restrain yourself. I will teach you to please a lady.'

'Oh! oh! oh! What shall I do?' I gasped. She increased my trial by playing with my testicles with her cool hand, and by covering my mouth with her dewy little unfolded rosebud.

At last I felt her flush.

'Now,' she said, 'good man to have withstood so long – now – now' – in a soft, low tone – 'now – fuck me!'

A sigh – throb – throb – throb – throb – throb . . . throb . . .

'Oh, you angel!' she groaned as she gave herself to the love fit.

'Love makes life worth living,' Clarissa whispered as she kissed both Bridget and myself. 'No wonder it is said to make the world go round!'

Yes, I learned a lot at Cambridge University.

CHAPTER EIGHT

Eighteen ninety-eight turned out to be a good year for me. I graduated from Cambridge with Second Class Honours, still called 'the Gentleman's Degree' I believe, since a gentleman does not work too hard. Mind you, only a lazy bounder would get a Third. Firsts went to the swots, of course. After that, I formally took my Seat in the House of Lords. My maiden speech, as I recall, urged that our rampant Empire should thrust forward boldly into virgin territory, and it was quite well received.

I appointed capable professionals to attend to my lands and my investments and rented a well-appointed town house in Mayfair, hiring only the barest minimum of servants. Five is surely enough for any single man; anything beyond that is ostentatiously extravagant. I had no cause for complaint. I was furnished with introductions to the highest in the land should I choose to enter more intimately the worlds of politics and diplomacy. The circle of that good, old rogue, Frank Harris, was still going, and Harris was now Editor of the still more influential *Saturday Review*. Others had not been quite so lucky.

Oscar Wilde's case against the Marquess of Queensberry had gone every bit as badly as Frank Harris had forecast. After Queensberry's side had produced a number of male prostitutes, Wilde's case collapsed. Oscar was then tried and found Guilty of acts of sodomy and other acts of gross indecency upon young men, on account of which he was sentenced to two years of imprisonment with hard labour. On his release, he had fled into exile in France. I gathered that his conversation was as witty as ever and despite the hideous tortures of his humiliating imprisonment, he yet retained his former essential nobility of soul and goodness of heart. Unfortunately, one gathered also that he was very short of money and in poor health. I think on one occasion at the Café Royal, I gave Frank Harris or Robert Ross or whoever else was collecting for Oscar a hundred pounds. God knows, the poor bugger needed it! He was a martyred great man, in my view.

The brilliant Aubrey Beardsley had died of consumption. Apparently his last Will & Testament contained instructions to burn 'by all that is holy, all obscene drawings', making especial reference to his illustrations for *Lysistrata* by Aristophanes. The instant I heard this rumour, I employed agents. I wanted to buy obscene Beardsleys before they could be burned. Fortunately, I located one of Beardsley's executors famed in artistic and decadent circles as publisher of *The Yellow Book* and later, *The Savoy*. There, Beardsley's exquisite drawings had been brilliantly titillating but I wanted to lay my hands upon the frankly pornographic.

Leonard Smithers was a clever but most eccentric man of business. His emporium was by the Charing Cross Road and it was a most curious enclosure. In the front of the store, many respectable citizens browsed amidst the 'best-selling' books of the day and the perennial classics of yesteryear. This area smelled of wax polish. A whispered and discreet enquiry to the grizzled, bespectacled shop manager, who always wore a floppy bow-tie, enabled one to pass on up the rickety, wooden staircase to encounter another, much smaller sanctum of books. This room was devoted entirely to two subjects: the Occult – and Pornography.

Customers prowled among these shelves as if they were beings obsessed and the smell was of stale and sickly incense. At the time, however, I had only a mild and passing interest in the occult and so went instantly in search of good pornography, in time purchasing many rare and choice items there. One could, of course, depart after that but there was, if one felt so inclined, a third floor to explore. There were two ways of getting there. One was to ask the Collection Manager:

'Is Dr Boyers in? It's about my medicine.'

Leonard Smithers always took copious quantities of narcotics. His trading in books and paper with the East gave him access to the finest quality of supply. Now, in our present degenerate days, when place-mongers and bureaucrats unite to rob an Englishman of his God-given right to his freedom at his pleasures, I believe it is forbidden by Law to imbibe of these oriental substances in a purely self-regarding action. This is a national disgrace!

I have never taken debilitating quantities of drugs and at the time I was acquainted with Smithers, I had no acquaintanceship with drugs at all. That was to come in due course. Even so, I was aware that Smithers dealt in opium, hashish and cocaine. In those days, obviously one could buy them at any pharmacist, although the old-fashioned apothecary's shops were usually better, yet I have been repeatedly assured that Smithers sold a better quality of substance than could be obtained anywhere else in London. Those who progressed up the creaking wooden stairs to the third floor, which smelled of jasmine and roses, did not look any the worse for their indulgence than anyone else one might meet on a fine day in Piccadilly.

The other way to the third floor was to ask the Collection Manager:

'Ah – do you by any chance have anything better?'

'Better . . .?' He would glance upwards from his chair, looking mildly puzzled.

'Well . . . you know . . . *better* . . .'

'Best have a word with Mr Wright. Yes, he'll be pleased to see you if you just go up the next flight of stairs. First on the right.'

Dr Boyers, the man of medicine, and Mr Wright, who could help one to 'something better' were of course both Leonard Smithers. His price for a set of Beardsley's *Lysistrata* drawings was outrageously high, especially since the artist had specifically instructed Smithers to destroy all of them and Smithers had assiduously spread about that rumour.

I was glad of Smithers, though, when I gloated over the nakedly bared cunts, the curvaceous female bottoms and the huge, pulsating phalli upon the men that Beardsley had drawn with such care and attention to every lascivious detail.

Smithers's shop was only one of my very many pleasures. I remained in friendly touch with Frank Harris, occasionally contributing to *The Saturday Review*. I tried to look up Aleister Crowley but for the time being, he had vanished. I had many other good men friends, though, some especially notable, and we shall pass on to these in due course. It is appropriate at this juncture, assuredly, to turn to the women who were giving me so much pleasure.

I made friends with Lady Clarissa and on occasion journeyed back to Cambridge to enjoy her four poster bed with her and Bridget. London women are very compliant, especially if you say a few sweet nothings and give them a sovereign, so I did not lack for sexual quality of life. During this period, I was nevertheless continuously delighted by letters from Rosemary, whom I still occasionally saw and within whose limbs I writhed.

My darling,

I miss you so much. Last Sunday was so pleasant. Do you recall how we lazed by the Serpentine, I wearing my hat of green velvet? There was a cream-coloured scarf knotted around my neck. My Point D'Esprit was knotted in the centre under a large cabochon of pearl and crystal and a white upstanding aigrette. My hair was in curls of rococo.

Down by the Serpentine, you took my body. No one could see on account of my long, flouncy skirt. We looked just like another couple canoodling on a warm Sunday afternoon, yet it was one quiet fuck after another. I am so desperate for your fucking once again that I have resorted to Onanism. I place my finger in my cunt, fondle my clitoris and think of you. This morning I had an orgasm amidst my bubble bath as I lazed in the tub, all the while thinking of you and your lovely member.

Oh! Thank you so much for our last delightful weekend together! After that, as you are aware, I departed for North Wales, which is so beautiful. First of all my hostess drove me in her Victoria to Llandudno to see the Little Horn and the Big Horn, both of which reminded me of you, and then we went on to Caernarvon to see the castle. I have never seen such beautiful countryside in all my life. Then I was introduced to the beautiful Isle of Anglesey. What a charming town Beaumaris is! especially if one arrives on May Day, or its eve, otherwise known as Walpurgis Night, the sacred eve of the Witches and the first day of Summer to follow. It is the second great Sabbat of the year, the first being All Hallows Eve, a holy night in which the spirits of the dead are called up by the living so that their souls can be put at rest.

Beaumaris Castle is so lovely and year after year, they carry on the same tradition. In the morning and at mid-day before a blazing sun, the Maypole dance was done beautifully by both adults and children. The phallus was crowned with flowers and hung with multi-coloured ribbons, yellow, red, green and brown to represent the four elements of air, fire, water and earth. I was so glad, though, when everybody left and I could imagine just you and me together in this castle.

The moon was full and I was rampant with desire, tingling all over my body as though I consisted solely of twinkling stars. I thought of you kissing me under the Maypole. First of all it was on my lips and then my breasts, followed by my belly and then to my cunt. Right now I can feel your lovely penis, your gorgeous cock and prick, your stick and tool. Why is it that the full moon makes one go so crazy?

But I digress. As you are aware, I had arrived here to take up my new post as Governess/Tutor to the Hon Edward Fenchurch, son of my hostess. If I have taught you as well as I should, you will no doubt be enjoying a good sex life as you read this, for you have told me how much you relish hearing the details of my tutorials.

Edward was reclining on the principal drawing room sofa, reading a book, with a glass of port wine at hand. He was wearing a white shirt with a stiff wing-collar and drainpipe trousers of a claret colour. The instant that he saw me, he snapped his book shut and hastily put it down. I wondered idly what it might be. Chaucer? Dickens? Shakespeare? My sharp eyes discerned from the spine that it was merely some piece of popular trash, all purple prose and lascivious ladies and languid young gentlemen. I made some pleasant remark which put him at his ease and we introduced ourselves to one another. I joined him for a glass of port. He was really rather charming. I accepted his invitation to show me his library.

There must have been at least three thousand beautifully bound books there but the first unusual feature was a bed in the corner of the room. I wondered if he had ever shared this bed with anybody else and so chose to interrupt his learned discourse on his library's joys.

'Edward . . .' I asked, 'are you a virgin?'

'Yes . . .' he replied, blushing furiously. 'You l-look a-bb-b-bsolutely beautiful,' the poor darling faltered, adding embarrassedly, 'sorry, please excuse me.'

'No,' I replied sharply. 'I shan't. Just stand there.' He froze stiffly to attention. I could see his member throbbing against his tight trousers, which appeared to be splitting at the seams. I undid his flies and hauled his trousers down to his knees, then I unbuttoned his underpants. That acorn I call the head of the penis was ready for me and I took it within my mouth. He was as nervous as a cowering puppy and could only shake and tremble as I sucked his lance of a cock. Within a minute he had gushed his juices, depositing his springing sperm into my mouth. It was of a delicious, salty flavour. At the same time I was vividly conscious of the scents he had placed within the library to adorn it: lavender and roses and the smells of herbs such as mint, horehound, oregano, borage and chives. Then I gazed fondly at his beautiful black hair that was slightly curly, his pale skin, his beautiful blue eyes with their double set of eyelashes and thought: How many and multifarious are the pricks!

'Edward, have you ever touched a girl before?' I queried.

'I did kiss my cousin Virginia on the mouth a few times,' my sweetheart admitted shyly, 'and once I fondled her breasts.'

'Like this?' I replied and removed my blouse. 'Please unlace my stays,' I requested. There was more fumbling on his behalf but eventually my corset was removed. We lay down on the library bed and he started to suck on my left breast, caressing my right with nimble fingers and

gentle palms. For a naive, 18-year-old lad only just out of Eton, he was proving himself to be quite a quick learner.

'Why is it,' he asked with an enchanting, child-like simplicity, 'that your nipples are getting so big?'

'My lovely, you do arouse me,' I murmured back, then reached out idly for more port wine, passing the glass to him. Our intoxication raised our spirits and he began to frolic and sky-lark and play silly, teasing games with his tongue. 'Would you like to see more?' I asked and proceeded to slip off my petticoat and knickers. The moment he saw my cunt, my vulva, my yoni, he started to lick it. His tongue penetrated my oyster to touch my black pearl; I couldn't stop throbbing and crying out my joy as I was overtaken by one orgasm after another. He bit gently and tickled more with his own dick throbbing once more in remarkably renewed vitality. 'Now is the time, now is the time . . .' I sighed and he at last thrust his pestle into my mortar. His pubic hair was as soft and silky and as glossy as the hair on his head.

How his kicky-wicky throbbed, pulsating in my box! I came not once more, not twice more but thrice more. When he came, his orgasm was even longer than his first. I discern excellent potential in this young man and shall ensure that he fulfils his immediate ambition, which is to go up to Cambridge. At some future date, it may be in your interest to meet him.

Well, my darling, I hope that this letter has pleased you and that all is well. I look forward to hearing more of your own doings in what some ghastly prude has called 'this repository of shameless sin that is the disgraceful capital of our great Empire'.

All my Love,
Rosemary.

CHAPTER NINE

One of the most intriguing and delightful men I met during my 1898-99 period in London was an exquisite novelist of modest reputation, Arthur Machen. I came across him by word of print, having purchased and read with great relish his magnificent translation into twelve volumes of the *Memoirs of Casanova*. His Editor's Introduction was excellent too. Instantly I sent for more books by Machen and read with growing delight *The Great God Pan* and *The Three Imposters*. One of the pleasures of having money is that it makes it fairly easy to locate people and so having ascertained the address, somewhere in Verulam Buildings, just off the Gray's Inn Road, I promptly sent an invitation to Mr Machen, accompanied by a note expressing my appreciation of his literary work. I was gratified by his instant rejoinder in which he looked forward to meeting me and complimented my choice of venue. 'How did you know it was my favourite chop house?' his letter ended.

Burton's, just off the Strand, was in fact my own favourite chop-house and I had guessed correctly that Arthur Machen would be a man of discernment. There is virtually nothing like it left in London in our benighted days. One sat before a roaring fire in a room where the walls, tables and chairs were all of stout old English oak, and huge hunks of well-hung meat sizzled upon the spits. The turning roasts were basted continuously but entirely in their own juices. Any novice at the spit who was sufficiently ignorant as to pour the juices of lamb over the beef would be sacked instantly – and quite rightly too! One could also choose steaks and chops of pork or lamb which were grilled to perfection upon griddles of naked flame. Some rejoice in well-roasted mutton, and the house saddle of mutton, carved at the table with ceremonial pride, was a source of evening gladness to many. King Edward potatoes, deliciously flowery in scent and packed with deep yellow Jersey butter, accompanied these carnivorous delights. To drink, there was good house burgundy and claret; although I tended to prefer a pint of their best nut-brown porter.

Arthur Machen turned out to be a youthful-looking man in his thirties, slightly shy in his gentlemanly manner, wearing a bottle-green velvet suit with a neat emerald green bow-tie. He had an enchanting baritone voice whose lilt recalled the Welsh days of his youth. He also had a gratifyingly gargantuan appetite for meat and drink. We agreed to start with the oxtail soup with cottage loaf freshly baked, then the porterhouse steak for him and the mixed roast and grill for me; and we would go on to treacle pudding with extra cream. By the time I had ordered, we had drunk a bottle of claret, so I ordered two more and also two pints of porter. The meal was superb and the bill was under a sovereign. Splendid value! But my guest's conversation gave me more.

'Casanova, yes,' he smiled gently and fleetingly, 'how wonderfully entertaining. But what does he really tell us? That men and women are attracted sexually to one another, little more. I see no sacred truth in his writings.'

Naturally I asked him what he held to be sacred truths. He told me that the Supreme Truth could be expressed in one word and that word was: *Ecstasy*.

'If it is an orgasm, then I have been blessed with it,' I said.

'It is an orgasm,' he replied, smiling enigmatically, 'but it is much, much more than that. Oh,' he sighed irritably, 'there is too much Reductionism and Nothing But-ness in this world. Suppose I were to tell you a tale of a man who worked as a clerk in the City, yet who at night worships and commits abominations behind drawn drapes with a delicately-dressed doll . . . what would you call it?'

'Masturbation,' I said.

'Is that all it is?' Machen queried feverishly. 'What about the sexual and emotional energy that has been invested in that delicately-dressed doll? The auto-erotic act is magical, perhaps? And yet it is sinful.'

'Sinful . . .?' Now it was my turn to query.

'Sorcery and sanctity,' Machen responded, 'these are the only two ecstasies. And Sorcery is sinful. In it one commits the sin of self-love when one should reverence and worship the Universe around us.'

'I agree with you there,' I returned, 'but I'm damned if I know what's wrong with having a good, healthy wank!'

'You're missing the subtlety, Horby.'

'I don't think I'm missing anything, Machen,' I returned genially. 'All right, let us not have individual wanks. I have an appointment later this evening to see a young girl birched by an older woman at a luxurious establishment within easy walking distance from here. This establishment is also renowned for the excellence of the brandy and champagne it serves to its more regular clients. If you don't fancy the sight of the birching, you can enjoy the charms of some of the sexiest stunners in London – and I'm your host.

There we can surely worship your "Universe around us", wouldn't you say?'

'That's a very kind invitation,' Machen replied with dignity and all the while there was a roguish twinkle in his intense, dark eyes. 'And there was a time when I would have accepted it only too gladly. However, I am a married man and my wife is not well. I wish you joy of the occasion, though.' He smiled warmly, then jovially toasted my health with his foaming pewter tankard of porter. 'It's just that, in common with Casanova, you are reducing Sacred Mysteries to the level of pricks and cunts. You do not, with all respect, appear to comprehend the sacrosanct nature of the Holy Grail.'

'That's where you're wrong,' I replied, 'for it is a hole and it is a cunt and it brings forth ecstasy. That's my Holy Grail.'

'No, you don't understand,' he replied with the quiet intensity of a sincere mystic. '*Ecstasy* is a withdrawal from the common life.'

I recall no more of that part of the evening save that we shook hands warmly, vowed to discuss these matters further and departed on our separate ways. I headed for a side-street just off the Haymarket, where Mrs Smythe was awaiting me. To all appearances, this was a quiet Queen Anne house. A maid instantly answered the agreed ring of three bells and I stepped inside and strode straight to the well-stocked bar.

Twelve gentlemen in evening dress were taking brandy. Mrs Smythe, a blonde, buxom lady whose bustle's obtrusion was almost obscene, greeted me warmly and introduced me to the other guests, with most of whom I was already quite well acquainted. I glanced at my white invitation of stiff card, embossed and engraved in gold:

TONIGHT
AT MIDNIGHT

'The naughty Miss Arabella Troubridge will be birched for scandalous sexual misbehaviour by her Governess, Mrs Beatrice Peel, with all due and appropriate humiliation.'

Mrs Smythe proceeded to usher us into a box of plushly-cushioned seats, overlooking a small stage. The walls were festooned by pictures of flagellation. A beautiful brunette stood at the centre of the stage, hanging her proud and pretty young head in shame.

Her hands were tied behind her back with thongs of leather. Upon her front, there was a placard which read: 'I AM TO BE BIRCHED FOR SEXUAL MISBEHAVIOUR.' Her pretty face was delicately flushed. Mrs Smythe strode to the centre of the stage and declared: 'Gentlemen, welcome to a lecture on the salutary effects of corporal punishment. Miss Arabella Troubridge here has disgraced herself through her lewd and lascivious behaviour towards young gentlemen in a manner which I would blush to repeat. She will therefore be punished by the celebrated disciplinarian, Mrs Beatrice Peel.'

Mrs Smythe gave way to Mrs Peel. She was a tall woman whom I judged to be around thirty. She had glossy black hair piled high upon her head, ice-blue eyes and rosy red lips. She wore a tight, sheath-like dress of scarlet silk. She was not wearing a bustle but her neat waist and voluptuous rear indicated that she did not need one.

'Good evening, gentlemen,' she said in a high, clear, cut-glass voice. 'I am about to show you the virtues of the birch. Some have recently argued in favour of the cane but the cane punishes merely the equatorial zone, so to speak, whereas the birch punishes the whole bottom. As you may know, a birch-rod is a bundle of flexible twigs of the birch-tree bound at one end so that the other forms a spray. This spray is then vigorously applied to the bare bottom of the culprit, either until it – the spray – is worn away or until the birching is deemed completed.

'By its unique combination of penetration and "spread",' Mrs Beatrice Peel continued in her maddeningly crystal-clear voice, 'it punishes like no other instrument: not deeply – a birch leaves no lasting bruises though its stripes can sustain for days – *but sharply as a good rod should.*' Her voice rose briefly and harshly in an access of obviously deeply-felt passion.

'There is a ritual attached to the use of the Queen of Rods. Birchings are always inflicted on the bare bottom, under conditions of the greatest possible shame and preferably in the presence of witnesses. Miss Arabella Troubridge, my recalcitrant pupil, is undergoing her period of preliminary shame. She has spent the afternoon constructing two birch rods under my direction. Now, you naughty young Miss! It is time for the rods!' A shame-faced Arabella bowed her head yet further. A moment later a buxom maid appeared bearing two birches bound with pink satin ribbons and placed a flogging block at the direct centre of the stage. She handed the rods to Mrs Beatrice Peel, who pursed her lips, and curtsied submissively.

'*Kneel*!!' Mrs Peel commanded and Arabella obeyed her. 'And what do you say now?'

The delectable Arabella knelt before her governess and raised her anxious face in an attitude of begging.

'Please, Madam,' she said softly, 'I have behaved disgracefully and I deserve to be birched. I humbly implore you to punish me.'

'Arise!' snapped Mrs Peel. 'Go to the flogging block

which awaits you and bend over!' Arabella obeyed. Her thrusting bottom swathed by her tight black bell-skirt was quite an enticing sight. The maid stepped forward and, in a gravely methodical manner, pulled up the miscreant's skirt and then her petticoats. Her lacy, frilly drawers were then pulled down to her ankles so that one had a full view of her posterior charms. What a perfectly rounded white bottom she had!

'Thrust your bottom upwards, Arabella,' Mrs Peel commanded, 'as though it is imploring just correction for your transgressions.' Arabella submitted and did her all to present her buttocks properly. 'You have shamed yourself by your sexual misconduct towards young gentlemen and this cannot be allowed. You will therefore receive twelve strokes of the birch, counting each one of them.'

'Yes, Madam.'

Mrs Beatrice Peel eagerly seized a birch then took up her position by the subjugated Arabella, thrusting her own bottom outwards in an action of deliberate authority. The birch descended with a faint hiss. Arabella's bottom jerked on impact and she squealed 'One!' Faint red marks appeared upon her pearly white cheeks. The birch hissed through the air again. Arabella's bottom twitched furiously as she gasped: 'Two.'

'Birching should be administered at the slowest possible pace,' Mrs Peel resumed her lecture. 'It is a perfect combination of smacking and lashing.' She applied a third stroke and Arabella moaned as she counted it. Her governess glanced at the rod. 'About fifteen fine twigs of no more than fourteen inches in length makes an ideal instrument for punitive correction at close range.'

'Four!' Arabella exclaimed as her buttocks took on a hue of faint crimson.

'Instead of a single sharp weal,' Mrs Peel explained, 'there are a greater number of finer, fainter weals, and a great deal more blushing, over a far wider area.'

'Five . . .' Arabella sighed as the birch thwacked her buttocks and her hips jerked on impact.

'It is the most profound of chastisements,' said Mrs Beatrice Peel, her face flushing with her own excitement.

'Six . . .'

The seventh, eight and ninth strokes followed at a leisurely pace. Arabella screamed, kicked and cried out, her bottom switching from side to side. It was quite plain that she suffered the punishment physically as acutely as the degradation hurt her pride. It was indeed a terribly humiliating ordeal. On the tenth stroke, she began to howl, as well she might, for her bottom was now crimson.

'Shame, tears and a sore bottom, that is the essence of a good birching,' Mrs Peel declared with relish.

'Eleven . . .!' Arabella sobbed after the next swish. She writhed and choked at the pain and ignominy of the punishment. Yet as she cried, she looked remarkably beautiful and alluring in her sorrow. Her distress made her so unusually attractive that I hoped I might find an opportunity for consoling her.

'A sound thrashing should always provoke tears,' Mrs Peel declared with absolute finality as her birch swished down for the final stroke. On the twelfth stroke, Arabella could only mutter the word through her sobbing and her bottom went into an obscene dance, raising itself high in the air then twitching rudely from side to side. I was hypnotised by the sight of her scarlet, glowing buttocks.

She had to spend five minutes decorously draped over the flogging block in order for the audience to witness the sight of her punished posterior.

'The birch should *never* cut the skin,' Mrs Beatrice Peel

remarked, 'but it should *always* produce tears of repentance.'

Eventually the maid restored the knickers to Miss Arabella Troubridge's fiercely burning buttocks, pulled down her petticoats and smoothed down her skirt. The birched young miss was then permitted to rise. After drying her eyes, she had to curtsey to Mrs Peel, kiss the rod that had chastised her so sorely and thank her governess for her just punishment.

'You will be taken to the drawing-room for one hour of thoughtful penance, standing in the corner,' Mrs Peel maintained relentlessly, and the beautiful, subjugated girl was led away. The gentlemen all applauded this uniquely erotic performance.

I would guess that each one of us was possessed of a rampaging erection as we entered the drawing room to partake of the finest brandy and champagne. Miss Arabella Troubridge was now standing obediently in her corner, hands behind her back, with her skirts and petticoats pinned up and her knickers around her knees, her birched bottom on full display so that one could watch its changing colours. Some men bid outrageous sums for the right to be the first one to have her. Others were desperate to enjoy the favours of Mrs Beatrice Peel instantly, and again extraordinary sums were bid for the right to first favours. It was small wonder that Mrs Smythe grew more charming by the minute as the bids increased.

For myself, I resolved to have the pair of them, though not at a price artificially inflated by present excitement and so reserved their attentions for the following week whilst taking Ellen, a sexy, slim blonde as the quick fuck for the night that I needed. After I had spurted again and again within her and was lying in her arms, I thought about the words of Arthur Machen. Ecstacy? Certainly! But I didn't want to withdraw from the common life at all.

CHAPTER TEN

Curiously enough, I encountered Arthur Machen the following evening in Oxford Street. In common with myself, he had just purchased one of those gold-knobbed walking canes of ebony which were all the rage at that time. He promptly insisted upon returning my hospitality and I agreed to join him at a small but delightful Italian restaurant he had discovered in Soho.

'To stimulate our appetite,' he suggested, once we were comfortably esconced, 'I recommend their house salami, which is made from the best end of a well-hung pheasant. The veal in Marsala is very good here and so are the chicken breasts stuffed with butter and garlic. To drink, let us have a Chianti. It may not be very good but the flasks are charming.'

His choice of food and wine turned out to be exquisite and the service was both friendly and impeccable. We returned to some earlier themes of conversation. I asked after his present literary work and he replied that he was working on stories with a sexual theme, based partly upon his own experiences or else upon tales told to him by others, provisionally to be called *Ornaments in Jade*.

'For example,' he said, 'I recently encountered a very dull fellow I had known in my youth, at school. He's now something in the City. One never thought of him as being a man likely to attract female attention but I suppose that money works wonders. He invited me to dinner and to meet his young wife: I think he had a villa in Harlesden or somewhere else equally deplorable. You can well imagine my astonishment when I met his wife. She was one of the most delightful women I ever encountered before my marriage. Naturally, I gave no sign of recognition and neither did she. The evening passed away without interesting incident. She looked very bored by his company whilst enjoying the results his prosperity had brought her. She went to bed early and I left early. A week later, I encountered him in the Strand and asked if and when I could visit once more. "My dear Machen," he replied, "you know I always liked you very much; your poor father was very kind to me; it's a great pity. But, to tell you the truth, Elizabeth is particular; she has evidently heard some stories about you (I am afraid, Machen, you have never lived a very strict life), and she says that as a married woman, she would not care to meet you again. It grieves me, I assure you, to have to say this; but after all, one would not wish one's wife . . ."

'I just burst into a wild peal of laughter,' said Arthur Machen, then drank some good Italian brandy. ' "My dear fellow," I told him, "I congratulate you again. You have married a wonderful woman. Good-bye." And as I went on my way, I was still bubbling with unconquerable mirth.'

We wandered out into the quiet street, feeling a dreamy delight in all things, and this street seemed full of fantasy indeed in the dim flare of the gas-lamps with a single star shining through the scudding clouds above. We walked on rather aimlessly, not quite knowing where we were going in our intoxicated condition, turning from one crooked street to another and continuing to discourse. It had started to pour with rain and there wasn't a hansom in sight.

'Where the hell are we?' I enquired.

'Confound it! I don't know,' Machen responded. We walked on a little farther when suddenly, to our great joy, we found a dry archway, leading into a dark courtyard. There we took shelter, too thankful and too wet to say anything. Before us there was a great house, towering grimly against the sky. It seemed all dark and gloomy, except that from some chink in a shutter, a light shone out. 'Hang it!' Machen exclaimed. 'I know where we are now. At least I don't exactly know, you know, but I once came by here with young Ernest Dowson and he told me there was some club or something down this passage. I don't recall exactly what he said. Good God! How amazing! There goes Dowson now. I say, Dowson, tell us where we are!'

Dowson greeted us. He was a slim, elegant young man with a consumptive cough. However, I was a great admirer of his poetry and so was delighted to meet him in person.

'Well, gentlemen,' said Dowson, 'you may come with me if you like. But I must impose a condition: that you both give me your word of honour never to mention this club, or anything that you see while you are in it, to any individual whatsoever.'

'Certainly not,' we both agreed. The mouldering house towards which we moved might have been an embassy of the preceding century. Dowson whistled once, knocked twice at the door and whistled again. It was opened by a man in black. There were a few whispered enquiries and then we passed inwards.

'Now, one thing,' Dowson muttered: 'You are not to recognise anybody and nobody will recognise you.' I was reminded of his finest poem so far: *I Have Been Faithful to Thee, Cynara, In My Fashion*. The butler led us into a huge salon, brilliantly lighted with electric lamps and adorned by paintings of gorgeous women, either unclothed or clothed so tightly that little was left to the imagination. Men were standing in knots, walking up and down or else smoking at little tables with gorgeous and elegantly gowned women. Conversation was going on but in a low murmur, and every now and then, someone would stop talking and look anxiously at the door of the other end of the room and then turn around again.

I was sitting on a sofa with a brandy, lost in amazement, since virtually every face of every man present was familiar to me. The veritable flower of Rotten Row was in this strange club-room: several young noblemen; a young heir to a steel magnate who had just come into an enormous fortune; some fashionable artists, musicians and literary men; two eminent actors; and a well-known Bishop. What could it all purport? My information services had given me to understand that they were supposed to be scattered far and wide over the habitable globe and yet here they were. Suddenly, there came a loud knock at the door, and every man started. This heralded the appearance of a strikingly beautiful young lady with flaming red hair and an almost obscenely low cleavage.

'Good evening, gentlemen,' she announced in a rich, throaty voice. 'Welcome to another meeting of The Vanishing Society. Formal proceedings will, as is customary, commence at midnight. Meanwhile, you are enjoined to enjoy yourselves.' She slipped away, which was a pity as I had my eye on her. However, there was a beautiful, slim blonde with flecks of freckles upon her impish features sitting nearby and so I propositioned her. In no time at all, she had led me to her boudoir and was lying lasciviously upon the bed to await the dictats of my pleasure.

I requested her to lie on her front, to pull up her skirt and petticoats and to pull down her knickers, exposing her preciously unmarked bottom, shaped like a ripe peach. My pestle was still burning with the thought of the birching my eyes had witnessed so recently and the feeling within my loins which it had aroused. It was glorious to feel her cool white buttock cheeks against my hot belly as my stiff prick penetrated her slim quim.

'OH! . . .' Her body quivered more vivaciously than if she were raising her bottom to receive the birch. Ellen moved ravishingly. She now lacked the ordinary means of defence which women possess when fully clothed and I could see how my ardent longing agitated her satin-smooth form and her vagina became increasingly wet in answering my swift thrusting.

The contact of my hands with Ellen's soft, cool buttocks in all their delicious plumpness, communicated a strong fire to my veins and caused my brain to whirl. I was in a state of violent commotion and the abrupt turn of her head to shoot me a lewd glance from half-closed eyes greatly increased my enthusiasm, making me fully aware of her own state. It was very evident that my rhythm was agreeable to Ellen. She pressed her arse against me more than there was any occasion for; and it is these voluntary and gratuitous caresses which I have always found to be the most irresistible and intoxicating. I could not keep my hands away from her breasts and we found ourselves locked firmly together, my arms around her bosoms, her ankles around mine, her bottom thrust defiantly into my belly and my prick throbbing within her cunt.

This contact with her flesh, initially touched solely by my hands, had been enough to set me on fire. Now, as my whole body pressed against hers. I was fully ablaze with pleasure. She was a volcano of sexual passion. Her bum was soon covered in the juices of her lust. I sighed joyously over her throbs and the convulsions she occasioned and felt.

How I loved passing my hand over her delicate and pretty

thighs to scratch the backs of her knees! How she shuddered and reddened as I shoved with my rude invading prick her soft, naked flesh – yet how she liked it! Suddenly she turned over on her back.

She enveloped me with her warm thighs, giving me such a squeezing that I can remember it until now, and making me kiss her behind as well as in front. It was so enchanting to thrust back between her lovely legs, in such close contact with her person.

What a curious sphinx-like affair women possess at the front of the lower end of their dear little bodies! What folds of flesh there are. How deliciously they unfold. What sweet moisture they exude. How they expand!

'You have a very impudent fellow,' Ellen murmured languorously.

'Try and conquer his impudence,' I rejoined.

She lay back and drew me further onto her.

'You sexy bitch!' I exclaimed.

She resigned herself to my fury, responding with short, thick gasps and upward thrusts of her hips. Her arms twined around my shoulders. Her passion startled me. Her legs wound around my body. She pressed me further into her, slipping a long, cool finger into my anus and wriggling it. I sucked upon her breast, enjoying the sensation of myself inside her and the workings of her mind and her body upon mine. I was entirely engulfed in her beautiful body.

She felt the throbbing of my member and its agitations were all understood and appreciated by the corresponding organ of her own feminine constitution.

Throb! Throb! Throb!

'Oh Ellen! O you darling sexy bitch!' What ecstasy was mine then! What rapture! What satisfaction!

'Oh!' Ellen moaned, 'fuck me again and again and again! Just fuck me!' But briefly, teasingly, I withdrew my shaft from her cunny and, with an appetite still ravenous, I placed my head between her thighs to kiss her, bite her and tickle her with my tongue.

I took delight in my nakedness as my head was swathed within her frilly garments and when I had excited her to the highest pitch, she sprang up, placed me roughly down upon the bed and threw herself upon me. Putting a cushion under me, she soon forced my prick far into her burning flesh, and produced, by her delicious violence, the spasm of love.

When we returned to the drawing-room at a quarter to midnight, the scene had not changed very much. There were a few more wealthy young gentlemen. Some ladies and gentlemen had departed from the room but were slowly returned in dribs and drabs, their facial expressions suffused with every sign of sexual satisfaction. Young Ernest Dowson looked especially pleased with the buxom wench he had chosen and I wondered that she hadn't smothered him. I asked Arthur Machen if he had chosen to avail himself of the Society's delights. He looked up from his brandy to reply that this was entirely a matter between himself and the Universe. He was always so discreet!

The throaty-voiced young lady with flaming red hair appeared again. This time she was holding a fan of peacock feathers.

'The President is awaiting you, gentlemen,' she said, waved her fan in the direction of a corridor, and vanished.

We filed out to find ourselves in an even larger room but it was lit only by two black candles placed in candelabra fashioned in the form of a serpent. The President sat at a long table and the flames barely illuminated his face. Even so, I recognised it. It was that of an infamous Duke who was numbered among the largest landowners in England. As soon as the members had entered, he said in a cold, hard voice: 'Gentlemen,' – for the ladies had disappeared – 'you know the rules of The Vanishing Society.'

He opened a huge, leather-bound volume, then shut it abruptly with a swift slam.

'The Book is prepared,' he announced. 'Whoever opens it at the black page is at the disposal of the committee and myself. We had better begin.'

Someone began to read out the names in a low distinct voice, pausing after each name, and the member called came up to the table and opened at random the pages of a big folio volume that lay between the two candles. The gloomy light made it difficult to distinguish features but I heard a gasp behind me that was at the crossroads of rapture and terror.

After opening and looking at the book, each man left the room. There was left only a fellow I knew vaguely as Manderville, a polished idler of the pavements, who was also known as a victim of addiction to gambling and debt. There was foam upon his lips as he stumbled towards the table and his hand shook as he opened the leaves. As he opened the book at the black page, he emitted a sound that was both a gasp of relief and a shriek of horror.

'Kindly come with me, Viscount Manderville,' said the President and they went out together.

'We can go now,' said Ernest Dowson. 'I think the rain has gone off. Remember your promise, gentlemen. You have been at a meeting of the Vanishing Society. You will never see that young man again. Good night.'

'It's not murder, is it?' I enquired coolly.

'Oh, no, not at all. Lord Manderville will, I hope, live for many years; he has simply – vanished. Good night; there's a hansom that will do for you.'

I went home that night in dead silence. I didn't see Machen until three weeks later and our wallets both contained the same newspaper clipping:

> Viscount Manderville of The Albany has disappeared under mysterious circumstances. Lord Manderville was staying at Boleskine in Scotland and came up to London, as is stated, on business, on August 30th. It has been ascertained that he arrived safely at King's Cross and drove to Piccadilly Circus, where he got out. It is said that he was last seen at the corner of Montague Street, leading from Regent Street into Soho. Since the above date the unfortunate gentleman, who was much liked in London society, has not been heard of. Viscount Manderville was to have been married in September. The police are extremely reticent.

Machen and I stormed away to track down and confront Dowson. When we finally bearded him at some Strand tavern, he regarded us placidly then laughed in our faces.

'My dear fellows, what on earth are you talking about? I never heard such a cock-and-bull story in my life. As you say, Machen, I once pointed out to you a house said to be a club, as we were walking through Soho, but that was some low gaming den. I'm afraid that Azario's Chianti was rather too strong for you.' Some disreputable acquaintance of his hastened to assure us that Dowson was in that tavern on the night in question.

Eventually, Machen and I found the archway where we had taken shelter on that rainy night and knocked on the door of the great gloomy house, whistling as Dowson had done. We were admitted by a respectable mechanic in a white apron, who was evidently astonished at the whistle; in fact, he suspected that we were drunk. The place was a billiard table factory and had been so, as far as was known in the neighbourhood, for many years. The rooms must once have been magnificent but most of them had been divided into three or four separate workshops by wooden partitions.

Later I learned that Manderville owed more than three million pounds. He was never seen again, to my knowledge. That night, Machen and I were both quiet and thoughtful. He walked away to have a drink and ruminate, perhaps transforming this extraordinary experience into a well-wrought piece of fiction, while I went away to forget these perplexities by having a good fuck.

CHAPTER ELEVEN

'Oh! oh! oh!' cried the Hon Maud Kitteridge as she came within my arms and hard against my loins. This had indeed been a very good fuck but it was under the unusual circumstances of being watched by her mother. Lady Kitteridge was renowned as being one of the most decadent women in England. She loved to watch her daughter being fucked by a wealthy young man who might choose to marry her. On this occasion, in a quiet town mansion in Belgravia, both mother and daughter had stripped to their chemises of white lace, which exposed most of their breasts and their graceful legs to just below the groin. I was grateful to Lady Kate Kitteridge. She had led her daughter to a waiting pile of pillows on a raised dais. With gentle but firm pushing and prodding, she had caused her blushing daughter Maud to place herself face down on the pillows. The majority of these pillows were piled beneath her satin-smooth belly, thus lifting wide her graceful buttocks.

With stroking and whispered consolation, Lady Kate had soothed her daughter into closing her eyes and relaxing. Then, quickly uncovering thin golden chains at the innocent's feet, she had cuffed her daughter's ankles to the bedstead, splayed wide apart. Maud had twisted herself up and turned her head with the gesture of a panic-stricken gazelle but her legs were firmly anchored wide apart and open.

Before Maud could resolve to turn her pang of doubt into action, her mother had seized her wrists and now the slender arms of this tender, twenty-year-old beauty were chained out too, holding her spread-eagled and gently struggling in position. Her movements were slight but visibly excited. One couldn't tell if she were struggling with her golden chains or testing them with delight.

'She is prepared for entry,' Lady Kate had intoned, 'but be gentle with her . . .' Yet as I penetrated, Lady Kate knelt and grasped her daughter's heaving buttocks. Digging her nails into Maud's softest flesh, she finally stilled her squirming movements.

It was just the sort of fuck I needed after my experiences with the mysterious Vanishing Society and I relished every throb of my orgasm. However, I wasn't expecting an extra treat.

Slowly and methodically, Lady Kate pressed outward with her thumbs, spreading Maud's bum cheeks wide apart to expose the bud of her daughter's nether eye. Kate's scarlet lips glistened with pleasure as she directed my face into this most delicate place, to kiss and wet it with my tongue now plunging eagerly into this garden of delights. The girl uttered muffled cries which mingled both pleasure and fear. All the while, her own devoted mother held fast her quivering flanks, her slim fingers even guiding my once more rampant rod to its own lewd goal.

I was past pity for Maud, of whom I was genuinely fond. I buggered her slowly. Maud cried out and whimpered uncontrollably as my horrifyingly swollen member slowly stretched and splayed open the tender flesh and muscle of her tiny, delicate entrance. But the wicked Kate soothed her daughter by the skilful and distracting application of her finger-tips and scarlet nails to Maud's front portal.

After a few moments, Maud's cries subsided for, having

inched the bulbous head of my member into her sweet anus, I paused in my onslaught. Maud, her prim but grimacing face half-crushed against the pillows, whined softly. Then, with sudden sadistic relish, I plunged the entire length of my rod deep inside her. Her entire body stiffened with shock and she let out one long and blood-curdling shriek . . .

'*More* . . . Give me more! Oh, GOD!' And she slumped upon the bed, rattling her chains and gasping and shuddering in a climax of frantic intensity. Lady Kate withdrew her fingers from the frontal entrance. After that, she unchained her daughter and called a maid to take her for a hot bubble bath. Some might condemn Lady Kate as an evil mother but the fact remains that on account of sessions such as these, Maud soon married one of the richest landowners in England, and one gathers that they are very happy together. No doubt he too delights in her rosebud.

On occasion, one simply can't stop fucking and now it was Lady Kate's turn. Even in the dim light, nothing smaller than a bowler hat could have hidden my member's clear desire. My informer stood proudly, eager for his reward. My hands lay at my sides. Kate pressed my thighs apart and bent forward slowly. I waited until her hungrily parted scarlet lips were but a breath from their objective, waited calmly, for I knew the precise, correct instant that would call to me loud and clear. And so it did. But as she chewed my dick with over-eager forcefulness, I slapped her with my open palm across her left cheek.

She sprawled across the floor, stopping her fall with her right arm. I leaped out of the bed and was over her in an instant. Her face was full of surprise, but it was excited surprise. She brought up her free hand as if to ward off another blow but I snatched her wrist in one hand and with the other seized locks of her thick, golden hair, dragging her impish face up to mine. All in a burning fit of anger, I hissed: 'You will never bite me that way, *bitch*!'

Her pretty face contorted and she mouthed the word 'please'. But that only stoked the flames of my angry lust. By the two handles of her wrists and her hair, I dragged her towards the bed. She half-stumbled to her feet in an attempt to sit upon the cushions but I snarled 'No!' and despite her muffled squeals, pushed her face down upon these cushions with her knees still upon the mattress. I let go my hold on her hair and immediately captured her other hand, to pinion both wrists behind her at the small of her back. I pressed the wrists together with my left hand and with my other began peeling down her stockings. When I had them both to her knees, Kate wiggled her hips in an attempt to thwart their complete removal but I'd have none of that. I slapped her hard across her quivering bottom and said closely into her ear: 'Lift your legs, bitch.'

Really! the things that second cousins do!

She whimpered into the cushions at my threat but she immediately did as she was told. I ripped both stockings down to her ankles, tossed off her high-heeled shoes and then had her legs completely naked. One stocking I threw onto the sofa but the other I used to bind her hands together swiftly against her back. Throughout all my rough usage of her, Lady Kate whimpered: 'Ooh! . . . oh, *no*, Horby . . . oh, don't do this . . . *no*!'

But she made no especially loud outcry and although her bound hands writhed behind her, although her full hips and flanks trembled in pathetic half-attempts to avoid my usage, she gave no firm resistance to me. Lady Kate was actually *enjoying* my brutal treatment.

She continued to kneel upon the bed, her face buried in the cushions. I shifted around behind her, pinioned her calves to the mattress by pressing them between my shins and jerked her shoulders over to put her in a favourable position for entry. Kate moaned softly and wiggled her buttocks to facilitate my entrance at her frontal gate. But that was not my goal. I put some moisture to my fingertips and amply greased her nether eye. She spasmed her bottom away as soon as she realised my intent and whimpered: 'Oh! No . . . no. You will injure me terribly if you . . . I have never,,,'

'Your daughter has,' I replied, then smacked her flank with all my might. Then I seized a hank of her hair and pulled it hard, so that her head came back and her spine arched painfully. I leaned over behind her delicate conch-shell of an ear and snarled: 'Shut up, bitch! I'll fuck you as I please!'

Then I balled up her remaining stocking and, her head still pulled back by the hair, stuffed the silken ball full into her mouth. There was nothing left for her. I placed my rod against its goal and guided just its tip through the tiny gate. With my thumbs I splayed her arse cheeks apart and then, with one brutal twist of my hips, plunged my shaft half-way in.

Lady Kate groaned from so deep within that I could feel the agonised vibrations around my root. Another twist of my hips and I was in her to the hilt. She moaned again, but this time I was sure there was a different quality to her noise, one of greater satisfaction. Pleasuring this witch was turning out to be a joy indeed. I commenced pumping her with total abandon, as if I were walking within the widest of passageways. Kate now took to sobbing uncontrollably but as she did so, I could not but note that her whole body was writhing in time to my phallic tattoo.

Her sobs grew even wilder and I realised that this sexy bitch was close to cresting. As the climactic fit finally took her, Lady Kate started to spasm in her sphincter muscle with amazing strength and completely undeniable rhythmic urgency. In my dizzy state, there was absolutely nothing I could do except pound my belly against her gulping buttocks and spout and fill her up with my own delirious spunk!

As my last contractions shook me, I collapsed forward onto her. I slept in her arms that night and slept contentedly. I did not arise until mid-day and I promised that I would see her again, but I now had another appointment.

This was for luncheon at the Café Royal with my good old acquaintance, Frank Harris. As usual, he was hosting the best table in the room. Unfortunately, Oscar Wilde wasn't there. He had been released from prison and had (understandably) fled into exile in France. It was forbidden to mention his name in polite society. One can picture my delight, therefore, when I walked into the Café Royal to hear Frank Harris bellow:

'No, no, my dear Duke, I know nothing of the joys of homosexuality. You must ask my great friend Oscar about that. However,' Harris became whimsical as he stuck his big cigar defiantly in his mouth, 'if *Shakespeare* asked me, I would feel compelled to submit.'

This was understandably too much for a table guest, that brilliant minor novelist, essayist and cartoonist, Max Beerbohm. On the back of an envelope he busily sketched out a drawing which would later be published with the title: 'If Shakespeare asked me . . .' This shows a naked, broad-buttocked, furiously masculine Frank Harris stroking his fierce handlebar moustache and reminding himself that he has to go through with it because it is Shakespeare. Meanwhile, a rather fey Shakespeare, looking slim and elegant, is looking at Harris with perplexity and going 'Yeuch!'

Harris was then at the height of his power, though. He

was editing *The Saturday Review*, arguably the most stimulating journal ever to appear in London. John Galsworthy, later to win fame for *The Forsythe Saga*, reviewed the novels. H.G. Wells, a rampant stud if ever there was one, was in charge of the most interesting Science pages. Bernard Shaw was the drama critic. His play about prostitution, *Mrs Warren's Profession*, had just been banned by the Lord Chamberlain even though Shaw, a tolerant chap, led a sexual life of the utmost moral rectitude. I knew that he was short of money, though, and was not at all surprised when he proceeded to marry a rich woman. I always felt that sex was regarded by him as being a dreadful nuisance.

It was very enjoyable seeing Frank Harris and his entourage once again and I was in need of three dozen oysters. Oh! how they remind me of cunts! They must be the most delectable food in the world! I knocked back champagne and brandy but then my knob started to twitch once more so after a time I made my excuses and left for Leonard Smithers's pornography shop.

There I bought the latest edition of *The Pearl*, *A Man With A Maid*, *The Romance of Chastisement*, *The Petticoat Dominant or Woman's Revenge*, *The Lustful Turk* and a volume of *My Secret Life*. Although I had thoroughly enjoyed my time with Lady Kate and her daughter Maud, I now wanted to go home, read pornography and relish the pleasures of auto-eroticism.

There are many arguments to be made in favour of masturbation. One meets nicer people; one doesn't always have to look one's best; and you don't have to take your penis out to dinner and listen to its problems. However, my intention to have a good read and a quiet wank were abruptly interrupted by the sudden intrusion of Aleister Crowley.

CHAPTER TWELVE

I was very pleased to see 'old Crow' again and naturally I asked him about his activities, gladly accepting his invitation to go back to his Chancery Lane flat for burgundy and port. He informed me that he had been living as Count Vladimir Svareff 'because I wanted to see how London tradesmen treated a Russian nobleman, which is very well', and as Sir Aleister MacGregor 'because I recently bought myself a Lodge at Boleskine on the shores of Loch Ness.' Certainly his chambers in Chancery Lane were luxuriously appointed. He served wines that were of truly velvety seductiveness and told me about his continuing quest for wisdom, understanding and truth. He had joined a society, he informed me, in which the secrets of inner light reposed, and were I to be interested, he would be prepared to vouch for me. I accepted his kind invitation.

Crowley was rhapsodising about this paragon of Temples pervaded by sweetness and light when there was a fierce ringing upon the doorbell. Crowley went away and returned calmly in the company of three beautiful and utterly furious young women, all of them exquisitely dressed in silk and satin and lace and tulle. One of them shoved Crowley backwards into the room.

'Horby,' Crowley smiled coolly, 'may I present Miss Amelia Edwards, Lady Lauderdale and Mrs Price-Hughes? Ladies . . . Lord Horby.' This approach appeared to cut no ice with the ladies whatsoever.

'How *dare* you!' shouted Amelia, who was a noted actress.

'You monster!' shrieked Lady Candida Lauderdale.

'Beast!' Davina Price-Hughes picked up a Japanese vase and hurled it at Crowley. He ducked and it smashed against the wall behind him, splashing him with droplets of water.

'Never dull where Crowley is,' he murmured.

'No discretion!' Amelia snarled.

'He's appalling!' Candida screamed.

'The cad!' spat Davina.

'To what do I owe the honour of this most unexpected, charming and delightful visit?' Crowley gently enquired.

'The sheer audacity!' Amelia exclaimed indignantly.

'The arrogance . . .' Candida hissed.

'What impudence!' Davina fumed.

'Some sherry?' Crowley queried.

'You've been deceiving all of us,' snapped Amelia.

'I thought I was the only one,' sighed Candida.

'But you didn't know that we knew one another,' Davina sneered.

'Or would you prefer port?' Crowley responded nonchalantly.

'We're putting you on the spot, Aleister Crowley,' Amelia declared in a tone of finality.

'You'd better choose one of us, Sir Aleister MacGregor,' Candida insisted.

'Or else, Count Vladimir Svareff,' Davina threatened.

'Oh, very well,' Crowley muttered. He sat down, took off his shoes and removed his socks. 'These need a wash,' he said, 'and there's a hole here that needs darning. Any volunteers?'

The silence that followed was abruptly interrupted by three female gasps of pompous indignation.

'Well!' squealed Amelia.

'The *insolence*!' Candida gasped.

Mrs Davina Price-Hughes smiled at Crowley. He rolled his socks into a ball and tossed them at her.

'Catch,' he said, and she caught it perfectly. 'Tomorrow evening at six, Davina.' He rose and opened the drawing-room door. 'Well, that's it, then. Good evening, ladies.'

Candida and Amelia were too dazed to do anything other than stumble away unsteadily. A proud Davina whisked her skirts and strode majestically out of the chambers, carrying Crowley's ball of socks as though it were the apple of Paris.

'Good, that's all settled,' said Crowley as he poured more wine for us. 'Sex-mad bitches, that's their trouble. My flat-mate doesn't understand them at all. He just doesn't seem to be interested in sex.'

'Flat-mate?'

'Well, he's my guide, philosopher and friend,' Crowley answered. 'Engineer. Bit down on his luck. Invited him to move in. Splendid fellow.' Suddenly there was the turn of a latch-key in the lock, the slam of a door and a tall, gaunt man strode into the room wearing cheap but comfortable clothes. Crowley introduced him as his flat-mate, Allan Bennett. 'Allan thinks that the pleasures of the flesh are enough to leave one cold,' Crowley resumed, 'and they've driven him into celibacy. He claims to have discovered greater joys.'

'There are drugs,' said Allan Bennett, 'which will open the gateways of matter.' He had fierce, honest eyes and he spoke with a burning intensity. I had no idea at that time that this man would in time bring Buddhism to Great Britain. 'These drugs come naturally from plants.'

'Why don't you show him?' said Crowley. 'Unless, of course, my dear Horby, you are frightened by false fires. If things go wrong, I doubt if there'll be a doctor in the house but I can recommend a first-class undertaker just up the road.'

I had never taken drugs before so I watched with fascination as Allan Bennett crushed a white powder with the edge of a razor blade, divided it into lines upon a book of Crowley's poetry and produced a thin tube of silver.

Meanwhile, Crowley packed a slim churchwarden pipe with thin dried sprigs of what looked like grass. Allan Bennett inhaled through the silver tube a line of the white powder, which was apparently called 'cocaine' and came from the coca plant in Peru. Crowley did the same and I followed suit. Within a few minutes, I began to feel most happy and talkative. Now Crowley's pipe came around. This was apparently something called 'cannabis' and it induced a most relaxing frame of mind.

'Magick . . .' Crowley sighed, 'there's just nothing like it. Care to see the Temples?' I nodded and rose to follow him. 'White Magick,' he announced at the entrance to the first door. I stepped inside to see an altar upon which were placed reverentially a wand, a cup, a sword and a disc. There were statuettes in gold and delicately engraven images of male and female Egyptian deities.

'Beautiful,' I said; and I meant it.

'Now come and see the Black Magick Temple,' Crowley replied. 'Never know, you might find that more interesting.'

We entered a second room and it was painted entirely in black. Above a golden, trapezoidal altar, there hung a human skeleton. On the altar itself, there were the horns of a goat and, between those horns, an obscene naked figurine of the Goddess Astarte with her legs spread wide apart.

'Beautiful,' I said; and I meant that, too. I also wondered why I found his Black Magick Temple to be more exciting than the White. But in fact, Crowley's good Temples and

Bennett's fine drugs had not inspired me to any flights of intelligent fancy. The truth is that I was feeling quite murderously randy and if I didn't make my excuses and leave, I would be in danger of creaming in my drawers and thus staining my trousers. I bade my farewells to Crowley and to Bennett, then staggered out into the street, pondering as to where I could prod my rampaging rod.

The very last thing I expected as I strolled casually yet eagerly beneath the gas-lit lamps of Chancery Lane was the press of a pistol at the base of my spine.

'Move!' declared a sharp female voice and I had no alternative but to obey. My captor marched me into a side-street. There, a brougham was waiting and the coachman in an old-fashioned stove-pipe hat stood alongside – armed with an ancient but no doubt still lethal blunderbuss. The pistol upon my spine motioned me to mount the steps and move inside this elegant carriage. Its owner stepped in behind me, motioning me to sit down with a gesture of her weapon, and it was then that I obtained a clear view of my captors. They were Miss Amelia Edwards and Lady Candida Lauderdale, who was still fondly fingering her pistol.

'Men!' she exclaimed.

'Disgraceful,' Amelia concurred.

'Men need to be disciplined and punished,' Lady Lauderdale declared. 'Wouldn't you say so, Amelia?'

'Oh, and strictly, until their bottoms burn!' Amelia gasped excitedly.

I was obviously in the hands of vindictive, sexy bitches.

Lady Candida Lauderdale was a woman with a voluptuous figure. Her breasts and her buttocks threatened to split the sheer satin of her shimmering purple gown. Her face, however, was surmounted by impudent blonde curls and upon her face there was an expression of prim but imperious mischief. Miss Amelia Edwards had by contrast long swathes of wavy black hair, a smooth and perfectly proportioned face and a delectably slender figure. She was clad entirely in black silk, though beneath her skirt hem, white petticoats rustled. Lady Candida clearly did not need a bustle but had chosen to wear one. Miss Amelia might have chosen to wear a bustle but had decided to accentuate her slim body by not wearing one. They were obviously good friends.

At gun-point I was ushered out of the carriage at a side-road which I judged to be just off the Marylebone Road. I had no choice other than to obey instructions and was marched inside a luxurious apartment. There my hands were fastened behind my back with hand-cuffs of steel and, to my great indignation, my pockets were searched. The only item which interested the ladies was a letter I had just received from young Claire, and Amelia Edwards really rather embarrassed me by reading it to me in her soft, mellow voice:

Dear, dear Horby,

To you I entrust all my beliefs and fantasies. I have a secret to tell you now and let this secret be safe under lock and key. This is my confession and I hope that you will keep it sacred. No one else apart from you must ever read these words.

I twitched indignantly in my handcuffs as Amelia read on remorselessly.

I must tell you the truth,' Claire wrote and Amelia read aloud. *I am now a spiritualist. My unconscious has been aroused. I now have power especially over men. They come to me for advice. Once a week, we hold a séance. There are usually 4-8 people in attendance.*

There is a man that sometimes attends our meetings. He is so young, so handsome and so strange. So very Russian.

Count Vladimir Svareff, I think is his name. The last time I saw him, he introduced me to something called 'cannabis' which he called 'the herb dangerous'. Frankincense was also being burned in the room.

We have talked about Literature, travel, Science and even the weather. It was evident that we had something in common. When I accompanied him to his flat in Chancery Lane, he produced both a bottle of absinthe and a planchette – a heart-shaped board supported by two castors. This was made of fine ebony and the letters were engraved in gold. We proceeded to undertake a séance. Our hands touched. The letters kept on forming messages. There was electricity between us. The planchette seemed to spin quicker and quicker. The word was so obvious: 'F-U-C-K.'

We consumed more absinthe and smoked more cannabis and then I accompanied him to his bedroom. He's quite a strange one! He sucked my toes, kissed my heels and licked both the backs of my knees and my bottom. After that, he licked my cunt greedily, though I wish it could have been you. I had one orgasm after another and then he put his member into my mouth and I had a good suck on it. Oh! How it throbbed and pulsated! It was such a sweet sorrow to have to leave him on the following morning in order to travel to see my distant cousin Dorothy, who had invited me to her house in Sussex.

It was a lovely, sunny day when I arrived and so I went out into the garden and there was Mr Hughes pruning roses. Mr Hughes has been Amelia's family gardener for years. Here Amelia squealed. *You know, Amelia Edwards, the actress, and a good friend of mine. He also works for Dorothy. He is a Welshman and still manages to maintain his youth. He has long curly hair and can be so obtuse at times but I greeted him warmly and enquired after his best remedy for aphids.*

I am so glad that Summer is here. The garden is so beautiful now and one does love to see freshly-cut roses on the table. After my arrival, I went up to my room as I wanted, to continue with my literary pursuits. It was suddenly apparent that Mr Hughes had entered my bedroom! I quietly entered to find him with his trousers dropped beneath his knees, his cock in his hand and a pair of my broderie anglaise *white knickers draped over his head.*

'What are you doing here?' I demanded indignantly.

'Nothing . . .' he mumbled.

'Call me "Mistress"!' I snapped, as I removed the freshly laundered knickers from his head.

'For you, anything, my Mistress,' he sighed.

'Will you obey me now?' I bound my knickers around his wrists and placed his hands in front of his swelling member. Producing a chair, I said sharply: 'Bend over!'

It was an old-fashioned love-seat and the gardener had to straddle both sides of the chair. I have spent many a pleasant moment sitting in precisely this chair while I have fondled a lover's pecker and he has caressed my cunt. Now I thought that the exercise I intended could conceivably be followed by a fucking on my bed beneath its lovely tasseled canopy. Within the cupboard of the room, there was a cane for the chastisement of idle servants. I produced this and poised and switched it in the air. Then I took off his shoes, garters and socks, the better to commence a light whipping with bamboo. He began to yell when I raised welts, yet I could discern that his rod was throbbing hard. With the final swish of my cane, he attained an orgasm. His sperm spurted and I mopped it away with my clean knickers, knowing that there would be more to come.

'Would you like to spank me, now?' I asked.

'Um . . . no, ma'am, as I have respect for you,' he answered.

'I demand your fealty and devotion,' I insisted.

'Oh . . .' he sighed, 'what else do you demand of me, Mistress?'

I could see that his rod was throbbing once more and so removed most of my items of clothing yet kept on my corset.

'Would you not say that these are luscious buttocks?' I teased. 'And that is why I deserve a spanking. A jolly sound spanking!' I promptly straddled my four-poster bed and he began to spank me. At first I felt just like a naughty girl being punished by an authoritative teacher; but suddenly there came a knock upon the door and my hostess and cousin Dorothy entered in. She has since changed her name to Dorothea as she is presently studying at the Sorbonne.

'Mr Hughes deserves a spanking,' she said coolly. 'He has no right to spank a woman.' With that, she removed her bright pink frock and underneath was a bright red basque. I had never seen Dorothy look so beautiful in her underwear before. I took her into my arms. She started to suck my tits. First of all, she fondled them and I could feel my clit being aroused, also my nipples. First it was my left and then my right. There were kisses down to my navel and then she put her tongue into my cunt. Mr Hughes looked on with amazement.

'Turn around,' I whispered to Dorothy. Once more, her lips descended to my vagina and her velvety tongue was within me. We lay down together on my bed. I placed my own tongue within her hot slit and our orgasms were of the ultimate. We then untied a panting Mr Hughes.

'Please larrup us, slipper and spank us,' we both requested simultaneously.

'I think both of you deserve a hot spanking,' he growled.

'Yes, please,' we both replied.

We both lay down on the bed and proffered our bottoms.

'My dear, beautiful ladies,' said Mr Hughes with his enchanting Welsh lilt. 'You should both be chastised on account of what you have done.'

'Yes,' I said and Dorothy agreed as we placed our arms above our heads and he smacked the pair of us gently. But suddenly I felt a hand down by my clitoris and from the feminine feel of its finger, I knew it to be that of my cousin. That finger penetrated my lower mouth and Mr Hughes kept on spanking my bottom. How I could feel my buttocks glowing! With my right hand, I started to fondle my cousin's pussy while she continued to stroke mine.

Abruptly, the spanking stopped and I felt a harsh, rigid stabbing sensation against my bottom. My arse has been penetrated by many a man before and so I was ready for this. At the same time, I was aware that he was sticking his forefinger up my cousin's bum. We continued to fondle the quims of one another and to kiss and caress at the same time. Mr Hughes's cock was meanwhile throbbing in my anus. Without warning, he took it out and proceeded to lick me and rim me. What a stallion! I thought as he inserted his tool back inside my arse.

There was a point, I knew, when he would be about to come and I knew he wanted both of us to share the juices of his magnificent pecker. He withdrew, then proceeded to spout his seed upon my bottom and upon Dorothy's. He then massaged both of our arses with his spunk.

This was good yet it was obvious that our gardener was

becoming fatigued – and I was still desirous of another fuck. I felt like a bitch in heat. I kissed Dorothy upon her lips and she inserted her tongue into my mouth and again started to fondle my copious breasts and then to suck upon them. She was as rampant as I was. Again her finger entered my cunt to toy with my lovely flower.

'I would like to give you more satisfaction,' said Mr Hughes.

'Then suck my pussy,' Dorothy answered and there he was, eagerly down on her. I watched as he bared his teeth to nip her clit and I saw his tongue enter her cunt. I was feeling even more rampant. Frankly, I was jealous. I also wanted to feel his agile tongue penetrate my vagina.

There was a penetration when I least expected it. His index finger had entered me and I started to squirm, wriggle and writhe. My orgasm was quick and yet I was ready for more, though a bit sleepy. We settled down in bed upon silken sheets, covered by an eiderdown. Despite my fatigue, I was still enduring sensations of horniness. My final words to the gardener before we went to sleep were: 'Will you come tomorrow?'

'Yes, my love,' he replied, 'I will come as often as you want.' Upon that final statement, we all went to sleep.

Darling Horby, do please write to me and tell me what you have been up to. Presently I find that the raptures of sexual activity are the only things worth recording. Words from you will enliven me so much.

All my love (and lust!)
Claire.

'Well?' Miss Amelia Edwards and Lady Candida Lauderdale demanded of me: 'What do you have to say to *that*!?'

CHAPTER THIRTEEN

'And what happened after *that*?' Ellen Terry exclaimed as I sat opposite her in her drawing-room about one week later.

Naturally, I was very pleased to be there. Ellen Terry was a beautiful woman and probably the most celebrated actress in England. The portrait of her painted by John Singer Sargent, where she is playing Lady Macbeth, on view at the National Portrait Gallery, is a classic of the art.

Now, it has been alleged by some disreputable rascals that Ellen Terry gave her sexual favours freely. This is not the case. She was faithful to every man with whom she was involved. I speak with the authority of a man who was trying to seduce her and who, on this occasion, did not succeed. What Ellen Terry enjoyed, however, were flirtatious attentions from handsome admirers: and she also relished hearing the details of sexual encounters.

'What did you say . . .?' she queried, licking the lips she had adorned in crimson.

'There wasn't very much that I could say,' I replied, 'since Lady Candida had whipped off her soaking wet knickers and thrust them within my mouth. Amelia had cast aside a high-heeled boot, peeled away a silk stocking and then knotted it tightly around my neck. Thus tied, gagged and noosed, I was led helpless before the outraged majesty of Womanhood.'

'I like it,' Ellen Terry sighed. 'Tell me more.' If my

imagination were not deceiving me, she was squeezing her thighs together very hard beneath her long, black, bell-shaped skirt.

'They marched me to a flogging block and chained me to it.'

'What, pulling down your trousers?' Ellen laughed.

'Yes.'

'And your underpants to expose your bottom?'

'Yes.'

I have never seen a woman move in such a swift and snake-like fashion. Suddenly she had grasped steel cuffs from beneath a pile of illustrated magazines in which she featured, and had snapped the locks around my ankles.

'And they tied your wrists like this, did they?' she enquired gently, taking off a long leather glove from her slim arm and binding my wrists with it. ' "Bend over!" Did they say that?' She pushed me over an arm-chair, then unbuttoned my trousers and whipped them down to expose my arse, bared to the world. 'Oh, Horby, was it like this? These ladies who had kidnapped you, what did they do to you? After all, let's not forget that I know them both.' She laughed gaily. 'I think you are here with me now in this same position as you were then, so do please tell me the story.'

'Very well.' I had no choice in the matter. I do not recall precisely the words I spoke to Ellen Terry that night but I do have before me a written record of what transpired, the gist of which I must have related to this beautiful actress from my captive position. My *Memorandum 56* reads:

'Now, Horby,' said the buxom Lady Lauderdale, 'here you are all tied up in bondage with your buttocks shamefully exposed. You insolent young man, you must realise that I am your governess along with my assistant Miss Amelia and that you are my slave. Don't you dare even try to speak!' she shrieked. This would have been difficult on account of her silken drawers filling my mouth. 'From you I shall expect and shall exact the most implicit obedience and the most abject submission. You will tremble hereafter at the mere rustle of a petticoat; by it, you are now to be governed. If you are sufficiently foolish to display your insubordination to ladies as you did today in the company of your friend Crowley, well, then, you must be punished.'

'He is too unruly for home!' Amelia broke in. 'Too indecent! Too anxious to know what young ladies have under their petticoats!' I blushed furiously. 'Yes . . .' she slid into a gentle bitchy cooing. 'I know all about it. The petticoat will have its revenge now and you, my dear sir, will be under it in more senses than one. But you are now kneeling at our feet, placed upon the flogging block. Oh, you will soon have due cause to rue your insolence.'

'Amelia,' Candida requested, 'strap this boy's elbows behind his back as tightly as you can.' Amelia grasped me firmly by the upper part of the arm. I was surprised to feel her strength. The little resistance I made was soon overcome. I cannot describe the mixture of sensations I experienced with her standing over me, my head level with her waist and at her pulling me about roughly as she delighted in fulfilling Candida's request. I noticed what Zola describes as 'a powerful feminine perfume' – the *odor de femme*.

At last two straps were buckled tightly round my arms, just above the elbows. In each strap was a small metal ring. Amelia passed a white cord three or four times through these rings and then proceeded to pull them as closely together as possible. Oh, how she hurt! I thought she would have broken my arms. I cried out, I resisted as much as I could but it was all too much for me. I writhed in my endeavours to get free but Amelia placed her slim knickered bottom upon my neck and kept me down.

'Tighter,' said Candida. At last, when my elbows were nearly touching each, Amelia tied the cords fast and stood up, looking very pretty with a flush upon her smiling comely face on account of her exertions.

'Now, Master Horby,' said Candida, clearly relishing this moment, 'you are in a fit state for punishment and you shall have it. Your behaviour was slighting to me earlier this evening.' Smack, smack, in my face, one on each cheek: one with the left, the other with the right hand! How those soft, lovely, dimpled hands stung! How my cheeks tingled! How I struggled in absolute helplessness to get free! 'You object to feminine domination, to petticoat rule . . .' giving me two smacks at each enumeration. 'I think I shall convert you. You see—' smack! smack! – 'you must endure it.'

I would not have believed that two dainty little hands could have caused such pain. Lying at the feet of Candida, in close proximity to her and seeing her graceful figure each time she raised her arms to inflict punishment was, I own at first, some assuagement of my pain. But at last the smacking she gave my cheeks made my head swim and I became so silly and bewildered, I was almost unconscious by the time she put the backs of her hands alternately to my lips and made me kiss them and thank her.

'Oh, please undo my arms and let me get up,' I pleaded but Lady Candida Lauderdale refused my request. Instead, she enquired of Amelia whether I had been rude to her or not.

'Indeed, Candida, very rude,' Amelia replied. 'So offhand and falsely superior.'

'Very well, Amelia,' Candida responded softly. 'Horby, you will be deprived of your trousers!' she snapped sharply. 'Take a long leave of them. When you will see them again, I do not know: they teach you all sorts of resistance and naughtiness and make you assume airs of ridiculous superiority which you do not possess. Amelia, take his trousers off.'

Amelia speedily unfastened the straps which kept me kneeling but ensured that my elbows were still confined as she busied herself in unfastening my garment. She pulled away the left leg first and I blushed with intense shame. Her hands then fumbled upon my right trouser leg. I cannot describe what I felt at being close to a girl in this heated condition with her hands busy about me, my trousers opened and violated and my person almost coming into actual contact with her swelling bosom as she proceeded with uncompromising rapidity and promptitude to tear away my clothing. I felt like a fowl about to be roasted and was stupefied by my humiliating position.

Presently, everything was unfastened and Amelia plucked my trousers and drawers from my heels, not hesitating to move her hands freely about my person, even putting her arm between my legs to effect her purpose. In the midst of my abasement, I noticed an incipient sensation of what I had felt when I first fucked Rosemary Radcliffe, and had lifted her garments to regard the magical secrets within. Truly the tables were turned on me, for now, before Candida and Amelia, my own legs, from the end of my shirt to my ankles, were bared and displayed, naked. My cheeks burned and I felt horribly defenceless.

'Now, Horby, how do you feel?' Candida teased me. Then she burst into verse:

> 'Georgy, Porgy, pudding and pie,
> Kissed the girls and made them cry.'

Amelia chimed in:

> 'When the girls came out to play,
> Georgy Porgy ran away.'

'To enforce your submission to the petticoat, the emblem of the female sex, and to demonstrate your domination by it, you will have one over your head,' Candida asserted self-righteously. She plucked a frilly white petticoat from her voluminous under-garments and handed it to Amelia. 'Please tie it together at the top – so! Now throw it over his head. There, now he is under the petticoat! Now, Horby, I shall cane your bottom for you as smartly as ever a boy's bottom was caned.'

I winced at her threat and at her talking so freely of my bottom. There was not much to hide it from sight and the ladies obviously were relishing this becoming prospect. What could I do, with my arms fixed immovably, my head wrapped in the white petticoat of Candida and myself overcome by the pungent odour with which I was then still insufficiently acquainted but with which I subsequently became only too familiar? I was also terrified to think of the caning in store for me.

'A male should always be caned with formality,' said Candida. I saw that before me, there was a full-length looking-glass. Behind me, Candida had picked up a whippy bamboo cane with an ebony handle and she poised and switched it in the air. With an amused smirk, Amelia spread herself upon the chaise-longue, her legs slightly apart and her right hand pressing softly between her thighs. Candida thrust out her beautiful buttocks, a gesture which I have known all dominant women to adopt, then informed me that she was going to give me six of the best and that I had to count the strokes.

'One!' I moaned. The effect of the cane was indescribable. Every stroke seems to penetrate to the core of your being.

'Two.' My bottom twitched from side to side. This was truly forcing me to sober up from the drugs I had taken earlier.

'Three . . .' That was a muffled sob. I heard Candida gasp and imagined the scene, the smallest glimpse of which was only vouchsafed to me through the petticoat of my punisher.

'Four . . .' I sighed as her cane branded my hide. I trembled at the crack of her cane and already began to repent and make resolutions of obedience.

'Five . . .' Obedience, alas! I did not know then that the infliction of chastisement, whether deserved or not, was an integral part of the discipline of these two handsome ladies, nor that I was being caned merely for being a male! A great deal of courage had left me with my trousers and, smothered as I was, I longed for some covering for my poor, sore bottom, lined with weals.

'Six!' I squealed, jerking my hips up into the air. Now a cool feminine hand stroked my burning flesh.

'You poor boy,' Candida said. 'Your bottom has been well whaled,' and Amelia sniggered with furtive pleasure as she adjusted her skirts. 'I trust that you will have learned your lesson and will know how to behave towards ladies in the future.' With these cool words, she walked over to Amelia, kissed her full on her ruby-red mouth, placed a slender arm around her waist and stroked her slim bottom. The two women left the room, giggling gently together, then I heard the front door slam.

After a time, a very fat woman entered the drawing-room, removed the petticoat and untied me from my undignified and painful position. As I recovered my trousers, she indicated that it was time for me to go.

'So I left,' I told Ellen Terry, 'what else was there for me to do?'

I could see that there was a sublime irony in the circumstances of my story. There I was manacled by this enchanting woman with my bottom bared for her delectation whilst telling her a story of similar circumstances. It certainly seemed to have excited her. It was impossible to tell just which particular instrument she had placed in between the thighs that made her skirts rustle so, but her face was highly flushed and suddenly she cried out. A shudder shook her body, then a wave of quivering.

'I enjoyed that story,' she told me softly as her hand withdrew from within her skirt and petticoats. She proceeded to untie me with every sign of satisfaction glowing upon her exquisite face. 'I trust that you learned something by it. I certainly did. Oh, isn't rôle-playing just such an absolutely wonderful game!? This is why I love to be an actress. I can be someone else each day and forget who I am. For example, tomorrow I am giving tea to Bernard Shaw. He seems to have no interest at all in sex save as an intellectual experiment.' She rang a bell. By now I had struggled back into my trousers. 'Today,' she continued remorselessly, looking more like Lady Macbeth than ever, 'I have played the part of a queen who delights in having her slave in bondage. What is life without variety?' A maid entered and proceeded to serve tea with thin cucumber sandwiches, scones with jam and Cornish clotted cream, also freshly made chocolate éclairs. 'I enter fully into and assume the identity of every rôle I take,' Ellen Terry declared. She sipped tea from a china cup most delicately.

It was very good tea. The cucumber sandwiches were exquisite, too.

'What fascinates me,' she continued, 'is whether there was any sequel to the punishment administered to you by Lady Candida and Miss Amelia.'

'There certainly was,' I rasped. 'I was all out for revenge.'

'How exciting . . .' she fluttered her blue-shadowed lids

demurely. 'Tell me more,' she added sweetly as her hand reached out idly for some hidden instrument of secret pleasure.

'Those ladies weren't the only ones who had guns,' I responded.

'Then give me more shots,' she answered languidly.

CHAPTER FOURTEEN

My *Memorandum 57* constituted the contents of what I told Ellen Terry that night. She appeared to be unhealthily thrilled by it, if one may judge by her use of the wicked instrument she kept by her and which seemed to depart from the floor into her skirts with bewildering rapidity. I told her of my plans to exact revenge upon Lady Candida Lauderdale and Miss Amelia Edwards.

It was hardly a problem to discover where they lived nor to send cards inviting them to tea. They arrived at my flat, no doubt thinking that I was one of those gentlemen who desired another session of bondage and caning. Over tea and chocolate éclairs I relaxed and observed their behaviour. After a time I decided that Lady Lauderdale could be a fucking nuisance. She was a cock-teaser, all promises and no follow-through. Amelia followed her lead. It was really rather a delight to produce a brace of pistols and have these delicate prick-teasers tied to their chairs by my servants. Amelia was looking rather delectable in her bound position, blossoming out in organdy and silk. Her thighs were admirable, though at that point I could only see so much. It is easy to do, one supposes, to show just so much and no more, to drive a man wild by letting him almost – but not quite – see that extra four inches. The hard part, one thinks, must be to keep him from knowing that you're quite aware of what you're showing. When I had first seen

Amelia, I had thought that she was catting for a lay. Meanwhile, my own arse had been caned.

Women like that can make a nervous wreck of you if you take them seriously. Three hours of a throbbing, unfulfilled dick within one's trousers make one ready to turn to masturbation. I stared hard at Amelia and Candida, now my bound prisoners and at my mercy.

Presently, both ladies were looking dreadfully shocked and terribly embarrassed. They hadn't dreamed that I could have them within my power so quickly. I pulled up the skirts and petticoats of both these bitches, then tore down their drawers. Then I unbuttoned their blouses and tossed them aside. It was a joy to contemplate the helplessly exposed teats, bellies and cunts of womanhood. I thought that the youthful Amelia had slightly better buds.

Candida had one of those big, deep navels, the kind that you could warm a chestnut within. She took care to keep her thighs apart so that the afternoon sunlight came through them. I viewed her from all angles. I was going to fuck that cockteaser, and not because she might be such an incomparable lay but because she made me so bloody angry. I would get my prick into her bush just once, just for the satisfaction of hearing her say a few well chosen words of apology . . . just to knock her off her high horse, take some of the starch out of her sails, put a spoke in her wheel, and many other phrases which add up to fucking the nonsense out of her. I untied her and threw her down upon the floor in front of the bound Amelia.

'How about a fuck?' I asked her, jovially.

'You won't get away with this,' she muttered back through clenched teeth.

'Oh, no, cockteaser,' I responded, 'you're going to find out what fucking is like. You're going to be raped on this damn floor.' She kicked, bit and scratched but I was too much for her. I had never raped anybody in my life before this but that was before I had encountered this sadistic teaser. I've seldom enjoyed taking off a woman's clothes as much as I enjoyed and relished the stripping of this bitch. I felt her up, and the more she squirmed and blubbered, the longer and harder my dick grew. Candida squeezed her eyes shut and I could feel her trembling under me. I might have felt sorry for her had it not been for her ill usage of my own person.

I ran my hands over her belly, played with her tits and then spread her legs further to inspect her fig. She was no virgin. Lady Lauderdale trembled within my arms. Still, she continued to fight like a cat whenever she could catch enough breath.

My cock was going for her cunt. I rubbed it against her struggling, straining thighs. She begged me, in a terrified whisper, to let her go.

'Please don't do this to me! I'm sorry that I was so beastly, it won't happen again! Don't shame me any more . . .'

She was far too late with her good resolutions. My dick had slid well within her mop and her thighs were throbbing to its rhythm. My fingers played with her breasts. Her belly quivered and quaked and I noticed that her nipples were erect, standing up, large and dark, in the centre of the dark eyes of her teats.

'NO . . . no . . . no . . . no . . . no . . .'

I thrust my all within her as my thumb penetrated her arse-hole. I forced it in as my balls brushed against her smooth legs. I kept her thighs spread as I gave it to the bitch very slowly. Her belly struggled to recoil from me and she moaned softly. She didn't want to look at me or have me see her face. I held her head and shook it to make her open up her eyes.

'Now, you bitch, how do *you* like it?' I demanded. 'Why don't you smile? Aren't you happy, you lousy teaser? Feel that prick in your cunt. I want you to feel it! Here, maybe this will help you know what you've got in there!' I fucked her so hard that it was impossible to tell whether it was the fucking or the struggling that made her toss herself all over the carpet. 'You won't be so tight when I've screwed you. It won't be so easy to keep your legs crossed from now on when you have some poor bastard sweating to lay you. Pity we're not all like Crowley, eh?'

For the first few minutes, her cunt fought me. However, nothing would make me take my cock out of her cunt. She found that it was no use. Her struggles became weaker. She was defeated. There was nothing for her to do but to let it be done. She twitched and lay still.

'Ah, now you're becoming reasonable,' I observed. 'We should have done this the other day. I think you enjoy being raped! You fucking teaser, you won't do your act so easily tomorrow. Listen, I've got at least three shots in my gun. Don't think that just one fuck is all you're going to get. I'll give you a night such as nobody but a whore ought to know. Maybe you'd like to be a whore?' She moaned. I was really fucking her hard by this time. I'd got the juice coming out of her by spoonfuls. 'Here's a little something to warm your cunt. Maybe there won't be enough to fill you right up to the edges but don't worry. You have plenty more coming. You'll jump a mile when you feel it.'

'Don't do that!' Lady Lauderdale begged. 'You can't do it to me!' I showed her that I certainly could. She squirmed and cried out. She was no longer fighting me. Oh, she didn't exactly throw her legs around my neck. 'Not another one . . .!' she gasped. 'Do I have to go through that torture again? Haven't you had your revenge?'

It was really nice to hear her beg after the way she had

treated me and I teased her nether lips with the tip of my prick, listening to her futile objections. I had been going crazy thinking of putting my prick up her cunt and now that the time had come when I could get it, I extracted every joy that I could. I tickled her bush with my cock. Then I shoved my penis deep inside her.

'Oh . . . don't . . .' she sighed.

'Shut up,' I snapped, 'or I'll come in your face. I'll shove my cock right down your throat.'

I withdrew my stiff prick from her vagina. I wanted to see all of her, to feel everything and to perceive just who and what I was screwing. I lowered my head to sniff her pubic hair. 'Come kidnap me at pistol point sometime, will you?' I demanded. 'Bind me, tease me, slap me and cane me? Just come here tomorrow and ring three times. Where there is love, I'll be there.' I moved my prick deeper within and felt her becoming limp under me. I smacked her bare arse. It was quite a treat to be able to do that. I grabbed her tits and I licked them. I could do anything I wanted to her. She was my helpless prisoner.

I stretched her cunt and let my prick head on right within her and she sighed with the pleasure of it. I lost sight of things and exploded inside her.

I still felt that I hadn't had enough. After a breather, I was back between Candida's thighs as Amelia writhed within her bonds. Candida was too weak to do a thing to stop me now. Her legs opened weakly once more and she did not even attempt to keep them together against me. I wiggled my cock beneath her buttocks. She did not try to hide her face any longer. One thrust and I was in. She simply lay there and let me fuck her. It was no effort to hold her.

'Don't fuck me any more . . . please don't fuck me any more . . .' She seemed too weak to talk above a whisper.

'Maybe I am fucking you too much,' I replied. 'Maybe I'm fucking you too much, even if you are a bitch. But I shall go to it. If there's anything wrong, you'll let me know about it, won't you? Yes, listen, you bitch, you! I want you to tell the truth. Am I hurting you or am I not?' I looked so damn fierce that her cunt was afraid to lie.

'No,' she whispered, 'it does not hurt me a bit. But I can't take much more. I promise I'll never mistreat you or anybody else ever again.' Which was all that I wanted to know, of course. I gave her an ejaculation of thick spunk that drenched her thighs. I said: 'Go on, lick it up, damn you. Maybe I'll let you suck me off if you like it and maybe you'd like to suck me off anyway. Can I trust you to take my prick in your mouth? Oh, I've been bitten by bitches, I'm telling you, I know what it's like. But how about it, you lecherous tart? I'll bet that you've tasted cock before now, haven't you? Oh, don't be so fucking coy. Did you ever have a prick in your mouth?'

I shoved my prick within her eager open mouth. Just when she was gaping and gasping for yet another ejaculation, I withdrew, spun her over on her face and snapped handcuffs on her wrists. It was after that an easy matter to fasten her with foot-cuffs at the ankles. Her voluptuous rounded bottom stuck up enticingly from the carpet. She squealed and sobbed but deserved every instant of this imposed humiliation. Now it was time to deal with Miss Amelia Edwards.

Every time the hollow voice of conscience whined at me, I recalled the punishment this woman had given me. This helped a great deal to keep me from feeling sorry for her. No doubt Miss Edwards had never been raped before this. But a bitch who acted in her manner might as well wear a placard: 'Forceful Entry Solicited.' She was enough to make any man feel violent, I thought, as I unlocked her chains and threw her down upon the floor.

'The first lay,' I muttered, 'is for pleasure only.' At that instant I thrust inside her and came. She cried as I sighed. After a few minutes of resting with my head upon her heaving breasts, I was ready to go again. 'Full measure,' I said. 'The second round is the one that really counts, the one that will take the nonsense out of you. Hell!' I laughed. 'Don't you see how it is? Now I've got you so that you won't ever mistreat *me* again. But that's not enough. I'm going to fix you so you will never mistreat *anybody* again and that means that I'm going to give you another. You see, I just can't bear to take my dick away from you.' I chucked her under the chin. I could feel the moist walls of her cunt twitch and tighten on my prick. She was still scared and it seemed that she was trying to find out if I were in condition to take her again. Amelia was remarkably good-looking in her prim way and almost succeeded in making me feel as though I were playing her a dirty trick.

'Don't do it anymore,' she pleaded. 'I won't tell the police, I promise, if you don't do any more to me.'

She wouldn't tell the police! Female logic is enough to drive any man crazy. She had spent an evening with Candida criminally tormenting me. But now *she* was going to refrain from informing on *me*?

'This one's for the time you kidnapped me at pistol point,' I replied, and shook her body with the force of my thrust. 'And this is for the time that you tied me up. And this is one for the caning.'

'You can subdue my body but not my will,' she hissed.

'Ah!' I exclaimed. 'Then I shall place a firework within your arse and light it. Or would you rather be a nice girl and fuck?' She tried to look reproachful but succeeded only in looking dazed. She was beginning to like it. I couldn't think about anything but my cock. It was lost up her vagina and I was coming.

The bitch didn't even close her legs after I was through with her. She kept them spread and waited for more. Luckily, after a pause, I was able to give her more and proceeded to roger her slowly for a long time. 'I find your hospitality bewitching,' I said. I pushed her onto her back. I grabbed her waving legs and pushed them up until her knees were on her nipples. My end of her was all arse and cunt – what else? My prick had disappeared into the centre of her bush. Oh! and didn't she wiggle? It was as though I had shovelled a bucket of hot coals into her furnace door. She reached down to my arse in response and stroked my balls. She was coming and she howled. I sucked her nipples, knowing that I had an exploding volcano on my hands. When I came again, it was rather as though the room turned over a couple of times. It always hit me hard in the pit of the stomach but I could hear her cooing for it had hit her too.

It was easy to snap the handcuffs and foot-cuffs back on her and to expose her bottom in all its embarrassed indignity. I took a riding crop and gave six strokes each to Candida and Amelia. Their white, quivering buttocks were well whaled. I watched their hotly blushing backsides tremble with some considerable satisfaction. After that, I departed for a country weekend in Hampshire. My maids had had instructions to release the ladies after an hour and to give them both a bubble bath. They needed it and I trust that they enjoyed their ablutions. After all, it was tit for tat.

When I finished telling this story to Ellen Terry, her blue-shadowed eyes were closed, her left hand with its mysterious instrument was deep within her voluminous skirts and she was sighing softly. Indeed, she appeared to explode with an internal convulsion. Since I was her guest, I waited patiently as her body throbbed. Then her hand reached out to unbutton my fly, to let loose my prick and to twitch it so skilfully within her soft, cool fingers, that I spurted into the air with my droplets landing upon her drawing-room carpet.

'Quite an afternoon,' she remarked softly.

One could hardly deny that.

CHAPTER FIFTEEN

My association with Aleister Crowley and Allan Bennett bore interesting fruit. In the early Winter of 1898, I was initiated into a magical society, the Hermetic Order of the Golden Dawn. Bennett was a longstanding and well-respected member. Crowley had joined only comparatively recently, but he was fast earning a fearsome reputation and he recommended that I join too.

In common with most human beings, I wanted to know the truth about the life we live, or in some cases, merely endure. Crowley was convinced that there was a secret Inner Sanctuary of Wisdom and that the Golden Dawn might represent it. I wanted that inner wisdom and that is why I presented myself for it. Certainly the price in financial terms was eminently reasonable.

Bound and blindfolded at Mark Mason's Hall, I was ready to endure whatever the Adepts of this secret Order might give me. Crowley had told me the history of the matter. At some point during the 1880s, a cipher manuscript had somehow been discovered by either Dr Woodman, a retired clergyman, or Dr Wynn Westcott, a London Coroner. One account states that it was found on a bookstall in the Farringdon Road; another, that it was in the library of the late bibliophile, Fred Hockley. An occult scholar, Samuel Liddell 'MacGregor' Mathers was called to assist and he soon ascertained that the code was relatively simple and could be solved via consultation with a work called *Polygraphiae* by the Renaissance scholar John Trithemius, available at the British Museum.

The Cipher Manuscripts yielded to Mathers's scrutiny. They contained the rubric of certain rituals of initiation and the true attribution of that mysterious pack of cards called the Tarot. This attribution had been sought vainly for centuries. According to Crowley and Bennett, it cleared up a host of difficulties in the same way that, in these later times, Einstein's admirers claim that he has done for basic problems of mathematics and physics. This manuscript also gave the name and address of one Soror Sapiens Dominabitur Astris, a Fräulein Anna Sprengel, living in Germany, with an invitation to write to her if further knowledge was required. Dr Westcott wrote; and S.D.A. gave him and his two colleagues a charter authorizing them to establish an Order in England. This was done. Soon after, Sr S.D.A. died. In reply to a letter addressed to her came an intimation from one of her colleagues to the effect that England must expect no further assistance from Germany and that enough knowledge had been granted to enable any English adept to formulate a 'magical link' with 'the Secret Chiefs', allegedly super-human beings. Such competence would evidently establish a right to renewed relations.

Dr Woodman died. Mathers forced Dr Westcott to retire from active leadership of the Order. He then announced to the advanced adepts that he had himself made the Magical Link with the Secret Chiefs, having met them in the Bois de Boulogne. This may well sound absurd but I took the Order with absolute seriousness. I remember asking Crowley whether people often died during the initiation ceremony. Frankly, I found it to be a rather flat formality. Even so, I saw myself as entering the Hidden Church of the Holy Grail. This state of my spirit served me well, for I felt I had experienced something new *despite* all the robes and pomp and ceremony.

If I had at all been looking forward to satanic orgies, then I was most bitterly disillusioned. I was most solemnly sworn to inviolable secrecy. The slightest breach of this oath meant that I should incur 'a deadly and hostile current of will, set in motion by the Greatly Honoured Chiefs of the Second Order, by which I should fall slain or paralysed, as if blasted by the lightning flash.' And now I was entrusted with some of these devastating though priceless secrets. They consisted of the Hebrew alphabet, the names of the planets with their attributions to the days of the week, and the ten Sephiroth of the Cabbala. I had known it all for weeks and any schoolboy in the Lower Third could memorise this 'secret knowledge' within a day.

In the robing room, my eyes and my facial expression told Crowley everything he needed to know and he laughed lightly.

'No, these are not great adepts masking their majesty,' he said to me softly and very quietly. 'They're merely muddled, middle-class mediocrities. Apart from Bennett and Jones over there, they're an abject assemblage of nonentities, as vulgar and commonplace as any other set of people.'

I thought that was much too hard, although I had been disappointed, for Arthur Machen was there, to my surprise, and we shook hands warmly. Unfortunately, he seemed to be very wary of Crowley. There was also a young poet whose work I quite liked called William Butler Yeats who later won the Nobel Prize for Literature. Crowley and Yeats appeared to dislike one another intensely, and this was probably due to professional jealousy, though I must admit that I prefer the poetry of Crowley. It is much clearer and stronger. I was pleased to be introduced to a man called Peck, the Astronomer Royal of Scotland, but he turned out to be disappointingly dull company.

Matters improved when we entered a communal hall where the men and women members could mingle freely. 'MacGregor' Mathers, who was visiting from his base in Paris, was certainly an imposing, martial figure. His wife Moina, daughter of the French philosopher Henri Bergson, was elfin and beautiful. According to Crowley, they never once fucked. He introduced me to a charming, pretty and intelligent woman, whom I knew by repute: Florence Farr. She had quite a figure and was very good-looking indeed. I'd been told that she had enjoyed affairs with Yeats, with Bernard Shaw and with Crowley, among others. She was a highly talented actress of note and I succumbed to her conversational charms. Ignoring Crowley's advice, to wit, that 'for her I've always felt an affectionate respect, tempered by a feeling of compassion that her abilities are so inferior to her aspirations,' I invited this delightful woman to dine with me the following week and she seemed pleased to accept.

Maud Gonne was another very beautiful woman present in the room. William Butler Yeats was running around her as though he were a puppy dog in the first stages of sexual heat and she was treating him with icy disdain.

'What a lank, dishevelled demonologist,' Crowley commented. 'He could take more pains with his personal appearance without incurring the reproach of dandyism.'

My own endeavours to attract Maud Gonne similarly came to naught, however. Only two matters seemed to interest her: the truths of the spirit enshrined within the Golden Dawn (which I had yet to discern); and freedom for Ireland. These days I gather that she was a prime mover in the agitation which brought about the Republic of Eire and that Yeats is still sniffing around her skirts, with equal lack of success.

I was surprised to see Constance Wilde there. She was the extraordinarily pretty wife of Oscar and everyone was very kind to her over the tragedy. She obviously was not looking for an affair. I exchanged only a few words with her, having been acquainted with her husband. To my surprise, she told me that he had always resented her membership of the Golden Dawn.

I did not care very much for Annie Horniman, even though she has in my lifetime done so much to further cultural causes. I refer to her founding of the Gaiety Theatre and also to the Horniman Museum in South East London. The Horniman tea family was indeed both well-intentioned and moneyed, but Miss Horniman herself struck me as being something of a forlorn Presbyterian prude. She continuously declared that 'our fleshy desires are a major obstacle on the spiritual path,' yet she displayed an irritatingly unhealthy and disapproving interest in the sex lives of other members.

A big, red-bearded man was briefly present and it was unclear as to whether he was a member or not. I was sure that I had seen him somewhere before and it turned out that this was Bram Stoker, business manager of the great actor Sir Henry Irving, presently enjoying great success as a popular novelist with a tale about vampires called *Dracula*. He had married one of the most beautiful women in the British Isles, Florence Balcombe, who had been courted in vain by Oscar Wilde.

There was also a slim young man there, elegantly dressed, called Arthur Ward. In later years he became very successful via the writing of popular novels under the name 'Sax Rohmer' which featured a Chinese villain called Fu

Manchu, though personally I much preferred his *Brood of the Witch Queen*.

Nevertheless, the Golden Dawn had so far not shed any particular ray of sunlight upon my path. Perhaps there was some hidden wisdom within the portals of its inner order, but I had yet to perceive it. It was a positive relief to return home and find another letter from my dear ex-governess, Rosemary Radcliffe:

My darling,

I have not been feeling very well recently. It seems that day after day, I suffer from the vapours. A week ago I fainted for no apparent reason.

Mother gave me good advice. 'Go to Brighton and visit your Great Aunt Elizabeth. It will do you the world of good.' My Great Aunt is a schoolmistress and something of an authoritarian figure but I do have respect for her. She married well but unfortunately this alliance did not last too long. After her marriage, she had a brief affair with a man a few years younger than her. I liked him. He used to wax his handlebar moustache and was always so debonair. Unfortunately, he also had a mistress. I think his mistress used to dye her hair. I believe she was also in possession of that decidedly decadent French innovation called a bidet.

I must not digress. I took the train to Brighton. Unfortunately, my Great Aunt was not there to meet me and so I decided to take a walk along the pebble beach. The sun was hot that day and there were many sunbathers along the shore. This was too much for me and I decided to take refuge under Brighton Pier. I found a lovely spot. Even though I was in the shade, I raised my parasol. I believe that sunlight can cause freckles and I do not wish for any more. The book I had with me proved to be quite interesting. The author was an American, one Ambrose Bierce, and this collected volume of short stories was called In the Midst of Life. *His macabre sense of humour amused me. According to his view: 'A bride is a woman with a fine prospect of happiness behind her.'*

The next moment I knew I was in somebody's arms. He was a man and I could feel his throbbing biceps. The heat was too much for me and I collapsed. Then I felt his lips upon mine and became a little more aware of the world around me.

'Who are you . . .?' I asked.

'Dubberly, Dr Dubberly,' he replied gently, 'and unfortunately my dear, the mid-day sun has evidently been a little too much for you.' Again I fainted. Perhaps it was on account of my tight corset. When I regained consciousness, I found that my blouse and bustle had been removed and the good Doctor was fondling my breasts. At the same time, he was giving me mouth to mouth resuscitation. His tongue was prodding within my mouth and I was feeling so rampant. I fondled his throbbing member. His prick was so hard in my hand. He came so quickly as his juices squirted and spurted over my breasts.

Although I had not yet been fully satisfied, I acceded to his invitation to accompany him to the Brighton Pavilion, erected by the Prince Regent, that notorious royal rake. This oriental extravaganza amazed me but my feet began to ache.

'Come to my hotel,' he requested. 'I am staying at the Metropole.'

'Please, I must go back to my Great Aunt,' I replied.

'I am of means,' he replied slyly. How could I possibly resist?

We sat sipping champagne in his suite and talked of literature, science, the Universe and the world to come. He spoke of his education at the University of London and of his subsequent career in Harley Street, where he had specialised in gynaecology. I told him of my days at boarding school. I had known this man for only a few hours and yet it was so easy to speak with him. As he spoke, though, I was a rampant bitch in heat.

The moon was beautiful that evening and I suggested a walk by the Palace Pier and West Pier. My gorgeous doctor agreed. It was a quiet night and the stars were bright. The Pleiades shone especially. On the promenade, with no one in view, I ran my fingers down his trousers, extracted his stiff cock and sucked it.

'Please, my dear . . .'

'There is no one here to hear,' I responded. He was amazed that I was eagerly able to consume six inches of his lofty member. One of my secrets is deep breathing. He was willing enough to spurt his juices within my tender loins and yet what I enjoyed most was the feel of his pulsating rod in my mouth. I fondled his arse. The more I caressed his bottom, the more he throbbed. I thrust my finger into unknown regions. He was grinding his tool into my mouth and there was a pause – abruptly followed by the spurting of his semen and I swallowed it all. My desire was to consume every single drop from his pecker.

It was certainly time for a return to his hotel suite. There and on the bed, he turned me over and I could feel the last droplets of his juices upon my bottom. My lovely doctor was pleasing me beyond belief. He again fondled my breasts and then again his mouth was glued upon my cunt, my gorgeous cunny. This man was after my pussy indeed. He kept on biting my erect clit, my lovely flower. His kisses were delightful upon the inner thigh and outer thigh and then down to the acutely sensitive backs of my knees. He delicately withdrew my stockings and sucked upon my toes. It was obvious that he was becoming aroused once more. I took his throbbing penis in my cool hand. The stars blazed through the glass windows of the hotel suite. He thrust inside me. Oh! what a joy to become familiar with his throbbing, stiff member! There was one pulsation after another and then he gasped in an ultimate orgasm.

After a time I realised that I had to return to the home of Great Aunt Elizabeth and Dr David Dubberly was only too willing to escort me. We arrived to discover that she was fast asleep and so we went to my bedroom. I took off all my clothes at his request but then slipped on my lacy, frilly night-gown. It is of white cotton with embroidery around the collar, the waist and the cuffs. He stripped himself bare. For a while we were felicitous, blissful and in paradise. I was purring with pleasure when I fell asleep, knowing that my lover had an easy escape route out of my ground floor bedroom window. My ecstasy was beyond belief, beyond paradise, beyond seventh heaven, utterly charmed and enchanted.

My dream was also beautiful that night. I dreamed that you *were my knight in shining armour and that I was your queen. I was in my castle like an oppressed Guinevere who waits to be rescued. Who were you? Sir Galahad? Sir Percival? Sir Bors? One of the three knights who won through to the Holy Grail? King Arthur? Sir Gawaine the hot-tempered who was humbled by the Green Knight? My intimation was that only Sir Lancelot could save me yet in the dream I was aware that I had to be loyal to my husband, King Arthur. Suddenly Merlin the Magician appeared and I metamorphosed into Morgan La Fay, the mighty sorceress, the temptress and the witch, the mighty bitch.*

I write this to you now on a beautiful morning. It is such a pleasure to watch the waves crash upon the sea-shore.

Great Aunt Elizabeth has just brought me a delicious cup of hot chocolate, topped with whipped cream. I don't think that this gracious woman has any idea of what I have been doing and I do not intend to upset her.

I am interested to hear from you that you are considering joining a Magical Order in quest of Hidden Wisdom and one hopes that you will find it. Please keep me posted but I am inclined to believe that the lessons I taught you were right and that Hidden Wisdom lies between the legs.

All my Love,
Rosemary.

CHAPTER SIXTEEN

I cannot honestly state that I made particular progress in my spiritual development as an initiated Neophyte of the Hermetic Order of the Golden Dawn. One advantage, however, was that it enabled me to make a further acquaintanceship with one of its senior Adepts, the beautiful Florence Farr, who invited me to tea with her in the newly created suburb of Turnham Green, a building development made possible by the District Line Underground Railway.

As I travelled upon the railway, I had my doubts about the Golden Dawn. Its financial charges were hardly extortionate but if one pays merely tuppence for peanuts, one does at least want nourishing and tasty peanuts. The Golden Dawn had sent me 'Knowledge Lecture I'. To be candid, I was not actually that interested in applying for examination in the matter of correspondences between the Hebrew Alphabet and the Tarot Trumps nor in matters of the sigils of Astrology in order to pass to the Grade of Zelator. What possible good could this do me? I had complained to Arthur Machen, who had gone on from the Zelator grade to take that of Theoricus, but he had told me that he was equally disappointed and that the Order 'had shed no ray of light upon my Path.' I had complained to Aleister Crowley, who replied that he had initially agreed with me but that elders whom he respected told him that he was as yet in no position to judge. He had gone beyond Theoricus to Practicus and thence Philosophus, swarming up the grades via his immense occult knowledge, and was poised to join the mysterious 'Inner Order' as an 'Adept.'

'What bunk!' I exclaimed as I took good Darjeeling tea and delectable apple tart with Florence Farr.

'You're only saying that because you do not understand it,' she replied.

'What's to understand?' I queried. 'There is the male and there is the female. Between them, energy! energy! energy! That's it!'

'You choose to miss,' she answered gently after a delicate bite at her delicious tart, 'the complexity of meaning enshrined within the symbolism.'

'Not at all,' I replied. 'The central symbol is the rose upon the cross. The cross symbolises the prick and the rose symbolises the cunt and so the prick and the cunt are united nobly within this symbol of higher consciousness.'

'Oh, Horby,' she giggled as she sipped tea. 'You are so crude.' She leaned back in her arm-chair with a rustle of her loose-fitting, flower-patterned dress. 'You know,' she continued in her high, clear voice, 'this trivial matter of sexuality has become such a major issue within the Golden Dawn. And I don't see the need for it. "MacGregor" Mathers, the Chief, is celibate even though he is married. His wife Moina abhors the sexual act. Yet they have a very good relationship together. Allan Bennett is celibate, too. I've never met a man so uninterested in sex as he is and yet he has true integrity.'

'Yeats?' I queried.

'Crowley's right in calling him "Weary Willie",' she responded. 'Poor chap. He will never make it with Maud Gonne, who is his true love. Frankly, when I had him, he was just masturbating within my vagina and thinking of her.

A woman can always tell these things. No, he is simply insufficiently virile for Maud. She's looking for some brave and handsome brute, a man of action.'

'Arthur Machen?'

'A good man,' she answered. 'Unfortunately, I've never had the pleasure of his sexual company. He has his fantasies but he is faithful to his charming wife and I gather that she is very ill.'

'And Crowley?' I was fascinated by this free and frank female.

'Oh, him!' she burst out laughing. 'What a charming joker! I rather like him, personally. But he must be careful.' Suddenly she looked serious. 'It is a hydra-headed monster, this London opinion, and it would not surprise me if all these hydra-heads were to move in one direction, namely, Aleister Crowley. This would be a remarkable achievement on the part of a young poet who has only just come down from Cambridge, but it only requires a serious purpose to stir mediocrity into serious suppressive action. The question before me,' she sighed, 'is: has Mr Crowley a serious purpose?' She crossed her thighs tightly beneath her 'aesthetic' dress. 'I do hope so.'

'And what's your opinion of George Bernard Shaw?' I queried.

'Another joker,' Florence Farr replied with a light laugh. 'Although I'm very fond of him. Mind you, he'll never join the Golden Dawn because he cannot believe that truth exists anywhere other than inside his own brain. You may have heard the story that he was a virgin until the age of twenty-eight. Isn't it extraordinary?' She kicked up her heels in mirth and merriment. 'It took an older woman to initiate him. After that, he was rampant for a time. Always burbled out all sorts of things before he came. I liked him. My opinion is that he doesn't actually like sex very much.

For him, it is two and a half minutes of squelching. My prediction is that he will marry the first wealthy woman who will enable him to write his plays in peace and quiet and that after that, he will fuck her only whenever she wants it, which might not be very often.

'You are quite right, Horby,' she resumed her discourse, 'in thinking that the symbolism of the Hermetic Order of the Golden Dawn is essentially sexual. Your trouble is, however, that you're incapable of seeing anything else in it other than organ grinding, and butchers' meat upon a slab.'

'Are you going to tell me more?'

'If you wish.' Florence Farr drained her cup of tea, rang a bell and then a maid entered to bring scones, strawberry jam and Cornish clotted cream. 'You don't discern the holiest act in the Universe. You do not understand its inner nature!' she suddenly burst out furiously.

'Then tell me more.'

'Persistent little bugger, aren't you?' she laughed. 'Just allow me to explain that through a loving union between man and woman, we can come to know God and Goddess.'

'Okay,' I answered, utilising the latest and most modish American slang. 'Let's do that right now.' She yielded readily enough to my lips. Her tongue was smooth and velvety. 'Let us,' I murmured, 'joyously, as friends who have nothing to hide from one another, become further acquainted with each other's capabilities and whims, and enter into a companionship which cannot but be wholesome for us both. I trust that you are more inclined to view me as a friend rather than an enemy?'

She had averted her face toward the back of the couch but I noticed that her long, slim fingers were squeezing my dick through my trousers. They seemed to quiver as if half afraid and half eager to essay new knowledge. I moved closer to her on the couch, now, and took her in my arms.

To my great delight, she did not draw away, nor did she withdraw her hand from my soft cock, which by its new tremors under her delicate touch once again informed me that its amorous energies were anything but exhausted. My left arm moved under her armpit and around, so that my hand might taste and cup and squeeze the sweet, shuddering goblet of her bubble and I bent to kiss the nipple of that other sweet love-turret nearest me, whilst my right hand stroked the shivering, silk-sheathed contours of her thighs.

'What lovely breasts you have, dear Florence,' I murmured. 'One might well spend an entire night praising them and adoring them. And to each facet of your luscious form, another night might be entirely devoted. In the pleasurable knowledge that as a woman who can inspire passion and adoration, you are in the foremost rank . . .'

As I sucked upon her nipple, I heard her sigh and saw her flush more deeply. At last she turned her face towards me, her eyes shimmering with a lovely light through those sentimental tears. Her lips trembled as if to speak and then she glanced down at her slim hand which was still lying atop my dick and she gave a little gasp of: 'Ohhh, how wicked I have suddenly become and it's all your fault, sir!'

I laughed aloud in my joy at seeing her thus happily reconciled to the inevitable and I said: 'Sweet Florence, give me your lips again and let us seal our bargain.' She smiled then and nodded, and then my mouth was back on hers, gently at first, until I felt the soft, moist petals within quiver in acquiescence and, very delicately, I advanced the tip of my tongue to hers. She quivered again and moaned a little and her fingers squeezed very slightly now my invigorated cock. Correspondingly, my left hand tightened on the soft thrust of her bubble, my fingertips brushing the sweet, soft crinkly bud until I felt it harden. And now my right hand, which had been dallying so gently and lingeringly over first one stockinged thigh and then the cream satin skin of the other, now boldly marched along her bared flesh towards the furry nest between them. With my forefinger, I began to tickle the lips of Florence's soft, moist and shivering cunt.

As she felt that titillation, she groaned a little, and then flung her arms around me, locking me to her as she sank back on the sofa cushions; and the shifting of her beautiful body granted me access to her most secret charms. Now it was obvious why she was wearing loose-fitting 'rational' dress. My forefinger unhesitatingly moved back to find that lodestone of her being, the crux and kernel of all her womanhood. Very gently, I began to rub the dainty button of sweet love-flesh, whilst my tongue foraged more audaciously still inside her nectared mouth.

When I at last released her lips, she was panting and sighing, her thick lashes fluttering wildly, incontrovertible proof that she was withholding nothing from me now. Exaltation filled me, along with eager lust to know that this 'Senior Adept' of the Hermetic Order of the Golden Dawn had now succumbed to the warm ebullience of communal passion. She moaned again and shook her lovely hand, closing her eyes and lowering her head demurely.

'Since I have taken,' I said, 'so many liberties with your person, it is only fair that you should take equal freedom with mine. Explore with that sweet hand and learn the nature of this instrument which rises at your command and droops at your neglect. Concentrate its powers and grant it deliverance from ennui and frustrating frigidity. Touch it where and as you will and learn its portents for that happiness to which Nature destined you in giving you so delicious a body – yes, and so sweet and hot and tight a cunt in which to accept my willing weapon!'

She kept her face averted but nonetheless, this lovely brunette began hesitantly and shyly, like a new bride on her eve of awakening, to graze and tickle, to press and squeeze, to explore, to observe the dimensions of my now thoroughly erect phallus. Her touch was velvety and soft, subtly different from that of many other women, and so the more enjoyable on account of that piquant distinction.

'You must touch my balls too, Florence, darling,' I whispered to her, 'for these are the sacs which contain the balm and the balsam of intense pleasure, a panacea to the most reluctant, the driest, the most frigid cunt.'

'Is – is that what you call my s-s-spot?' she naively queried, probably deliberately, while her cheeks and throat and forehead flamed at her own sweetly scandalous obscenity. I observed the quivering curve of her red, moist lips as she uttered that naughty, image-provoking word and my pulses raced in salacious ecstasy.

'Yes, my darling Florence, that and "pussy" and "cunny" too. The more imaginative the lover, the more descriptive the names for that Temple of Venus, that grotto of all delight, that haven of exquisite repose and languishing fulfilment.' I spoke in a mellow and poetic tone, to bring her still further from that path of spiritual prurience which can be found in those of little imagination who still believe that the art of fucking should be under a cloud, in the dark and secretive and sinful.

Her fingertips grazed my balls, which throbbed and ached, telling me that they contained the wherewithal to offer tribute to my newly acquired mistress. All this while, my finger was touching her clitoris, though I had not been too active, so as not to bring her too quickly to climax. I wished that climax could be shared with me, to seal a bond between us. For once thoroughly appeased of all her secret ardours, she would not deem me guilty of insufficient homage to her charms.

Her sweet cunt was moistening and the love-juices which had been gathering for so long were now readily manifesting as Nature graciously showed the felicitous bounty which comes only with candour and honesty between a man and a woman. She no longer clutched her thighs so perilously tight and though her muscles shivered and flexed as I brushed the tender lodestone inside her temple, Florence in no way withheld herself. Once again I kissed her and this time my tongue was met by her with a little moaning sigh that welcomed me to take the amorous initiative, knowing that it would be aided and abetted by my beautiful partner. I left off touching her clitoris to rim the twitching inner lips of her cunt with the tip of my forefinger; and they were swollen and moist with the sweet cream of this prelude to bliss.

With a little cry, she flung both her arms around me and dragged me down upon her, my chest mashing down the heaving goblets of her breasts as her tongue rapiered its way into my own eager mouth. Our tongues thus commenced a friction that was a portent of that greater and more glorious friction soon to be effected between us. I fitted myself to her and my stiff, throbbing cockhead rubbed her inner thigh and then prodded at the gates of her domain, imploring entrance. With another soft cry of acquiescence, she squirmed a little, as if to make room for me, and with a shout of joy I felt the tip of my flesh-spear probe easily now into her moistened cunt, and as my hands slipped under her bottom to hold her tightly, I felt myself press forward into that glorious tight channel to the very hilt.

She groaned, her eyes closed, her nostrils flaring wildly,

as I slowly drew myself back to the gateway of this paradise of pussy, only to sink back slowly again till I was buried up to my balls. Her buttocks jerked against my grasp and their contractions told me there need be no more words between us, only sweet fucking.

'You sound like Frank Harris,' Bernard Shaw commented drily when I mentioned that she was one of the finest fucks of my life. 'Be careful.' He nibbled at the peanuts I had offered him at my flat and sipped at the mineral water I had proffered.

'Careful? Why?'

'Frank is fast acquiring a reputation for being sleazy and second rate,' said Shaw, who was about to fulfil Florence Farr's prediction in marrying a wealthy but physically unattractive woman who would finance his plays and advance his career. 'In fact,' Shaw declared, 'he is not second rate. He is not first rate. He is not even tenth rate. He is merely his unique, horrible self.'

'So am I,' I replied.

'If you think,' said Bernard Shaw, 'that you have succeeded in a masterpiece of seduction, you are very much mistaken. Florence Farr is simply such a decent, gracious woman that she cannot find it in her heart to say "No," to any reasonable man who asks her nicely.'

'Oh, if only you knew, Shaw . . .' I sighed.

'And if only Oscar Wilde was still among us,' he retorted crisply. 'I mean no offence but you remind me of the young poet who said to Oscar: "Mr Wilde, there seems to be a conspiracy of silence about my work. What do you advise me to do?" Oscar replied: "Join it".'

I could see that much as I liked Shaw and admired his work, there was absolutely no point in talking to him about sex because Florence Farr was right and he didn't particularly like it. He regarded it as being an irritating nuisance brought about by biological exigencies. How little did he know! Later in the evening and after this interesting man had gone, I sat down at my desk and took up my pen to write about my encounter to one person who might understand, Miss Rosemary Radcliffe.

CHAPTER SEVENTEEN

My letter to Rosemary obviously told her all my news along with the account of my encounter with Florence Farr, as described earlier. George Bernard Shaw clearly wasn't interested in the details but I felt that Rosemary might well be and so I continue with my account. I transcribe directly from the letter.

After our first joyous fuck, I withdrew my right hand and edged it between us as my forefinger once more sought after the button of Florence's clitoris as I drew back from that charming nook which had held my cock so snugly. Oh! Her cunt was so tight it was as though she were virgin to fucking; yet it was so warm and welcoming, too. The moment my finger touched her love-button again, she uttered aloud: 'O! You gorgeous man!' in such a tone of panting rapture and wondrous delight that I shuddered with overwhelming lust. It was as if she had come upon the gates of Paradise! Flattening that tumescent nodule with my fingertip, I now thrust myself slowly back down into her depths and even I was not prepared for the convulsive and frenzied clutching of her arms and of her legs. Her stockinged thighs coiled over me as might attacking serpents, pinioning me to her with such ardour that my pulses hammered wildly in sheer erotic joy. My lips met hers and now our tongues were freely coming and going and I felt her fingernails dig deep into my tensioned back while under my left palm, her naked, velvety bottom weaved and lunged and wriggled uncontrollably.

Back I drew again and again to the brink of her sweet cunt, whilst my forefinger prodded and pushed and flattered her stiffening clitoris. Her moans and sobs and whimpers were accentuated by my dive towards her lovely lower mouth. I drank with savouring relish the juices of her rapture. Withdrawing, I quickened my gait and my finger furled and pressed and rolled the stiffening little button. Florence could not control her responses as her climax neared. Her legs threshed around me with their feverish lock, her nails gouged my back, her vivid blue eyes opened and rolled and glazed over, whilst her tongue slashed and stabbed and daggered at me, as she now seemed to thrust up her pelvis to meet my every down-digging plunge. She began to gasp and groan and her breasts surged wildly against my dominating chest, flattening their sweet turrets with such a brash exuberance as to belie completely the formidable prudish countenance she had put on at the Golden Dawn meetings.

Then suddenly she twisted her face away, her eyes wild and staring. She arched up her loins just as I thrust to the very hilt, and just as my penis thrust and flattened the love-button back into its soft pink protective cowl of love-flesh. She uttered a piercing scream that vibrated in my ears like all the angels of heaven singing that heralding of a new dawn.

'Ohhh! . . . ahhh! Ohhh! . . . I am going to die . . . oh, darling, hurry, oh, darling – oh! oh!! oh!!!' And with this she cleaved unto me, our bellies grinding together as I poured forth my last libation of the late afternoon and felt it met by the intoxicating torrent of her climax-cream. It was the little death of which the philosophers write and her lovely face was contorted in the sweet rictus of passionate fulfilment, displaying a blazing sun beyond a golden dawn.

'*Well, my darling Rosemary, you who have taught me so much*,' I ended my letter, '*you taught me how to pleasure a truly wonderful woman and I thank you from my heart for it. Please keep in touch and tell me of everything that is happening at your end. Loads of love.*'

Having sealed the letter, and given it to a manservant to post, I sat back with a glass of vintage port and for a time enjoyed the sight, sound and feel of a roaring fire of well-aged logs. What to do now? It had certainly been a fabulous afternoon with Florence Farr. Bernard Shaw had been his usual dry self in the early evening and I was glad that he had gone, though he was always welcome. I resolved upon a walk beneath the flaming gas-lamps, which add so much charm to the West End of our great city, and as I had had no supper yet, eventually resolved to enter *Robertson & Son: Music & Dinner*. The place was crowded and cheerful. Today, yes, in these degenerate days of the 1920s, I really regret the passing of these institutions. They were so – well, it dates me, but I'll say it – *jolly*.

One entered into a riotous but good-humoured hall that rather reminded me of a lower-grade version of Trinity College, Cambridge. There was a stage in place of High Table but beyond that, long tables and one never knew with whom one might be sitting. That was part of the charm. It was hardly a place to go for an intimate dinner with a lady friend one did not know too well. However, it suited my mood and I knew exactly what to order. Robertson's Roast Beef of Old England, served between slices of freshly baked and thickly buttered cottage loaf could put the spunk back into any man. Whilst I was waiting for it, I ordered a dozen of their good oysters with lemon and brown bread accompanied by a pint of the best stout that could be found in the West End, served in a foaming pewter tankard. The men sitting next to me seemed to be a party of lawyers so I chose not to join in their dismally dull conversation. Instead I enjoyed the song on the stage of Mr Robertson Jnr. It seemed to reflect the company in my immediate vicinity.

'What a mouth, what a mouth,
What a north and south,
Blimey, what a mouth he's got!
Now when he was a kid he was always in some trouble
And his poor old mother used to feed him with a shovel . . .
What a yap!
Poor chap!
He's never been known to laugh . . .
Oi!
If he did it's a penny to a quid that his face would fall in half.'

My oysters were excellent and three shillings for the dozen was a reasonable price. My beef, dripping with blood, arrived just as our Chairman, Mr Robertson Senior, who was wearing evening dress and stroking his legendary, waxed handle-bar moustache, was bantering with the audience.

'My dear sir!' he cried at one unduly noisy reveller. 'I have seen you here before. Now, have you spilled your glass again? Or, regarding your trousers, have you just pissed yourself?' The audience shouted with laughter. 'Now, we have a splendid bill with which to entertain you,' he continued, having silenced a fool, 'and next it will be the Wicked Can-Can Girls.' There was a loud cheer. 'Yes! Freshly from their recent engagement in Paris. Gay Pareegi, no less. But we want no barrack-room manners here!'

'Excuse me,' a soft, gentle and lilting voice said from just behind me, 'but could I possibly squeeze in here?' I turned to recognise Arthur Machen and gladly moved along to make room for him. 'I do so enjoy this place,' he said quietly, then he ordered two dozen oysters and a mutton chop with fried potatoes and onions with a pint of best bitter and a neat gin on the side. We greeted one another warmly just as 'The Wicked Can-Can Girls' mounted the stage.'

'Stunners,' Machen muttered; and I agreed with him. They had exquisitely pretty faces and superlative figures. I sighed longingly as they kicked up their long legs to reveal their frilly petticoats and silken, lacy drawers beneath.

'Not exactly your idea of "holy", is it, Machen?' I remarked.

'You misunderstand me, Horby,' he replied. 'If you'll pardon the pun, it is "holy" in more senses than one. If you know how to look and how to see, oh yes, there is ecstasy present here.'

'He's never been there before,' sang the first girl.

'Never been there before?' the others queried.

'Oh, he's such a bore
You don't ask encore
Not one to adore
And what is he for?
Is he into the gore?
Does he want a whore?
Or does he just jaw?
Is he sent from the Law?
Does he offer me more?
Can't do it, nor
Furnish an oar
Perhaps he's so poor

Q for queer – Cor!
That's life in the raw
That's what I saw
A scarecrow of straw
Waving a paw
And there's no need for more
'Cos he'd never been there before . . .'

The lascivious gestures of the girls, who had mimed the song with perfect choreography, including every erotic gesture with which I was familiar and many with which I wasn't, brought the house down in a positive *furore* of applause. Instantly the flower-sellers entered among the audience. Actually, it was a perfectly decent system. Whoever sent the best bunch of flowers was received by the leading lady after the show was over. I sent three dozen roses to her and hoped that no one had out-bid me. Two bunches of carnations would usually be enough to attract the favourable attention of a girl in the chorus line, though a simple sunflower or small sprigs of freesia, if well chosen, would bring one a chance at the stage door.

There is precious little to be said about the fuck that followed in a suite at the Cadogan Hotel. The Americans have, I believe, an expression for the matter and it is: 'Slam! Bam! Thank you, Ma'am!' At least they are contributing something to the cause of civilisation. To be candid I do not remember the girl for she was one among so many others but I gave her a good supper and a hearty champagne breakfast. That was around the time that some started putting orange juice in their champagne and calling it 'Buck's Fizz.' Myself, I have never seen the point in doing that but never mind. When I reached home, there was another letter from dear Rosemary.

My love, my dearest darling,

I miss you so much. I deeply desired to spend the past weekend with you, having the time to while away the hours but I have my duties and obligations to my Aunt. I think that she is a lady of mature years and in her home she was entertaining a most curious individual.

Tea was served. It was a rather strange sort of tea and one has reason to believe that it was laced with absinthe on account on its peculiarly bitter flavour. Our visitor was obviously a Westernised Oriental Gentleman and one wonders whether it is right to ascribe the appellation of 'Wogs' to these charming, civilised and cultivated people. This fascinating man spoke of Yoga and I was most intrigued by his words.

'Yoga,' he declared to me, 'is the union of our separate wills to the Will of God.' I was invited to his classes in Yoga. He spoke eloquently of the many Gods and Goddesses who epitomise the multifarious aspects of Brahman, the Unity behind all manifestations. There is a Trinity of three forces coming from Brahman: Brahma, the Creator; Vishnu, the Preserver; and Shiva, the Destroyer. Each one of these sometimes takes a body upon Earth. He informed me about Krishna, a man into whom Vishnu had entered, enabling him to become the greatest man on the planet at that time. He became so inspired that he wrote a sacred scripture called The Bhagavad Gita.

This intriguing Indian, a Mr Sru Sabathi Swami, was a rather lean and lithe man. (In later years, Aleister Crowley would tell me of how much he learned from him out in Madras in 1905 – Author's Note.) *He informed me of the existence of 'the Kundalini', the divine energy of the cosmos portrayed as a coiled female serpent lying dormant at the base of the spine and waiting to be aroused so as to strike into the higher regions of the brain.*

I await for you to arouse my Kundalini through my yoni, my flower, my most luscious cunt, for I am like a coiled female serpent. From time to time, I miss you so very much, my darling. Sexuality is the most sacred ritual of union and so I long for your lingam. As Mr Sru Sabathi Swami informed me, Shiva is often depicted as a phallus and worshipped for it. How I love these words! – lingam and yoni – your cock and my cunt! I long to feel your pintle throbbing inside me, ensued by your pulsating ejaculation.

My aunt looks somewhat younger than her years and one could be pardoned for observing that her visitor was younger still. Eventually they made their excuses and retired to another room for the furtherance of their purposes, mentioned as being a deeper study of Yoga. For my own part, I chose to retire to my own bedroom and recline beneath the canopy of the four-poster bed. I enjoyed the sensation of feeling the lily-white cotton sheets that smell faintly of lavender and there was an eiderdown of pleasing comfort in the event of inclement weather. I adorned myself with the exquisite silken nightgown that you had given me for my thirtieth birthday and slid between the sheets.

I lay there quietly for a few minutes and then turned over on my stomach, raising my nightgown in order to rub my fur pie against the bottom sheet. With one hand, I caressed my breasts and my other reached down towards my pubic nether regions. My nipples now became aroused and my vagina began to pulsate. When my clitoris, my dear praline, became moist, I allowed two of my fingers to enquire within and I began to groan with the pleasure of it. What exquisite ecstasy there was as the juices flowed from my fingers breaking and entering this sacred part of me!

My sleep was deep with pleasant dreams.

In the morning I awakened to discover our maid Josephine serving me the morning hot chocolate with whipped cream. She is a gem although one gathers that she is in possession of a questionable past. As I imbibed my beverage, she stood attentively by the bed and murmured pleasantries.

'Would you like me to run your bathwater now?' she enquired politely. The bathroom was en suite *and she hummed as the water flowed. Lying in bed with my legs crossed lazily, I could hear the sounds of the opening of bottles and could smell their drifting scents. I felt so languid that when I entered the bathroom and stepped into the tub, I asked Josephine to join me.*

'I have breakfast to prepare for the household,' she replied.

'Do not temporarily burden yourself with these trivialities,' I answered. 'I imagine that my aunt is greatly enjoying the company of her teacher of Yoga and would prefer not to be disturbed. They will not wish to be disturbed by the nuisance of breakfast prior to noon.' After all, my aunt is something of a merry widow, though some of her clandestine affairs have perhaps not been as surreptitious as could be desired by the censorious.

Josephine removed her clothing and climbed into the bathtub to nestle beside me.

'Face me . . .' I sighed to this beautiful, slim-buttocked woman as we interlocked our limbs. The temperature of the maid's water was perfect as we embraced amidst the soft bubbles her attentions had aroused.

'Miss . . .' she faltered, 'I have never done this before.' I knew this and in consequence, deliberately kissed her cheek. She blushed profusely with embarrassment. 'How is your gallant beau?' I enquired as I caressed her.

'He is not that gallant,' she lamented. 'He has left me for another.' I consoled her with a gentle kiss upon her cupid's bow of a mouth and took her in my arms. I then gently commenced to massage her shoulders so that she might be occasioned to be more at ease. She has a strange birthmark on her shoulder at the left and it rather resembles a star, so I kissed it.

'Turn, turn, turn,' I requested and my bosoms were now pressing against her back as I fondled her lovely small breasts.

'Oh . . .' she murmured. My hands descended to her slender waist and then to her mons veneris *and I fondled the lips of her moist and pouting clitty. She commencing to coo as if she were a dove then burst into a uniquely strange song:*

> *'Kimo, Kim: Where? Uh, there! my high, low!*
> *Then in came Dolly singing:*
> *"Sometimes medley winkum lingam up-cat,"*
> *Sing-song, Dolly – won't you try me – oh!'*

The "oh!" was exclaimed at that exquisite moment when I stroked her throbbing little button.

'I have been taking singing lessons,' she told me. 'I would like to make a career as a music hall singer and then perhaps my fiancé will return to me.'

'Let us arise from the bath now,' I replied, wishing to assuage the sadness of her tone. The bath towels with which we rubbed one another intimately were so fresh and clean! The skins of both of us glowed a pleasant pink.

'Would you like me to make your bed?' she asked courteously.

'Not yet,' I replied, 'let us lie down first.' We lay down nude and I kissed her bottom and stroked her inner thighs,

coming in time to fondle her cunny. Just as she was breathing a deeply felt sigh of sheer content, there was a knock upon my door.

'Have you seen Josephine?' my aunt's voice demanded. Fortunately she is too civilised ever to enter my bedroom without expressed permission even in her own house.

'Josephine is lacing my corset and will be down to the kitchen soon enough,' I called back. There was no alternative save to don our garments and step downstairs. I entered the drawing room to discover my aunt and her yoga teacher imbibing some variety of herbal tea. There was a scent of bergomot in the air which appeared to come from a censer on the principal tea-table.

My aunt's face was flushed, her hair was dishevelled and she was endeavouring unsuccessfully to present an immaculate appearance. A close observer could discern the love-bites upon her neck. As I have always informed you, Horby, my aunt has a certain element of the strange about her. Her first husband, Major Gray, died under mysterious circumstances. Her subsequent style of life, amply supported by the profits from his able business dealings, was criticised by one member of the family as 'ribald'. She married again after a year to a Dr Kellogg and it was said that they were very much in love but he soon perished from a heart attack. Dear Oscar Wilde told me that my aunt's hair had turned 'quite gold from grief.' Her third marriage was to an exquisitely handsome young scion of Captain Industry but he died, alas, from a brain tumour.

I am exceedingly fond of my aunt even though some may find her life to verge upon the side of the unconventional. She does not seem to care whether a man is young or old, just as long as he is a man. Sometimes I have found these conjunctions to be rather outré. *Every once in a while, I have known her to be friendly with a dotard. What terrible old men some of them can be! The instant that she is out of the room, they turn their lascivious attentions upon this innocent and unsuspecting person. I have never forgotten Colonel Ransome, nor his waxed handlebar moustache, his monocle and his claim to be a baronet, though I could not confirm his claim upon consulting Burke's Guide. He imitated a knighted squire quite capably in always calling me 'my dear.' In the early afternoon, after a bottle of brandy, he used to fall asleep in his chair with a smouldering cheroot in his hand. 'Suck my cock, caress my dick and drink my semen,' he kept muttering to me. On another occasion, he wandered into my bedroom wearing a white night-shirt with vermilion socks and murmuring: 'Fuck me, fuck me, fuck me,' before retiring to his room.*

I rather prefer young rakes such as the lithe and serpentine Mr Sru Sabathi Swami. Possibly I may learn something from him.

I send you all my love.
Rosemary.

CHAPTER EIGHTEEN

On approaching the Winter of 1898, I was experiencing a slightly jaded palate and looking for experiences of greater pungency. In particular I sought for something which could marry the joys of sexuality to my quest for a holy grail of spiritual meaning. Although Crowley was swarming up the grades of the Hermetic Order of the Golden Dawn with his usual loud exultations of enthusiasm, I had no interest in memorising astrological tables, the secret attributions of the Tarot cards and suchlike, finding it all to be worthy enough in its way but rather dull stuff on the whole. I whiffed the air for the scent of stronger meat.

I had a very interesting session in The Cheshire Cheese, Fleet Street, with H.G. Wells, whose appetite for good ale was as ravenous as mine. So was his appetite for women. His insatiable greed for the cunts of women rivalled that of Frank Harris, Crowley or, for that matter, my own. His success with the fairer sex was all the more remarkable in view of the fact that, initially, he had had precious little going for him and among these disadvantages was the matter of his appearance.

Wells was a short, squat man with a short, thick and bristly moustache. His voice made no endeavour to disguise the evidently humble origins of the speaker. There was nothing of the sycophant about Wells: he challenged every man he met. Today he has, deservedly, achieved world fame but at the time I knew him, he was barely known, always short of money and appreciated only by the discerning few. As the Reverend Sydney Smith said of Whewell, 'his forte was science and his foible was omniscience.' This had led good old Frank Harris to give him his first proper opportunity to make his mark upon London by employing him as Science Correspondent of *The Saturday Review*, then the most exciting publication in London. This enabled Wells to make appropriate connections and he was thus enabled to have published quite a number of astonishing works of fiction. 'A marriage of fiction and science,' I called it at the time and that French chap, Jules Verne, was doing something very similar. 'Science Fiction' was the term one of my sons used to me only the other day although this does not seem to have arrived at any significant development if one is to judge by the shoddy and lurid rags which this son mistakes for books. I'm sure that Wells regrets this lamentable decline in standards from his interesting and controversial but nevertheless literary work.

The Time Machine: that is actually one of my favourite books. Wells later established himself as a serious novelist, in the tradition of Dickens, and has since proceeded to write great works of popular education but I shall always treasure the effect which his early works of heightened imagination had upon me. On matters of sex, however, he was notably down to earth.

'If you want to attract women,' he told me matter-of-factly, 'be rich, be 'andsome or be strange. And I don't mean peculiar.' He wagged an admonishing finger at me. 'Fuck them well, treat 'em right and don't let *them* treat you wrong.'

Wells always spoke sense and was excellent manly company but his words on women, although always to the point, usually swiftly proceeded into the terminology of

Biology and became a matter of organ grinding devoid of atmosphere. Although he was a splendid fellow that night, and on many other nights, I found more sexual wisdom in the letter which awaited me after my swift walk home. It was from dear young Claire.

I can see why women were attracted to Wells, even when he was labouring under every conceivable disadvantage. The sheer dynamism of this fellow was incredible. His wide-ranging intelligence was formidable: and he genuinely liked women. However, I was about to learn more from Claire than I would from Wells.

My dear darling,

I have been to Paris, a city that I love so intensely. I embarked upon a visit to my pen-friend, Charlotte, since for several years we have been in correspondence. She is a student at the Sorbonne and maintains an 'apartment' as they call it, close to the University. Her English is absolutely impeccable and I wish I could state the same of my French.

As everyone knows, the journey from London to Paris is fraught with delays and difficulties. However, the journey from Victoria to Dover showed that the Pullman company, with its delectable cream and coffee coaches and its impeccable waiter service was doing its utmost to minimise inconvenience to its passengers. The kippers served were quite superlative and as I crunched the accompanying toast, served hot with deep yellow Jersey butter and Seville orange marmalade, accompanied by strong Orange Pekoe tea from Ceylon, it was good to discern that at least some of the standards within our great Empire were being stoutly maintained.

On my arrival at Dover, I was courteously escorted to the boat by a Pullman porter. Naturally I had booked a cabin for the crossing. Having had my belongings gracefully deposited, I proceeded to enter the bar on the first class deck. My intention was simply to take a schooner of tawny port. As I sipped it, the player at the grand piano commenced the essaying of popular works by Tchaikovsky and Rachmaninov. This bar was indeed rife with life. I was pleased to be wearing a hat with a peacock feather as I did not want to give the appearance, sitting alone, of a fallen woman.

This first class saloon bar was ribald with life and warmth, conveyed through the playing of the music, which seemed to caress my body. Suddenly there was a very gentle touch upon my left shoulder.

'Excuse me,' I heard a polite voice enquire, 'is there somebody sitting here?'

'I am waiting for my companion,' I replied.

'I do not think that your companion is about to join you,' he replied softly. His small, dark, almond-shaped eyes, which gleamed unforgettably, made an immediate impression upon me. 'Can I purchase another drink for you?' he enquired. 'Another glass of good tawny port, perhaps?' I was immediately attracted to him, especially since he strode away to the bar with the nonchalance of the true gentleman. He had exquisite looks and upon his return to my table, he spoke of his works as a mountaineer and poet. This man, I believe, had the capability to mesmerise me. He appeared to know so much about my life. Initially I was somewhat reserved and demure in response to his attentions but my resistance was melted by his jocular and waggish manner. He bought me another glass of port, this time insisting that it should be 'vintage port rather than starboard'. I could not resist his amorous advances and invited him to come back to my cabin.

He was carrying a case which contained a bottle of

vintage cognac. It also contained a vellum-bound book of poetry from which he read to me. I gathered that he was the poet. He served me a brandy and then he insisted that we give libations to Bacchus. The boat rocked slowly and gently across the Channel. I was aware of the aroma of hashish in my cabin, drifting slowly and softly in delicately formed rings from his curved pipe of meerschaum. The fumes were making me dizzy and I feared an attack of the vapours. I lay down upon my bed.

Before I could do anything to prevent the issue, he was unlacing my corset and then I could feel his finger penetrating my cunt. How sleepy I was! But his lips persisted in pressing upon mine and in demanding entrance. How his tongue did prod! There was not a part of my anatomy that his tongue did not reach, for this man was incredible in his knowledge in the arts of making love to a woman. I am sure that he has had many a paramour. His hands were so beautiful and his finger-nails so well manicured.

His tongue was all around my rings. He French-kissed my arse and the penetration was so delectably amazing in its rhythm. I realised that it was about an hour before the boat would be arriving in France. He seemed blithely oblivious to this matter of logistics and gave me another cognac from a flask he had cunningly concealed about his person. I have never known a man to be so arrogant and with a cock as stiff as his, who can blame him?

His rod penetrated me, ramming my cunt, pounding like a wild beast. As his rod throbbed, his fingers were fondling my cherry; and with regard to his other hand, I could feel his forefinger enter within my bottom. My orgasms were of the ultimate. At the same time, he was so exquisitely gentle. Our time together, I knew, was going to be so short. There was the knowledge that he could fuck me twenty-four hours a day. I was rather hoping that the crossing of the English Channel would turn out to be rather longer than it was.

However, it was necessary, after our gorgeous fuck, that we had to dress again in order to disembark. I watched with fascination as he adorned himself. He even wore suspenders to hold up his socks. His member was still throbbing as he tied on the waist-laces of my petticoats and after the donning of my long, pleated skirt, there were some moments to languish.

When we set foot in France, I fear I still looked a little flushed, though one trusted that all observers would attribute this to the joys of fresh sea air. A pleasant fat porter took my luggage to the Wagon-Lit suite in the railway carriage which awaited me. He assisted me in mounting the steps of this delightful industrial creation, decorated externally in deep royal blue.

Now, the gentleman with whom I had passed such a pleasant sea journey was the enchanting Count Vladimir Svareff who, I noticed, spoke French with an atrocious English accent, although he did speak the language fluently. He is a Russian aristocrat who recently graduated from Trinity College, Cambridge, and who mentioned you with praise. He also praised a friend of his called Aleister Crowley and gave me a volume of his poetry.

What a rake! But a charming one! That is my verdict on Count Vladimir Svareff who informed me as my train departed that he had urgent matters of business in Boulogne. Unless it is the gorging of oysters, I cannot imagine what it might be. The book with which he had presented me and which I read on the train between Calais and Paris was entitled White Stains. *Its purported author was one George Archibald Bishop, 'a Neuropath of the Second Empire', yet Count Svareff had informed me that it was in fact the writing of his good friend, Aleister Crowley. I had never known that there could be such erotic writing. My eyes scanned the pages and I felt glad, as the train jolted and then glided away, that I had a private compartment. I crossed my legs and continued to read, increasingly aware of the fact that there was a mounting pulsation within me. The more I read, the tighter I crossed my thighs. Anyone who accidentally entered the compartment would have seen my face flushing once again. For a few minutes, my fingers fondled my cunt and my juices flowed as I thought of this beautiful and literate man.*

Eventually I arrived at the Gare du Nord to meet my friend Charlotte and her twin brother Jean-Pierre, who greeted me with the customary courtesies of our Continental neighbours. By this time my exertions had left me feeling faintly fatigued and so I was relieved when they took a cabriolet to their apartment in the Rue St Germain.

Charlotte is very attractive and so is her brother. Upon my arrival, I was served with good coffee and then shown to my room. I needed to rest for an hour or so after which I intended to see the Eiffel Tower, The Louvre and the Cathedral of Notre Dame. Unfortunately I must have slumbered somewhat longer than I had originally intended. I endeavoured to arouse myself yet found this to be a difficult matter since I was experiencing asphyxiation. I coughed repeatedly for there was a sweet smell in the room as I drowsily awakened to the sound of chanting.

Had I been unwittingly drugged? Jean-Pierre had entered the room quietly, accompanied by perhaps a dozen acolytes, all garbed in robes of black. They circled me and chanted.

'What time is it?' I asked.

'Time? There is no time,' Jean-Pierre responded.

Suddenly I realised that I was naked and shackled by

metal chains to the four posters of the bed. My chains shook and rattled as Jean-Pierre forced me to imbibe a fluid from a silver chalice, holding my head by the hair as I drank. It had the bitter taste of absinthe laced with other wines and strange drugs. I had smelled hashish before – and not just on the recent Channel crossing . . . and he was smoking it. I felt so vulnerable in my nudity especially since I could not struggle.

I slipped in and out of consciousness as they chanted, occasionally raising my head. I endeavoured to comprehend the words of their strange but enticing chanting. I was so aware of my drowsiness and my nudity, I felt as if I had been martingaled. It was blatantly apparent that Jean-Pierre had a rampant erection beneath his black silk robe. I only had to watch the full-length looking-glass before me to discern the sight of his throbbing penis.

Abruptly he pressured his member into my mouth with its full force. His acolytes kept dancing and singing, all the while chanting: 'SATANAS! SATANAS! SATANAS!'

Suck me,' he said, 'suck me and succeed.' There was precious little else that I could do, bound as I was. Behind him, nine tall black candles flamed giving off the stench of brimstone. 'Pardon the pun and also the punishment,' he hissed just like the snake he was. 'We call this one Nectar Delecta,' he said softly. I was feeling somewhat dizzy as he shoved his cock up my arse. He buggered my bottom as simultaneously his finger was tickling my cunt's own trigger.

I was feeling so awfully vulnerable. Why was I chained down and why were there so many strange people in the room? Everyone had been watching with such unalloyed delight as he shot his manhood within me, all the white chanting 'SATANAS!'

There is a sequel to this, my darling, and I know that

you will enjoy it, but I am tired now and so shall close this letter with all my dearest love to you and my promise to write again tomorrow.'

As I pondered the contents of her letter, I could not help but wonder whether her subtlety or the plain, straight sense of Wells was right. 'Only one way to treat intelligent women,' Wells had told me. 'Simply fuck their brains out.' This makes excellent sense: but I could not help feeling that Claire's next letter might make more.

CHAPTER NINETEEN

Before receiving Claire's next letter, I made the acquaintance of one of the most beautiful women in London. This was Florence Balcombe who had married Bram Stoker, author of *Dracula*. Stoker was on the fringe of the Hermetic Order of the Golden Dawn, which is how I came to know him. His wife had been courted by Oscar Wilde, but perhaps she sensed that he adored her physical charms without wanting to fuck her for she spurned his advances and married Stoker, who was then business manager for Sir Henry Irving. Irving was the greatest actor of my generation. He was, however, a most arrogant bastard. I have never forgotten the occasion when he hosted a dinner where he, as first knight of the theatre, was ensconced at the head of his oak table beneath a portrait of himself painted by Whistler. Whistler was present that night at table and many praised the portrait.

'It is indeed a fine portrayal of me,' said Irving, 'but I forget who painted it.'

Florence Balcombe had invited me to sherry at mid-day. The maid admitted me to a well-furnished drawing-room, furnished me with a glass of quite exquisite amontillado and informed me that Mrs Stoker would be joining me shortly. I looked around the room to notice that it was festooned with prints of a peculiar nature. One set depicted various manifestations of the vampire. There were Gothic castles gloomily illuminated by a waning moon on the turrets of which men with long fangs sank them into the delicate throats of tender young ladies. Other prints showed beautiful young bitches sinking their fangs into the throats of tender young men.

These scenes had been exquisitely engraved upon wood: but there was another series of sets which had been etched upon steel or else coloured by the process of lithograph. Each print showed a beautiful lady dressed at the height of fashion. Each print emphasised her bottom.

I am among that breed of men who find the female bottom to be among the most beautiful sights in the world. What sight can compare to those wiggling, gorgeous globes? What man can resist the matter? The various artists had cleverly deployed their skills to portray Miss Florence Balcombe and Mrs Bram Stoker swishing her skirts and switching her buttocks in a wide variety of formal situations. Every convention of propriety had been observed yet she still came over as being a devastatingly sexy bitch with a bottom as stunning as her face. The first thing one noticed was her exquisite *derrière*, tightly wrapped by her long skirt, and the artist had suggested that it was twitching lasciviously.

The artist needed no skills other than accurate draughtsmanship as became apparent when Mrs Florence Stoker herself entered the room, ushered in by the maid. She had clear blue eyes, a straight nose and a pouting cupid's bow of a red mouth. Her thrusting breasts threatened to split the silk of her fussy and frilly white blouse. A belt of glossy and shining black leather gleamed in the mid-day sunlight to display her slender waist. Her hips and legs were adorned by a long, black, figure-hugging skirt which fanned out to knife-edged pleats at her thighs and cascaded over the ankles of her high-heeled leather boots. Petticoats rustled and swished within her skirt as she walked. I was instantly conscious of her bottom. She had obviously demanded tight lacing. Her stiffly-backed corset had clearly been tailored to make her buttocks protrude. No doubt her silken drawers had been run up by a lady tailor, containing a leather strip to separate the cheeks of her bottom and make her yet more enticing. A slight tremor of her left buttock made her pleats quiver at the ankles.

There is, I think, a delicious and delectable contrast between the demure face of a lady and the switching globes of her womanly arse. Then one regards her luscious mouth and thinks of her lascivious cunt. She switched her skirts mischievously as I praised her husband's novel *Dracula*.

'I am delighted that you have enjoyed it,' she said. 'Bram researched it exceedingly well, I feel.' I could not help but notice that there were love-bites upon her delicate white throat, concealed only partially by her silken, high-cuffed white blouse. 'Ah . . .' she sighed, 'there are definitely vampires in the world.' She crossed her thighs beneath her petticoats and, judging from the fluttering of her pleats upon her skirt, it looked as though she was squeezing them together tightly. I was just wondering whether to make a pass at her when I heard a heavy masculine tread of boots and her husband entered the room. Bram Stoker was a big, red-bearded man with a deep bellowing voice. He wore an immaculate tweed three-piece suit.

'Hallo, my dear!' he bellowed heartily. 'Hallo, Horby! Good to see you again! What's this? Sherry? No, I'm not having a bloody sherry. Is that any sort of a drink for a man? Maisie!' he shouted and a slender maiden eagerly entered the room. 'Bring a decanter of malt whisky!'

'We were discussing the matter of vampires,' Florence said as the maid brought in the whisky decanter and glasses. I noticed that Stoker had love-bites around his throat and started to wonder about the nature of their relationship.

'Vampires, hmmm . . .' Stoker mused as he knocked back some whisky. 'Now that's a very interesting subject, isn't it?'

'Have you ever met a vampire, Mr Stoker?' I queried. He and his wife responded with gales and storms of mirth and merriment. Their laughter was so fierce that I feared they might injure themselves internally.

'Of course I've met vampires, Horby,' Stoker responded gruffly. 'And vampires suck your blood as all the while they leave you sexually fascinated. Isn't that true, my dear?' He looked at his wife.

'Absolutely, my darling.' Florence smiled broadly at him, exposing long, canine teeth. 'But Lord Horby,' she continued, 'surely you are not entirely ignorant of these matters?'

'No,' I said, 'not at all. Although I'm always eager to learn more. For example, one hears strange tales about Satanism in Paris.'

'Yes, one does,' said Stoker. He rang a bell upon the coffee table and a maid entered with a tray of nuts: Brazil nuts, peanuts, cashew nuts, almonds, hazelnuts and walnuts. I noticed that Maisie the maid also had mysterious markings around her throat. 'There's Satanism in Paris, all right,' he said. 'Fellows like Huysmans, Stanislaus de Guiata, Sar Peladan and Dr Gerard Encaussee. Well,' he swigged Scotch, 'can't say that all of them embrace Satanism but there's certainly something strange going on there at present. Can't say I'm particularly involved.' To judge from his eyes, he was even more interested in his wife's buttocks than I was at the instant that she stood up to excuse herself for a few moments. 'Vampirism is a taking of energy,' said Bram Stoker, 'but what happens if there is vampirism committed upon oneself and one feels a different form of energy coming back? Ha! Ponder on that, my friend and explain it if you can. You are very fond of explaining things,' he added as his wife swept back into the room with a swish of her skirts, a rustling of her petticoats and a switching of her magnificent bottom.

'There's only one thing to do with vampires,' Bram Stoker declared. 'Let them take your blood and then take theirs. As for Satanism, can't say I'm that interested. Sounds like a childish parody of Christianity to me. No, no, I have my own pleasures, I assure you, sir!' He looked at his wife and she looked at him. I felt somewhat *de trop*, and made my excuses to leave. Stoker rang a bell to summon Maisie the maid to usher me out. The last sight I recall, on looking back, was of Mr and Mrs Bram Stoker embracing, with their teeth firmly embedded in one another's throats.

I walked home through the streets of London resolved to pass the afternoon amidst the joys of masturbation. Florence Stoker had aroused my carnal passions and it was a pity that I had been unable to enjoy her physical charms. I have always preferred to shove my cock into a woman's cunt rather than into my own hand but there are sometimes advantages in having a wank.

Upon my arrival home, I ordered my butler to bring me a bottle of my finest malt whisky, my favourite tumbler, a packet of Turkish cigarettes, my opium and hashish pipes and the necessary quantities of delectable substances. I instructed him to place these on a tray in the Library and then to bring another tray upon which would repose matches, an ash-tray and a plate of prawns accompanied by slithers of smoked salmon. His second knock disturbed my search for appropriate erotica, for I desired a book whose imaginative qualities would give me an appropriate orgasm. However, there was a letter reposing upon the second tray and it was from Claire.

My dearest darling,

I cannot begin to tell you all of the rhapsody and the thrill of my initiation into Satanism that has taken place in Paris.

I agree with Jean-Pierre. I agree with Charlotte. Satan is not 'the Evil One'. He is everything about God which the Church dislikes. Even so, I was frightened when I undertook my first initiation.

Picture me spread-eagled naked upon an altar. My erect nipples are shouting to the heavens and the cherry within my cunt is aroused and pulsating. I felt as though I was yet a virgin, nevertheless. I was aware of a circle drawn upon the floor of this medieval and disused church, tucked away in one of the seedier suburbs of Paris. Within this black circle, two signs had been inscribed in silver: the five-pointed Pentagram, which is the Star of Man; and the six-pointed Hexagram, which is the Star of Woman. The chanting of the name 'SATANAS' continued. All around the Church were tall, black candelabra. Whenever one extinguished itself, it was replaced by another lit with a taper.

A beautiful, dark-haired whore proceeded to pee in a stolen communion chalice. Jean-Pierre added wine to the mixture and we all supped from it.

'Drink this in remembrance of me,' all the congregation intoned. Next, Charlotte broke bread at the altar and proceeded to rub it between the thighs of all the women present.

'Eat this in remembrance of me!' she laughed raucously and we all did. In fact, the taste was delicious.

The name of 'SATANAS' was chanted repeatedly and they all began to whirl widdershins about the altar, dancing back-to-back and holding hands. At the climax of the dance and as the candles burned their brightest,

Jean-Pierre threw himself upon my prone, bound and helpless body. My pussy was now so wet that I did not want to wait any longer. I gladly kissed his lovely smooth knob. My legs were forcibly parted indeed but I could not wait for Jean-Pierre to place his thick pole in my cunny.

But instead of having his broad boner nestling inside my honeypot, I felt his staff in my pussy hair and I opened my eyes to see it twitch wildly and then ejaculate his gooey white jism all over my satin-smooth tummy. Poor Jean-Pierre let out a strangled cry of frustration for he had spent so quickly that he had not had time to fuck me first. So much for Satanism!

'Let us try again,' Jean-Pierre murmured but his cock had shrivelled somewhat and looked very sorry for itself. Jean-Pierre rubbed his dangling dick furiously to try and make it harden up again but to no avail. Then I tried to coax his wayward prick by lowering my titties onto his recalcitrant tool and this had discernible results. I let my lips beckon so that I could suck his cock and his shaft swelled up to its precious thickness. As he withdrew, I gestured to encourage him, ever eager to comport myself passionately upon the couch of love, and so I kissed him on the mouth. He undid my bonds to free my right hand as a test of compliance. I responded by fondling his stiff prick, boldly and yet sweetly stroking the head and fondling the balls. When I teased him by drawing my hand away he drew it back to his cock for I feel that he was truly appreciating my caresses. I could not help the fact that my blushes deepened and this sight appeared to have a most noticeable effect upon his growing hardness.

Now he thrust his hard, firm rod within me – how I writhed and squirmed and loved it! My juices flowed out of my cunt, trickled between the cheeks of my bottom and dripped upon the altar. I looked up as he was fucking me to discern a writhing, squirming Charlotte, twisting her hips ecstatically over a dildo. Behind her, there was a statue of a Goat-God with erect phallus.

Jean-Pierre plunged deep within me, causing me to faint briefly with a slight spasm of the hips. Arousing, I screamed out my pleasure as his dick slammed in and out of me and laughed with joy as his thumbs tickled my nipples. His hands were cupping my bottom, his right forefinger deep within my anus. I sighed deeply when his prick spurted its sperm.

Afterwards I was untied, led solemnly to the altar and requested to kneel before Jean-Pierre and Charlotte. I pledged myself to SATANAS as the embodiment of freedom of mind, body and spirit and swore that I would always oppose tyranny and superstition. I was then proclaimed to have attained the First Degree of the Lesser Orient Degree of the Grand Lodge of Satanism. One wonders what the Greater Orient Degree might be like, for I am informed that they have Lodges all over the World.

Although, darling, strictly between you and me, I'm rather inclined to think that Satanism is simply fucking with frills.'

CHAPTER TWENTY

One chap whom I shall never forget was Sir Richard Bellingham, the third baronet of that name. On account of the facts that he walked with a slightly hunch-backed stoop and was physically clumsy, he was indeed known by a number of unkind souls as Richard the Third.

Poor fellow! I shall never forget accompanying him to a country weekend, courtesy of the Duke of Devonshire. Richard Bellingham acquitted himself well at luncheon where he charmed the ladies, he shot well later in the day, he proved to be a delightful companion at dinner and he subsequently delighted the ladies again with his skills at dancing. When he retired to bed, it was with the plaudits of the entire household.

Unfortunately, Sir Richard had taken more than his customary glass of port. As he lay humming softly upon his four-poster bed, it suddenly struck him that an urgent call of nature had instantly to be answered. He had neglected to ask the servants the precise whereabouts of the lavatory and he did not wish to disturb anyone else in a misguided hunt for it. To his delight, he noticed that an old custom had been observed. A chamber-pot had been placed beneath his bed. Sir Richard duly employed it and thence fell asleep.

He awoke in the morning to a warm, sunny day and an utterly foul smell. Realising that he was responsible for the latter, he wondered how to rid himself of this embarrassment. On opening his bedroom door, he discerned a hallway of identical doors, a corridor which appeared to be thronged with busy maids. Deciding that he could not possibly walk past them bearing a pot full of turds, he closed the door and pondered his situation.

He could, he supposed, hand his pot peremptorily to a maid but Sir Richard's inner gentility forbade him to do that. Another alternative was to leave the pot beneath the bed. If so, Sir Richard would leave behind him a room stinking to high heaven.

Sir Richard sought after a better way of accomplishing matters and noticed the window. There was a piece of waste ground outside there, then a wall and, after that, a conservatory. The happy guests, of whom I was one, were enjoying a hearty breakfast in that very conservatory. Sir Richard decided to heave the contents of his chamber-pot onto the waste-ground, where they would be concealed by weeds. He heaved hard. Too hard, for the pot flew out of his hands, sailed over the wall and crashed through the roof of the conservatory to startle and alarm the guests at their kippers. They gazed aghast at the upended potful of turds that had been served to them so abruptly, then stared upwards to see a hideously ashamed young man at an upstairs window.

'Young man, I want a word with you!' old Devonshire shouted as Bellingham ran from the house. I'm told that he bribed a carter to take him to the nearest railway station, meanwhile hiding in a bundle of hay. Then it is said that he sailed to Tierra del Fuego where he served briefly as a diplomat and one can hardly blame him. Sir Richard III was ever afterward known as Richard the Turd.

Nevertheless, he was exceedingly kind in his introduction of George Nathaniel Curzon to me. These days, of course,

Curzon has been elevated to the peerage and has held Heaven knows how many offices of State. Only the other day, I chanced upon a rhyme about him:

> 'My name is George Nathaniel Curzon;
> I am a most superior person . . .'

There is some justice in this satirist's rhyme, as I felt when I lunched with Curzon and Bellingham at White's.

'As I have always maintained,' Curzon drawled, 'no gentleman wears a brown suit or eats soup at luncheon.' Since I myself was wearing a brown suit and had ordered brown Windsor soup, I was somewhat put out by his comment.

'Quite right, Curzon,' I returned, 'the *gentry* don't. But the *aristocracy* do.' He must have been very happy to receive his recent peerage. Fortunately his manners improved as the afternoon progressed. Good old Bellingham kept ordering more port and the quality of port at White's is sufficient to make one desirous of membership. My great-uncle, aged 89, is still known there as 'young Rowley', but it was a perfect setting for Curzon to unbend a little. He was perhaps the most stiff and frigid man that I have ever met and yet I doubt if he could have unburdened himself in anything other than stiff and frigid surroundings.

In his usual clumsy manner, Bellingham blundered into the subject of sex. Curzon pursed his lips.

'It's the first, damn it, Curzon,' he insisted, 'I always say it's the first. Oh, don't be such a drone and drear! Why can't we talk about these things? Didn't the first woman who initiated you into the joyous mysteries of sex have a lasting impact upon you?'

'It depends what you mean . . .' Curzon's voice was slightly strangled.

'In my case, that's true insofar as two women are concerned,' I said, thinking of Rosemary and Claire.

The long and the short of the matter is that the three of us retired to a smoking room with some bottles of vintage port and a box of cheroots. Whilst I will always take a West Indian cigar with cognac, preferably a cigar from Cuba or Jamaica, it has to be an East Indian cheroot to accompany my port. We drew lots from a match-box as to who would start the game. I came first and proceeded to tell them some of the tales related here. Curzon grew visibly more comfortable as I spoke.

'That was extremely interesting, Horby,' he said, gingerly fingering the match which had made of him the second lot. 'I wish I had enjoyed your good fortune. My governess was a termagant and a violent disciplinarian.'

'Tell us more,' Bellingham came in eagerly.

'Mrs Joan Smythe was a very beautiful woman,' Curzon sighed wistfully. 'Picture a mature lady in her early forties. Her blonde hair is piled immaculately upon her head and impeccably waved. She has piercing blue eyes, an upturned nose and a smiling pink mouth that turns downward at the corners. The thrust of her breasts threatens to burst the fussy and frilly white silken blouses that she wears. Her voluptuous bottom threatens to split the tight black bell-skirts she favours.

'She wanted to discipline me and to make me her slave and would stop at nothing to achieve her objective. At the age of fourteen, I was subjected to the indignities of petticoat government. For unkempt appearance, day-dreaming, tardiness, poor attitude, uncouth behaviour, furtiveness and/or bad table manners, I was sentenced to stand in the corner with my hands behind my back and my trousers down and around my ankles to expose my naked buttocks. Greed, slovenliness, secretiveness, sulkiness, inattention and any repetition of a previous offence was visited with a sound bare-bottom spanking across Madam's knee. The crimes of evasion, loutishness, disrespect, laziness and dirtiness meant that I had to bend over and present my bottom for punishment. Here Mrs Joan Smythe wielded either a leather tawse or a springy, wooden tapettee and she used to laugh as her well-timed strokes caused my buttocks to twitch and jump.

'Any repeat of the previous offences, plus any incident of swearing, lying, insolence and disobedience brought about a formal caning, leaving my bottom well and truly striped and wealed. But as Mrs Smythe used to say, the cane merely punishes the equatorial zone whereas the birch punishes the entire bottom.

'She used to birch me if there was any inclination on my part to fall back into previous offences. The birch would also automatically be invoked in cases of lying, stealing, rudeness, blasphemy, absconding, mutiny or self-abuse. She was particularly strict on the matter of self-abuse.

'Her spankings, whippings, canings and birchings made my bottom burn with punitive fire. It throbbed and glowed, quiveringly submissive to the majesty of her domination. More humiliating still was . . .' Curzon swallowed, 'the petticoating. Oh,' he arched his eyebrows, 'you have never heard of that, sirs? And I had fancied that the pair of you had been well brought up! Well, now, sirs, how would you yourselves feel, I ask, if your governess were to deprive you of your trousers? Eh? "Trousers down fast!" Mrs Smythe used to snap at me. I would be stripped and denuded. A giggling maid would lace me into a tight corset. I would have to step into the white, frilled, silken drawers she proffered with a smirk.

' "You're knickered now!" Mrs Smythe would hiss fiercely.

'I would be buttoned into a blouse and then Mrs Smythe would say, in a cooing, charming way:

' "Now step into your petticoat," and as I felt its folds clinging around me, she would tauntingly add: "Never forget that you are under petticoat rule." I then had to step into a long, flowing skirt. The feel of the soft, feminine materials made my penis rampant but the skirt, petticoat and knickers kept me subjugated to dominant female authority.

'Sometimes she used to keep me in petticoats for an entire weekend, especially if I had committed the offence of insubordination. To add to my humiliation, Mrs Joan Smythe was a great believer in the virtues of punishing before female witnesses and I have been soundly thrashed before laughing females on more than one occasion.

'However, there is one occasion that I shall never forget.

'I admit that I had been cheeky to Madam but she decided that I had repeated my offence of insolence. She reached for her golden bell and let it tinkle softly. Instantly her maid Millicent appeared.

' "This young male has insulted Womanhood," Mrs Smythe declared. "I want him petticoated and prepared for the birch." How Millicent giggled as she zipped up my skirt and secured the final clip! I had to walk into the drawing-room with my skirts swishing around my legs and curtsey to Mrs Smythe, humbly imploring her pardon for my terrible misbehaviour. I then had to lie over her crafted flogging-block. Millicent drew up my skirt and petticoats, then drew down my knickers. Ahead of me, there was a full-length mirror. Millicent had settled onto a sofa and was sipping tea, the better to enjoy the sight. Mrs Smythe had proudly thrust out her buttocks and was swishing her birch in the air.

'She gave me six strokes. By the end, my bottom was just

jumping in pain as Millicent squealed with pleasure. I had to kiss the rod and thank my governess for the punishment then go and stand in the corner, my hands behind my back to hold up my skirt and petticoats; my drawers reposed, in undignified fashion, around my ankles. My blazing bottom was on display, punished for all the world to see. Two beautiful society ladies of my acquaintanceship came to tea and the ladies twittered about trivialities as I stood shame-facedly in the corner.

'Suddenly Mrs Smythe sharply instructed me to pull up my knickers and let down my petticoats and skirt. I had to turn and curtsey to the lady visitors, a matter made all the more awkward by the rampaging erection they aroused in me.

' "Now face the wall again!" snapped Mrs Smythe. "Hands behind your back!"

'The ladies chattered as this subjugated boy stood there in penance, his loins swathed and entrapped by ladies' soft garments. When they finally left to continue their chatter, Mrs Smythe approached me. Her long, pink finger-nail scratched my neck. Then her cool right hand snaked through my skirts to finger my furiously throbbing member.

'She tickled it and teased it as I had to stand rigidly with my face pressed against the wall,' said Curzon. 'My buttocks were blazing from her birching. Her flicking and flickering fingers made me writhe and squirm in an involuntary fashion and in a spasm I spurted my seed into the knickers I wore as a punishment, which she herself had worn and moistened only the previous day.

'I will never forget that woman . . .' he sighed languidly, 'swishy though her birchings were.' He looked mildly regretful as though he rather missed them. 'Whatever I may say against her, she was so imperiously beautiful.'

CHAPTER TWENTY-ONE

Now it was young Sir Richard Bellingham's turn to tell us of his own first meaningful sexual experience as the three of us passed the port. Curzon's tale had certainly been a good one and I could not resist a quiet smile over the mental image of this 'most superior person' standing humbly in the corner, petticoated and with his bottom birched in front of delicate damsels. The tale of Bellingham, I guessed, would be of a different nature.

'Gentleman, as you are no doubt aware,' Sir Richard began, 'I have throughout my short life hitherto suffered from a series of comical misfortunes. I do not know why. My ill-luck with a pot of turds is of course generally known in certain circles. I have to say that I envy you gentlemen. You, sir,' he looked at me, 'enjoyed the most delightful introductions to the female sex. You, sir,' he looked at Curzon, 'may have suffered pain but it is clear to me that you also experienced pleasure from your first introduction to these matters. My own was not as fortunate. No governess ever initiated *me* into the mysteries of sex. I am sorry to state that I was a virgin until the age of twenty. At the time I was an undergraduate of Trinity College, Cambridge, which is how I came to meet Horby here. In any event, I lured a most attractive young lady of the town to come and take tea with me, in my rooms. I thought that wearing my gown might impress her, and I spared no expense over the occasion. The College servants duly prepared cucumber sandwiches and pastries, reposing on the finest silver that Trinity possessed. In my eagerness to bed the young woman, I had removed my underpants and was wearing very tight, drain-pipe trousers with one of those new-fangled zip-fastenings. I felt that my slim figure was thus displayed to best effect.

'The initial stages of the afternoon could not have gone better. Madeleine arrived and appeared to be enchanted by my reception. I rang a bell and the College servants I had paid entered instantly, bearing silver pots of India and China tea.

'I could see that the young lady of the town was impressed by my hospitality. As soon as the servants had withdrawn and this most attractive, strapping girl had finished her tea, I ventured to make a pass at her. She yielded easily enough to my advances and as the gay cavalier I was purporting to be, I lifted her up within my arms and carried her to my bed.

' "Oh . . ." she moaned as she lay there before me, her tawdry town finery swishing in rich profusion around her legs. I concealed my inner excitement and gave her a very firm look as my prick throbbed lustily within my trousers.

' "My dear . . ." I stated sternly, just as I had fancied a worldly Don Juan might do; and I followed this with my wicked but genial grin. "I shall now lead you to the gates of Paradise!" With that, I ripped down my zip to expose my throbbing member to her. Unfortunately and owing to the lack of underpants, my zip caught my scrotum in its toils and my next word was simply: "Ow!"

' "Darling . . ." her lids were closed dreamily, "will you soon be coming to me?" She cooed so sexily. How do you explain that the reason that you can't is because your balls are trapped in your fucking zip and it hurts like hell?

'I had to sit down on the bed and slowly and steadily disentangle my scrotum from my zip, during which time she fell asleep. When I finally freed myself and aroused her, I myself was no longer aroused for the pain had caused me to lose my erection. She looked extremely disappointed, swished down her skirt and petticoats, rose to thank me most charmingly for "a very pleasant afternoon tea" and left. The last sound I can remember hearing from her was that of high-pitched giggles. I gather that she subsequently informed other girls of the town that I was merely a sherry trifle without the sherry.'

'*Tsk, tsk.*' That was Curzon.

'When *did* you lose your virginity, Bellingham?' I enquired.

'Oh, brothel in Bateman Street. Not much to be said about it. A fuck is a fuck, after all. Ever go there, Horby?'

'Many a time and most enjoyably,' I replied. 'Often with Crowley. Did you know him at all?'

'No, can't say I did, particularly.' Bellingham's face puckered with disapproval. 'Very eccentric sort of fellow. Not a friend of yours, is he, Horby?'

'A friend, certainly,' I replied, 'though I don't know him that well.' It was time to take another cheroot. 'Bellingham, are you seriously telling me that your life hitherto has not vouchsafed you the smallest memorable sexual satisfaction?'

'Yes, there certainly has been one,' Bellingham returned, 'but it was of so strange a nature that I have never told this to anyone before. You will probably think that I'm mad if I tell it to you. But since we're all being frank, perhaps the moment is appropriate. After Cambridge, I entered into Government service as our friend Curzon here is well aware.' Curzon nodded lazily. 'This involved undertaking missions in the cause of British Empire interests, many of which were fraught with danger. Now, on one occasion, when I was working to uncover a foreign spy network based in London, I found myself to be the object of several murderous assaults.'

Bellingham was a big, beefy, red-faced lad, only too eager to serve Queen and Country, though his manner of doing so was somewhat eccentric.

'I fought off these assaults successfully though sometimes more by accident than by design. Indeed, while I knocked one of my assailants clear into the Regent's Canal, on another occasion I was saved only by the fact that the revolver placed in my face failed to fire. I took the blackguard's gun away, gave the fellow a good, hard pistol-whipping and handed him over to the police. On another occasion, some fellow went for me with a knife. In common with all these Johnny Foreigner types, he was too clever by half. His intention was a quick, neat slit to the body but, you see, you can't beat good, old English cloth, what? I could feel his knife sawing slowly through my Harris Tweed jacket and I had his wrist by the time it reached my Guernsey sweater, oh, and the leather vest beneath it. Poor chap. I think he's no longer with us. But the whole operation, I admit, did make me feel a trifle nervous at the time.

'Now,' young Sir Richard Bellingham continued, 'I had a rascally acquaintance of the name of, let's say, Bill Smith. He was quite a character. "Always tell the truth but lead a life so improbable that no one will believe you" – that was one of his frequent and favourite sayings.' Sir Richard chuckled. 'How true. How very, very true. To my knowledge,' he resumed, blowing a perfect smoke-ring from his cheroot, 'most of his money came from illicit erotic literature, some rather seedy Soho gambling dives and a few opium dens in the East End of London, which is not to deny that he was, nevertheless, superbly genial company. Oh, how Bill loved to laugh! On one occasion, he tried a bet with me. The terms were that within three months, I had to walk a route between the Underground stations of Kilburn and St John's Wood that did not pass a single pub. I explored this matter meticulously in my leisure hours.

' "Well, you won that bet, Bill," ' I said when I paid up. ' "One cannot go from Kilburn Underground Station to St John's Wood Underground station on foot without passing a pub."

' "You don't *pass* the pubs, you fool!" he roared with laughter. "You go *into* them!"

'I was a little disturbed when I did not see Bill for some weeks. On making a few enquiries at various public houses he was known to frequent, I discovered merely that he was "away", which is the slang of his class to denote that the villain is in prison. However, the Metropolitan Police co-operated fully with my enquiries and according to their intelligence, he was not, in fact, "away." It was around this curious time of my life that certain peculiar aspects of it increased in intensity.

'Unknown to me, during that period there was a war going on between various low-life gangs of thugs for control of the streets and a number of regrettable places of dubious business. I had been seen imbibing beer with Bill Smith in many of these locations and no one was aware of my own position. Not did it help that I was ignorant of many expressions of slang. I would walk into a Kilburn High Road public house with a cheerful smile upon my face, blithely oblivious to the tension between three rival gangs, the members of which would be murdering one another later that evening. The local people would greet me in friendly fashion, making earnest enquiries after my health. "Oh, jolly good!" I'd say, "oh yes, in a good mood. Just bought myself one of those new typewriter things." Then I would be surprised at the suddenness at which the place became silent. I simply didn't know that to them it meant a Colt repeating revolver.

'One night I went out for an evening stroll along the Kilburn High Road and was possessed by the horrible sensation that I was being followed. When I crossed the road, so did two burly, hairy thugs behind me. I noticed that as I increased my pace, so did they. Fortunately I knew, or thought I knew, the area quite well. I marched proudly along the old Roman road of Watling Street, recalling that the area had grown up in the Middle Ages because it was one day's travel by horse and cart from the London Docks to the inn and the blacksmith, were one transporting goods to the North of England. Just as my strolling pursuers and I were approaching Maida Vale, I sprinted down an alleyway and whirled through a series of left and right turnings, all the while conscious of a hard pounding of footsteps in the distance. I nipped into what I had anticipated to be a short cut – but it turned out to be a dead end.

'There I was in a small square of Queen Anne houses. In the distance I could hear the heavy tread of boots. I looked around to discern that a blue door, with a number "56" wrought upon it in gold, was ajar. I stepped within and closed it, only to be confronted by the sight of a strikingly beautiful young woman with bright blue eyes and masses of flaming hair, wearing a tightly belted black ball-gown of silk. There was both fire and light in her blazing gaze.

'I apologised profusely for disturbing her and endeavoured to explain my predicament. She listened sympathetically and invited me to partake of some refreshment, being obviously a cultured and wealthy woman. As she served me with a glass of vintage Krug, I noticed the diamond, sapphire, emerald and ruby rings, set in platinum, which graced her left hand and sparkled in the candle-light. The room in which we sat was simply but charmingly furnished. There was a table of oak and two stout chairs of the same wood. It puzzled me to notice that two places had been set and I wondered who else she may have been expecting. Along the walls, there were delicately framed prints by Doré, Moreau, Whistler and Beardsley.

The strange lady, who asked me to call her by the curious name of Nuit Babalon, served me Persian gold caviar with thin, dry toast, chopped egg and chopped onion, accompanied by ice-cold Russian vodka. To follow, there was goose liver paté, studded with Italian truffles. Moist white, lightly grilled toast accompanied that, along with a bottle of chilled *Gewürtztraminer*. We then tackled a cold lobster each, with a dozen oysters as a side-dish. There was mayonnaise and tartare sauce with exquisite capers, also brown buttered bread and a bottle of chilled Pouilly Fumé to refresh our palates for the next course. This consisted of Steak Tartare accompanied by a small portion of buttered spinach and with it a bottle of vintage Château La Tour. It was hard to find room for the subsequent board that groaned with a delectable selection of ripe cheeses, raspberry tart with cream, a bottle of vintage Château d'Yquem, crystallised grapes, Blue Mountain coffee and Hine cognac.

'I find it very hard to recall the precise nature of the conversation vouchsafed to me by this extraordinary woman. All I can state for certain is that she had wit, she had intelligence, she had beauty – and that we went to bed together that night. Never have I known such sensual ecstasy. Moreover, every erotic thought that passed through my mind and my nervous system somehow seemed to be transmitted to her. Every spoken obscenity evoked another orgasm.

'She had the sweetest and yet the most wicked, wet, welcoming cunt of any woman that I have ever fucked. The juices of her cunny poured down the soft satin bottom cupped by my hands. I sucked her erect nipples, I licked her cunt, I kissed her gorgeous arse and communed with its rose-bud and the seed of my long, rock-solid shaft spurted within her orifices time and time again. She sighed softly when I came within her cunt. When I came within her mouth, she swallowed my semen greedily. She squealed with delight when I penetrated her bottom and came within her nether passage. She shouted obscenities with joy as I fucked her cunt again. No woman has ever satisfied me so completely.

'When I awoke in the morning, she had gone, leaving me a note which stated that it had been a delightful night but pressing matters required her attendance. It also invited me to sup with her at eight o'clock this coming evening. I wrote that I would and departed.

'There was no menace at all on the Kilburn High Road as I walked along it that evening to see a woman with whom I had fallen in love. But I was to receive another kind of shock altogether. Her house was in darkness and outside it, there was a sign stating: "TO LET".

'The following morning saw me call upon the estate agent in question. I purported to be a potential tenant and he showed me around the house. It was empty. Everything had gone. The agent assured me that the house had not been occupied for three months. The freeholder, he informed me, was an elderly gentleman of private means who led a quiet and reclusive life. Considerations of health had led him to move to another property he possessed in the South of France but he was interested in either selling a lease-hold or else letting a tenancy, though the agent had never actually met him.

'I returned to the house about a month later to find that builders were wrecking the place. They had no idea why they were doing that, informing me that they were simply obeying the agent's instructions. I returned to the estate agent and made enquiries after previous tenants but he had no information at all about any ladies and when I insisted that I had enjoyed a splendid dinner in the house as the guest of a beautiful woman, he looked at me as though I was mad.

'Meanwhile I was learning from the newspapers and from local gossip that a number of people vaguely acquainted with me in the district had been killed. Their bodies were customarily found in the Thames with bricks in their coats. As I endeavoured to make sense of this, I received an unsigned letter in feminine, spidery handwriting. The writer was sorry but it could not be helped. There was no hope for the future but the memory would never fade.

'No, it never would and I still nurse an aching grief. I was bursting to tell at least *someone* of my bizarre experience but I feared that no one would believe me. Eventually, I encountered Bill Smith on the Kilburn High Road. He was wearing a high silk hat, probably from Lincoln Bennett, and wore morning dress that could well have been tailored by Pope & Bradley. His highly polished boots were probably hand-made by Wildsmith and his golden fob had to be either Garrard's or Carrington's. He informed me that he was extremely pleased over the way in which his business was expanding. Hailing a hansom, he took me to luncheon at the Savoy, which seems to be letting in all sorts of flash coves these days. Over our port, I told him the story and he burst out laughing.

' "No," he said, "I don't think you're mad at all. The people who attacked you – or me – the people who the papers say ended up brick-drowned in the river, them's the ones who're mad. Now, your story, squire. I can't make any more sense out of it than you can. I don't know the explanation and I don't pretend to know it. It's a funny old world, guv'nor, and don't believe nobody who tells you different. For all you know, I might've met this lady too. But would you believe me if I told you the story you've just told me? I doubt it. But I've survived by a bloody miracle, me old chum, and that's why I accept your story. What do I always say? Always tell the truth but lead a life so improbable that no one will believe you".'

CHAPTER TWENTY-TWO

I had certainly been intrigued by the tales of Curzon and Bellingham but I was even more fascinated to find a letter from Claire on my return home. Doctor Johnson has declared: 'Sir: it is the ultimate ambition of every man to be happy at home' and I shall not argue. It was a pleasure to pull up a chair before a roaring fire with a decanter of Madeira at my elbow so as better to peruse the ensuing missive:

My dear darling,

I continue to stay in Paris, a city that I love so intensely. My experience of Satanism has been interesting enough but to be truthful, I find this mere inversion of Christianity to be limited and somewhat puerile. It was therefore a joy to meet gentlemen called Sar Peladan and Dr Gerard Encaussee, who writes under the name of Papus, in a Montmartre cafe. They informed me that they were involved with something called the Salon de Rose-Croix *and took me to an exhibition of Art. I was astonished by the exquisite beauty of paintings there, especially those by Moreau and Redon. When they informed me that they were Rosicrucians, members of a society dedicated to realising the inner light within oneself, a society which had endured for hundreds of years but which had its roots thousands of years before that, I eagerly asked if I could participate in their hallowed ceremonies.*

That is how I found myself once again (sigh) to be spread-eagled naked before robed and chanting men and women as tall candles blazed, only this time there was no bondage. The Temple, adorned by strange and exquisite works of painting and sculpture, was full of smoke and the aroma of incense. A man in a hooded black robe was censing the room from a chalice he bore upon a chain. Above me hung a sparkling crystal chandelier upon which the flames of the candles glittered garishly. All the robes of the participants were in jet black and I longed to see the faces of the 'brothers' and the 'sisters' as they circled the Temple anti-clockwise.

A gong was struck three times and its sound resonated within my ears. Suddenly there was absolute silence as they all removed their robes. Then a beautiful goblet of engraved silver was being passed around the room and everyone drank of that chalice. I noticed four men and four women, all of whom were physically beautiful, and the energies between whom created a sexual polarity, as the chalice passed from woman to man and from man to woman.

When the cup returned to the thickly bearded Sar Peladan, he raised my head and tipped the vessel to my eager lips. It contained, insofar as I could judge, heated wine with ginger and nutmeg, which I believe to be an aphrodisiac. A hookah, one of those oriental smoking pipes filled with cooling water, was freely available to all present and was now proffered to my lips. It contained tobacco mixed with hashish, of which I am very fond. I lay back and sighed with pleasure.

Again the gong resounded and someone began to play a glockenspiel as the murmuring chant became louder while everyone leaped around the circle in a mania of frenzied joy. Occasionally I was aware that someone was fondling my breasts, kissing my navel and touching my cunt as the music and chanting reached a crescendo.

'Ah, Sar Peladan . . .' I murmured as I felt his hot breath upon my cheek as he ripped my thin silk kerchief from my neck.

'Do not call me that name,' he rasped in response. 'I am Bacchus. This is a ceremony in honour of Bacchus and this is how we celebrate the Bacchanalian rites. You, my beautiful one, will now be called Diana of the Ephesians in honour of that many-breasted Goddess.' I saw that he was wearing an interesting pendant upon his muscular chest. It was a five-pointed inverted star and in the centre was a strange image that was neither beast nor human. What came to mind was the idea of a goat crossed with a man sitting in a crossed-legged position.

He removed that pendant and began once again to circle me in an anti-clockwise fashion. Every once in a while he would halt his dance and place this ornament between my breasts, uttering words that were incomprehensible to me. I was only too well aware that whatever else, I was in a state of delirium. My cunt was crying out to be appeased. Something deep within me desired to be honoured, venerated, worshipped and adored. I sucked the stiff cock of Bacchus, the God of rampant fertility and divine drunkenness. What a ribald one! I knew that he wanted to penetrate me.

The light touch of his lips upon my clit made me squeal aloud with the joy of it and then his ramrod of a penis penetrated my vagina. My nipples were utterly erect as he touched them. Yes, I felt like a rampant bitch as I was fucked; Diana, the many-breasted goddess of the Ephesians.

'Much wine had passed with grave discourse
Of who fucks whom and who does worse,'

he whispered. I do not know whether it was the poetry of the Earl of Rochester or his stiff erection which caused me to enter upon a series of writhing spasms.

I had just reached this enlivening point of Claire's letter when there was a ring on the doorbell. Why is it that these calls always occur at the wrong time? I had my penis in my hand and would have come within five minutes but the card that my butler brought up was from Sir Richard Bellingham. With an irritable sigh, I put down Claire's letter and requested Alfred to admit him to the first floor drawing room and to bring the best vintage port.

Sir Richard was rather drunk and flushed, as usual.

'Just had a bloody good fuck!' he announced. 'Nothing like a bloody good fuck after plenty of fucking good bloody port and nothing like plenty of fucking good bloody port after a bloody good fuck! Fucked yet this evening, Horby?'

'Not yet.'

'All the more fool you,' said Bellingham. 'Oh, just did it up against the wall like dogs, y'know. Up against the wall like dogs. Sixty seconds,' he continued remorselessly, 'and oh! – I tell you, how I came. All that shivering and dissolving, oh! – eh, Horby?' He chortled in his joy. 'And all this for just five shillings. Why, that's only fivepence a thrust! Good value that, old chap, to say the least. Anyway, just popped by. Thoroughly enjoyed our session today. Hope you don't mind my unannounced intrusion. Hmmm, good port. You know, old Curzon's really rather a good sort though I thought, mind you, that his tale was a little bizarre. Not to my own taste at all, that sort of thing, but I did once go for something bizarre myself with somewhat unsatisfactory consequences. Would you allow me to relate my mournful tale?'

'By all means,' I replied, though I would, in all truth, have preferred to continue reading Claire's letter.

'I was tired,' said Bellingham, 'of having sex in the same old way all the time. Thought I'd branch out a bit. Y'know, be a little more adventurous. So I went down to the Haymarket and picked up the sort of tart who enjoys her own suite of rooms, informing her that I would like to experiment with something bizarre. On arrival, she asked me if I were previously experienced in modes of the bizarre and I replied that I wasn't. You have to bear in mind my naivety at the time. Why, it was only shortly after I came down from University.

' "Very well," she replied sweetly, "we shall start with a little *soixante-neuf* – sixty-nine. And you, *mon cheri*, place your head here." I followed the guidance of her hands. She placed my head beneath her thighs. And then she farted horribly. It was terrible. She murmured an apology then once more pressed my head down beneath her thighs. At this point, she farted again. This was perfectly insufferable and I leapt to my feet and drew on my coat.

' "Where are you going?" she asked.

' "To hell with 'something bizarre' and your bloody '69'," I roared. "I'm not staying there for another 67 of those!" '

'Could only happen to you, Bellingham,' I murmured.

'S'pose so,' he responded ruefully, then helped himself to another glass of port, which he drank as though it were beer. 'Cunts, you see, that's what I'm after. But what I ask you is what do these cunts really want?'

'Satisfaction,' I replied, suddenly possessed of an idea. 'I was reading a letter on this subject by a very fine woman friend of mine just as you called and naturally discretion forbids me to mention her name. Interested?' He nodded eagerly so I requested the butler to put more coals on the fire, fetched the letter myself, for it would not do for it to fall into the wrong hands, and read the continuation of Claire's letter into his eager ears, having explained its Parisian and ceremonial contest.

I opened my legs wider, he withdrew his rampant rod, and then with a tickling of its tip, he once more parted my pink-lipped slit. Then I drew him to me, taking hold of his throbbing cock and inserting his knob within my eager and waiting cunny. His tight little backside quivered with anticipation of the joys to come.

"Go on, don't stop now, I want you to fuck the arse off me!" I demanded and my earthy instruction had the desired effect and with his hands on my lily-white buttocks, Bacchus drove himself deep within the glistening wet crack of Diana. How I enjoyed the swiving! This was hardly the first voyage into manhood of Bacchus, who had a natural understanding of how to perform. To my delighted surprise, he did not pump his prick in and out of my juicy cunt in peremptory frenzy but thrust home at regular slow intervals, enabling us both to enjoy our coupling to the full. I was enjoying myself immensely in my role as Diana and shrieked out: 'Yes! Yes! Yes! Make me come now, you gorgeous god! Ram home your thick shaft, Bacchus!'

I let out a fierce war-whoop as my bottom rolled violently on the satin cover which graced the altar. My fingernails clawed instinctively along the back of Bacchus as he grasped my shoulders and started to ride me like a cowboy on a bucking bronco in a Wild West circus. My legs slid down as I arched myself upwards, working my clinging cunt back and forth against the sides of his rock-hard stiffness. I leaned forward to obtain a closer view of his proud tool pounding in and out of my cunt and as he became ready to spend, touched his balls as we rocked and rolled to and fro. Bacchus was sent over the top, his torso went rigid and his cock spurted spasm after spasm of frothy white seed inside my welcoming channel of love. I too now began to shake and expressed my satisfaction with a long drawn-out cry as we writhed furiously in a tangle of arms and legs.

After our frenzy had subsided, we rested for a time upon the altar as the chanting of Om mane padme hum continued – later I would be told that this means: 'Hail to the Supreme, the jewel within the lotus.' By this is meant the male and the female united in the divine act of sexual sacraments. I let my hand slick up and down his glistening, semi-erect prick which was still wet from a coating of my cuntal juices. I rubbed the rubicund crown of his cock until his shaft had risen back up to its previous, erect, stiff state. The congregation switched to a different and more rhythmic chant.

'Pan! Pan! Pan!' These words echoed on the stone surroundings and resonated in the air. I took his cock between my lips, teasing his knob against the roof of my mouth with my tongue. A strangled gurgle of delight came from his throat as I stroked the tip of my tongue along the underside of his shaft to make it twitch. He thrust his slippery rod deep inside my mouth and I helped him by gobbling up as much of his tool as my orifice would sustain until his wiry pubic hair brushed against my nose. In no time at all, his lusty member pulsed within my mouth and he gave a hoarse yell as he jetted spurts of creamy spunk down my throat and I swallowed all of his copious emission, pulling him hard inside my mouth as he delivered the contents of his big, hairy balls in a sensual tribute *to me. I continued to swirl my tongue around his knob until I had fully milked him of his libation and his member began to shrink back to its normal size. It was delicious. His seed had a wonderful tasty tang to it.*

'Pan! Pan! Pan!' the congregation yelled in the course of a mad, swirling dance accompanied by the rapid, whirring, thumping beat of the tom-tom. With a low moan, he plunged his head into my pubic bush and I pressed my thighs together as he paid lip service to my love box. Then I partially released him, enabling him to part my swollen cunny lips with his fingers whilst his tongue left a warm, wet trail along the insides of my soft thighs. Then he started to lap at my crack and soon enough my yelp signalled that Bacchus had found the clitty of Diana, which he playfully nibbled between his teeth, and I writhed and squealed, my hips rotating wildly as he brought me swiftly to an exciting little climax. He lifted his head and I lay back and gasped.

'Oooh . . .' I sighed, 'I just love a God-Man who knows how to lick out a pussy. Now fuck me, please, sir, if you would be so kind.'

His straining shaft shot up in salute once more and my cool hand grasped his rigid stiffstander.

'My, that's a fearsome weapon and no mistake,' I murmured with some relish as I slid my hand up and down his thick and throbbing pole. He rubbed the tip of his knob against my rolled cunny lips and I purred with pleasure as he whispered: 'Just lift your lovely backside up a trifle, my dear.' Obediently I raised my luscious arse two inches or so, which allowed him to slide his hands underneath and clutch my soft rounded bum cheeks and I wriggled up so that his knob could now slip between my pouting pussy lips and the subtle lubrication of my tight channel of love allowed him to push forward with

complete ease. He carefully inserted about three inches of his cock into my cunt and for a moment we both lay still as we gathered strength.

'Pan! Pan! Pan!' came the chanting with the hypnotic beat of the tom-tom. Immediately we locked into a lewd rhythm of long, sweeping strokes as his sinewy shaft squelched its way in and out of my juicy little cavern. I squealed as he pistoned his prick backwards and forwards, keeping hold of my quivering buttocks as his body slewed one way and then the other. The dancing men and women were eagerly excited by the sight of the grand fuck of Bacchus and Diana, openly rubbing their genitalia as they danced and chanted.

'Pan! Pan! Pan!' I panted as I pushed vigorously to meet his every thrust and my cunny creamed time and time again as the soft, moist walls squeezed his delighted love truncheon, nipping it tightly with my muscles as we abandoned ourselves to a moment of being utterly consumed in a veritable frenzy of lust. I raised my head so that I could again see his cock, glistening with my love juices, emerge from every long, plunging stroke and when he prodded his rod back into me, we whimpered with sheer ecstasy at the sibilant sound of his cock sliding into my tingling pussy.

'Go on then!' I shouted joyously. 'Fill my hole with your sperm!'

'Pan! Pan! Io Pan!' *they all cried in unison as I jerked my hips wildly. With an enraptured shriek of release, he jetted a fountain deep inside my soaking womb. I spent simultaneously with him, milking his cock of every last drop of spunk and he rolled off me quite shattered by these voluptuous exertions.*

The tom-tom was now silent. Solemn organ music played as a handsome man and a beautiful woman came forward. Each one bore an antique spoon. The man's was of gold and the woman's of silver. Behind them, a young girl held a silver chalice, studded with diamonds, emeralds, rubies and star sapphires. With exquisite delicacy, they scooped our love juices from my cunny and placed them reverently within the chalice. A man added brandy to it. a woman added herbs and a man added spices. A woman stirred the mixture and a man was the first to sup from this chalice.

In ancient myth, one is never told about the components of the Greek nectar and ambrosia *or the Indian* soma. *One is told only that these are the foods of the gods and goddesses. I can only state that this liquor was the most extravagantly delectable beverage that I have ever tasted, as smooth as velvet, warming, soothing, nourishing, and yet it had sharpness and bite. Immediately after, I fell into a trance wherein all seemed to be bliss, a permanent and ecstatic union between the male and the female, the goddess and the god, in which all things fornicate all the time.*

There were reverent prayers to the Horned God and the Sky Goddess, then the Temple was closed and so ended a truly beautiful occasion. I will write you more about this and would, only my right hand is exhausted from writing and my left from masturbation. All my love . . .

'Well, Bellingham,' I exclaimed, 'what did you think of that, eh?' But Sir Richard was dead to the world and snoring peaceably in the armchair opposite. He had unbuttoned his flies and his right hand still grasped his now flaccid penis. As I asked the butler to put him to bed, I reflected that some men have absolutely no religious sensibility.

CHAPTER TWENTY-THREE

'Is there such a thing as Magick, gentlemen?' I asked one evening over supper at a private room at Kettners in Soho. (Alas, I gather that these convenient private rooms are no longer available at this otherwise excellent establishment).

'Depends 'ow you mean,' said Bob Fitzimmons, Heavyweight Champion of the World.

'Harumph!' John Sholto Douglas, Marquis of Queensberry, coughed. 'Yes, you'll have to make yourself a little bit clearer than that, Horby!' he barked.

I was enjoying our dinner of Dublin Bay Prawns followed by rare roast sirloin of beef with thin potatoes fried in the French manner and individual portions of buttered spinach. The bottles of Pol Roger and Nuits St Georges had gone down well, too. Many friends of mine have been at a loss to explain my friendship with the Marquis of Queensberry, especially in view of my friendship with Oscar Wilde. It was Oscar who called Queensberry 'The most infamous brute in London'. Queensberry was an infamous brute indeed and he did ruin Oscar, was an abominable husband to his wife, an appalling father to his sons, and treated his various women atrociously. He was mad and he was bad and therefore I found him interesting for, on occasion, he could be most enlivening company.

One interest we had in common was the grand old British sport of Boxing. How Queensberry and I used to reminisce over a few pewter pink tankards of port about the great days of the prize-ring in dear old Regency England! Queensberry had rescued the prize-ring from oblivion by the Rules named after him and which enshrine a code of hard but fair sporting combat between men. I admired him for doing so but unfortunately the Championship of the World had for a time been rudely seized by the United States of America. Bob Fitzsimmons was the man who had brought the Heavyweight crown back to our fair shores.

Although his manner was pleasant enough, the man was a physical freak. He had slight, spindly legs and the torso of the World's best blacksmith, which indeed had at one time been his trade. His ruby red hair was a mass of messy tufts which straggled away from his freckled forehead. He had eaten six rare and bloody thick slices of beef with great relish and the three bottles of wine that he had drunk only served to reinforce his geniality.

'This Magick lark,' he said, reminding me.

'I'm talking about a ceremony that is completely out of the ordinary involving sacred rites of passage between Man and Woman,' I replied.

'Oh, yeah, I get it,' he responded, 'you mean like all the rites surrounding the Heavyweight Championship of the World, right? Tell you the truth, I couldn't've won that without my wife. That 'Gentleman' Jim Corbett, who's no gentleman, incidentally, was stabbing my face silly with that left hand of his. Just couldn't get my jab past his. Then suddenly, after I'd been knocked down and was bleeding all over the place, Rosie, bless 'er 'eart, shouts out: "It 'im in the slats, Bob!" All of a sudden, I knew just where I was going wrong. I was going for Corbett's head, trying to slam that conceited, insulting prat in one shot that'd break his jaw when I should've been digging to the body. Then I remembered another one of my wife's sayings: "Kill the body and the head will die." Well,' Bob Fitzsimmons shrugged his shoulders modestly, 'the rest is history, ennit? I hit Corbett right under the heart with what they called my "solar plexus punch" and the papers are still talking about it like I invented something new. Corbett turned lime green that afternoon when he went down and I won the Heavyweight Championship of the World. Now, I'd already won the Middleweight Championship of the World and I'd done that before I met her. Believe me, though, I don't reckon I'd be World Heavyweight Champion without my wife's words of . . . what was it you called it? – oh, yeah, it was Magick.'

'Full credit to her, but it doesn't seem to stop you from fooling around with all these other floozies, eh, Fitz?' The Marquis winked at him roguishly. 'Must say all this "Magick" stuff's a little lost on me. Good of your wife to help you out of a jam like that but after all, that's what wives are for.'

'Just a moment and with all respect . . .' Fitz held up a cautionary hand that looked fit to break bricks. 'Please don't misunderstand me. I do screw around and so do many men, at least those who can. But at the end of the day, for me the one and only is my wife.'

'Would you say that there is something holy about certain women?' I asked.

'Oh, yeah.' The Heavyweight Champion of the World nodded nonchalantly. 'Some.' He looked reflective. 'Some. The rest are just cows and sows and bitches.'

'Ho! ho! ho!' roared Queensberry. 'Ha! Did I hear you say "holy", Horby? Well, I say that *all* women are holy, without exception. And why? Why, they all have holes in 'em!' He exploded into guffaws of laughter at the humour of his own joke as the waiter arrived to prepare our crêpes suzettes. 'Ho! ho! ho!' Queensberry bellowed, his short, squat body shaking as his thick, stubby fingers brushed his bristly moustache and mutton-chop whiskers, 'every man worth his salt knows that all women are just walking cunts!' He beamed with self-approval as the waiter poured cognac and curaçao upon the sizzling pancakes. 'And that's why I succeed with women the way you don't, Horby! You're full of all this romantic piss 'n' wind. Me, I just fuck 'em. Why, I betcha I can lay any woman in London faster than you can, Horby!'

'You're on,' I said as more brandy was poured and abruptly ignited to burn in blue with a hard gem-like flame. 'All we need to decide now is which woman, by what rules and for what stakes.'

'Jane Scrimshawe!' barked the Marquis as the flaming thin pancakes were served.

'No good,' I replied, 'I've already had her.'

'Oh . . .' The Marquis looked thoughtful.

'Allow me to make a suggestion, gentlemen, since I'm a betting man myself,' Bob Fitzsimmons interposed. 'Choose a woman and a time limit. If neither of you makes her within that time, then all bets are off. Whichever one of you seduces her first must afterwards explain to the lady the nature of the bet however things go in the relationship afterwards. Knowing the nature of the bet, she must promise the winner to acknowledge it to his rival. Now, there's quite a lot of sporting ladies out there, and knowing what I do about their natures, they'd be amused rather than aggrieved. Let's face it, the ladies are always flattered when there's two stags contending for them.'

'Jolly good!' Queensberry pronounced in his rasping, stentorian tones. 'I say I have ten thousand pounds which declares that I can seduce any woman Horby cares to name within three months and ahead of him.' He waved for brandy. His bet was somewhat larger than I had expected but naturally I took it. 'Name your woman, sir!'

'Lillie Langtry,' I replied. Bob Fitzsimmons gasped at my sheer audacity but Queensberry remained impassive. I had only named the most devastatingly beautiful woman in Great Britain, who was celebrated all over the United States of America as well. I had also named a mistress of the Prince of Wales.

'Bet taken,' Queensberry said firmly, 'and our fine friend Fitz here is our witness to our wager.' We all shook hands. 'Going to take a side bet, are you, Fitz?' Queensberry chuckled. 'Why, if you bet on Horby here, I'll even give you odds of 2-1.'

'Done at ten grand,' said Bob Fitzsimmons. 'Horby.'

'Ho! ho! ho!' Queensberry rocked with laughter so vigorously that I feared he might rupture himself. 'Bet taken of course, my dear fellow! But please explain the nonsensical line of reasoning that led you to undertake this foolish bet?'

'Simple,' Fitz responded. 'You're richer but he's rich enough and he's slimmer than you. Besides which, you're a fair man so you'll pay up.'

'You'll see, Fitz,' the Marquis bared his teeth with the joy of forthcoming battle, 'you'll see. And you'll see when you pay me.'

'Lillie Langtry?' Fitz tossed back a gulp of brandy. 'I don't reckon that any of the three of us is risking anything.'

'Want to put five thousand on All Bets Orf?' Queensberry taunted him.

'No,' said Fitz. 'I never hedge my bets.'

'Then put five on your next defence of your Championship,' the scarlet-faced Marquis demanded, clearly inwardly incensed by Fitz's backing of me. 'Your judgement is obviously out, don'cha know? Your next challenger, Jim Jeffries, outweighs you by two stones and twelve pounds.'

'Ten grand, chief,' said Bob Fitzsimmons. 'The bigger they come, the harder they fall.'

I promptly backed him with ten thousand pounds.

'What's life without a wager!' Queensberry guffawed.

Suddenly the Marquis was in a jovial mood again. He tossed gold sovereigns upon the table to pay the substantial bill of fare with a joyous aplomb.

'If a waiter's good, tip him well, I always say,' he declared, 'and if he's no good, why, throw the bloody fool out of the nearest window and tell the manager to stick him on your bill!' We rose. 'And now gentlemen, let's tackle the finest brothel in London! Everyone up to it?'

As we left Kettners and strolled towards Piccadilly amidst the flaming gas lamps, I was thinking of my bet. It was ten thousand pounds to seduce Lillie Langtry, whom I had never even met – and the World Heavyweight Champion had backed me with ten thousand pounds too. My heart sank like a stone as we reached Piccadilly and Queensberry was suddenly hailed with shouts of joy from a gleaming black Victoria in which reposed elegant young bucks and dandies and which was presided over by Lillie Langtry, looking more radiant, luscious and beautiful than in any drawing or photograph.

'John!' she cried out at Queensberry. 'What a delight to see you! We're just off to Bertie's. Hop in!' I gritted my teeth. Bertie was, of course, the Prince of Wales and I was only distantly acquainted with him. Furthermore, there was only one seat left in the carriage.

'I shall be delighted to join you, my dear Lillie.' Queensberry elevated his high silk hat, then turned to Fitz and myself with a wolfish grin and said: 'I trust that you can excuse me, gentlemen? Ho! ho! ho!' He cackled raucously. 'A most enjoyable evening!'

As Queensberry mounted the carriage steps, Fitz and I

looked at one another, thinking of the money that we might be losing.

'I reckon you're losing on points so far, Lord Horby,' Fitz commented as the carriage of laughing idlers drew away, 'but he's not exactly going to make Lillie Langtry while she's with the Prince, is he? I reckon you're just going to have to knock 'er out fast. Hit *'er* in the slats.'

'That's right,' I muttered, wondering just how I was going to accomplish that. There wasn't much I could do except take Fitz to London's finest brothel where Queensberry and I were equally well-known. Unfortunately, my mind wasn't really on the job and I gave the girl I chose little more than two and a half minutes of squelching. I kept wondering how to win my bet.

Bob Fitzsimmons, however, did not seem to be troubled at all as he enjoyed one girl after another at my expense. After his eleventh fuck, I could see why the great Champion John L. Sullivan had called him 'a fighting machine on stilts.' The man was a fucking machine on stilts too. I fucked another girl half-heartedly while he had two more. By the time we left the brothel, it was dawn in Regent Street.

'Where're you going now?' I asked.

'Where d'you think I'm going, mate?' he replied. 'Back to the wife, of course.'

It was at that moment that I heard the clattering sound of horses' hooves as a brougham came by and a familiar voice shouted out: 'Horby!' It was my gorgeous Rosemary Radcliffe, looking more beautiful than ever and inviting me to join her within. I was overcome by a rapture of delight on seeing her again. I introduced Fitz and invited him to join us but he declined with a wicked grin.

'No,' he said as he shook my hand with his right and

hailed a hansom with his left. 'You just enjoy yourself. And my money's still on you.'

It was such a joy to be with Rosemary again and to accompany her to a small and elegant town house in St John's Wood. She was, she told me, now the mistress of a wealthy international banker but she made me swear never to mention his name in this connection. Over scrambled eggs on toast with vintage champagne, I briefly informed her about what had been happening to me and asked after her life since the last communication I had received from her when she had been enjoying life as a guest of her Aunt in Hastings.

'My darling, sometimes I wonder how life can be so strange,' she replied, kicking up her legs to make her skirts rustle so sexily. 'I've just been re-reading *Alice's Adventures in Wonderland*. It's a strange story with characters such as the Gryphon, the Mad Hatter, the March Hare and the Cheshire Cat. The Cheshire Cat always has a mad grin upon his face. You might wonder why I am referring to this work of literature, and yet, dear Horby, you have a mad grin upon your face at the present time. You see, a while ago my health was not as good as could be desired and so I took advantage of my doctor's invitation to stay with him at Whitby Bay in Yorkshire. Dr Foster is an elderly, well-educated gentleman who prescribed a restorative regime for me. He has a wonderful bedside manner.

'He is a top Harley Street specialist who is very civilised and humane. He was always presenting me with appetising gifts of Turkish delight, butterscotch and crystallised fruit. He has always stood up for better conditions in the workhouses. However, he is known most widely for his books about sex. According to his written words, women do not enjoy the matter. Have you ever heard anything more ridiculous in your life? You *know* how much I relish the pleasures of cunnilingus and copulation. You *know* that I will never say "No" to a good fuck. At times I have lain languidly upon my bed and have fondled my cunt as I thought of you . . . as I've written letters to you, my other hand has been probing my pussy. The fact is that within sixty minutes and via masturbation alone, I can climax twenty times.

'I must admit that I was intrigued by the tales he told me of his son whom he criticised as being "a dilettante" and "a lazy young rake", fickle, lacking in manners and something of an infidel. I couldn't wait to meet the rogue. However, that was yet to come. One night in the Conservatory, where we were dining, he told me about his wife. This room was absolutely sublime with a magnificent view onto the raging seas bursting upon the rocks beneath. In the centre of the interior was a fountain fashioned from a statue of a young boy and water spurted from his penis into a pond filled with water-lilies. It was then that he told me that his wife of thirty years had died recently. It had been a riding accident and she had died in his arms.

'Comfort and solace were what this dear old doctor needed and so I placed my arms around his neck and he rested his head upon my shoulder. He pulled away nervously and poured generous quantities of brandy for both of us, after which he lit his pipe hesitantly. He spoke to me about his friend, Bram Stoker, author of *Dracula*.

' "This is where Stoker stayed when he was writing that vampire novel, my dear," he told me in between puffs of his gnarled briar pipe. "In the novel, this is where Count Dracula comes ashore." Shivers tingled up and down my spine. "My family is related to the Stokers." The candles on the table flickered and I was aware of a draught in the room. I looked out of the windows to see the night sky, the full moon and its shimmering upon the water. A thousand, a million stars and then he took my hand in his. There was trepidation in my heart as he put his hand upon my breasts and felt my quivering palpitations.

'Suddenly I was aware of a strong wind, a rushing, mighty wind outside as the windows rattled alarmingly. In the distance there was the baying of a wolf. He kissed me on the cheeks and on the lips. Clearly his libido had been aroused. I looked out of the window and glimpsed an object in flight. What was it?

' "Calm down, my dear, there is no need for fear," he whispered and then he kissed me again. His hands were upon my breasts once more and then my chemise was all unbuttoned. He led me to his bedroom. My nipples were so aroused. Gradually I removed his clothes. I wanted to see his fine nudity. I took his member into my mouth and sucked. Abruptly he shot his juices down my throat and I swallowed them with great delight. As he caressed my cunt, I wondered how an intelligent man could write so disparagingly of sexuality and womanhood yet still retain so great an appetite for the matter.

'He kissed the nape of my neck and then my cunt again. How he licked my cunt! How I relished the feel of the rough edge of his tongue! I did so want him to penetrate my fig. My welcoming pussy was waiting. He entered me – and how he did ram it in! His stiffly erect phallus probed the deepest regions of my vagina. As his organ pulsated, his fingers teasingly tickled the outer lips of my labia. At moments he would give me a butterfly kiss upon the cheek followed by a nibble on my ear-lobes accompanied by nips, slaps and delightfully peculiar pinches. I could feel my juices starting to flow even more profusely.

'Unfortunately, Dr Foster is in truth just a mite too old for my liking yet I appreciated the sheer lust of the man.

His intellect certainly appealed to me yet I know that a younger man can satisfy me so much more. While he was prodding his stiff rod into me, I began to have other fantasies and yet it was so apparent simultaneously that he knew how to pleasure a woman. There is no denying that he made me feel so incredibly orgasmic. It was apparent that he had had many years of experience, this gentleman who claimed that 'the fairer yet weaker gender' did not enjoy sex. Possibly he had fucked his wife to death? If so, I hope I go in the same manner.

'At around dawn, when he had spent himself inside me with a series of throbbing ejaculations, I was feeling rather fatigued yet, despite his advanced years, he wanted to continue swiving me. I reminded him that he had an occupation to which he was obliged to attend.

' "The only obligation I want for myself at present," he breathed heavily, "is to fuck you." However, he agreed to a break and I made him a breakfast of eggs and bacon, fried tomatoes, liver with onions, toast and kidneys, accompanied by kippers and a pint of stout. He rubbed his abdomen with joy, then realised that he had his duties to perform within the area.

'He had just left and I was about to retire to my bedroom for a sleep which I needed badly when there was a pounding upon the door, rather like peals of thunder. A maid showed a tall, straight man into the room and he introduced himself as Douglas Foster.

' "Is father around?" he enquired casually. He appeared so young, rampant and virile yet he was so pale about the face. He was dressed completely in black. When he smiled, I felt wholly entranced. From the instant I set eyes upon him, tired as I was, I wanted his prick to enter my cunt. There was a certain fascinating charm about him, even though his attitude was rather glib and glossy, yet his remarkable physical beauty appeared to be ageless. It was so obvious that he was a squire of many dames, a Don Juan, a Lothario. I sensed that there was an element of the vampire about him. I wanted to compare father and son, for I can play the game of vampires too.

'His prick entered my cunt as he took me on the kitchen floor and I wondered: is there no peace for the wicked?'

CHAPTER TWENTY-FOUR

'And so I plunged my rampant rod between the lascivious lips of her eager cunt and she quivered and sighed in a series of ecstatic spasms, her love juices flooding my spurting member,' I told Rosemary Radcliffe over a healthy bottle of restorative morning Armagnac.

'And that was your latest fuck?' she enquired.

'No, it was the one before last and it was luscious!' I enthused. 'My latest fucks were a couple of sloppy ones in a Haymarket brothel.'

'I'm sorry to hear it,' she replied with some cutting asperity. 'What could have brought about this limp tragedy?' I told her about the bet over Lillie Langtry with Queensberry and Fitzsimmons. Bless her! She burst out laughing. 'You silly boy! You twerp of a toff!'

'I'm not a toff!' I returned indignantly. 'A toff looks down his nose at people, hence the expression "toffee-nosed". By contrast, a gentleman treats everyone as an equal.'

'And a lady?' she queried archly.

'A lady can be gracious to anybody.'

'I see . . .' She laughed richly in a series of deep, throaty chuckles. 'So you'd claim to be a gentleman now, would you, Horby? Wouldn't some call you a bounder? Or even a cad?'

'I can explain to you the precise differences between a

gentleman, a bounder and a cad,' I retorted. 'The gentleman, the bounder and the cad get a girl pregnant. The gentleman will marry her because his code obliges him to do so. The bounder will not marry her but he will pay for an abortion or else pay maintenance for the child. The cad will leave her in the lurch.'

'And so you'd marry her?'

'If it were dynastically appropriate.'

'And if it weren't?'

'Abortion or maintenance.'

'You bounder!' she squealed. 'You're not a gentleman at all. And as for your "dynastically appropriate" marriage, would you spend much time with your wife and child?'

'The child, yes,' I replied, 'whenever I could spare the time. But never the wife.'

'You cad,' she said. My answer was to dive beneath her voluminous skirts and press my lips to her gorgeous cunt. 'Ohhh . . .' she moaned as I tongued her clit, 'you bounder and you cad, sir!' And as I licked her juicy, sweet cunny, she began to sing:

'She's a most immoral lady
She's a most immoral lady
She's a most immoral la-a-dee!
And she lay between the lilywhite sheets with nothing on at all.
"Oh, Sir Jasper, do not touch me!
Oh, Sir Jasper, do not touch.
Oh, Sir Jasper, do not . . .
Oh . . . Sir Jasper . . . do . . .
Oh, Sir Jasper!
Oh Sir!
OH!!!" '

'She's a most immoral lady . . .' I hummed as I licked her. I dipped my head closer to inhale the tangy aroma of a heady wet cunt.

'My God, that's marvellous!' she exclaimed as I lovingly licked the delicate edges of her pouting crack, sliding my hands beneath her dimpled buttocks as I tucked my head in deeper between her thighs. I moved my wicked tongue suddenly to draw circles across Rosemary's flat belly, then returned my attention to her crisp nest of curly cunny hair. All the while I pressed her darkly red, rubbery nipples repeatedly between my fingers.

I could imagine her throwing back her head and closing her eyes as I slid my tongue inside her cunt, the tip of my tongue flicking and nudging her tiny, erect clitty which was now pushing out of its hood. Then I began to eat her in earnest, forcing my tongue deep inside that trembling wet slit, pushing and probing against that sweet mouth.

'Ooooh! Suck my pussy, darling! Suck harder now and make me come!' she panted in a sensual frenzy, her body twisting furiously as I continued relentlessly to nibble at her clitty. I lifted my own flushed face for a moment to breathe in great gulps of air and then I dived back between Rosemary's thighs, sucking and slurping with great passion, noisily lapping the love juices that were now flowing freely from her cunt as, with a huge wrench, the aroused young lady brought herself to the brink of a gargantuan orgasm. She wrapped her thighs around my head as she screamed out: 'Yes! Yes! Yes! I'm there, you darling!'

And then the floodgates opened as she came off with a tremendous shudder, deluging my mouth and chin with a sharp stream of love juice which poured out from her cunt but I eagerly swallowed her copious emission, smacking my lips as I gulped down the pungent essence.

I was aroused by this exhilarating encounter. My gigantic

prick urged me to clamber aboard her.

'It's just as well that I'm not looking at your thick dick,' she murmured as she gripped my large shaft with her fingers, 'or I might be worried that you'll split me in two with that colossal cock of yours.' Turning over, she knelt forward and pushed out the cheeky white globes of her buttocks, so smooth and splendid, to give me an excellent view of both her arsehole and her cunt. This presented me with a problem. To coin a sporting metaphor from the snooker room, should I go for the pink or the brown? But she must have discerned that this question was going through my mind for she said with genuine feeling: 'Oh, darling, please don't even think of trying to go up my bottom. Your prick is far too big for the tradesman's entrance!'

'No need to worry, I'd much rather fuck your juicy cunt,' I replied gaily, grabbing a cushion and inserting it under her tummy so that Rosemary's hips and wobbling backside were raised up into the air. Then I moved between her legs, prodding her knees further apart as, holding my gleaming shaft in my hand, I judiciously guided my massive uncapped knob into the crevice between her bum cheeks and pushed forward until my helmet slid inside her squishy honeypot. I settled myself on my knees and bent my body forward so that my hairy chest brushed against her back and then I slid my arms under hers to cup her pert breasts which I held in a firm grip as I started to pump in and out of her throbbing orifice.

My prick thickened and swelled even further as her magnificent arse slapped lasciviously against my thighs. She caught my rhythm and my shaft see-sawed in and out of her. The diminutive wrinkled rosebud of Rosemary's rear dimple quivered and winked with every stroke as I pounded away with great gusto.

Reaching behind her, Rosemary caressed my bollocks as she rocked to and fro, her long hair whipping from side to side as she writhed under my relentless pistoning. She waggled her bum, working it round and round with her hips, rotating to allow me the maximum penetration, and then this lusty young woman threw back her head again in total abandon as a primordial sound came out of her, from deep within, and her body shuddered with the force of a breathtaking orgasm which coursed through every fibre of her being.

I was now also ready to spend and my torso stiffened as with an anguished cry, I managed one final thrust forward, my balls banging against the back of her thighs as my cock squirted hot jets of jism inside her love channel. My climax was so powerful that it seemed as though I was being shaken to pieces by the force of my spend and I could manage only one last drawn-out bellow before I collapsed on top of Rosemary, my glistening body bathed in perspiration.

There were a few moments of delicious rest and then Rosemary became the aggressor. She started by licking my wiry pubic bush and then she moved her face slowly from side to side, enjoying to the full the voluptuous grazing of my swelling stiff cock against her soft cheek. With a salacious giggle, she made strands of her silky hair and then made a web around the base of my shaft, stroking it slowly and feeling it throb and pulse under her delicate touch.

She moved her head upwards and across the smooth wide dome of my knob and kissed the minute eye out of which some droplets of moisture had oozed. Then her tongue circled my helmet, savouring these juices as she drew my dick in between her generous red lips and sucked with an intense verve as, instinctively, I pushed forwards and backwards as her warm fingers fondled my heavy, banging, hairy balls.

She slurped happily on her fleshy sweetmeat as my stiff shaft slid in and out of her willing mouth. Then my body began to shiver uncontrollably and I gasped: 'I can't hold back, Rosemary, I'm going to have to let go! Brace yourself!' and she started to swallow in eager anticipation. This was just as well for with a rasping growl I shot my load and a potent stream of hot, sticky seed spurted down Rosemary's throat. She continued to suck and nibble greedily upon my shaft, draining my trembling tool to the dregs of my abundant ejaculation.

'Ah, that was grand, Horby,' she commented quietly. 'I do so love sucking off a nice thick prick like yours. I could happily gobble it for a full hour.' She gave my now flaccid shaft a farewell kiss. 'Of course, this could never happen as all you men squirt off far too quickly. Bet you're not up to it again.'

'A bet?' I queried. 'You're on.'

CHAPTER TWENTY-FIVE

'Aboard the good ship Venus
By Christ, you should've seen us
The figurehead
Was a nude in bed
With her mouth around a penis,'

Rosemary sang as I brought her champagne and brandy singing:

'Frigging in the rigging,
Frigging in the rigging,
Frigging in the rigging . . .
There was fuck all else to do.'

Now Rosemary sang again:

'The captain of this fucker,
He was a dirty bugger.
He wasn't fit
To shovel shit
From one place to another.'

'I know a different version of that verse,' I said.

'The captain's name was Carter.

'By gad, he was a farter:
When the wind wouldn't blow,
And the ship wouldn't go,
They used Carter the farter to start her.'

Now is was Rosemary's turn:

'The first mate's name was Topper.
By gum, he had a whopper.
Twice round the deck,
Once round his neck,
And into his arse for a stopper.'

I responded with:

'The second mate's name was Green.
He invented a wanking machine.
On the ninety-ninth stroke
The fucking thing broke
And mashed his bollocks to cream.'

She riposted by singing:

'The cabin boy was Ripper.
He was a fucking nipper.
He stuffed his arse
With broken glass
And circumcised the skipper.'

I replied:

'The cook, her name was Mabel
And, by Christ, she was able
To give the crew

Their daily screw
Upon the kitchen table.'

We both joined in for a rousing chorus of:

'Frigging in the rigging,
Frigging in the rigging,
Frigging in the rigging – yeah!
There was fuck all else to do!'

It was an hour later and I had just fucked her again in straight and joyous fashion. Now we needed to relax and talk about things. I hadn't yet had a night's sleep but this did not matter since she had had such an invigorating effect upon my loins. It was wonderful to hold her warm, soft, smooth body in my arms: but I also needed some advice.

'This ridiculous bet of yours with Queensberry concerning Lillie Langtry,' Rosemary broke into my thoughts. 'You may have wondered why I was so amused when you initially mentioned it to me. The fact is that I know Lillie, only too well.' She burst out laughing. 'I know her through the gentleman whose mistress I am. Lillie is always in debt and his bank lends her money. The same is true for poor old Bertie too. How he must be aching for the Queen to die so he can fulfil his role at last! Oh yes, Horby, it would be a relatively easy matter to obtain for you an introduction to Lillie Langtry. As for fucking her, any person of common sense would term that feat impossible at present.'

'Why so?' I responded. 'Report has it that she is a rather fast and foxy lady.'

'Oh, indeed. But ever since she's been with Bertie, she has taken no other lovers. The Prince is fiercely jealous. He would never allow her to be fucked by another man. He would end the relationship instantly. from some reports I gather that he might even engage rogues to give the offending man a sound beating. She knows that her reputation is so notorious that she could never be Queen of England but she also knows that her fortune is secured forever should she become the mistress of the King. As Balzac says: "Every woman's fortune lies between her legs".'

'So you're saying that there's no hope for me with her?'

'I didn't *quite* say that,' she giggled mischievously. 'I said that this would appear so to any person of common sense. It's just that women have uncommon sense.' She drained her glass and called for more. 'And I should now,' she continued, 'since I'm a witch.'

'Yes,' I said simply. There was nothing else I could say.

'I was initiated into Witchcraft at the age of puberty by my grandmother,' Rosemary stated calmly. 'We lived in a remote country hamlet in Cornwall. I shan't weary you with the details – perhaps another time – but I learned the ancient secrets of the Craft of the Wise. That's how I can help you to seduce Lillie Langtry.'

'More . . .' I muttered.

'We'll do it this evening,' she answered briskly. 'There's a room upstairs where the moonlight shines through so beautifully. We shall need patchouli leaves, cloves, basil, passion flowers, all of which can be purchased in the locality, and sweet red wine. I suggest ruby port. You will have to powder the herbs and then mix them together by the light of the silvery moon upstairs and with a thick red candle burning in the centre of the room. While you're doing this, it is absolutely essential that you concentrate completely on Lillie Langtry. Chant her name over and over as you work this love spell, visualising yourself and her as passionate lovers. Then pour this love philtre into a flask and seal it with a kiss.'

'Yes,' I said. 'What do I do then?'

'Pour the bloody mixture into her wine, you fool!' She shrieked with laughter. 'Do you honestly think that if you keep the wretched flask of love philtre in your cupboard for three months, that it's going to do the blindest bit of good? Your principal problem, dear Horby, is one of logistics. How do you get the philtre into the wine glass without anybody noticing?'

I sincerely hoped that Queensberry had not beaten me to it, for he certainly hadn't informed me of same, when I met Lillie Langtry on the ensuing Saturday. I really can't thank Rosemary enough for giving me the opportunity. She certainly managed the matter with accomplished finesse. She introduced me to her suitor and the instant that I saw his gaunt, white and cadaverous features, I knew that it was the son of Dr Foster of Whitby. The first and last I'd heard of him from Rosemary was that on entering his father's kitchen, he had fucked her upon the floor. This man, who asked me to call him 'Douglas', was immaculately garbed in white tie and tails and his left hand sported a huge ring of star sapphire. He found the idea of my bet to be quite wickedly amusing and announced his intention of assisting me. He had, he said, invited Lillie Langtry to come for a cruise upon one of his boats at lunch-time on Saturday, returning in time for tea and cruising from Richmond towards Hampton Court and back again. I was welcome to join the party.

The boat was a steam-powered motor yacht with a number of private cabins. The crew of three men looked after the boat. The staff of three women looked after the food and drink. The passengers were the man I can't resist calling 'the Black Douglas', Rosemary, Sir Richard Bellingham, who seemed to gad about everywhere, the rather sphinx-like yet beautiful Mrs Ada Leverson, well-known in artistic circles; and myself. Only one person was missing before we could cast away and that was Lillie Langtry. I gathered that she always made a point of being late.

As I waited nervously, I fingered the glass phial in my trouser pocket. I had followed Rosemary's instructions exactly. At last! AH! A Victoria clattered up, with the driver dressed in ostentatious Regency fashion, and there was Lillie Langtry with six laughing, champagne-swilling beaux.

They escorted her to the deck and spent a seemingly endless time in essaying their farewells. Once they had gone and the boat was moving, I lost no time in joining the circle that gathered around the one they called 'the Jersey Lily'. She was astonishingly beautiful. Her thick brown hair was waved in thick serpentine coils to crown her head. Her eyes were of cold, gleaming azure. Her nose was straight, short and disdainful. Her mouth was a pink Cupid's bow. Her pert-looking breasts strained against the silken fabric of her white dress. Her waist was so slender yet her bottom was thrust out proudly, as though she did not need to wear a bustle. Her skirts trembled slightly in the soft south wind. I wondered how to open my conversation with her.

'You know, you're terribly beautiful,' Sir Richard Bellingham was telling Ada Leverson.

'And you know, you're terribly obvious,' she replied. Clearly this direct approach was going to cut no ice with the ladies present. My opening pleasantries were no better and no worse than those of any other man. Lillie Langtry responded by being impersonally pleasant.

'I often wonder, you know,' she remarked teasingly as she fluttered her peacock-feathered fan, 'what exactly it is that constitutes a bore.' Her voice was just like a soft violin. 'Gentlemen, you all look rather clever, which I don't pretend to be, but perhaps you can assist me?' Instantly all the men were competing for her attention.

'A bore is someone who talks when you want him to listen,' said Bellingham, ever eager to be first off his marks. Lillie giggled.

'A person of low taste,' said Douglas, 'more interested in himself than in me.' Lillie chortled.

'When you ask a bore how he is, he tells you,' I said and Lillie burst out laughing.

'A bore is a snore,' she said and of course all the men burst out laughing, though actually I thought she'd been the most succinct of all of us.

She was certainly well-disposed towards me but from the way that she positioned her body, I could discern that Rosemary's words were accurate and that she did not have the slightest intention of sleeping with anyone on the boat. She was merely charmingly sweet to one and all.

The sun was blazing at mid-day. I offered to fetch her a glass of red wine. To my immense relief, she nodded. I took two glasses from the bar then pretended to be enraptured by the sight of the river glistening in the noon-day sun. No one was looking when I poured the contents of my phial into Lillie's glass. She took it, sipped some and became increasingly animated.

'Isn't the sun a beautiful sight?' I declared heartily.

'It is,' she replied dreamily, 'and I feel rather overcome by it.'

'Let's take a stroll aft,' I suggested and she accompanied me. We gazed at the willow trees along the river bank, regarding with pleasure the other sailing boats and rowing boats. One rowing boat came past with three laughing men, reminding me of *Three Men in a Boat* by Jerome K. Jerome. 'Ah . . .' I breathed. 'Lovely.'

'Yes, it is lovely,' she responded, 'but perhaps it is the

heat of the day that is making me feel just a little bit faint.' The obvious strait-lacing of her corset was probably as responsible for that comment as my love potion. 'Is there a cabin here where I could just rest for a while?' I assured her that there was. 'Would you please escort me to it? I do not know if I can quite manage the steps.' Naturally I guided her down the steps and into the cabin I had earlier arranged with Douglas and Rosemary. The instant that we were within, I kissed her and she laughed.

'You're a wicked sexy bitch,' I said.

'Yes, I am a wicked bitch,' she replied. 'Why don't you give me a good spanking? I'll enjoy that, it'll liven me up and I'll wager that the sight of my jiggling bum cheeks will stiffen your cock a treat.'

'I'll give it a try,' I responded as this lithe woman spread herself face downwards over my knees, thrust down her knickers, whipped up her skirts and petticoats and, turning up her exquisitely pretty face towards me, said: 'Go on, I don't mind, really I don't.'

I smoothed my palm along the soft contours of her alluringly rounded buttocks, stroking, pinching and rubbing my fingers along the dark crevice between them. Then, placing my left arm over the small of her back, I held her firmly in position and, raising my right hand, I brought it down upon the middle of her right bottom cheek with a loud smack, the sound of which resounded throughout the cabin although I had not applied any great force. Again my hand rose and fell as I began to slap her delicious bum, firmly but not too hard, which made her wriggle and yelp as her bum cheeks changed colour from alabaster white to a rosy coloured hue.

I continued the spanking, slapping her shapely cheeks alternately and my sizzling hand rebounded from Lillie's chubby, elastic buttocks. She writhed like fury on my lap and the thrilling friction of her naked belly rubbing against my cock soon sent my shaft swelling up to his customary majestic height.

'Oh, stop!' Lillie yelped. 'Stop! My arse is burning!' and I was glad to finish the 'punishment' because my hand was now burning too. I turned her over and kissed the darling girl, sinking my tongue inside her mouth, and my hand stroked through her fleecy pubic thatch as she in turn grasped my pulsing prick and frigged it as our melting kisses urged us further down the path of ardour.

My fingers probed downwards and caressed the folds of Lillie's cunny, and her body started to shake with erotic excitement as we fell from the bed to the floor, and as the boat rocked, my thumb found her clitty which I began to rub, and this made her cling to me even more tightly. But now I broke off our kiss and I moved my lips down towards her jutting raspberry nipples, tracing tiny circles with the tip of my tongue around the stiffening little red bullets.

She moaned with delight as she lay down on the floor, opening her legs as my fingers ran over her wet, open crack. I raised myself above her and, positioning my cock with my hand, guided my helmet between the inviting cunny lips into the depths of her juicy cunt. Our bodies moved in sensuous rhythm as I pounded into her, sliding my prick inside her honeypot until my balls banged against her bottom as she lifted up her arse (which I noticed had quickly lost its reddish tinge and was now as beautifully milky white as before) to receive the full length of my sinewy shaft.

I thoroughly screwed Lillie Langtry's cunt with a slow, circular motion and she moved excitedly underneath me as my shaft explored every last part of her sopping love box. From her ardent shivers of delight I could see that she was enjoying this marvellous fuck as much as myself. This greatly pleased me.

'Oh, Horby, how gorgeous, how lovely, how you make me spend!' Lillie yelled. 'Oh! Oh, I can feel my juices gushing! Spunk into me, you big-cocked man!'

I had prolonged the pleasure for as long as I could, slowing down my thrusts and sometimes letting my shaft rest inside her tingling cunt to feel these delicious throbbings of cock and cunny in perfect conjunction but I was now more than ready to release the sperm which had been boiling up within my balls. So, summoning up my remaining reserves of strength, I pumped my prick faster and faster in and out of her dripping crack, my balls slapping against her shiny, moist bum until I exploded inside her, filling her slippery slit with spout after spout of salty spunk as Lillie reached the peak of her mighty orgasm.

There was no fending off this lascivious girl. After taking a few breaths, she kissed me vehemently on the lips, forcing her tongue between them and then she sat between my legs, leaning forward to take hold of my pulsing shaft and easing down my foreskin to bare the smooth rigid crown of my renewedly rigid penis.

She turned over on her tummy and, still holding my twitching boner in her hand, delicately swirled the tip of her tongue around the ridges of my helmet, making me gasp with delight. Then ever so gently, she eased my shaft inch by inch between her lips, sucking furiously as she engulfed my knob, sheathing it in her mouth as her tongue darted all along the sensitive underside of my moistened cock. I jerked my hips upwards as Lillie sensuously sucked my dick in a quickening rhythm, sending thrilling warm spasms of joy from my groin all over my body. After just a couple of minutes of this sweet palating of my prick, I had to whisper to Lillie that I could not hold back for very much longer.

With her mouth still filled with my glistening shaft, she nodded and she gently squeezed my balls as a stream of my creamy jism hurtled out of my cock and into her mouth. Game little bitch that she was, she swallowed my entire gushing emission, draining my shaft of its salty essence whilst a wonderful orgasmic wave swept over me, and then she opened her lips to release my fast deflating tadger and panted: 'Oh, your spunk has such an invigorating taste!' She moaned softly. 'Oooh, I'd so love it were you to screw me again.'

'I don't know if I'm up to that,' I replied honestly, 'but I would like to eat your pussy and I trust that this will be to your satisfaction.'

I began by kissing her two elongated crimson nipples whilst I cupped her firm buttocks in my hands, squeezing them lecherously as I slid all the way down until my lips were only inches away from her soft strands of pussy hair, and she parted her thighs to make her moist, swollen cunny lips more accessible to me.

Lillie let out a delighted gasp as my tongue moved over every inch of her juicy, damp crack and she breathed a long sigh whilst my eager tongue delved everywhere in the folds of her cunt, probing and sliding from the top of her slit to her bum-hole, licking and lapping up the odoriferous love juices which were now being expelled from her pussy.

I stiffened the tip of my tongue and started to lick the soft, puffed inner lips and inhaled the unique feminine aroma as she moaned again with unslaked desire. Then suddenly I thrust my tongue between the lips, pushing into the warm, wet channel. Her hips gyrated madly as I tongue-fucked this luscious woman, licking her cunt up and down and feeling her clitty grow harder each time my tongue flicked across it.

Now it was time to concentrate on this swollen bud and I

nibbled at her jerking love-button whilst I moved my hand up and slid first one and then two fingers into her wetness. Her cunny was hot and tight and she bucked as I twisted my fingers inside her, arching her body with joy when I tickled her clitty with the tip of my tongue.

Again and again I drove my fingers inside her, feeling her vaginal walls clutching my digits as my lips paid homage to her clitty, kissing and sucking the erectile flesh as Lillie writhed beneath my erotic ministrations. The throbbing vibrations of her body excited me as well and my turgid prick swelled up yet again as my hips twitched and I continued to tongue-fuck Lillie towards the ultimate peak of pleasure. She reached her climax with a throaty shriek as the orgasm burst inside her cunt in a mighty explosion and my face was flooded by a fierce, fresh outpouring of cuntal juice which I gulped down as Lillie now shivered all over with the might of her climactic spend.

Afterwards we both felt very warm and gentle towards one another and began to joke and laugh about things in general. I told her about my bet with Queensberry and as Bob Fitzsimmons had correctly forecast, she was 'amused rather than aggrieved'. In fact, she hooted with raucous laughter. It was easy to see why everyone adored her, including and especially the future King.

'But that man Queensberry!' she gasped between her dreadful giggles, 'that dreadful oaf, I'd *never* go to bed with him. The very conceit of that useless fool in even imagining that he had a chance in hell with me! Anyway, what on earth made *you* think you had a chance with me, you bloody rogue?'

'I wanted you because I adore you,' I replied. 'He wanted you to win a bet.'

'You're absurd!' she laughed and I did not disagree. I was

thanking Rosemary from the depths of my heart for her advice on the love philtre.

We returned to the deck and had a most enjoyable cruise. Lillie of course could not continue the affair with me but we remained friends and I still treasure the memory. I duly collected my ten thousand pounds from Queensberry. Unfortunately, I had to hand it back again since Bob Fitzsimmons had lost his Championship by an 11th round knockout to America's James J. Jeffries. Fitz duly wired Queensberry ten thousand pounds, which bet must have added extra pain to his physical defeat, but Queensberry had to wire back ten thousand pounds owing from the ex-Champion's 2-1 bet on me. What was lost on the fighting was won on the fucking.

CHAPTER TWENTY-SIX

'Spank 'em, that's what I say!' cried Sir Richard Bellingham. 'Just spank 'em! What they need is a sound thrashing and after that, a jolly good rogering!' He drained his pint of port. 'Another?'

'Very kind, Richard, but it will have to be on another occasion,' I answered.

'Got anywhere to go? Like to come with me for a fuck?'

'Some other time, thank you, Richard.'

'Dear me.' His expression became one of deliberately supercilious indignation. 'What *can* you be up to this evening?' I laughed easily. 'Trouble with you, Horby, is that all you're interested in is this mystical windy stuff and I'm just interested in fucking. Too kind to women, that's your trouble, Horby.'

We shook hands warmly outside the Strand tavern, for Sir Richard was good at heart despite his many faults, and went on our separate ways in pursuit of separate pleasures. The air was pleasant, the sky was of deep royal blue, the gas lamps were lit and I hailed a cab to take me to Kensington. My purpose was to meet Mrs Arabella Mornington-Stuart.

On the boat and after our tryst, I had talked with Lillie Langtry quietly about my search for the holy grail and of my belief that the holiest sacrament was sex. She had murmured quietly that perhaps she agreed but that I ought to meet Arabella Mornington-Stuart, to whom she could arrange an introduction. I might find her to be 'extremely interesting'.

When I mentioned the name subsequently to Rosemary, she burst out laughing, refused to say why and declared that she too would gladly furnish me with an introduction. 'It might prove to be a very educational experience for you,' she said. I was sufficiently intrigued to hire a reputable private detective to gather information concerning my hostess. At length, an invitation to sherry arrived, which was how I happened to be in a cab, clip-clopping in a westerly direction towards Kensington. At least it wasn't West Kensington. 'West Kensington is where you drive until the horse drops dead and the cabman gets down to make enquiries,' dear old Oscar Wilde had said.

I alighted outside a mansion block. Mrs Mornington-Stuart lived on the ground floor and I was admitted to her chambers by a maid. A very dry fine sherry was served to me the instant I had taken my seat in the large, somewhat fussily furnished drawing-room. There was an antique grand concert piano of the kind that Chopin might have played, wherever I looked there were delicate porcelain ornaments and the walls were adorned by prints of fashionably dressed women in erotic poses.

Arabella Mornington-Stuart, who now swept into the room, was a very handsome woman indeed. Her face was imperious and haughty, with flashing blue eyes that could flutter demurely beneath blue-shadowed lids. She wore a very tight black dress of silk with lace adorning its frontage. Beneath it, her breasts thrust forward and her bottom thrust out behind. As she seated herself delicately to take her glass of sherry, her dress slid up momentarily to reveal a glimpse of white lace petticoats and a peeping ankle. It was deliciously well turned.

After the necessary formalities and preliminary introductions had been complied with, she naturally enquired gently after the purpose of my visit. I mentioned Lillie and Rosemary and she glowed with approval. She had a somewhat shrill and authoritarian voice yet this only added to my interest. I mentioned my own interest in the holy grail.

'Woman bears the holy grail,' she replied. 'Woman *is* the holy grail. And Woman manifests in three forms: The Virgin, The Mother and The Crone.'

'And what is the best way for Man to understand Woman?' I asked.

'Worship the Goddess within her. Submit to her.'

'I'm not surprised to hear you say that,' I replied, 'because I believe you taught that to a friend of mine. Chap called Curzon. George Nathaniel Curzon. Only he knew you under the name of Joan Smythe.' My detective had done his work well and she acknowledged my shot instantly but if I expected her to be at all put out, I was very much mistaken. She burst out laughing.

'You're quite right,' she returned, in between wicked chuckles, 'I do have a habit of choosing whichever name is appropriate to any given situation. Obviously your private detective has told you more. Tell me.'

'You run a flagellation brothel in the Haymarket,' I said, 'or else you are a governess to pupils found by their parents to be a nuisance.'

'Quite correct,' she replied. 'You *are* well informed.'

'Allow me to call you Mrs Smythe, then,' I said, 'for I first heard of you from Curzon.' She inclined her head graciously. 'I would be very interested indeed in witnessing a practical demonstration of your most interesting theories.'

'I'd be delighted,' she replied with a twinkle in her eye, and the price was agreed and business transacted in a trice.

I would be seeing a demonstration within an hour behind a screen disguised as a looking-glass.

'I wonder which role I shall take tonight . . .' Mrs Joan Smythe mused. 'The Nurse, The Governess or The Dame . . .'

I had no cause for complaint as I reclined in an upstairs drawing-room. There was a bottle of tawny port and a glass upon the Sheraton table before me and a wide plate-glass window giving me a superb view onto the salon beneath. This, I had been assured, had been disguised as a looking-glass so that the participants present would be unaware of my spectatorship. This seating had cost me a small fortune and I sincerely hoped that the resulting exhibition would justify my expenditure. For the present, everything was in darkness and one could see nothing at all.

After a time, I discerned dim light, then a maid entered to light some candles. I discerned eight tall black candles, blazing within serpent-headed candelabra. I also discerned a tripartite statue which extolled the external feminine. There was a young girl, a wife and a lady of mature years with their marble arms intertwined and gracing the altar. Incense was burning, filling the room with smoke though from where I sat, it was impossible, obviously, to ascertain the precise nature of the smoke. It cleared slightly as the lights came up and I could see someone standing in the corner, hands behind their back, though whether a male or a female, one could not tell. Certainly this person was wearing a bright, pink satin frock with frilly petticoats and high-heeled black shoes of shiny patent leather. A placard adorned the back of this personage and it shouted: 'TO BE BIRCHED'.

A gong resounded throughout the room beneath me, beaten by the buxom maid. Mrs Joan Smythe entered the room and calmly seated herself upon a throne beneath the statue and before the altar, which, as I could now make out, resembled nothing less than the flogging-block used at Eton. The maid tolled the gong thrice more. Three women quietly entered the room and took seats opposite Joan Smythe. I started involuntarily since I recognised all of them.

How could one ever forget Lady Candida Lauderdale and Miss Amelia Edwards, with whom I had had so extraordinary an encounter in the previous year? How could one forget Ada 'The Sphinx' Leverson, whom I had recently seen on a steam-yacht in the Thames being acidly witty at Sir Richard Bellingham's expense? All four women bore chalices filled with red wine. The chalice of Mrs Joan Smythe was of gold, those of the other three ladies of silver. Mrs Smythe handed the maid a small tankard of red wine made out of pewter, from which she drank greedily. All five women in the room were dressed in long gowns, nipped in sharply at the waist and with foundation garments which accentuated the curves of their breasts and buttocks. The maid wore white. Mrs Joan Smythe wore black. Ada Leverson wore blue, Candida Lauderdale wore red and Amelia Edwards was adorned in a sunny yellow. Through the ventilation shafts, I could hear the rustling of their petticoats.

The maid struck the gong once more. Joan Smythe arose.

'In the Names of Juno, Diana, Venus and Minerva, also in the sight of Isis, who includes all, I declare this Temple open. Tonight shall witness a sacrifice to the Goddess. Come forward!' she commanded the penitent who had been standing obediently in the corner. I saw as they turned that this was a young male dressed in womens' clothes and looking very shame-faced. 'Curtsey to the ladies.' He did. 'Bring me the birch you have made for me, pickled in my urine.' He obediently fetched a birch-rod, standing in a vase, from the opposite corner of the room, knelt before her and proffered it to her. 'You have been exceedingly rude to Mrs Leverson here. Curtsey to her, kneel before her and beg her pardon.' He did so. 'Do you forgive him, Mrs Leverson?'

'He needs to be punished first,' she replied.

'Definitely,' said Miss Amelia Edwards.

'Without a shadow of doubt,' declared Candida Lauderdale.

'Come and stand before me!' Mrs Joan Smythe demanded. 'Now, you know why you are here, do you not?'

'Yes, Madam,' the young male replied humbly.

'Then tell me.'

'Madam, I was rude to Mrs Leverson and failed to treat her with proper respect.'

'A catalogue of sins for which this,' she shook the birch, 'will settle the score. You remember what you must do now?'

'Madam, I do most solemnly repent of my offences and I ask if you will be so good as to punish me for them.'

'I will!' Joan Smythe replied with relish. 'Bend over this block!' The maid fastened the block's strap to the further platform, having looped it around his waist. The second strap was passed around the backs of his knees, securing his legs together. The maid then clipped his wrists together before him with a pair of steel hand-cuffs, whipped up his long pink skirt and frilly white petticoats and drew down his lace knickers to reveal his white, bared, boyish bottom. 'I am going to give you twelve good hard strokes of the birch on your bare bottom. It will leave marks and it will make you cry but bear it as bravely as you can and that will be the end of the punishment. Head down! Lie still! And,' she tapped his buttocks with her birch, 'present your bottom properly for punishment.' The young man began to whimper. 'If I were you, young man, I should save my breath.' Her first stroke landed and he writhed upon the block, weals gently rising upon his bum cheeks.

'Up again!' she commanded as the three ladies sniggered. She thrust out her bottom majestically, rustled her skirts with her left hand, then brought the birch down with a whistling hiss to make his buttocks jump. 'Measured strokes,' she murmured, 'whose force is partly dictated and controlled by the weight of the descending rod. One should thrash the target with a good portion of one's strength of arm.' On the third stroke, his bottom started to glow as it writhed.

'Serve him right,' said Ada Leverson, smiling all the while.

'Indeed,' said Mrs Smythe, who appeared to be giving a lecture on the romance of chastisement. 'When administering this sort of birching, remember that you are emulating the Goddess, who favours this position for dealing with a naughty Cupid.' The birch hissed through the air once more and the culprit's bottom executed a naughty dance. 'Be regal and firm,' she continued calmly. 'Deal with the matter almost as you would a spanking, except that there is always a note of extra formality present when the birch is employed.' Her fifth stroke raised a squeal in addition to a weal. 'A good birch can be as accurately applied as a cane,' she continued with maddening calm as the audience of ladies visibly squeezed their thighs together beneath their petticoats. On the sixth stroke, they all crossed their legs tightly and looked longingly at one another.

'The spray covers more ground,' Mrs Smythe continued, 'and the effect of this most ancient of rods is a perfect combination of smacking and lashing!' Her seventh stroke made her victim's bottom lurch crazily from left to right and back again as the three lady witnesses laughed. 'Ha! The intriguing phenomenon of "the dancing bottom"! You see,' she dealt the eighth stroke which made his jerking bottom shift up and down, 'instead of a single, sharp weal, there are a greater number of finer, fainter weals, and a great deal more blushing, over a far wider area.' The ninth stroke made the penitent's arse shoot diagonally to the left then downward to the right. 'It is the most profound of chastisements.'

The tenth stroke evoked a severe jiggling of a sorely red bottom.

'Are you sorry, now?' Ada 'The Sphinx' Leverson called out.

'Yes, I'm sorry, Madam,' the culprit sobbed, 'well and truly sorry.'

'You had better be,' snapped Joan Smythe, 'for such impertinent insolence to a lady.' Her eleventh stroke drew a cry from him as Candida Lauderdale and Amelia Edwards giggled with pleasure.

'That'll teach him a lesson,' said Candida.

'It's about time that he submitted to women,' Amelia declared prissily.

The twelfth and final stroke of the birch saw the young man weep with pain as his bottom shot everywhere that was not tied down.

'Do not be dismayed by the apparently severe physical effects,' Mrs Smythe said calmly. 'The flush will fade within an hour and even the worst of the weals will be gone within two days.'

The culprit whimpered and cried upon the block as the ladies cracked open a bottle of champagne and toasted the punishing work of Mrs Joan Smythe, regarding the young man's twitching, glowing, scarlet bottom with visible sexual pleasure.

'It would be unreasonable, wouldn't it,' Joan Smythe

laughed, 'to proceed to the next stage until the culprit can speak coherently?' As the young man's buttocks, all purple and scarlet, continued to twitch with the pain of his chastisement, Joan and Ada embraced to kiss one another's protuberant breasts as Candida and Amelia also kissed, touching the curves of each other's beautiful bottoms.

Now Mrs Smythe stood up once more. I have always noted that dominant woman love to thrust out their buttocks defiantly as if to say: 'Kiss my arse,' and she was no exception. The maid untied the gently sobbing culprit. Slowly he arose from the flogging block and turned to face her.

'Now make the final act of contrition,' Mrs Smythe said sternly.

'I thank you must humbly for the whipping you have given me,' he responded, then knelt and kissed the rod.

'Do you worship the Goddess in her Triple manifestation?' Joan Smythe demanded.

'Yes, Madam, I worship the Goddess in Her every manifestation . . .' he sobbed.

'Then I forgive you. You may kiss me.' She turned her voluptuous bottom towards him and he had to kiss each cheek and the cleft between through the soft silk of her black dress. 'You may arise and tidy your clothes. Now go and stand in the corner.' He obeyed. 'Face to the wall. Hands behind your back. Mary!' The maid came and her hands flickered up beneath his feminine attire to draw his lace knickers down to his ankles. 'Now raise your skirts and petticoats to display your punished bottom for the delectation of ladies whom you have offended.' He submitted to this indignity and the ladies cooed with delight over the sight of a birched, petticoated and wholly subjugated male. 'You will stand there and reflect upon your misdeeds and your sexual misbehaviour as we watch your bottom change colour,' Joan Smythe chortled, 'and then you will spend all evening, when we are ready, in service to us.'

With that, all the ladies embraced one another with quite extraordinary lasciviousness. I was eager to watch further but just then, the lights in my room behind the two-way mirror went out and a huge, fat woman entered the room.

'That's it,' she said. 'It's time for you to go.'

'But I'd like to say goodbye to my hostess . . .'

'She says goodbye to you.'

'If money's a problem . . .'

'It's not a problem,' the huge maid shot back. 'You're welcome again but it's time for you to go now.' There was clearly no advantage to be gained by arguing. 'The cab's all ready for you' she added.

As I went home in the cab I mused over Mrs Joan Smythe and her three lady friends of my acquaintanceship who worshipped the Goddess in their strange way. I reflected that Joan Smythe was also known in other circles as Arabella Mornington-Stuart.

I also thought about the male who had been humiliated and birched. It was Sir Richard 'Spank 'em' Bellingham.

CHAPTER TWENTY-SEVEN

How I love it when it rains in the morning! I can look out of my bow-window and watch all the damn people getting wet as the butler brings me my breakfast tray and my morning post along with my newspaper. I never address my morning's literature, though, without taking a hearty breakfast. Usually I enjoy porridge with treacle and cream in the winter months and Scottish kippers in the Summer. Bacon and eggs with kidneys and a fried tomato are usually best after that, I find, and there has to be plenty of hot toast with deep yellow Welsh butter to go with it. Then, over strong Ceylon Orange Pekoe tea and more toast with butter and bitter orange marmalade from Seville, I can peruse my morning newspaper and my correspondence in peace and quiet.

There was very little of interest in the paper other than a report that we were becoming involved in some utterly pointless and entirely stupid war against some primitive tribe called 'Boers' in the wilds of South Africa. The next letter brought news from the City that my shares in gold and diamonds had doubled in value. This was good news but I was given much more pleasure by noticing that the next two envelopes were respectively from Rosemary and Claire.

Rosemary's last account of her stay at Whitby Bay had left her helpless underneath the kitchen table being fucked by the cadaverous Douglas Foster, son of Dr Foster with whom she had been staying. My Document 272 omits her twittering about trivialities and begins at a moment when they are in bed together:

' "Can I be your queen, nymphet and beautiful Jezebel?" I requested, for I felt so shameless.

'He did fuck me, caress me and kiss me. However, I found it somewhat strange that he wanted to nibble upon my neck. Sometimes it would just be a light bite and then every once in a while I felt as if he were nipping in search of my jugular vein. At around midnight, I did not want to rest for a while but upon his insistence, we proceeded to enjoy a nightcap. We squeezed our bodies together, this strange young man and I, and he told me more tales of his family. I was so intrigued. He mentioned a castle, which I believe was in Transylvania and spoke to me of Vlad the Impaler, also quoting to me from the old family friend, Bram Stoker "What manner of man is this, or what manner of creature is it in the semblance of man?"

'I looked upon my lover and began to wonder. There was undeniably an air of arrogance upon his face and I knew again that his desire was to dominate me. I looked upon his pale face and, following his courteous request, proceeded to fondle his cock. He was aroused within a matter of seconds and once more I sucked his member as he penetrated my throat. There was a throb, another stiff throb and then yet more throbbing. He was endeavouring to ram his stiff rampaging penis down my gullet as I sucked on him like a bee greedy for honey, at the same time gently fingering his testicles. We were both rampant with desire and I increased his by pushing him away.

' "Please fuck me," I pleased. As his penis entered my vagina, the pulsation was as great as any I have experienced between my thighs. How he did fuck me! We both

came several times by the early hours of the morning, I was feeling rather exhausted and fell asleep in his arms. There was great comfort in our embrace as I whispered into his ear:

' "Can I be your concubine?"

' "Yes, oh yes, definitely, yes." I fell asleep, deeply desiring his continued presence, yet when I awoke in the morning, he was gone.

'Now, this had been an extraordinary sexual encounter. I did not mind the bite on my throat at all, for it could be easily covered with a silken scarf; and I hope that he did not mind the teeth marks I had left in his flesh. However, there was a curious sequel.

'When Dr Foster returned from his many labours of medicine and charity and I praised his courteous son, he turned slightly pale and said that he did not know what I was talking about. As far as he was concerned, he had no son and I must have confused the matter for it could have been one of the farm labourers playing a joke upon me – hardly likely, I thought, in view of the man's dress and manners. Yet my subsequent interrogation of the maid who had admitted him elicited nothing other than stammered words. She purported not to know anything other than that he was a long-standing friend of the family.

'I put this to Dr Foster.

' "A friend of the family, oh yes," he responded gruffly, raising a tumbler of malt whisky to his lips. Suddenly, he burst into song.

' "Doctor Foster
Went to Gloucester
In a shower of rain.
He stepped in a puddle
Right up to his middle
And never went back again."

'After that, he drained his glass, sighed very heavily indeed, as though he were the Dr Frankenstein who had created a monster, and went up to bed.'

I called for more thick-cut marmalade and another pot of tea as I spread lashings of butter on my toast. Hot white toast is always the best, I say. A moment later, I knifed through the envelope from Claire:

My darling Horby,

At the present time, as you know, I am suffering from stress. Upon the recommendation of my mother, I felt it was essential to leave Paris for Vienna where I would find one of the greatest mental specialists in the world, Doctor Sigmund Freud.

How I craved to be in Vienna, that legendary city of art, literature, culture and Gemütlicheit. *The waltzes of Strauss hummed in my head along with visual images of the blue Danube and of the Black Forest, as I sat in my compartment entering notes into my diary. In the background there was that lovely rhythmic sound, so hypnotic, of the train wheels clattering over the railway tracks.*

Even though I was the only passenger in the compartment, I began to feel oppressed. I opened the curtains and the windows and removed my hat. I was feeling so constrained by my corset of dreadful whalebone stays. I unbuttoned the top of my blouse. To any casual observer, I would have appeared to be a capricious, licentious, lewd, unchaste and lascivious young woman. I unlaced my boots and removed my hot damp knickers. Would brilliant, young Dr Sigmund Freud be willing to see me? I wondered. I have seen a photograph of him and he is a gentleman who has often wandered through my dreams and fantasies. I longed to lie upon his couch feeling sleepy, languid and lethargic. There would, I knew, be so much to see in Vienna.

LATER

I have at last arrived in Vienna, my darling, and what a dreamlike city it is! There is music in the air as I wander the streets and travel idly upon the trams. Today I went to visit the Winter Riding School, which was originally built by Emanuel Fischer von Erlach. It is also known as The Spanish Riding School on account of the Hapsburg connection between Austria and Spain. I witnessed the haute école *performance of the Libizza stallions. These are a gorgeous cross-breed of Andalusian, Arab and Neapolitan horses, bred not only for battle but also for equine ballet. It was pleasing to be invited to one of their functions. I met a beautiful young man there. How gorgeous he looked in his riding attire: a double-breasted jacket, skin-tight white britches and highly polished knee-length riding boots of black leather!*

I was fascinated by these stallions, absolutely fascinated. 'Why are they so white?' I queried.

'They were not born white,' the charming Arch-Duke and heir to the Empire, Francis Ferdinand replied. 'Only the best are chosen. Most are born black or grey. Within a year, if their skin does not change, they must be discarded.'

'Have any of these horses been gelded?'

'Certainly not!' His Imperial Highness responded indignantly. 'This is The Spanish Riding School, after all.' He snorted at the thought. 'Perhaps you would care to view my own principal stallion?'

He led me up a staircase and onto a balcony from which one regarded a panoply of sand. I fear I paid little attention to the chandeliers and mosaics in the chamber behind me. A pure white stallion was led into the pit below by a sturdy groom.

'Is it necessary,' I asked, 'that their eyes be blinkered?'

'Only in the beginning.'

'Are those hoofs cloven?'

'Definitely not,' was his answer. Then he led me away from the balcony and into his chamber, calling loudly for coffee. It came laced with whipped cream and a scattering of chocolate flakes. The maid also added a slight sprinkling of cinnamon and nutmeg. Beside our cups, two generous glasses of brandy reposed.

'Put your cup down,' he sighed. I responded willingly as he began to caress and suck my tender ear-lobes. His tongue positively throbbed *into my ear. Then he threw himself upon me.*

'This is Vienna,' he breathed heavily, 'the city of Mozart and Strauss. Can you not hear it in the air? Stay with me this evening. Tomorrow I shall show you secrets of our magnificent city.' He had crisp cotton sheets upon his bed and as we lay down next to one another, I knew that his libido had been aroused. He was so concupiscent, lustful, lickerish and altogether goatish, adding to my own dreamy state of libertarian licentiousness. I did so much want to fornicate with this exquisite member of royalty.

Suddenly he entered me. My juices were running freely as I accepted his member so willingly – and how he did throb! He sucked upon my breasts and then rubbed his head between them, making me feel so motherly momentarily. As he continued to fuck me like a howitzer, I ran my fingers up and down his spine. I wanted to tease and yet delight this lascivious young man.

'I am the best, the best!' he cried out as he came, then panted: 'I am superior, supreme beyond belief. Have you ever experienced anything more superlative than this?'

I had, actually, but thought it unkind to tell him so since so far he had certainly been very good.

'Would you not say,' he continued remorselessly, 'that my prick is not just a Prince, not just an Arch-Duke, it is,' he thrust hard, his royal member stiffening again, 'every inch a King, no?!'

'I cannot deny it,' I replied, for I wanted him to come again. That was just as well, for this time his every penetrating thrust was deeper than the last one, touching even the inward lips of my womb. Every single pore of my skin was aroused and even my toes were twitching. Abruptly he grabbed my hands and held them above my head. I felt deliciously imprisoned in a state of constraint. Our fingers interlaced in our conjoinment. His orgasm was magnificent! Oh! What gratification, what bliss and such euphoria we both enjoyed as he spurted forth within my perfumed garden of sensual delights!

Finally we fell asleep. I lay abed on my dreamy awakening in the early hours and thought of Mozart, now no doubt in residence amongst the angels. As the Arch-Duke Francis Ferdinand stirred lazily into renewed life, he muttered something about taking me to the State Opera House. I relapsed into a dream state in which my lever was taking me down the beautiful blue Danube, accompanied by the music of Johann Strauss. Shakespeare has written: 'To sleep, perchance to dream.' How lucky I was to enjoy both!

For some hours I drifted in and out of this deliciously somnolent state, but at some point I was aroused by a slight tickle. My eyes flickered and then I was aware that my beautiful lover was still in my arms. I submitted so willingly to the caresses of his eager hands. I gasped as his stiff shaft penetrated me once more. Thrust! Thrust! Thrust! And how his tongue did tease my nipples!

'More! Please, more!' I shrieked with delight. It felt as though his tongue was everywhere upon the delicate skin of my upper body. I came so quickly when I allowed his forefinger to penetrate my arse. Basking in the euphoria of post-coital glow, I knew that I wanted him to fuck me again.

'You're quite a rampant young filly,' he growled.

'And you're my ribald young stallion,' I replied.

'What would you be if you weren't a lady of leisure?' he enquired. In return I sang:

'I wish I was a pretty little whore.
I'd always be rich and I'd never be poor.
In my pretty little house with my shiny red light
I'd sleep all day and I'd fuck all night.'

He laughed and pinned my shoulders to the bed with a carefree abandonment. What exhilaration and ecstasy there was as he prodded his rod into me once again! I am sure that we attained orgasm simultaneously and I was desirous of more yet wanting also to see the sights of Vienna.

Of course, there could be no one better than the Arch-Duke to guide one through the multifarious delights of the Imperial Palace and to relate the tales of the Holy Roman Empire, although (and obviously I refrained from saying so) it wasn't Holy, it wasn't Roman and it wasn't really much of an Empire. I found his stories of the relics it housed to be rather more enlivening, especially when he showed me the Sword of Charlemagne; and the Spear of the Roman centurion, Longinus, which is alleged to have pierced the side of Jesus Christ on the Cross.

Upon his insistence, we visited St Stephen's Cathedral. He was the first Christian martyr and according to the

Bible, he made such an insufferably long and boring speech that everyone concurred in stoning this insufferable prig to death. Nevertheless, the Cathedral named after him has a gorgeous Gothic tower that raises its eminent head above the city. It aroused me just to look at it. We climbed the steps to its summit to behold an incredible panorama of Vienna. His hand was so gentle upon my shoulder as he pointed out various beauties of the cityscape as his other hand casually fondled my bottom.

'There, mein liebchen, *is the* Schloss Schonbrunn. *This was the modest summer palace of the Hapsburgs from the late 17th Century onwards. It has merely 1400 rooms.' I was so glad that there were merely the two of us at the top of this magnificent tower, gazing upon this inspiring vista. My aesthetic joys were unbounded as he pointed out a wide variety of sights and then lifted my frock to shove his stiff member into my bottom, having an instant earlier taken the necessary step of whipping my knickers down to my knees. We went up against the tower wall like dogs for a quick bum-fuck that was so rapid and frigging fast, yet when he came within my squeezing anus both of us felt exquisitely good.*

It was a pleasure to accompany this gentleman to what he termed 'a simple local restaurant.' The waiters and waitresses danced attention upon him in this charming and informal establishment. I enjoyed the best Wiener Schnitzel *with roast potatoes and* weinkraut *followed by apple* strudel *that I have ever tasted. A cheerful flask of young red wine was a perfect accompaniment, especially since it was followed by the largest glasses of brandy that I have ever enjoyed.*

He informed me that he had matters of State to which he was compelled to address his attention and so one of his carriages delivered me back to my hotel. Before I depart into a deep slumber, I think also of you and your phallus. I am loving my time in Vienna and yet I yearn, desire and hanker after you. I miss you so much and yet realise that there remains a long, difficult and laborious journey of self-discovery before me. I am so glad that I have a private sleeping compartment within the privacy of my own mind. Without contact with you, Life would be virtually unendurable in these exquisitely private moments. I lust after you and crave for your arms and your loving.

All my love
Claire.

As I finished my breakfast, I wondered briefly if healthy women ever truly thought about anything other than sex. And then, of course, sitting here all these decades later, still enjoying my tea and toast and marmalade, I recall that the Arch-Duke Francis Ferdinand, of whom Claire wrote, had been assassinated in Bosnia in 1914, to trigger off The Great War.

We had no inklings of forthcoming horrors in those spacious days, no, no. I believe that after breakfast on the morning that I received these charming letters from Rosemary and Claire, I passed the day enjoying the great luxury and blessing of idleness, concerning which so much cant and false doctrine have been preached. Probably I spent hours in my library, perusing my collection of erotic literature. In any event, my Document 272 notes that the next communication from Claire arrived courtesy of late afternoon post, which indicates that I must have rung for tea at five-thirty. Darjeeling is best at this time of day, I find, and I like it accompanied by thin cucumber sandwiches, scones with butter, raspberry jam and Cornish clotted cream and a light strawberry tart or chocolate éclair.

A letter from Claire in Vienna came with these delights. Now, in those days it really was the *Royal* Mail Service. I don't know what it's coming to in these damn benighted days. It seems as though nothing bloody works properly any more in this preposterous decade of the Twenties, even though the Thirties will probably be worse. I don't like the sound of that ranting fat lunatic in Italy, Mussolini, and I forecast that he is a portent of worse things to come. This is what happens when the ignorant are allowed a say in politics. They'll elect any illiterate brute who reflects their worst aspirations. Now in my day . . . but I digress. Let us turn to Claire's subsequent letter. I shall omit her preliminary pleasantries as not being germane to the narrative in hand:

. . . and then I had my consultation with Dr Freud. He is an extraordinary man, wiry in build, bearded and most energetic, pacing fiercely up and down the room as I lay upon his leather couch and waving his glasses in the air quite frantically.

'Zo, vas iss your trouble?' he asked in that charming Viennese accent of his.

'I don't have any, to my knowledge,' I replied. 'My mother just thought it might be a good idea if I came to see you. Anyway, if I do have a trouble, surely it's your job to tell me what it is?'

'Ach, zo,' he muttered and made a note. 'Patient resistance.'

'I don't know about that, Dr Freud,' I replied. 'You strike me as being a pretty good fuck.'

He blushed furiously and turned his back.

'Zo,' he said, 'zo you do not think that you zuffer from ze sexual repression?'

'Not at all, Dr Freud,' I returned dreamily. 'When are

you going to put your throbbing hot cock within my warm moist cunt?'

'Sexual hysteria . . .' he muttered.

'Oh, yes . . .' I sighed in answer.

'I shall spank you, you naughty girl.' He turned towards me and waved an admonishing finger.

'Oh, yes . . .' I giggled. 'When?' He sighed once more and turned his back, crossing his hands behind him.

'Clearly not ze Electra complex,' I overheard him mumble to himself. He shook his head in puzzlement, then reached for a small steel phial on his mantlepiece, opening this to tip out a quantity of white, grainy powder onto the clip-board upon which he had been making notes. I watched with considerable fascination as he chopped up this mysterious powder with a cut-throat razor then, taking a slim hollow tube from the mantelpiece, inhaled a small pile alternately through each nostril.

'Ach!' He grinned with pleasure. 'Das ist richtig!'

'What are you doing, Dr Freud?' I queried.

'Cocaine,' he replied. 'It is a wonderful white powder which we have from the coca leaf of Peru, Bolivia and Columbia. It kills pain,' he felt his jaw thoughtfully, 'and it is invaluable for stimulating the brain and the central nervous system.'

'Can I try some?'

'Of course, my dear. This may assist our dialogue.'

He chopped up two piles for me as though he were a well-seasoned practitioner at this game. I promptly inhaled them. Certainly this cocaine substance cleared my sinuses and I was conscious of a euphoric effect, not unlike the sort of thing you might feel if you were having sex on your own.

'Dr Freud,' I said, 'just what are these theories of yours

that have made you so unpopular? Why, I've heard that you're a danger to society.'

'Not at all, Madam,' he answered briskly as he resumed his intense pacing of the room. 'My theories are simple. First, zere is zumzing within you which is like a rampaging beast with every animal desire. Zis I call ze libido*, ze unconscious mind, or in my presently developing theory, ze* id. *Zen, zere is zumzing zat represses zis, zumzing zat zes ziz is wrong. Ze Christians call zis ze conscience. It is ze result of education in society. My term here is* super-ego. *These forces of unrestrained animal instinct and societal constraint fight a continuous battle within the human psyche.' His dark eyes were so active and alive at that moment. 'Well, zere has to be a mediator, no?' he smiled delightfully, 'otherwise we would all go insane. And it is* rationality *which I call the* ego. *My theoretical work consists of an endeavour to comprehend how these three factors function within the individual and within society. My practical work consists of applying my discoveries in order to assist my fellow human beings.'*

'Admirable, Dr Freud,' I said, 'wholly admirable.' He tweaked his moustache and preened himself.

'I am execrated by many members of society because of my adherence to the truth of my sexual theory,' Freud insisted fiercely. 'Believe me, the roots of all of our thoughts are sexual. We must never abandon the sexual theory!' His voice resounded throughout the room. 'For,' he added darkly, 'if we do, we will be engulfed in a black tidal wave of occultism.'

'But Dr Freud,' I said, 'isn't your idea of these rapacious animal instincts that have to be repressed just the same as the Christian doctrine of Original Sin? I wonder why they call you a danger to society.' I laughed. 'You are not a threat at all.'

'You are a very strange woman,' he replied. 'Ve-ry strange.'

'Dr Freud,' I pleaded with him, 'you are such an intelligent man. Your theories really will advance human knowledge, I am sure of it. I especially endorse your insistence on your sexual theory. You're right! Are you any good in bed?'

'When I am aroused,' he answered, 'and when there is cocaine in my blood, then I come to my wife like a lion.' He looked so sincere and intense at that moment but I could not resist the temptation of tempting him. 'Mr Medicine Man,' I sighed as I shifted my thighs and allowed my skirts to rustle, 'come show me your sexual theory by leaping on me, you lithe, lean body of muscle.'

'Zis is a most gracious invitation, my dear, but as a married man I must regretfully decline it,' he explained apologetically as there came a knock upon the door. 'Now were I single, it might be a different story . . . yes, vas ist das?'

'Sigmund,' came a gentle female voice, 'when will the session end? I have your favourite chicken soup with kreplach for your lunch and I have made especially for you your beloved gefillte fish and there is chopped liver also if you want it.'

'Ah! Delicious!' Freud exclaimed. 'My darling, I will be with you shortly. And you, my dear,' he put on his glasses to give me a severe "intellectual" look, 'you must come again zo zat we may continue zis most interesting analysis. I don't know quite who is being analysed,' he chuckled as he escorted me to the front door, 'you or me.'

'You're such a clever man, Dr Freud,' I said. 'If only you'd just let me suck your cock!' As he went back to his chicken soup, he wore the expression of a worried retriever.

Now, Dr Freud is certainly a very intelligent man and in my opinion, His Imperial Highness, Franz Ferdinand, is rather stupid, yet I received more pleasure from my evening with the latter. I knew I'd made a sensible decision when His Imperial Highness knelt on the carpet in front of me and began to lick my thighs whilst his hands pulled my bottom closer to him. I rested my hands on the top of his head as he forced his face further into my moist depths, working his tongue in deeper and deeper as he searched for my fleshy clitty. When he found it, he kissed and sucked this ambrosial morsel which sent me into a series of sensual spasms and I purred like a kitten as he worked his tongue all around my love button, which was ever so erect.

'Aaah!' I screamed out as, with a tremendous heave, I worked myself off on his tongue, drenching his face with my cuntal emission in a shuddering orgasm; and I was delighted to observe that he greedily gulped down my piquant love juices. 'Fuck me,' I pleaded.

He raised himself on top of me and I grabbed hold of his stiff cock, the better to place it by the opening mouth of my honeypot. He eased his prick forward and let his knob slide between my clinging cunny-lips. Once firmly esconced inside me, he began pumping in and out of my sopping slit and I clamped my hands around his neat, tight bum, pulling him forward so that every last inch of his shaft was crammed inside my cunt. Our pubic bones mashed together and I started to move my hips up and down in time with his own thrusts, and soon enough his shaft was slithering in and out of my avid vagina at a great rate of knots. Our movements speeded up even more until I felt the sperm bubbling up in his balls and with a gasp, he shot a raging torrent of sticky seed into my love channel.

Dear God! What a wonderful fuck! He slammed his shaft back and forth until he had emptied his balls and then I requested him to rest, which he did, lying on top of me with his head down on my soft bosoms whilst I played gently with his exhausted, limp prick.

Well, Horby, as you can discern, Vienna is a most interesting city and I intend to stay here for a while. Perhaps you might care to come and visit me. I think of you fondly always.

All my love,
Claire.

I smiled fondly as I put down her letter. Solitary afternoon tea would never be quite the same again.

CHAPTER TWENTY-EIGHT

'*Of course* I enjoy a good birching, Horby!' Sir Richard Bellingham exclaimed. 'Don't you? Frankly, I don't care if it's my bum that's being birched or some delicious little female botty that I'm birching. Great heavens, man, it's all in fun. And let's not forget that pink rosy bottoms make for a damn good fuck!' He sat back contentedly, as though his arse was even then glowing pleasantly, and grinned cheerfully. 'If I'm going to be birched, don't mind if I wear ladies' garb, quite frankly. Find it adds extra spice and all that. Another drink?'

I had no cause for regret in accepting Bellingham's invitation to dine with him. He had chosen 'Barter's', an oyster bar just off Victoria. Barter's was in fact an offshoot of 'White's Noted Oysters' and offered the finest in plain wood surroundings. I was perfectly contented to drink malt whisky with him as we awaited the arrival of two men who had been described to me by Bellingham as 'my mystery guests.' 'Always have the best! Cheers!' Bellingham declared heartily. 'Bottoms up and all that! Money . . .' he grumbled, suddenly moody. 'Don't like the stuff, actually, but it calms my nerves. I know what I need. I need a good sinecure. Nearly had that one once. Did I ever tell you about the time that I was appointed a Sex Adviser? No?

'Well,' he continued, 'there was Mr Cohen and Mr Levy and a Mr Goodheart here, namely me. Mr Cohen said: "I like this proposition and I am putting up ten thousand pounds." Mr Levy said: "I like this proposition and I am putting up twenty thousand pounds." I said: "Well, I'm jolly well putting up a hundred thousand." We went away, they organised whatever and we all came back for our next business meeting. Mr Cohen said: "I have put up ten thousand pounds so I shall be the Chairman." Mr Levy said: "I have put up twenty thousand pounds so I shall be the Managing Director." I said: "What about me?" "You," Cohen and Levy turned to me with arms outstretched and genial grins, "why, you will be The Sex Adviser." "Sex Adviser?" I queried. "Yes," said Cohen and Levy, "when we want your fucking advice, we'll ask for it." '

'Are you serious?' I chuckled.

'I never am,' he replied. 'Ah!' his eyes flickered towards the door of the oyster bar. 'Yes, yes, yes . . .' he rose to greet Arthur Machen, who was in the process of having his cloak removed. I always found it a joy to see Machen apart from his occasionally infuriating Welsh habit of spending the first ten minutes on customary courtesies. Mind you, one cannot criticise his courtesy, which is all too rare in this day and age. Whenever Arthur Machen said 'How are you?' he really expected one to tell him and he always listened with the utmost interest. Whenever Arthur Machen said 'Thank you' for passing the salt, it sounded as though he really meant it.

Unfortunately, he did not look like a particularly happy man on this particular evening as he stared morosely into his glass of white port and I was aware of the reason: his beloved wife, the actress Amy Hogg, had died recently.

'Strange days,' I heard Machen murmur. Bellingham looked surprisingly sympathetic.

'What are you working on now, Machen?' Bellingham asked.

'It has the provisional working title of *The White People*,' Machen responded thoughtfully. 'It is about Witchcraft and sexuality told from the point of view of a child-like and disconnected mind.'

'Well, that sounds jolly interesting,' Sir Richard declared uneasily. 'Ah! Crowley! Late as usual, eh?'

I was astonished to see Crowley joining us since neither Bellingham nor Machen liked him but as usual, the man seemed to be utterly unconcerned. He greeted everyone cordially and we all acquiesced in taking platters of three dozen Colchesters and three dozen Whitstables with another three dozen Limerick oysters for good luck. Lemon and hot pepper sauce are the essential accompaniments along with much buttered thin brown bread. Bellingham properly ordered pints of stout, in case one wanted that, and a couple of bottles of ice-cold Gewürtztraminer.

'I adore oysters!' Sir Richard exclaimed enthusiastically. 'They remind me so much of women's cunts.'

'True enough,' said Machen, 'but let us not forget that they are also oysters. Also that they may be the symbol of something divine.' Crowley nodded slightly but approvingly.

'Oh, you mean the pearl?' Bellingham retorted, his bushy eye-brows raised. 'Yes, pearls do look rather divine draped around the slim white neck of a woman one is fucking.'

'To an Initiate,' said Crowley, 'Holy Mass can be the same as fornicating with a prostitute.'

'Trust you to say something so crass,' Machen commented acidly. Bellingham beamed broadly. He had brought these two men together for the pleasure of seeing them clash.

'And trust you to comment so acidly,' Crowley responded levelly. 'I've never understood why you dislike me so much, Machen, especially since I can say, without any intent to flatter, that I am a strong and genuine admirer of your work.'

'You profane the sacred,' Machen returned.

'How so?' Crowley looked all pained innocence as Bellingham and I slurped our oysters. Yes, they were almost as delicious as cunts.

'I did not like,' Machen stated, 'your behaviour to a friend of mine, Mr Crowley. Oh, and kindly don't look so innocent, you know perfectly well what you've done. I have this friend, a good artist once upon a time, and a happily married man, who visited a small town in Wales in order to undertake a week's sketching. At his small hotel, he met a man – we shall call him Smith – who proved to be excellent company and to whom he rhapsodised about the virtues of his wife. Smith meanwhile delighted him with his powers of dazzling mimicry. He was some sort of an actor by trade, apparently.

'Well,' Machen downed his pint of stout swiftly and replaced it on the table with a resounding thump, 'Smith left the hotel. My friend left one day later. His train was held up by about five minutes just prior to entering Paddington Station. A train went the other way, and he could have sworn that he had seen the face of Smith, only he had shaved off his beard and now looked the very spitting image of my friend. When he arrived home the maid greeted him as if he had returned the previous night and had just gone out for a stroll. So did his wife. His cigarette case, which had mysteriously gone missing during his sojourn in Wales, was resting comfortably on the marital bedside table.

'It's sad,' Machen sighed. 'He gave up painting altogether and disappeared, some said to America. His wife was dead within a year and some said it was suicide. Are you proud of what you did, Crowley?'

'Is this accusation true?' I demanded.

'Oh, absolutely true and no question about it at all,' Crowley answered. 'Yes, I fucked that bitch.' Machen looked quite white with fury. 'But I suppose that you, Machen, thought that in her reposed some lie known as "the purity of Womanhood".' His voice was as a sharp sneer. 'You see, I knew her when she was a student of Art paying for her studies via prostitution, and I couldn't resist having a fuck with her for old times' sake, especially given the fact that her husband was such an ugly, old, untalented, staid, semi-impotent Royal Academician. All right, the dismal old fart gave up painting. That's a mercy on the human race. And actually she didn't kill herself. You're being far too sentimental for the sake of fiction. The last letter I had from her, why, the dear girl was running a successful brothel in San Francisco, California.'

'You broke up a happy marriage, Crowley,' Machen stated patiently.

'It couldn't've been that happy,' Crowley returned acerbically, 'if all it took to break them up was some nonsense that was no more than another branch of athletics.'

'Is absolutely nothing sacred to you . . .?' Machen sighed.

'I can make the profane sacred,' Crowley riposted.

'No, you can't,' Machen returned. 'I don't deny that everything you touch turns into gold. It's just that it's Fool's Gold and will vanish in the morning.'

'You obviously speak with the bitterness of experience,' Crowley replied, 'and your own is valid for you. I think you're a shrinking violet at heart.' Machen blanched. 'I am not. I essay every experience. If I am a fool, then I am a bloody fool and I spell it with a capital "F".'

'Well spoken, sir,' Sir Richard Bellingham applauded.

'Can't stand you, Crowley, but it can't be denied that you do talk some sense on occasion.' He slurped another oyster with evident enjoyment and quaffed some wine. 'Anyway, gentlemen, sorted out your fucking for this evening?'

'Yes,' said Crowley.

'I have an assignation,' said Machen.

'Glad to hear it!' Sir Richard roared. 'So do I. How about you, Horby?'

'The same,' I said. Actually I was lying. What I really wanted, for once, was a quiet evening at home. The trouble is that one can never tell other men that or they might think that one is peculiar. If I needed a fuck later that night, I could always take my carriage to the Haymarket but at that moment, despite the invigorating effect of the oysters, I just wanted some time to myself. We had coffee and brandy and departed on our separate ways.

My quiet evening enjoying the pleasures of solitude? Alas, it was not to be. I arrived home to be presented with Rosemary's calling card, urgently requesting that she see me tonight. The message on the card did not say why but I felt that I could not let her down and so ordered the carriage for a journey to her home in St John's Wood. Although her hospitality was of its customary excellence, it turned out that there was no emergency at all. Although Rosemary enjoyed the pleasures of solitude, she also abhorred the pains of loneliness and simply needed a friend to whom she could talk. Eventually, over her exquisite vintage Armagnac, I asked her to continue with her story of the mysterious and cadaverous young man up in Whitby.

'He was such a beautiful young man,' she said dreamily. 'I really enjoyed being fucked by him. It was so obvious that he was an experienced squire of dames, a Lothario, a Don Juan and actually something of a vampire, though that did not frighten me since I have similar tendencies myself.

'I could not resist comparing him with the elderly gentleman he declared to be his father and who had denied all knowledge of him. The old man was definitely so knowledgeable and possessed of a most caring and considerate nature which I did truly appreciate, yet his alleged 'son' was like a rampant young stallion. How he has shoved his ramrod into me! I knew that I was meant to be his concubine. How he did titillate me so as to arouse my juices!

'The last time I fucked with him, his beautiful phallus kept on probing every inmost recess of my cunt. My difficulty was that I did not wish to be perceived as being a woman of easy virtue. I think he had encountered many a young hussy during his life and I did not intend to be just another notch-mark on the barrel of his gun.

' "You must come to my castle," he requested. "It is so beautiful and there are so many exquisite rooms. Please: come to my castle."

' "Where is your castle?" I enquired.

' "I have two," he replied. "One is in Transylvania. But the other, just outside Vienna, is most pleasant at this time of year."

' "Can I come and visit you there?"

' "Yes, if you behave yourself."

' "But I already have."

' "No," he replied, "you have not."

'He gazed at me fiercely.

' "I must spank you," he pronounced solemnly, "as you have been a very naughty girl. I am a Count and I demand some visible respect." He seized my wrists and held them by the golden bed-stead above my head.

' "You are hurting me!" I cried out to no avail. He responded by prodding his thick, throbbing rod into me.

' "My darling, you have no understanding of the true

meaning of pain but as you are so beautiful, I shall not overdo the measure of grief I intend." I was amazed that this beautiful young man could copulate whilst carrying on a most bizarre conversation. His rod was giving me a curious mixture of tenderness and pain. He began to nibble my neck and whispered sweet nothings, all the while squeezing me within his arms.

'Then it was as if time were standing still. There was no longer any conversation between us. How he caressed my quim! It was apparent that my strange lover was reaching the point of orgasm. At the instant that he shot his seed into me, his forefinger penetrated my anus and my hands reached for his testicles. What a glorious spending there was!

'Unexpectedly, he removed his prick from my cunt and I saw that it was rising again with rapidity for he forced it into my mouth. I took his pulchritudinous member deep into my throat and how I did suck on it. As Shakespeare says, "Where the bee sucks there suck I." It was apparent that there was still quite some juice left. I tickled his member with my tongue, forcing him to release his sperm with an expiring gasp so I could take his seed right down my throat.

'I then allowed his tongue to enter my quim. How rampant was my lover! – yet there was a strange and peculiar element about our mating. It seemed that he could continue for hours and yet there was something macabre, eerie, weird, unearthly, eldritch even, about this encounter. Yes, there was something untoward. After a while, I stood up in front of the looking-glass as I wanted to rearrange my hair, so as to match my lover's inimitable elegance. Was it my imagination or could I not see his reflection? The thought was swept from my mind by the feel of his arms around my waist and I knew that his fire had been kindled once more. Yes, the sensation was glorious as he took me standing up and from behind yet when I looked into the mirror, once again, all I could see was me. If I stared ahead, I could not see him reflected, but I could feel his penis thrusting inside me. For no reason, I began to cry, weep, and caterwaul.

' "Please, my love, do not cry any more," he whispered softly as he nipped my neck again. "I love you and do not wish to see you in such pain. I will always be here for you." How mesmerising his voice was! "Can't you feel my presence? I will always be here to attend to your needs." We came together in a sensational orgasm and I collapsed back upon his bed.

'How sleepy I was! I was nevertheless also aware of a fluttering of wings and of a cool breeze entering the room with its curtains blowing in the wind. Then there was silence. It was as if black velvet had been draped upon my body. "To sleep, perchance to dream," as the poet has it.'

CHAPTER TWENTY-NINE

'What manner of man is he?' I demanded of Rosemary, who appeared to be enjoying a phantasma of masturbatory lassitude. I noticed the marks on her neck.

'You have met him,' she answered calmly.

'Yes, the man I call "The Black Douglas", though he's certainly a charming host. Unfortunately, all too little is known about the fellow. He claims to be the son of Dr Foster of Whitby yet you inform me that Dr Foster, a randy old goat by your account, denies it. He also claims to be a European count with two castles. Has old Dr Foster been marrying European countesses on the quiet? You also proceed to inform me that he is a wealthy banker of international repute, who is presently lending money to, among others, the Prince of Wales and Lillie Langtry. In addition, you describe in lavish and lustful detail the excellence of his skills as a lover. Who *is* this man?'

'I really don't know,' Rosemary replied honestly, 'but he is rather fascinating, knows how to treat a lady and is a fantastic fuck to boot! But if you want to find out more about him, I can discern an excellent opportunity for so doing. He has invited me to play croquet with him at mixed doubles and to nominate the opposing team. I nominate you and any lady of your choice for the occasion. Anyone in mind, Horby?'

'Too many,' I replied. 'To see or not to see, that is the question.'

'You do make me laugh.' She chortled in her joy. 'Douglas was frightfully cross with me the last time I came over to play croquet though. Well, what d'you expect if he will invite one to play croquet at twilight? He was positively furious about Henry in the bushes.'

'What were you doing with Henry in the bushes?'

'Fucking him, of course, you fool!' she expostulated. 'Really! For a man of your intelligence, you're sometimes quite surprisingly naive. And you know what the moral of the story is?'

'No?'

'Ha! ha!' she kicked up her long lissom legs and giggled. 'The moral is that women have no morals.' She tossed back her Armagnac and poured more generous quantities for both of us. 'But let us to our muttons, or rather, to our lambs.' She gave me a very sharp look. 'Next Saturday at three.'

'Yes,' I said and then flung myself upon the irresistible Rosemary.

'Forbear, you bounder!' she shrieked in mock astonishment. We enjoyed an exceedingly friendly fuck.

'The Black Douglas' had a house on Chiswick Mall, overlooking the River. His front lawn had been manicured quite exquisitely and the croquet hoops were perfectly positioned. For my companion and croquet partner of the day, I had chosen Miss Emily Ward-Bishop, the very proper daughter of a clergyman, principally because I had not yet fucked her and had ambitions in that direction. She was a pretty and prim young woman, with impeccably coiffed chestnut hair, set off to perfection by her straw boater, wearing a tight white blouse and green pleated skirt which did much to adorn the charms of her nubile figure.

'The Black Douglas' gave us a most hospitable welcome, though he was looking leaner and more cadaverous than ever. Rosemary, tightly dressed in shocking pink, appeared to be relishing the occasion.

'I see no point in a game without a wager,' he declared and I promptly proffered a ten thousand pound bet which he accepted. We proceeded to the croquet lawn where all logistics had been immaculately organised. A manservant and maidservant had set up a table on which reposed a silver bowl of cold fruit punch, laced with copious quantities of wine and spirits, for the players to refresh themselves at their will.

'I'm not terribly good at croquet, Horby,' Emily whispered to me. 'And you have bet a tremendous amount. I'll do my best but what happens if I let the side down and we lose?'

'Then I think you'll deserve a jolly sound thrashing,' I responded, and to my delight, this prim young lady giggled.

'Ooooh, yes,' she said. 'Then perhaps I should make sure that we lose.' She tweaked her long skirt and made its pleats flutter demurely.

'You had better not,' I growled, 'or else it will be the most severe and the most expensive spanking that I have ever handed out.'

The afternoon sun, reflected in a brilliant gleam from the river, blazed down upon us as the game began. I have a passion for croquet. It is the epitome of repressed violence. One also enjoys the delectable sight of women bending over, thrusting out their bottoms as their faces evince a fierce determination, just as they sometimes do prior to fucking. Their mallets arise to hit the balls and one is reminded of the clitoris.

Rosemary opened the game with a perfect shot straight

through the first hoop. She swished her skirts airily in triumph. Emily showed that she could play well too, if not as perfectly, for her ball struck the edge of the hoop, then rolled onto the other side. The ball of Douglas bounced off the hoop and so did mine. The ladies both passed their balls through the second hoop and took more punch. Douglas clocked my ball to make croquet, then, placing it behind mine, he made croquet by sending my ball spinning into the stick in the centre, sending me back to start.

'Oh, bad luck, sir!' the bastard sneered as he then proceeded to tap his own ball casually through the first hoop. I set out manfully again, got through the first hoop and endeavoured to do some catching up, so as to assist my partner. Emily did not appear to be in need of my assistance, however. She had executed a perfect croquet upon Rosemary, sending her ball whirling into the rose bushes, before passing through the third hoop. Her excellence of play, or possibly another glass of fruit punch, inspired me to croquet Douglas and send his ball shooting into the compost heap before I passed through the second hoop. 'Oh, bad luck, sir!' I said.

It was an increasingly grim game as afternoon wore on, with many vicissitudes of fortune. Rosemary at one point sent my ball flying into the magnolias but five strokes later, I knocked hers into the rhododendrons. Douglas kept aiming at Emily's ball and missing. He was, however, a very good partner to Rosemary, often making croquet with her ball so as to croquet her into an enviable position. It was an even match which came to its climax at the final hoop, with just the stick to strike after that. There were ten thousand pounds resting upon the matter. Rosemary's ball went through the hoop, as always. Emily's did the same. Douglas looked greedily at my exposed ball but thought better of it and instead passed through the hoop and I chose to imitate his example so as to enjoy a final show-down before the phallic totem pole of the thick, red croquet stick, stuck in the centre of the lawn.

Rosemary swung her mallet. There was a click and her ball hit the stick. That meant that we could no longer win, but we could draw, in which case the bet was off. I felt ready to explode with inner fury as Emily hit her ball and missed the stick. Douglas smiled with snarling satisfaction as his ball hit mine. He took his time placing it carefully, then casually knocked mine into the stick, sending me back to the beginning of the course again. 'Hard cheese, old chap,' he grinned, as his own ball cannoned against the finishing stick.

I felt angry and disconsolate as we returned inside the house. Perhaps it was the effect of the fruit punch, but I felt so furious with Emily and the shot that she had missed, that I seized her and turned her rudely over my knee, whipping up her skirt and petticoats and pulling down her frilly knickers to reveal her satin-smooth white buttocks. Douglas and Rosemary appeared to enjoy the sight as well they might.

'You badly behaved bitch!' I exclaimed, giving her bottom a resounding smack. 'You muffed your shot and let the side down, you naughty girl, so I am going to administer a sound spanking . . .' I smiled. 'All spanking,' I glanced at Rosemary, 'is beneficial. Having her bottom spanked well and in the correct manner brings satisfaction, contentment and well-being. Spanking has an irresistible fascination. It never palls for every spanking is a new experience and no two spankings are alike. The secret of why people enjoy spanking is quite simple. The warmth and tingling generated in the bottom cheeks is delightful.' My hand came down heavily on Emily's upturned arse and she moaned. 'Once experienced, one usually longs for it again. It is quite impossible to describe the sensations produced in the bottom cheeks by a carefully administered spanking, given in a relaxed atmosphere,' I declared as I brought down my hand with an echoing thwack once again. Emily's bottom squirmed and quivered beneath my firm discipline.

'Is there pain in a spanking?' I resumed my discourse, bringing my palm down hard to emphasise my point upon her gradually reddening bottom as Rosemary and Douglas watched with obvious pleasure. 'Yes, there is. However, the pain there is soon enough diminishes and a delightful afterglow replaces it. As the pain goes, warmth comes. There is no gain without some pain.' Emily cried out as my hand once more smacked her firm white buttocks to add a further blushing redness to the mildly blushing cheeks. 'People on the whole put up with much greater pain than that experienced in spanking for far less enjoyment.

'There are many degrees of severity,' I continued remorselessly with another hard smack that made her bottom wriggle and writhe. 'It may be summarily administered with much sound and fury; or laid on in silence with due solemnity after a grave admonition. A good spanking is the archetypal "nursery" form of punishment.' I smacked Emily hard again and she squealed. 'A man should just stiffen his hand into a flexible punishing surface and apply it again and again – and again, for good measure – to the increasingly rosy bottom of a squalling and writhing culprit sprawled upon his lap, *sans pantalon et sans dignité*.'

Emily squealed as I continued to punish her. She was totally defenceless and her shame was publicly exposed as her hips writhed and her face blushed as red as her bum cheeks.

'Here is a true and good spanking!' I laughed with glee as I chastised her further. 'As the punisher, I have fully bared the young lady's bottom before witnesses for proper correction. Even a severe spanking can be considered . . .' – *smack*! and she shrieked, 'a childish correction and therefore shaming, especially if administered publicly.'

'Oh, stop, please!' Emily cried out, 'I promise you that I'll be good in future!' Smack! Smack! Smack! 'I'll be good,' she sobbed.

'It is a punishment suitable for all age groups. Being less of a formal punishment than most, it may usefully be accompanied by a flow of spoken directives, impromptu scoldings, expressed hopes for repentance and preferably, the guilty culprit's cries of penitence.'

'O!' she yelled. 'I'll be such a good girl. I'll never ever do it again!'

'Lie still and make less noise!' I snapped back. Douglas grinned wickedly, exposing his long, canine teeth; and Rosemary smiled slyly.

'Oh, you weren't expecting this, were you?' I taunted Emily. 'Well, my girl, when young ladies behave like mischievous little girls, I treat them like little girls and that means . . .'

Smack! *Smack!!*

'Ow! *Ouch!*'

'A bare, reddening bottom. There!' SPANK! 'I hope you feel ashamed.' I turned to Rosemary and Douglas. 'One should apply the strokes with one's hand flattened yet relaxed, fingers very slightly apart yet extended. Aim initially for the exact centre of the bottom. Smack as hard as you like but remember to keep up whatever level of severity you have initiated. If you are striking at the correct angle, a tiny quantity of air will be trapped between your hand and the culprit's skin at the moment of impact: the explosion caused by its expulsion creates a notable increase in the percussive effect.

'Ouch! *Ow!*' she squealed and writhed.

'*Smack!* Smack!' I smiled. 'Keep the rhythm as unvaried as you can.'

'Do not stiffen the fingers,' I indicated calmly, 'and spank at a rate of not slower than 10 to the minute.' SPANK! 'After a few strokes you will be able to see, from the reddening of the skin, where your blows have been landing. Compare this with your point of aim and adjust accordingly. Start to range more widely, punishing first one buttock, then the other, then the two cheeks together, then a low blow, then a high blow, and finally a thigh. Do not follow too rigid a pattern or the naughty girl may come to anticipate you. The important thing is to distribute your slaps around the "circuit" as evenly as you can. If you have done so, you will be rewarded by the sight of a perfectly roseate behind, glowing evenly all over with only a few traces of livid blue finger marks where sharper blows have struck home.'

SMACK!

'Ooooh . . .' she wailed.

'Ideally,' I said, 'the next SPANK! should arrive before the culprit has fully absorbed the effect of the last. This promotes a rapid loss of self-control and so the weeping state usually signals the end of the punishment.'

Emily began to sob in penalty and repentance.

'I believe that most spankings should be administered with the single object of making the culprit cry,' I declared firmly. Emily wept salty tears as her blazing, burning bum cheeks twitched to and fro over my lap. 'Now, my dear, the sternest part of the punishment is over.' I slipped her off my knees and she had to stand in front of me with her proud head with its swan-like neck hung in shame, her knickers around her ankles and her skirts and petticoats held up obediently. 'Your punishment was for your own good,' I stated kindly. 'Now go and stand in that corner.' She shuffled towards it submissively, her lacey drawers dragging on her ankles. 'Face to the wall. Hands behind your back!' Holding up her skirt and petticoats, she obeyed, a spirited but subjugated, prim young lady.

Sherry was served as Douglas, Rosemary and I relaxed to enjoy the sight of Emily's spanked bottom gradually changing colour as the sun set. Her ears burned visibly and her face must have been flushing as furiously as her bottom on hearing our remarks upon the changing colours of her arse in the sun's dying rays.

'What a rosy glow!' Rosemary remarked merrily. 'How divinely decadent it all is! Horby,' she smirked mischievously, 'I had no idea that you possessed such enthusiastic expertise on the subject of spanking young ladies!'

'Oh, it's just an interest of mine,' I returned airily with a casual wave of my hand. I gazed contentedly at Emily's scarlet, glowing bottom, reflecting that it was the most expensive sexual pleasure that I have ever purchased, as Rosemary commenced a tale of the Prince of Wales.

CHAPTER THIRTY

'This is hardly the most decadent occasion that I have ever attended,' said Rosemary.

'Which was?' Douglas asked lazily.

'Oh, I don't know!' She burst out laughing. 'One was certainly a dinner hosted by the Prince of Wales.'

'One can well believe it,' he replied. 'Pray, what happened?' He called for more sherry. 'What was Bertie up to this time?'

'It was an invitation to a supper party in Belgravia at a house owned by a friend of his,' she answered. 'I wondered what to wear, for I wanted my outfit to be immaculately correct. I wondered also if I were going to meet the Empress of India, our grand matriarch and mother of this rakish son, though I doubted it somehow. I laid my clothes out upon the bed with great care. There were my white cotton knickers that had been so carefully hand-washed. They were whiter than a snowflake falling down from heaven and even more delicate. It was essential that I wear a bustle, my finest satin petticoats and silken seamed stockings. My lacy, high-heeled boots would add further to my ensemble.

'I know you do have a penchant for women who wear high-heeled, tightly laced boots, don't you, Douglas?' She fluttered her dark-shadowed lids demurely and he grinned lustfully. 'Do you remember one of our more beautiful evenings? All you wanted me to wear was my scarlet corset and my boots . . . but I digress. On my arrival I discerned that the rooms shone and sparkled with the splendour of ostentatious vulgarity. Six men and six women sat down to dine as candle-light was reflected by the crystal chandeliers enabling light to play, gleam and twinkle all over the room.

'It was pleasing to be placed next to Prince Edward, though it could not be said with truth that he was truly a physically attractive man. I cannot state in all honesty that I am strongly attracted by pompous, stout, middle-aged, florid-faced men with fulsome moustaches and pointed beards. Nevertheless, he had extraordinary charm. I was especially enchanted by the excellence of his manners. After a delicious soup made from venison and strongly laced with red country wine, there was a dish of asparagus in hollandaise sauce, accompanied, naturally, by a finger-bowl. One of the guests was some chieftain from Africa, and unfortunately, he mistook the nature of the finger-bowl and solemnly drank its contents. The Prince promptly silenced all suppressed sniggers by taking his own finger-bowl with the utmost gravity, as though he always finished his asparagus in this fashion, and drinking its contents. Therefore everyone else had to do the same thing too. Well!' Rosemary looked warmly approving, '*that's* what I call the manners of a king!

'The feast proceeded and I acquired an increasingly high opinion of the Prince, delighting greatly in our verbal intercourse as we gazed into one another's eyes. Oysters were served, lobster, scallops, ox tongue, grouse and roasted suckling pig, one for each guest. Accompaniments included truffles and artichoke hearts, buttered pea pods, creamed swedes and sweet young potatoes. The atmosphere became increasingly jovial and I began to feel more and more euphoric, especially when warm mead was served to accompany the Madeira Trifle. There was a hint of ginger in both. The Prince, who had entreated me to call him "Bertie", now arose and solemnly lifted his glass to toast: "The Queen."

' "To the queen! To the queen!" we all shouted.

' "The Queen, Duke of Lancaster," said Arthur Balfour, Cabinet Minister and nephew of our Prime Minister, Lord Salisbury.

' "The Queen!" the radical poet Wilfred Sedgewick cried out.

' "And since when, Mr Sedgewick," rumbled Prince Edward, "have you been so solicitous over Her Majesty's health?"

' "Ever since I have had the honour of knowing Your Royal Highness," Sedgewick returned insolently. The Prince refused to accept this insult at the table and instantly rang a small silver bell by his right hand. At once, the biggest man that I have ever seen entered the room. He must have been at least six feet nine inches in height and weighed at least eighteen stone, most of it finely tuned muscle. He stroked his thick handle-bar moustache thoughtfully as he watched the Prince's eyes flick angrily over to the hapless Wilfred Sedgewick.

' "Boris," said Prince Edward, "that one." His finger touched a button beneath the dining table. A trap-door opened beneath the dining chair of Wilfred Sedgewick, and he uttered a strangled cry as he dropped from view. Boris nodded with grim satisfaction and left the room with a softly measured tread. The Prince casually touched another button and the trapdoor slid shut. "Now, to return to where we were, prior to being so rudely interrupted . . ."

'Without warning, I had dived under the dining-table well beneath the tablecloth to tear open the flies, release the prick and lick upon the dick of the Prince of Wales.

Everyone else carried on as though nothing had happened or nothing else was happening. The fact that his stiff penis was in my mouth did not stop him from proposing another toast. It was so apparent from his stammering and breathless speech in praise of Womanhood, that he was close to orgasm. Did the other guests really become aware of what was happening as they cheerfully swigged back their port? *Oh, what a grand banquet!* I thought as I sucked hard upon his fat prick! How I would love to have seen the exact look upon his face! I could imagine the tweaking of his moustache and a sly smile upon his lips.

'The tablecloths covered my movements. For all the other guests knew, I might have been searching after a lace handkerchief I had accidentally dropped beneath the table. I let him enter more deeply into my throat. My face flushed with hot pleasure as I nipped, nibbled and licked his swollen member. At last he shot his juices into my mouth and the taste was rather brackish and briny. As he came, our hands met in a strong and warm embrace. I did not see the precise expression upon his face but I am sure that it was one of contentment.

'I arose and reseated myself with a proper dignity, carelessly waving the lace handkerchief I had *accidentally* dropped . . . and surveyed a table now groaning with bowls of maraschino cherries, grendalla, wild strawberries, pomegranates, mangos and passion fruit. At that moment there was a loud cry from within the house, followed by a splat-like sound.

' "Oh, don't worry about that, ladies and gentlemen," said the Prince, "that is merely one of Mr Sedgewick's jokes falling flat. Y'know, he once said to Oscar Wilde: 'Mr Wilde, there appears to be a conspiracy of silence about my poetry. What would you advise me to do?' 'Join it,' said Wilde." Prince Edward guffawed. "Should Sedgewick put more fire in his poems, eh? No, no, he should put more poems in his fire. Ha! ha! ha!" Prince Edward roared and of course we all laughed with him.

' "No, please, Boris . . .!" came Sedgewick's anguished voice from the back garden and it was followed by a resounding splash.

' "The cess-pond," Prince Edward muttered with evident satisfaction. "Something to be said for Boris and his Cossacks, y'know. Never thought Sedgewick's poetry was up to much anyway." Well,' Rosemary smiled gleefully, 'it was quite an evening.'

'What happened then?' Douglas demanded.

'Why, I fucked with him in a private bedroom, of course,' Rosemary responded. 'What else d'you expect?' She patted her hair. 'And as to what he was like, that's private also.'

'An enlivening tale,' I said, then added sharply: 'Emily! You may pull up your knickers and let down your petticoats and skirts. Hands behind your back again. Face to the wall. There's a good girl!' She stood obediently in her corner, her bottom still glowing beneath her long, green pleated skirt that trembled and fluttered at her well-turned ankles.

'So that's the story of how I came to suck the cock of the Prince of Wales,' Rosemary said coolly.

'I wish you'd tell us more,' Douglas commented, appearing amused rather than aggrieved. I was still endeavouring to ascertain the nature of this man. Clearly Rosemary adored him. Obviously, too, he was a man of mystery whose very existence had been denied by his own alleged father and a housemaid. My private detectives were working upon his case and so far there had been precious little information. 'Douglas Foster' was indeed well reputed in the circles of international finance, yet no birth certificate linking him to the Dr Foster of Whitby could be traced. It occurred to me that Rosemary might have been relating fiction to me. After all, she had suggested that the fellow was a vampire yet he had nevertheless played croquet with me in the afternoon sunshine and won ten thousand pounds. He did indeed appear, according to my information sources, to own castles in both Transylvania and just outside Vienna. 'Too many sherries are too mild at this time of day,' he was murmuring, then he waved idly for malt whisky. 'Naughty Miss Emily,' he said in that curious, slightly foreign accent of his. I saw her buttocks twitch with the pleasure of being mentioned and her skirts flutter once again. How cunning women are at the art of being noticed! For I saw him regard her with a pleasure equal to my own. 'Is she going to be consigned to the corner and in disgrace all evening?'

'Not at all, I am inclined to be merciful,' I retorted genially. 'Emily, you may come out of your corner now, provided that you apologise like a well chastised young lady who is resolved to behave better in future.'

She turned to us and addressed the company with a delicious curtsey.

'Sir,' she spoke to me, 'I apologise humbly if I have at all offended you in any slightest manner. I deserved my punishment and I thank you for its stern administration. In offer of recompense for my inexcusable behaviour upon the croquet lawn this afternoon, I pledge to you ten thousand pounds as a just fine in view of the bet which you so bravely undertook.' She curtseyed to me and then to Douglas and Rosemary. 'Sir. Madam. I accept my punishment before you and trust that I shall never again be seen to be at fault.'

I wanted to fuck her so desperately at that instant and penetrate to the essence of her penitential grace – though rather than penitence, there'd be a penis tense. Instead I postponed the matter so as to enjoy further and later delights, took her in my arms, kissed her and gladly forgave her, urging her to sit down by me on the sofa, which she did somewhat delicately and gingerly.

'Emily, your gracious offer to cover my bet cannot possibly be accepted,' I told her, 'though I do thank you for it.' She happened to be one of the richest heiresses in England but much as I appreciated her gesture, I did not think that it would be right to accept it.

'Then allow me at least to cover five thousand pounds as your partner,' she returned with quiet dignity.

'Ah! This sort of thing makes me proud to be a snob,' Douglas observed, though Rosemary looked at him quizzically.

'I'm not a snob,' Emily retorted indignantly. 'A snob is a very bad thing to be.'

'On the contrary,' Douglas returned somewhat sniffily, 'it's a very good thing to be.'

'No,' I said, 'with all respect, it isn't.' Whatever else Douglas might be, he was displaying the behaviour of the *arriviste*. 'And I put ten thousand pounds on the matter that a snob is a low class person, which matter is to be decided by reference to Skeat's Etymological Dictionary backed up by the Oxford English Dictionary in case of doubt.'

'Bet taken!' 'The Black Douglas' barked back somewhat drunkenly. The works of reference were produced by his servants. It was easy to demonstrate that the original meaning of "snob" in the medieval era denoted a person of the lower classes and was used so in Chaucer's time. In Shakespeare's time, it was London slang for a shoemaker to the aristocracy. The Oxford English Dictionary was defining it as "undue deference paid to wealth, rank or station."

'And it's clear how the expression came about,' I said, quietly rubbing in my advantage. 'If you go to Oxford or Cambridge University Colleges, then as now you have to commence your career by signing your name in a book presented to you on arrival within the Porter's Lodge. In the Middle Ages, however, you had to add your rank in society. Now, the poor scholars, unlike the aristocracy and gentry, were indebted either to a wealthy patron or else to the Church. They had to write SINE NOBILIS OBLIGATORE BENEDICTIO . . .'

'Are you sure that's right?' Rosemary queried.

'No, I'm not precisely sure, for my Latin is dreadfully rusty despite your teaching,' I returned. 'You always said that my Latin was awful. What it means though is: "Without Nobility, Obliged to Benediction." S.N.O.B. That's beyond dispute.'

'Well, well . . .' Douglas lit an Egyptian yellow cigarette. 'I always count it a day lost if I don't learn something new. You've just won yourself ten thousand pounds, Horby. Just as I won ten thousand off you at croquet.'

'So it's evens,' said Rosemary, 'not odds and sods.' We both nodded.

'You're an interesting fellow,' Douglas mused aloud. He did not seem at all disconcerted by the fact that he had neither gained nor lost on our betting. 'Tell me, do you think that sex is sacred?'

'Yes.'

'Do you think that it can be central to religion?'

'Yes.'

'Have you ever seen it done so?'

'No.'

'Would you like to witness it?'

'Maybe.' He offered me a silver box which contained a selection of cigarettes and I chose a Russian one, made from Yenidje tobacco imported from Turkey, wrapped in black and adorned by a gold tip. 'What exactly is involved?'

'I don't want any money from you or from anyone else, Horby,' Douglas stated. 'My proposal is that you and Emily join Rosemary and myself to witness a ceremony at my castle near Vienna, in one week's time. We shall travel by *Wagons-Lits* and my chauffeurs will meet you at the station. Agreed?'

'Agreed,' I responded firmly.

'Agreed,' Emily answered, though somewhat timidly.

'Good!' he exclaimed. 'Splendid! It is better than I hoped.' With that, he jumped upon Rosemary, bit her neck, tore off her clothes and commenced fucking her on the floor. I looked at Emily, she looked at me and we decided to do the same thing too. My spanking of Emily had aroused me greatly and my cock was pushing the front of my trousers like a steel bar. I pulled away Emily's clothes as Douglas and Rosemary began their fuck. It was a joy to stare at her glorious nudity. Her bottom still glowed in the light of its evening punishment. Her beautiful breasts, crowned by large, nut-brown nipples, jiggled up and down as she offered herself to my delicate attentions. I also noticed that this demure young miss had for her own reasons neatly trimmed her pussy hair into an inverted pyramid before I knelt on the carpet in front of her and began to lick her thighs whilst my hands pulled her warm bum cheeks closer to me. Her hands were on top of my head, forcing my face further into her moist depths as I worked my tongue in deeper and deeper, searching for her fleshy clitty. When I found it, I kissed and sucked this ambrosial button which sent her into a series of sensual spasms and she purred like a kitten whilst I worked my tongue all around her erect love-nub until my jaw was fairly aching.

'Aaaah!' she screamed out as, with a tremendous heave, she worked herself off on my tongue, drenching my face with her cuntal ejaculate in a shuddering orgasm and I gulped down her tangy love juices until she released my head and her cool hand reached downwards to caress my achingly stiff member. I made her roll onto her front. Her bottom was absolutely breathtaking in its configuration and its satiny smoothness. It possessed a mobility, an agility and a musculature which promised the most lubricious joys under the assailing onslaught of my possession of her flesh. There was at her chinkbone a most adorable kind of dimple, so that the prominent jut of her buttocks became that much more accentuated. But before I tortured myself further with viewing the palpitating globes of her behind, I felt that I had to see her cunt. Again.

Oh, I turned her over to roast her white flesh with the fires of my gaze. Her face, scarlet and contracted, glistened with beads of agony and shame-sweat as she writhed and moaned in a tumult of distraught emotions. Ah! What a delight it was to view her triangulated aperture of flossy down, extending from the lower abdomen and growing in rich profusion right over the lips of her delicious quim, disappearing below the orifice and doubtless growing along the intimate and humid connecting groove which led to her nether hole! Words cannot sufficiently describe that exquisitely salacious picture Emily made with her silken knickers rucked down just beneath that appetising cunny, stretched by the slight spread of her shaking, stockinged thighs, with the sweet delicately rounded goblet of her belly adorably marked by that tempting kiss-nook which was the navel.

I was shuddering with desire and my eyes were blazing. My dear Rosemary was being fucked just a few yards away from me and I could hear her panting and certainly her cunt was full and plump and fleshy and prominent, but at that instant, the cunt of Emily had, shall I say, an even more seductive allure for me. At first glance, even though the silky hair concealed its conformation, it appeared that the outer labia were somewhat more pronounced and also that the aperture might well be deeper than sweet Rosemary's tender slit. I now placed my left palm on this wonderfully submissive girl's slender hip and to my astonishment she yelled out: 'Ohhh, no, for God's sake, no!' Her hips jerked upwards convulsively as though I had struck them with a red hot poker. 'Don't touch me, you horrid villain!'

'You are extremely sensitive, it would appear,' I told her, forcing my hoarsening voice to remain mockingly calm, to show her that she could expect no wavering or indecision from me. And I thrust my thick, throbbing ram-rod within her.

'Damn you!' she shrieked. 'Damn you for your brutal, vulgar and vicious conduct to me, a helpless woman . . .!' she gasped. And now she tried desperately to clench her thighs and wrench herself backwards and away from my probing penis. I still had my left hand on her upper thigh and I now snapped her garter viciously, stinging her tender flesh again and drawing a little: 'Aagh! End this horror! Haven't you had revenge enough on me, you dirty brute?'

'I have hardly begun to wipe out your first sarcastic remark of this afternoon, my charming lady,' was my answer. Emily uttered a gurgling scream and in a supreme effort of maddened fury, spat fully into my face. How I relished this outrageously unladylike manifestation of her spleen! For now she had not added not one but several fresh pages to the ledger of her account. She would be soundly punished for what she had done – after I had fucked her.

But the overpowering sensation of being inside her cunt took full possession on me now. How wonderfully tight and warm she was! I felt myself sheathed and clamped upon within her cushioning quim and I had no desire to move for a moment, so rapt was I in tasting the myriad sensations of my sweet confinement. With my fingers digging into the cheeks of her bare, glowing behind, feeling the sporadic flexions and the quiverings of that satiny flesh, I once more bent my head to lick her nipples, sucking her left one noisily, to embarrass and to spite her, yet also to suggest that we were the tenderest of lovers rather than the deadliest of enemies. When she felt that thrust, the frantic jerkings to which her body gave vent provided me with a most delirious pleasure, for she was providing her own friction to my stiffly imbedded cock.

'Beast! Monstrous rapist! Filthy degenerate!' she screamed, in a sobbing, strangled voice. 'Ohhh . . .!' she panted as I came with a shuddering sensation that shook me from the crown of my head to the tips of my toes. 'Ohh . . .' we both breathed together.

'Yes, Emily is one of my pupils,' Rosemary informed me the next day when I was rhapsodising about her. 'Did you not realise?'

CHAPTER THIRTY-ONE

'I think women can be such a dreadful bore,' said Sir Richard Bellingham, 'except when one's fucking 'em.' He quaffed his pint of port and ordered more.

'Don't agree,' I said. We were sitting in the Cheshire Cheese, Fleet Street, with Machen and Crowley. Sir Richard seemed to have set up an unofficial club just for the pleasure of watching these two men disagree with one another.

'You never do seem to agree with me, Horby,' he retorted languidly, 'which is why, no doubt, I find your company stimulating.' At that moment we were interrupted by Wilfred Sedgewick, that awful poet, who looked as though he had at least had a bath since Rosemary's tale of the Prince of Wales having him flung into a cess-pit. Nobody looked pleased to see him.

'My dear Sir Richard!' he cried out effusively. Sir Richard looked up morosely from the thick slices of rare beef wedged between thickly buttered slices of cottage loaf, accompanied by lashings of horseradish and English mustard which he had just been enjoying. 'How is your charming wife?'

'Dead.'

'Oh, my dear Sir Richard, I am exceedingly sorry to hear that. But I trust that your dear mother is well?'

'Dead.'

'This is tragic! But surely your dear father who was always so kind to me is still enjoying his customary robust health.'

'Dead.'

'Oh . . .' Wilfred Sedgewick looked about to cry. 'I am so sorry.'

'Dead, dead, dead, everybody's dead.' Sir Richard snorted disgustedly. 'Don't you understand, you bloody fool? Everybody's dead while I'm eating. Now be a good chap and piss orf!'

'That was unkind,' Arthur Machen said as Sedgewick slunk away.

'Yes,' said Bellingham. 'Why don't you go and talk to him if you find him so interesting?' Machen did not.

'He's an atrocious poet,' Crowley remarked. 'Have you ever heard of anything as bad as this?' He produced a piece of paper from his wallet. 'It is so appalling and abominable, such an affront to the human aesthetic spirit, that I treasure it among my prize possessions.' He read:

"Philosophy, as quantity, be less
When knowledge as a quantity be more
Than quantity, philosophy can score;
Hence quantity less quality possess
Sensation never can put under stress;
Since semblance of condition cannot store
Shades protean as quality before
Proportionate of quantity duress:
Since semblance of condition unity
Possess by holding unit under stress
As quantity, however, change will stay;
While quality as mere diversity
Stress more or less of quality, more or less
Enforced, with dying force will melt away."

The three men put their heads upon the table and groaned in agony at the sheer awfulness of the purported sonnet.

'Shall we kill him now or later?' queried Sir Richard.

'Poor fellow,' said Machen, 'looks as though he's in need of help. I'm going to send him a pint of port to console him in his misery.'

'It's written under the name of Wm Howell Williams,' Crowley informed us as Machen ordered a drink to be sent to this lonely wretch, 'and is part of a breath-taking work entitled *Sonnetical Notes on Philosophy*.'

'Heaven help us all,' I muttered.

'But will it?' Bellingham demanded. 'You see, gentlemen, that's the question, isn't it? Is a fuck just a fuck or is there more to it than that? That piece of bad verse – and I agree with Shakespeare and "Tear him for his bad verses!" – could be compared to holding an uninspired limp cock in one's hand on a wet afternoon whilst farting uncontrollably. So let's get back to basics. Is a fuck just a fuck, I mean is it merely organ grinding, or is there something more to it than that? You see, I've been invited to a castle near Vienna to witness sex as a religious sacrament and I've been informed that I can take some trusty companions if I chose. Interested?'

'Certainly,' I said, 'but if we're speaking of the same castle, I've already been invited. This coming week, isn't it?'

'I haven't,' said Crowley. 'Not formally.'

'I can see why,' said Machen.

'And where's your invitation?' Crowley retorted.

'Here,' Machen replied simply.

'Coming, then, are you, Machen?' Bellingham asked. 'Do you good, y'know.'

'I'd be interested,' Machen replied, 'but a series of previous engagements precludes that eventuality.'

'As you wish.' Bellingham shrugged. 'How about you, Crowley?'

'Normally I'd be only too delighted,' Crowley replied, 'it's just that I have urgent personal work at present.'

'Such as?' Bellingham enquired scathingly.

'Sir Richard, we are all members of the Golden Dawn here,' Crowley responded with dignity. 'As such, I'm sure you will appreciate that I have sworn to undertake the Operation of *The Book of the Sacred Magic of Abra-Melin the Mage* as translated by our leader, S.L. 'MacGregor' Mathers, which requires six months of solitude, fasting and prayer.'

'And where will you get that?' Machen enquired sceptically.

'I've just bought a hunting lodge at Boleskine, on the shores of Loch Ness,' Crowley returned casually, 'and that's where I'll be going.'

'So it looks like just you and me, Horby, eh?' said Bellingham.

'I was thinking of bringing a lady friend.'

'Why, so was I!' our host exclaimed. 'Being met at the station in Vienna, are you?' I nodded. 'That finance chap?' I nodded again. 'Look, old boy, why don't you go to Vienna *my* way, eh? I've chartered a carriage on the Golden Arrow to Dover, there'll be cabins on the boat over to France, and after that it's *Wagons-Lits* plus my carriage of hospitality all the way until we reach Vienna. There, my dear fellow! How about that?'

'Excellent,' I replied. 'My companion and I are pleased to accept your invitation.'

'Just make bloody well sure that your Victoria is at Victoria on time, Horby.' He smiled genially. 'Now, Crowley, I'm awfully sorry that you say you can't come, but the puzzling thing is that it seems to be for reasons of sacred

Magic, fasting and prayer when members of the Golden Dawn are presently accusing you of dirty and disgusting debauchery.'

'That is their problem,' Crowley responded, 'not mine.'

In common with Bellingham, I was vaguely aware of savage quarrels within the Golden Dawn. Crowley had swarmed up the grades and was eager to enter the Inner Order, that of the R.C., or Rosicrucians, whilst Bellingham and myself had made little progress under that schema and I suspected that Sir Richard didn't take it seriously at all. Machen had originally taken it very seriously indeed but appeared to be slightly disillusioned. In time, this burgeoning quarrel would affect the lives of all of us, but that night, conviviality was restored.

We went for a walk in the moonlight and along the Embankment, admiring the moon's glistening sheen upon the still waters of the Thames. We walked well, we talked well and later on we drank well. It was a men's evening.

'*The Book of the Sacred Magic of Abra-Melin the Mage . . .*' Arthur Machen mused aloud. 'Crowley, do you seriously believe that you are going to obtain the Knowledge and Conversation of the Holy Guardian Angel?'

'Yes,' Crowley replied simply.

'Good luck,' said Machen, 'for you will need it.'

Frankly, I didn't give a toss about any Holy Guardian Angel at that time in my life. I was simply pleased to be sitting on the Golden Arrow with Emily and it was just in time for tea. Now, in those days, they really knew how to run railways. Bellingham had booked an entire Pullman carriage for us and another one for himself and his lady companion, whom I had yet to meet. Douglas had taken another one, where he was comfortably ensconced with Rosemary, and I was a welcome guest in either carriage as long as I wasn't interrupting anything by tactlessly cutting it short. My hope was eventually to see a sight both sacred and exquisitely erotic while thoroughly enjoying the journey.

The train moved away from the station and after the inevitable period of peering at the drabbest and weariest, dreariest South London suburbs, we were at last gliding through the countryside, enjoying Assam tea with hot buttered crumpets and muffins. We had the whole carriage to ourselves. I chose to ask Emily which man had influenced her most.

'It was when I was an adolescent,' she replied, then delicately sipped tea. 'I used to be so frivolous, flirtatious and light-hearted, as playful as a kitten being tantalised by a ball of wool. I suppose I still am. Oh, I can be so capricious! Only yesterday morning I lay in bed till mid-day, feeling a bit naughty and skittish and intending to be rather revealing and flagrantly flaunting in the evening, quietly frigging myself all the while . . . but I digress. I was speaking about my uncle.

'I knew that my uncle was something of a debauched rake but although I'd been warned about his wickedness, this only served to spice my fascination for him. Even though he's getting on in age, he always looks so dapper and debonair, and he loves the company of a beautiful young woman. I was glad to accept his invitation to join him for supper at Robinson's in Kensington, an establishment renowned as much for its discreet debauchery as for its unimpeachable discretion.

'My uncle has written many a treatise and sometimes these are of purely academic interest. He loves to pontificate upon such topics as Astronomy and Literature. He's also an excellent painter and some of his pictures have been exhibited at the Royal Academy. He does mix with a rather bizarre coterie of personages. According to my mother, some of his works have been somewhat licentious. Many of his works have been published and some, I am informed, have been banned. I think this has rather embarrassed my mother, who refers to his writing as 'impure literature' and who does not consider it fit for the eyes of the young. Oh . . .' she sighed lasciviously, 'in life there is such beauty, love – and aberration. No one can escape the passages of existence.' She bit into a crumpet and spilled melted butter on her delicate chin. 'There is such joy when one hears the cry of a new-born baby. Shakespeare wrote so well of our journey through life. It is a wheel which forever turns and we are all bound by this wheel until we are confronted by death. How unbearable life would be without it!

'There is a high-walled back garden at Robinson's. The company gazed upon it with pleasure. In its centre, there stood a pole, My tutor Rosemary Radcliffe had taught me all about the Seasons of the Witch. Tonight was October 31st, All Hallows Eve, Samhain, the ending of the old year and the beginning of the new, the renewal of a cycle. Yule at the Winter Solstice, 21st December is the shortest day of the year as the evergreen Holly King is crowned as Lord of Misrule. There's Candlemas on 2nd February followed by the Spring Equinox, a time of equal day and night. One dances around a great big prick – whoops! sorry, the Maypole – on 1st May and the sun which gives us life is at its mightiest at the Summer Solstice. There's Lughasad or Lammas at the beginning of August to celebrate the harvest and then the Autumn Equinox when the nights grow longer and the Sun King becomes the Lord of the Shadows. Tonight, however, I agreed with my uncle that I would be the sacrifice on All Hallow's Eve.

'Robinson's has a long-standing connection with my

uncle's family and gladly permits him to use their cellar-room to celebrate his religious devotions. This was how I came to be lying naked upon a stone slab. Upon the altar there were marble statuettes of a fully erect, red-tipped Priapus and a lustful Venus to honour the Horned God and the Great Goddess of Earth and Moon and Sky and Stars. Cakes and a chalice of wine reposed before these figurines, illuminated by a tall black candle. Around the room there were more candles: white for air; red for fire; blue for water and green for earth. There was a thick incense of frankincense, sandalwood, frangipane, chypre, orris root, woodruff and a slight touch of civet. That scent is of a strong, pungent perfume from the anal glands of a cat. I massaged my underarms, forehead, heels, inner thighs, bottom and cunt with the oil of civet. What a grand celebration we were about to have!

'I lay upon the slab, enjoying the tense silence as eight figures, robed and hooded and masked in black, entered the room. The rays of the full moon flickered in through the cellar's one barred window. A figure whom I instinctively knew to be my uncle took a thick staff from the altar and pounded the floor thrice, five times and thrice again.

' "Who dares to enter?" I enquired, for it was what Rosemary had coached me to say.

' "I do." I recognised his voice immediately, especially appreciating its resonance as that of a tintinnabulation, as the ringing of bells by an experienced campanologist. "I have brought the young Goddess an apple and a pomegranate."

'I spread my legs and allowed him to enter my secret lady's chamber, my most holy sacred temple. He kissed me tenderly upon the lips and then upon my cheeks. His beautiful lips brushed the tip of my nose as his hands fondled my breasts. How my cunt was being aroused! I longed to feel the penetration of his gorgeous member.

'When he fucked me, it was not in an earthly manner. There was something so holy and sacred about our making of love. I wanted to embrace every single part of his body and I stared into his beautiful eyes as our toes twitched together. His penis throbbed and pulsated within my cunt. Oh, how I wanted to be dominated and constrained! My vagina squeezed him repeatedly in its endeavour to extract and gulp all his juices. He came with a great cry that mingled triumph with an inner anguish.

'Ohh . . .' she sighed, 'Believe me, I felt initiated and the promise of my tutor Rosemary had been kept.'

'Your uncle sounds like a rather remarkable man,' I observed.

'Oh, he is,' she returned, 'I really do admire Uncle Douglas and I'm so happy to be invited to his castle at last.' Then she saw my surprise and added: 'I thought you knew that we were related.'

'Well, well,' I murmured, 'one learns something new every day, thank heavens.' I kissed her full lips then slipped my hand beneath her skirts and petticoats. Her knickers were loose and it was easy to finger her luscious, moist pussy. I had just intended to frig her all the way to Dover, and it would turn out to be an astonishingly rewarding journey, but my joys were rudely interrupted by a loud knocking upon the carriage door.

'Open up!' cried Sir Richard Bellingham, 'or are you just being a pair of anti-social turds?'

'The door is open,' I sighed. Bellingham entered bearing bottles of vintage champagne, followed by a strikingly beautiful and buxom woman whom I had met once before, Mrs Davina Price-Hughes. I had last seen her winning Crowley's sexual attentions at his Chancery Lane flat by agreeing to wash his socks. We greeted one another graciously and drank some champagne as the Golden Arrow, bound for Paris, clattered cheerfully through the Surrey countryside and I ached to frig Emily, knowing that her cunt was itching for it.

'Pullman class for lots of money!' Bellingham exclaimed. 'And it's worth every penny! First class for the bourgeoisie, second class for the mediocre and third class for the poor – but everyone gets to travel. Third class prices are so astonishingly inexpensive. What could be fairer than that?'

'Quite agree,' I replied, 'and the great advantage of the Pullman is that one pays for some privacy.' Davina looked at Bellingham and fortunately he took the hint.

'Well, just wanted to say hello and to introduce Davina,' he said. 'See you at Dover, then.' Just as he was leaving with Davina a liveried attendant entered to ask if Emily and I required more tea and crumpets.

'More crumpets?' I returned. 'Yes, definitely.' As the carriage emptied, I returned to frigging Emily.

CHAPTER THIRTY-TWO

The instant that more hot buttered crumpets and a pot of freshly made Assam tea had arrived, I returned to the rather more serious matter of pleasuring Emily's cunt with my finger. I applied my right forefinger to Emily's dark curls and Emily, with a sudden squeal, lunged her bottom backwards in a futile and faked ladylike endeavour to evade my profanation, only further exciting my lustful desires. The first touch I had of those soft downy ringlets upon her pudenda made my cock throb further with priapic anticipation. They had a softness and curliness to them that bespoke an absolute treasure trove of Venus beneath that protective foliage. My left hand moved round to palm her covered bottom over both cheeks, bridging the shadowy gap which separated their contracting hemispheres, and thus I could force her back to the peregrinations of my invading finger. She glanced back at that ungentlemanly hand while tremor after tremor rippled through her body. For a moment I was playfully content to press my forefinger here and there over the large mound and to feel the soft curls of that delectable quim. But now the time had come to explore once more her innermost secrets. And so, leaning forward in our railway seat, my left palm pressing hard against her naked, squirming posterior, forcing her to thrust out her loins willy-nilly, I began to probe with the tip of my searching finger. Her outer lips formed a soft gash in that lovely mound and they were as yet relatively dry – a condition which I meant soon enough to alter – but deliciously crinkly-soft to my discriminating touch.

As my fingertip brushed that sensitive outer gateway to Emily's love-channel, she uttered a low, sobbing groan, twisting her face to this side and then the other, her eyes tightly closed and her fists tightly clenched but the trembling of her jaw and the flaring of her nostrils told me that she was not at all impervious to what she was experiencing. Her breasts too entered into this tumultuous anguish, thrusting out with panting exhalations and her stentorous breathing gave the lie utterly to her every facial attempt at indifference. To my great delight, as my finger passed slowly along that delicious aperture, first at the base of the outer lips and up to the top, then down to the other lip and to its base where it joined its sweet sister, I felt the membrane twitch and flutter and quiver. For all her purported prudery and prim *hauteur*, Emily was hardly the cold statue of righteousness which she liked to present to the world.

I proceeded to tickle the outer lips of that soft pink chalice relentlessly back and forth until gradually I could feel them twitch and tremor and flutter almost uncontrollably, until I could hear her gasps and whimpering moans exude more frequently from between her tight lips and until I felt the spasmodic contractions of her bottom muscles and the squirming, restless, uneasy movements of her smooth behind against my restraining left palm.

Slyly then, I probed deeper and I found the smaller, more delicate and slightly moist lips of the inner membrane which led to the vaginal sheath, the furrow down which at not too far distant a moment I knew my raging prick must needs slake its hungers for her tasty woman-flesh. At length I could restrain myself no longer.

Tearing down her knickers and lifting up her petticoats and skirts, I lifted her bodily into the air, with her back to me, then placed her cunt upon my prick, prodding my rod into her with a joyous abandon. She screamed and I roared and we both came with gasps and emissions of juices as the train reached Dover.

However sinister I might find 'the Black Douglas' at times, so far I really could not fault his travel arrangements nor the service of the Golden Arrow. Emily and I finished our crumpets and took more tea as the railway servants directed us towards the formalities of embarkation. This we accomplished in a trice, then we strolled aboard the boat to rejoin our party. Douglas and Sir Richard had obviously hit it off and Rosemary and Davina were talking animatedly over drinks. I took a large malt whisky and Emily chose to have another glass of champagne. As usual, Bellingham was entertaining the company with another of his preposterous stories.

'Once upon a time,' he began, 'there was a vicar and he was a very good, dear, sweet, kind man. He went for a walk one day by the river and what did he see but a shivering little frog. "Oh, little frog," he said, "what's your trouble?" "Oh, thank you for your kindness, Mr Vicar," the frog replied. "What's this?" said the astonished vicar, "a talking frog?" "Oh, yes, Mr Vicar, and I'm so lonely and so cold," said the little frog, "for the other frogs don't like me at all because I can talk. Oh, I'm so lonely and so cold." "There, there, little frog," said the good, kind vicar, "your troubles are over now." And being such a good, kind man, he put the little frog in his pocket and took him to his home, where he gave him warm milk and bread and a pool of warm water and a nice basket of straw. "Rest easily tonight, little frog," said the vicar. "Thank you, Mr Vicar, you're very kind," said the frog. The vicar then climbed into bed and slept but in the middle of the night he was awoken by sounds of piteous crying. "Why do you cry, little frog?" the vicar asked concernedly. "Oh, Mr Vicar, I am so lonely and so cold." And the good, kindly vicar carried the frog into his own bed, tucked him up nicely and slept peacefully. Yet when he awoke in the morning, to his complete stupefaction, the frog had changed into a beautiful thirteen-year-old boy. And that, my Lord,' Bellingham finished, 'is the case for the Defence.'

It was an appropriate note on which to hear the ship's siren, weigh anchor and cast off, setting sail, so to speak, upon the seas, whilst watching the white cliffs of Dover gradually recede from view. Now my prick was starting to itch again and some servant from somewhere had given me some bits of paper informing me of the location of my cabin, which is where I led Emily, having made the conventional excuses about sea-sickness. Its evident luxury made precious little impression upon me since I was much more interested in Emily's cunt and the expressions my manipulation of it evoked upon her lightly freckled and demure face.

I rushed her to the vast, soft bed, held her down, pulled down her knickers and whipped up her skirt and petticoats, to bare her womanly glory. Just above the inner lip of her vagina, my right forefinger moved to discover the nodule of her clitoris, that fleshy little jewel, that lodestone, that kernel of passion which is the key to Woman's emotions and which should unlock the door to all of Emily's portals no matter how hard she fought against the prospect of my mastery and domination.

As my fingertip touched this tender morsel, Emily uttered a stifled groan, her head falling back, her eyes wide and exorbitant and her nostrils flaring delicately as a feverish spasm swept her entire body. Yes, her flesh shook under the shock of this impress and my left hand felt the convulsive jerk of her agile muscles under the satiny skin of her naked bottom. To distract her a little, I withdrew my hand only to suddenly run it up under the leg of her rucked-down drawers to find the stocking top. I detected the tight and flouncy rosette garter high on her thigh, which kept the black silken sheath in such an impeccably unwrinkled caress of her long shapely leg. Plucking it out, I snapped it wickedly and drew a startled little cry.

'Ohh! D-don't!' she squealed but this was followed by a convulsive wriggling that made my cock jump with virile ecstasy. Again my right forefinger pressed against the nodule of her love-button, pressing it back into its protective cowl of soft, pink protective loveflesh, then releasing it so it could bob up. This manoeuvre also produced a whimpering gasp and a convulsive twist from the frantic, helpless beauty and she restlessly turned her face from side to side, her eyes again closed, her soft lips grimacing to show her chattering teeth as she shuddered with truly mixed emotions.

Now my finger withdrew but only to attack the inner lips of her cunt again and to rim them with soft, tickling caresses, round and round, till I felt them to be more open than usual, twitching and quivering in that insidious attunement which indisputably showed that, whatever she might sometimes say, Emily was very much a warm-blooded female.

I stared eagerly at her cunt, passing my right forefinger against the centre of that hidden grotto and pressed it on between the fleshy lips of Emily's channel of forbidden pleasure. She caught her breath and tilted back her head, her eyes desperately closed as tight as she could get them, and abruptly her body went rigid. It was a magnificent spectacle to observe how the muscles of her sleek calves, so beautifully and provocatively sheathed in the clinging black silk stockings, flexed and trembled from the nervous stress upon her system in her beleaguered helplessness. I foraged my finger onward, past the smaller inner labia of her slit, until I felt myself intrude well within that tender, mysterious groove which nature has afforded for the gratification of my sex. Up to the hilt I plunged my finger and I looked down upon her triumphantly. For a moment, her teeth were chattering again and all her muscles were in mobile tension as she stiffened and then quivered in a compound of fury, shame and the sheer joy of lust. Once again her pale white cheeks were dyed a flaming scarlet hue and the pulse-hollow in her gentrified throat was even more visibly hammering from her agitated senses.

It was a rough crossing upon the Straits of Dover through the English Channel that evening but there was a rapture, a most sensuous rapture, in rocking and rolling with the boat upon the waves. Whisking my finger out of her cunt, I cupped her breasts, tickling her nipples with the tips of my forefingers as I stared into her congested face. My cock prodded against the silky hairs of her mount; and, sucking in her breath again very sharply, Emily executed a violent, convulsive spasm of rapture with the intent of placing her most vulnerable niche at the disposal of my person. Once more our congress was quick but I shrieked out as the rod I had pronged into her let fly with its Gatling-like spattering of sperm and my own body heaved and sighed in awe of the ecstasy that shook me.

For a time we held one another closely, merely enjoying the motion of the boat upon the fierce swelling of the sea, then we returned to the upper deck, just in time to see the flat sands of Calais coming into view. Sir Richard and Davina and Douglas and Rosemary had made it to the bar slightly ahead of us but judging by the relaxed joviality of the men and the flushed satisfaction of the women, it was obvious that they had all enjoyed the crossing too.

'Sodomy?' I heard Douglas say as we entered to take refreshment. 'I'm not saying that it can't be enjoyable but it has always struck me,' he continued with a cool arrogance, 'as going around the tradesmen's entrance.'

'That,' Rosemary returned rather typically, 'surely depends upon the woman involved. The tradesmen's entrance to a castle is assuredly preferable to the front door of some seedy suburbanite.'

'You're making me feel hungry,' said Bellingham.

'There'll be dinner on the train to Paris,' Douglas replied.

'And no doubt it'll be jolly good,' Bellingham responded as he tossed back a glass of cognac. I glanced at Davina, who had upon her face that quiet smile of satisfaction which declares her happiness at having just been buggered and buggered well and truly. 'But I'm sure,' he continued, 'that we won't be able to eat what I really fancy right now. Roasted swan! Aren't elegant women like swans?'

I could discern, looking at the slim white necks of the ladies of the company, a certain analogy.

'No, you won't be able to eat roasted swan on the Golden Arrow, Richard,' said Davina. 'Swans are rightly protected by Law. The only people in England allowed to eat swans are the Royal Family . . .'

. . . and the dons at High Table of St John's College, Cambridge,' Sir Richard completed her statement. Suddenly he burst into a limerick.

'There was a young man of St John's
Who wanted to bugger the swans.
But the loyal Head Porter
Said: "Sir: take my daughter;
Them swans is reserved for the dons." '

We downed our drinks as the boat docked and rejoined our separate carriages of the Golden Arrow, though Douglas asked us all to meet up in the dining-car he had chartered in about half an hour. There was some kerfuffle, what with Bellingham insisting that he wanted to pay for it and Douglas refusing his kind offer, but in any event, we all changed our clothes and sat down to dine. It was a good and simple French meal of *moules mariniere* followed by three rare chateaubriands between the six of us with an exquisite sauce bearnaise, portions of buttered spinach, French fried potatoes sliced as thin as wisps of straw and green salad, followed by a board stacked with an astonishing selection of ripe cheeses, then *tarte tatin*. To drink we had many bottles of Pouilly Fumé, Château La Tache with the steak, Château Mouton Rothschild with the cheese and Château D'Yquem with the pudding. Our coffee came with green Chartreuse and Romeo y Julieta Coronas from Havana. A horde of porters descended upon us upon our arrival at the Gard du Nord and this was just as well, for each one of us had a minimum of fifteen trunks and cases.

I love the cream and russet brown colouring of English Pullman railway coaches but the deep blue and gold lettering of the French *Wagons-Lits* carriages shows that our Continental neighbours can manage these matters equally well. Once again, a carriage was assigned to each couple and I surveyed mine with pleasure. It was a joy to hurl Emily upon the bed once more.

I pulled off her clothes and slipped away mine as the train pulled out of the station and one heard that delightful sound of the wheels clattering along the railway tracks. My prick was in violent erection, as one may well imagine, since I hadn't come for a while, and its head was swollen and purplish with pent-up ardour. I reached around and palmed the lower cheeks of Emily's bottom, luxuriating in the warm satiny smoothness of those impudent and resilient globes, in the frantic contractions with which all the muscles now came into play as she realised that another defeat was now imminent.

Putting my lips to one of her nipples, I took it between them and nuzzled it delicately, flicking it with my tongue, and she uttered a hoarse shout, absolutely beside herself at the liberties I was taking with her fair person.

'Ohh-no, no, you beast, I won't let you have me completely, I'd sooner die . . .'

Still maintaining my strategy of keeping my left palm against her quivering bottom, I shifted my right in front of us and used all five fingers to attack her cunt. This time I went directly to the tender hidden lodestone of her clitoris and I began to rub it insistently and lingeringly, making her thighs jerk convulsively with the erotic stimulus. I could see that beads of sweat were gathering in her finely-downed soft armpit-hollows, and the scent of her sweat and of her naked flesh now began to overpower the musky perfume in which she had liberally doused herself. Her eyes rolled, her nostrils opened and closed convulsively and at a more accelerated pace while she made a frenzied effort to clench her thighs.

I cannot tell you what maddening pleasure I experienced as I kept my left hand firmly pressed against her jerking, squirming, contracting naked bottom and my fingers pressed against the nodule of her very life. As I continued to suck and nibble at her nipple, I felt it stiffen and turgify, indisputable proof that despite my rude and harsh treatment of her after the croquet game, she was a young woman of ardent flesh and blood, quite capable of being stimulated to the point of yielding to the good fucking I intended to give her.

Now inarticulate groans erupted from her gaping, wide,

crimson mouth as she relentlessly turned her face from side to side. It was evident that all of her senses were now being tumultuously awakened, try as she might to deny them. She had set me a magnificent challenge and I was extremely grateful to her.

I swore to myself that I would topple her from this pedestal of inner exalted aloofness. I took my fingers out of her cunt, letting her gasp and shudder and slowly bow her head, while long rippling tremors of enervation swept over her. Nothing would prevent my penetration of her soft, fleshy cunt. Later, to be sure, she would be further stripped and made to be even more acquiescent to my desire, I savouringly promised myself.

This brief respite left her more agitated than ever, judging from the spasmodic heavings of her naked breasts. The sweet tit-bit at which I had sucked and nibbled glistened with my saliva and it was darker and stiffer too. I was at last reaching something within her aloof and disdainful spirit, bringing her to a sensual awareness of herself, though I could only speculate on what emotions were truly aroused by my doing so . . . Now my thick throbbing prick delved through her thick verdure, pressing open the fleshy outer labia of her slit. I laughed as I launched my savagely rigid weapon towards its goal.

At the instant she felt the tip of my prick touch the entrance to her womb, Emily uttered a wild cry and began to struggle with all her might, wriggling backwards, twisting from side to side, wildly scraping my back with her long crimson finger-nails, turning her contorted, scarlet face in every direction as she supplicatingly besought some supreme reprieve. But this time there would be none for her!

She groaned as she felt my prick press within the inmost lips of her citadel and then suddenly, almost miraculously, her bare arms enfolded me to draw me closer to her. I quickened the stabbing momentum of my thrusts. How the cheeks of her bottom clenched and flexed and jerked against my digging fingers! Her eyes were hugely dilated, glazed and unseeing as they stared into my looming face and her mouth attacked mine with a voracity which could not have been believed on first meeting.

To feel her naked bubbies flatten against my heaving chest, to feel our bodies clash in a sweet conflict, to feel best of all the clamping, tightening, constricting pressures of her vaginal walls against my embedding prick was to taste the most bounteous rapture of which man is capable upon this ephemeral earth. I ground my teeth to hold her with me to that apex of amorous ecstasy. Now at each time my prick delved down to the hilt inside her, Emily uttered a little whimpering sigh and clutched me all the tighter, and then her legs came into play as she wound her calves tightly against my sinewy legs and gave herself up totally to wanton abandonment.

I quickened the rhythm, matching it to the passage of our train over the sleepers, but feeling myself almost upon the brink of explosive fury. I felt her bottom jerk and bound and arch as she met me, move for move, plying me with her velvety flesh, digging herself against me to take every inch into her most vital depths.

And then abruptly, with a wild cry, Emily twisted her face to one side, her nails pitilessly digging into my buttocks, and a loud shriek clamorously burst from her. I felt her body heave and buck against mine as, with a final savage fury, I drew myself back and thrust myself to the hilt and then felt my prick vibrate with the hot lashing vigour of my seed into her warm, tight sheath. As she felt that hot jismic tribute burst against the tender flesh of her womb, Emily uttered another loud cry and pressed her lips to mine as she lifted herself to absorb all of me.

And then it was over and she lay moaning and gasping, with me atop her, my limpening prick still burrowed in her quaking cunt. The moment of truth had come for Emily. She was beyond all dissembling now, all her body vibrated and shook with the tempestuous elemental fury that had overpowered her and made her mine, as our train raced away across Europe, for at last she had opened her eyes unto me and within them I had seen a shining secret glory of blue and gold.

After a superlative night's sleep I awoke to order big cups of steaming black coffee for both of us. These proved to be excellent, as the coffee usually is in French trains, but Emily asked to be excused from the breakfast table. I decided to attend. Now, although I am an Englishman to the roots of my being, I am not one of those awful chaps who expects bacon and eggs with toast, marmalade, kidneys, sausage and so on when I am travelling on the Continent. For a start, the continentals simply aren't up to doing it the way an Englishman likes it. Secondly, the climate is different and in consequence other foods are appropriate. I was glad to see, therefore, that 'the Black Douglas' had once again arranged matters impeccably in the dining-car. One simply came whenever one wanted to in order to have whatever one wanted. I was pleased to see that apart from two liveried attendants, it was empty, for I simply can't bear it if anyone is brilliant at breakfast.

I needed a pot of coffee to revive me and I wanted a basket of croissants with Normandy butter and the confiture of the peach and the apricot. I ordered another pot of coffee and another basket of croissants, with all accoutrements, to be brought to Emily, who assuredly deserved it after her endeavours of the previous day and night. I enjoyed the delights of solitude as I ate my croissants, which were of surpassing quality, drank my good coffee and stared out of the window at the passing French countryside. Every sane man adores the pleasures of solitude and abhors the pains of loneliness.

I had just reached the latter mood when Rosemary wandered in to join me. She certainly looked as though she had relished the delights of the previous night as much as I had. She greeted me warmly, sat down opposite and ordered tea.

'Tea?' I queried. 'In France?'

'Oh, yes,' she replied, 'have you not noticed that the *Salon de Thé* is a French institution for the upper classes?' She also requested a *Croque Monsieur*, a dish with which I was then unfamiliar. When I saw the melted cheese on toast covered with a thin slice of ham and a delicately fried egg, it looked so enticing that I ordered one for myself. It was delicious so I ordered one to be taken to Emily. I also ordered a Buck's Fizz. This turned out to be a mistake for the French attendant shrugged his shoulders at the ignorance of foreigners and said:

'*Champagne et jus d'orange, milord?*' as though I were some sort of imbecile. They brought me champagne and they brought me orange juice and they brought me glasses but the implication was that if Monsieur, the eccentric English milord, wished to do something as barbaric as putting orange juice into champagne, they did not wish to be implicated in this horrendous crime.

Really! The French, sometimes! Well, I don't give a damn so I mixed it myself and, without making a fuss, had some sent to Emily. Rosemary, who declined my offer and who asked for a large Fernet Branca, was treated with rather more respect. I overheard one attendant say to another: 'The English are mad. Champagne and orange juice? And they even roast gigot of lamb with *sauce menthe*! Why, I once even had to serve an English milord who wanted melon *with* smoked ham! Strips of ham placed upon it! Have you ever heard of such barbarism? I do not know what the world is coming to when things like this can be done.'

'Ah! That's better!' Rosemary said as she threw her Fernet Branca down her throat in glorious glee. 'Nothing like it for restoring the system and digestion after a heavy night!' The attendants glanced at her approvingly. 'Best medicine, I can tell you, Horby. Anyway, looking forward to the visit?'

'Very much so,' I answered. 'Though I do wish I knew more about your friend Douglas. Delightful host, I must admit.'

'Horby, you amuse me,' she smiled. 'Well, why create an artificial mystery when there are already far too many real mysteries in the world?' She laughed. 'Very well, I must admit that I have slightly misled you in the cause of giving you some further and higher education. Remember Dr David Dubberly of Brighton, principal subject of my letter to you when I was staying with my Aunt Elizabeth?' I nodded in recognition. 'He is the same man as Dr Foster of Whitby. As for Douglas, he isn't Dr Foster's son at all and that letter to you was pure fiction. Douglas isn't his real name anyway. I first fucked him somewhere else.'

'This is brilliance at breakfast,' I grumbled irritably. 'Just tell me, who the fuck is he?'

'Easier done than said,' she responded coolly. 'You will see in due course. We should be in Vienna within a couple of hours.' She took a glass of champagne but pointedly avoided the orange juice. 'It's said that his mother, the Countess, was a vampire. Now that's just too silly for words, isn't it?' She shrieked with peals of girlish laughter.

Well, now, Horby, I think he is awaiting me and if you will kindly excuse me . . .'

'Fine,' I muttered and we returned to our respective carriages. Emily had obviously enjoyed her breakfast and was staring entranced at the gentle rolling greenery of the landscape. To my delight, she turned towards me with a shout of joy.

What's the best thing to do after breakfast? I can't imagine anything much better than a nubile young girl taking down my trousers and underpants and proceeding to suck hard upon my freshly renewed, rampant, raging penis. Her tongue tickled me with such delightful delicacy. I'm afraid that I can't give any sort of accurate description of the scenery since my attention was focused on Emily's mouth, her full lips and what these and her tongue and the teeth that nipped my foreskin were doing to my stiff ram-rod. There are cocksuckers whose skills equal those of the demure Emily, daughter of a Bishop, but I have yet to meet a better one. As she sucked my cock, she frigged herself with the fingers of both hands and my prick brought forth its juices to spurt into her mouth and down her eager throat just as the train halted with a judder in some European station or other.

CHAPTER THIRTY-THREE

'Heavenly,' declared Sir Richard Bellingham, 'absolutely heavenly.' The mysterious Douglas had organised a fleet of horse-drawn carriages to meet us at Vienna station and Emily and I were sharing one with Davina and him. They both looked as if they had relished almost as enjoyable a time as Emily and myself. 'As opposed to hell,' Bellingham continued in his usual way, producing a hip-flask of silver encrusted with the family crest from the poacher's pocket of his Norfolk jacket and offering it around. It contained good brandy. 'Unlike hell. And what is hell? I know. It's a hotel where the plumbing is French, the cooking is Dutch, the waiters are German, the attitude is English and the women are American. Anyway, after all this, I'm jolly keen to see if this strange but curiously likeable chap Douglas can lead us to the gates of an even higher form of Paradise.'

'I hope he has a good wine cellar,' Davina murmured dreamily. 'I could do with some more good wine.' She cradled herself in Bellingham's arms and he held her closely with a tenderness which both surprised and impressed me.

'Oh, I'm sure there'll be that, my dear,' said Bellingham. 'The question is, though, will he be specialising in Burgundy or Bordeaux? Y'see, Horby, that's a real clue to a man's nature. And I admit that the subject can be debated,' he continued, his words echoed by the clip-clop of the horses' hooves, and backed by the jingling of the brasses hanging off their saddles. 'Dr Johnson said: "Claret is for boys. Port is for men. But," ' he held up his hip-flask triumphantly, ' "he who aspires to be a hero must drink brandy!" '

'And who drinks Burgundy?' I enquired.

'In my experience,' Davina replied, 'mainly debauched aristocrats. Claret buffs tend to come from the gentry or else the educated professional classes.'

'Yes . . .' I reflected, 'I always think of claret as being like an exquisitely delicate woman and of burgundy as being a full-blooded rich whore who does it for pleasure.'

'Oh, Horby,' Emily sighed, 'you're so crude sometimes.'

'He's right, though,' said Bellingham. 'Another way of putting it is that claret is the queen of wines but burgundy is the king.'

The journey passed pleasantly and we were pleased to see that the castle of Douglas stood high on a hill surrounded by dark and thick woodlands. We were greeted formally and courteously by liveried footmen and uniformed maids who showed us to our suites. We were given to understand that wine would be served in the main drawing-room in an hour but meanwhile, for our delectation, there was vintage champagne in an ice bucket and a bottle of genuine Napoleon cognac.

On entry, we were greeted in silence by a gentleman who, though in court dress, wore a very 'practicable' sword. He requested us to sign an Oath that we would keep silent about all we saw for twenty-one years. I have kept that Oath but I am released from it at the time of this writing. On satisfying him, we were passed through a corridor to an anteroom, where another armed guardian awaited us. On presentation of our signatures, he proceeded to proffer court dress, the insignia of the Sovereign Prince and Princesses of Rose-Croix, and a garter and mantle, the former of green silk, the latter of green velvet, and lined with cerise silk.

'It is a Low Mass,' he whispered. In this anteroom were three or four others, both ladies and gentlemen, busily robing.

In a third room we found a procession formed and joined it. There were twenty-six of us in all. Passing a final guardian, we reached the chapel itself, at whose entrance stood a young man and a young woman, both dressed in simple robes of white silk embroidered with gold, red and blue. The former bore a torch of resinous wood, the latter sprayed us as we passed with attar of roses from a cup.

The room in which we now were had at one time been a chapel; so much its shape declared. But the high altar was covered with a cloth that displayed the Rose and Cross; while above it were ranged seven candelabra, each of seven branches. The stalls had been retained; and at each knight's hand burned a taper of rose-coloured wax, and a bouquet of roses was before him. Above the altar was a great banner proclaiming in black: DO WHAT THOU WILT SHALL BE THE WHOLE OF THE LAW; and at the base there was a banner stating: LOVE IS THE LAW, LOVE UNDER WILL. To my right, on the Chapel wall, a banner announced: EVERY MAN AND EVERY WOMAN IS A STAR. To my left, a banner shouted: THE WORD OF SIN IS RESTRICTION.

In the centre of the nave was a great cross, a calvary cross of ten squares measuring, say, six feet by five, painted in red upon a white board, at whose edge were rings through which passed gilt staves. At each corner was a banner, bearing lion, bull, eagle and man, and from the top of their staves sprang a canopy of blue, wherein were figured in gold the twelve emblems of the Zodiac. Knights and Dames being installed, suddenly a bell tinkled in the architrave.

Instantly all rose. The doors opened at a trumpet peal from without and a herald advanced, followed by the High Priest and Priestess.

The High Priest was Douglas and the Priestess was Rosemary. Their hands were raised and touching as in the minuet. Their trains were borne by the two youths who had admitted us. All this while an unseen organ played an Introit. This ceased as they took their places at the altar. They faced West, waiting.

On the closing of the doors, the armed guard, who was clothed in a scarlet robe instead of green, drew his sword, and went up and down the aisle, chanting exorcisms and swinging the great sword. All present drew their swords and faced outward, holding the points in front of them. This part of the ceremony appeared interminable. When it was over, a young man and a young woman appeared, bearing the one a bowl, the other a censer. I recognised the pair of them: the man was Francis Ferdinand, Arch-Duke of Austria-Hungary and heir to the throne, and the other was my dearest Claire. Singing some litany or other, apparently in Greek, though I could not catch the words, they purified and consecrated the chapel.

Now the High Priest and High Priestess began a litany in rhythmic lines of equal length. At each third response, they touched hands in a peculiar manner; at each seventh, they kissed. The twenty-first was a complete embrace. The bell tinkled in the architrave; and they parted. The High Priest then took from the altar a flask curiously shaped to imitate a phallus. The High Priestess knelt and presented a boat-shaped cup of gold. He knelt opposite her and did not pour from the flask.

Now the Knights and Dames began a long litany; first a Dame in treble, then a Knight in bass, then a response in chorus of all present with the organ. This Chorus was:

'EVOE HO, IACCHE! EPELTHON,
EPELTHON, EVOE, IAO!'

Again and again it rose and fell. Towards its close, whether by 'stage effect' or no I could not swear, the light over the altar grew rosy, then a strange shade of purple; purple beyond purple, it was a light higher than eyesight! The High Priest sharply and suddenly threw up his hand: instant silence.

He now poured out the wine from the flask. The High Priestess gave it to Claire who bore it to all present.

This was no ordinary wine. It has been said of vodka that it looks like water and tastes like fire. With this wine, the reverse is the case. It was of a rich fiery gold in which flames of light danced and shook but its taste was limpid and pure like fresh spring water. No sooner had I drunk it, however, than I began to tremble. It was a most astonishing sensation; I can imagine a man feels thus as he awaits his executioner, when he has passed through fear and is all excitement. I recalled some words of Arthur Machen: 'There is a wine so strong that no earthly vessel can hold it'.

I looked down my stall and saw that each was similarly afflicted. During the libation, the High Priestess sang a hymn, again in Greek. This time I recognized the words; they were those of an ancient Ode to Aphrodite.

The male attendant now descended to the red cross, stooped and kissed it; then he danced upon it in such a way that he seemed to be tracing the patterns of a marvellous rose of gold, for the percussion caused a shower of bright dust to fall from the canopy. Meanwhile the litany (different words but the same chorus) began again. This time it was a duet between the High Priest and Priestess. At each chorus, Knights and Dames bowed low. Claire moved around continuously and the bowl passed.

This ended in the exhaustion of the male, who fell fainting on the cross. The female immediately took the bowl and put it to his lips. Then she raised him and, with the assistance of the Guardian of the Sanctuary, led him out of the chapel.

The bell again tinkled in the aperture.

The herald blew a fanfare.

The High Priest and High Priestess moved at a stately pace to each other and embraced, in the act unloosing the heavy golden robes they wore. These fell, twin lakes of gold. I now saw Rosemary dressed in a garment of white watered silk, lined throughout (as appeared later) with ermine.

The vestment of the High Priest, Douglas, was an elaborate embroidery of every colour, harmonized by exquisite yet robust art. He wore also a breastplate corresponding to the canopy; a sculptured 'beast' at each corner in gold, while the twelve signs of the Zodiac were symbolized by the gem-stones of the breastplate.

The bell tinkled yet again, and the herald again sounded his trumpet. The celebrants moved hand in hand down the nave while the organ thundered forth its solemn harmonies. All the Knights and Dames rose and gave the sacred sign of the Rosicrucians, the Sign of the Rose and the Cross, of male and female united in love and lust.

It was at this part of the ceremony that things began to happen to me. I became suddenly aware that my body had lost both weight and tactile sensibility. My consciousness seemed to be situated no longer in my body. I 'mistook myself', if I may use the phrase, for one of the stars in the canopy.

In this way I missed seeing the celebrants actually approach the cross. The bell tinkled again; I came back to myself and then I saw that the High Priestess, standing at the foot of the cross, had thrown her robe over it, so that the cross was no longer visible. There was only a board covered with ermine. Rosemary was now naked but for her coloured and jewelled head-dress and the heavy torque of gold about her neck and the armlets and anklets that matched it. She began to sing in a soft strange tongue, so low and smoothly that in my partial bewilderment I could not hear all; but I caught a few words, *Io Pan! Io Pan!* and a phrase in which the words *Iao Sabao* ended empathetically a sentence in which I caught the words *Eros*, *Thelema* and *Sebazo*.

While she did this, she unloosed the breastplate and gave it to Claire. The robe followed; I saw that they were naked and unashamed. For the first time there was absolute silence.

Now, from an hundred jets surrounding the board poured forth a perfumed purple smoke. The world was wrapt in in a fond gauze of mist, sacred as the clouds upon the mountains.

Then at a signal given by the High Priest, the bell tinkled once more. The celebrants stretched out their arms in the form of a cross, interlacing their fingers. Slowly they revolved through three circles and a half. The Priestess then laid the Priest down upon the cross and took her own appointed place. The organ now again rolled forth its solemn music.

I was lost to everything. Only this I saw, that the celebrants made no expected motion. The movements were extremely small and yet extremely strong. This must have continued for a great length of time. To me it seemed as if eternity itself could not contain the variety and depths of my experiences. Tongue nor pen could not record them; and yet I am fain to attempt the impossible.

I was, certainly and undoubtedly, the star in the canopy.

This star was an incomprehensibly enormous world of pure flame.

I suddenly realized that the star was of no size whatever. It was not that the star shrank but that it (= I) became suddenly conscious of infinite space.

An explosion took place. I was in consequence a point of light, infinitely small, yet infinitely bright, and this point was without position.

Consequently this point was ubiquitous and there was a feeling of infinite bewilderment, blinded after a time by a gush of infinite rapture. (I use the word 'blinded' as if under constraint; I should have preferred to use the words 'blotted out' or 'overwhelmed' or 'illuminated'.)

This infinite fullness – I have not described it as such but it was that – was suddenly changed into a feeling of infinite emptiness, which became conscious as a yearning.

These two feelings began to alternate, always with suddenness, and without in any way overlapping, with great rapidity.

This alteration must have occurred fifty times – I would rather have said a hundred.

The two feelings suddenly became one. Again, the word 'explosion' is the only one that gives any idea of it.

I now seemed to be conscious of everything at once, that it was at the same time *one* and *many*. I say 'at once', that is, I was not successively all things but instantaneously.

This being, if I may call it being, seemed to drop into an infinite abyss of Nothing.

While this 'falling' lasted, the bell suddenly tinkled three times. I instantly became my normal self, yet with a constant awareness, which has never left me to this hour, that the truth of the matter is not this normal 'I' but 'That' which is still dropping into Nothing. I am assured by those who know that I may be able to take up the thread if I attend another ceremony.

The tinkle died away. Claire ran quickly forward and folded the ermine over the celebrants. The herald blew a fanfare and the Knights and Dames left their stalls. Advancing to the board, we took hold of the gilded carrying poles and followed the herald in procession out of the chapel, bearing the litter to a small side chapel leading out of the middle anteroom, where we left it, the guard closing the doors.

In silence we disrobed. Then Rosemary entered the room and greeted me lovingly. I asked her, if that was a Low Mass, might I not be permitted to witness a High Mass?

'Perhaps,' she answered with a curious smile, 'if all they tell of you nowadays is true.'

Little did I realize that this was only the end of the beginning of my sexual education.